The Angel Max

Also by Peter Glassgold

*Boethius: The Poems from On the Consolation of Philosophy,
Translated out of the original Latin into diverse historical
Englishings diligently collaged.*
SUN & MOON PRESS, 1994

The Flaxfield by Stijn Streuvels.
Translated, with André Lefevere, from the Dutch
SUN & MOON PRESS, 1989

*Hwæt! A Little Old English Anthology of
American Modernist Poetry.* Translated and edited
SUN & MOON PRESS, 1985

Living Space: Poems of the Dutch "Fiftiers."
Edited with an introduction
NEW DIRECTIONS, 1979

PETER GLASSGOLD

The Angel Max

Harcourt Brace & Company

New York   San Diego   London

Requests for permission to make copies of any part of the
work should be mailed to: Permissions Department,
Harcourt Brace & Company, 6277 Sea Harbor Drive,
Orlando, Florida 32887-6777.

Library of Congress Cataloging-in-Publication Data
Glassgold, Peter.
The angel Max/by Peter Glassgold.—1st ed.
p.   cm.
ISBN 0-15-100220-7
I. Title.
PS3557.L3515A8   1998
813'.54—dc21   97-24178

Text set in Granjon
Designed by Lori McThomas Buley
Printed in the United States of America
First edition
A C E F D B

For Suzanne

"History is placed where it is and hope is full of wishes."

—GERTRUDE STEIN

CONTENTS

Part One

Part Three

Part Four

Part One

I

First Memories

MY FATHER OWNED a roofing company in Riga. He died when I was three, after breaking his back in a fall. Two men carried him home in a blanket, up the stairs and through my play blocks, my mother behind them screaming "Osip! Osip!" They laid him out on the kitchen floor still alive, silent and staring. My mother tended him for a few days, while a neighbor took me in and fed me honey bread and sugar water and showed me how she made rock candy.

That was early summer of 1869. Later in the year my mother and I returned to Kovno, where she and my father had come from and where I had been born. We moved in with a relative of my father's named Pyotr Mikhailovich Kraft, a widower who had two small children of his own. He put me on his knee one day and asked my permission to marry my mother. I said yes, he gave me from his pocket the jellies I was waiting for, and they were married under a bridal canopy set up in the parlor.

The gathering seemed huge and hilarious to me and my stepsisters, Sophie and Nina. We giggled over everything, the unintelligible sounds of Hebrew, the crunch of the wineglass under Pyotr Mikhailovich's foot, the severe looks the rabbi sent our way. My mother picked me up and danced around the room. Someone shouted her name, "Fanya and her bridegroom!" Then Pyotr Mikhailovich danced with both his daughters at once. Someone shouted, "Jacob our father and his wives!" There were cakes and finger foods, vodka and caviar, sweet wine and plum brandy. The girls and I ate ourselves sick in our excitement and thought it was the best time we'd ever had.

Less than a year later, my mother died of childbed fever. After the baby had been born, I was allowed into the room. My mother was propped up by pillows, looking pale, with dark circles under her eyes. A loose strand of red hair lay matted against her cheek. "Maxie," she said to me, "I would like you to meet your new brother." I looked at the small purplish object asleep in her arms and asked if I could have a pony instead. She laughed, and then she was gone from our lives.

For several days, everyone in the household went around disheveled, and all the mirrors were draped in black. I lifted the cloth on the mirror over my mother's dresser and looked, afraid of what I'd see—my mother's grieving face, a grimacing demon, or, worse yet, no image at all. Marya, one of the servants, found me staring into my own eyes. "Holy Mother of God!" she cried, and crossed herself. I ran off before she could hit me.

When the days of mourning had passed, Pyotr Mikhailovich called Sophie, Nina, and me into his study and said he would always take care of us, no matter what, and gave us each a treat from his pocket. We hugged him and wept. He called us his little macaroons. But afterward in the playroom, Sophie said that we children had to watch out for ourselves, that we had to mind our baby brother, and that she was in charge, being the eldest. I said I should be in charge because I was a boy. "So?" said Sophie. We turned to Nina to see whose side she was on, only to find her over by the window tracing faces on the foggy glass.

Pyotr Mikhailovich hired a nurse for the baby and sent my stepsisters and me off to a Russian day school within walking distance from home. It was what Americans call a one-room schoolhouse, in which the older children in the grades took charge of the younger ones like Nina and me, so Sophie seemed to have had her way after all, except for the baby. The nurse was strict. We were allowed to view little Mishka for only a few minutes in the late afternoon. Sophie and Nina would coo and babble at him, pick him up and fondle him when the nurse let them. To me he looked like a boiled yellow turnip, and I didn't care to touch him.

We could afford to go to a better school than we did, but my stepfather felt the three of us, orphans as we were, should stay together for now. This restricted his choices. He had to find a Russian-speaking school that admitted both kindergartners and grade-school children, girls as well as boys, and Jews. Earlier my mother had been our teacher, and we had a schoolroom of our own in the house. At the age of five, I spoke Russian and German. In both languages I could count to a hundred and recognize many whole printed words, though not all the individual letters. Sophie was almost two years older. She knew both alphabets backward and forward and could read all our storybooks. Not much was expected of Nina, who was only four and in the habit of going off by herself whenever she could. On the first day of school, when asked to give her name aloud, she astounded everyone by writing it in full on the blackboard, in a proper Cyrillic hand: Nina Petrovna Kraft. But that was all she could write.

We lived a mile south of the Old City, in a neighborhood of comfortable villas with old, shady oaks and thick-rooted beeches whose gnarled trunks I imagined as peasants' faces. One day as we were leaving for school, Sophie said, "Let's go the other way," and we did, straight into a line of trees that quickly became wooded marshland. We played all morning among the muddy rivulets and autumn leaves and returned home at midday for lunch. At school that afternoon, Sophie said our father was un-well. She used this trick successfully three or four more times, until Pyotr Mikhailovich received a concerned letter from the schoolmaster asking after his health and noting its effect on our attendance. We had a serious talk in his study, with no candy. Most fathers would have birched us black-and-blue. Without rais-ing his voice, with no accusing frown, he read us the letter and said, "Children, how could you?" In a moment we were weeping and asking his forgiveness, Sophie most of all.

I was relieved not to go running with my stepsisters anymore. At school, some of the boys had begun calling me a sissy because, they said, I played only with girls. Their taunts were terrible. Once one of Nina's friends broke the point of her pencil and stood there, sobbing tragically. Her name was Fanya, like my mother.

"I can fix it," I said. She solemnly handed me the stub, and I proudly shaped a new point with my pocketknife. She thanked me with a smile and vanished among her girlfriends. Then the boys circled me like a wolf pack. I fought my way through them, butting and punching. They kept a distance from me after that, for the remainder of my time there.

At home and on our secret outings, Sophie and Nina in their own way caused me more trouble than the boys at school. They wanted me to play with their dolls and just for fun to dress up in their clothes. Getting into bed at night, or in the bathhouse, I caught them trying to look at me. On one of our adventures in the marsh, we came across two hutches in a small clearing. I rushed up to them. "Be careful," said Sophie, "there might be a witch inside." "Baba Yaga! Baba Yaga lives there," Nina whispered. But the hutches were abandoned. People had lived in one, judging from the charcoal remains of a hearth. Pigs had lived in the other, judging from the lingering smell and the packed, clayey floor. Bees droned overhead in the warmth of a late autumn day, while we played house and the-farmer-feeds-the-animals. Suddenly I had to relieve myself and dashed out behind the pigsty. As I made water against the back wall I sensed on either side my stepsisters eyes on me and the source of the unstoppable stream now foaming at my feet. When finally I could button up, Nina said, "I have one, too. I'll show you." I said no. "She does have one," said Sophie. "Show him." "See?" said Nina, lifting her dress. But I had already turned and run.

When in early winter my stepfather asked me if I wanted anything special for my sixth birthday, I said, "A room of my own." "I see," he said. He offered me a sourball and then took one for himself. He asked about the fighting at school. I was amazed he knew about it. I told him I wasn't getting into fights much now but had no friends to play with. Pyotr Mikhailovich rolled his candy in his mouth thoughtfully. He asked if I'd like to go to a school for boys only. His suggestion took me by surprise. "We'll think about it, Maxie."

For my birthday, I was given a room of my own. My stepfather and the servants led me in blindfolded, my stepsisters trailing behind. It was a boy's room, with pictures of wild animals over the bed—reindeer, a mother Kodiak bear and her cubs, a family of wolves—all my old toys, and some new ones, including adventure books with pictures. Over a small writing desk hung engraved portraits of a beginning gallery of heroes: Moses, who had led the Hebrews out of slavery; Tsar Alexander, who had freed the serfs; and Abraham Lincoln, who had freed the slaves in America. On the bed was a new school uniform: a blue tunic with bright brass buttons and a matching cap with a band of gold.

II

What We Spoke

MY NEW SCHOOL was on Kanto Street, not far from the river. In wintertime, at midday break and after classes, we would run down to the Neman and play on the ice. The spring thaw set in violently. Every year when the first groans and cracks echoed through the streets, students and teachers would cluster by the riverbank. All along the water's edge were knots of people come to watch the breakup of the ice. But the best spot was a half-mile away, on the other side of town, where merging currents of the Neman and the Neris sent ice floes whirling and grinding against each other and great chunks rearing up and spinning out of sight. The noise was tremendous. People side by side had to shout to be heard. Here stood students from an all-girls' Russian school, there Lithuanian dockhands, farther on some German businessmen, a Polish peddler and his family, a party of Latvian timber merchants and, a hundred yards across the Neris, a broken line of Jews. People pointed excitedly and tried to yell over the icy tumult, but between the groups of viewers there were unbridgeable silences, scarcely a smile or a friendly wave.

There were similar silences at home. Sophie and Nina when I approached them now turned their backs and spoke a private language of girls. Frieda the housekeeper, Ruth the cook, and

Basya the kitchenmaid all spoke Jewish among themselves but German or Russian to everyone else. Kazys the gardener and Marya the housemaid joked with each other in Lithuanian, but when responding to others in Russian, they hardly laughed at all. Polish, my stepfather said, was forbidden in the province, and everyone pretended not to understand it. When he remarried, his new wife was from Poland, and I was afraid she'd get into trouble with the tsar. But Vera Andreyevna spoke a refined Russian with sprinklings of French and by her manner forbade the use of other languages in her presence. She had a paid companion with whom to speak French, who was also a kind of governess for Sophie, Nina, and me, teaching us good manners and, of course, French.

Each language was an enormous room of a different shape, with windows cut in different sizes and patterns and set higher or lower. The furniture in each room was different, too. I dreamed of a faraway land where only one language was spoken and I would be with my mother once more. In my imagination, I called that land America.

Vera Andreyevna's arrival drew my stepsisters and me together again. It was our intention to drive the governess insane. We thought that if Madame left, so, too, would Vera Andreyevna. Sophie suggested we do it quickly by sewing dead mice in her pillow. I thought that would only cause trouble. As a compromise, we agreed to leave a mouse on Madame's bedroom slippers one night. Meanwhile, we would act up during our lessons, talk and cough with our mouths full, wipe our noses on our sleeves. After a few weeks of torment, Madame's bare foot bearing down on a dead mouse triggered a burst of screams that announced her dawn departure. After her, however, another Madame appeared, and then another, and another, until there was no longer any purpose to our scheming.

I was eight when Vera Andreyevna swept in. It wasn't long before she had us children moved to a wing of the house near the servants' quarters to make room for her own babies, who arrived one after another in three successive years: Nikolai, Boris, and Vasily. We called them Nikki, Nakki, and Nokki, after three fussy old brothers in a children's book. Sophie and Nina still shared a bedroom, and Mishka, who was only three, was doubled up with me. I appealed to Pyotr Mikhailovich. He explained quietly that I would have to look after my little brother until he was old enough to care for himself—and then I could again have a room of my own. When would that be, I asked. In four, maybe five years, he said, not much longer—an eternity—and gave me a caramel. "Trust me, Maxie." He said this, I thought, with some sorrow and squeezed my shoulders with his large, puffy hands. I was beginning to feel I had no firm place in my stepfather's house, even if I had taken his name. I'd better remember to behave. Mishka's head still looked like a cooked rutabaga, but he could talk and understand everything I told him. I terrorized him with folktales from Grimm. Then he'd crawl into bed with me, and I'd tell him the wonderful adventures we were going to have with our mother in America. He asked me once what language they spoke there. "English," I said. He asked what it was like. I said it was like everything. "No matter what anybody says or how anybody says it, everybody understands."

III

Lessons

MADAME'S ROOM WAS the largest in the servants' quarters and in earshot of us older children. She saw us off to school in the morning and instructed us in etiquette and French twice a week. Our progress was slow, in the former on principle, in the latter because of the steady turnover of Madames. She was Vera Andreyevna's lieutenant, her watchdog and mouthpiece, and much of our lesson was given over to warnings about household rules and to sermonettes. We were to adore the Russian royal family and to pray for the restoration of the Bourbons of France. We were to deplore the populist *narodniki* and the French Communards, who, if anything, were lower than the foul spawn of the upstart Napoleon, but not as low as the English, who were innately stupid and brutal, a degenerate tribe of Teutons. Vera Andreyevna's intention was to turn us into good Russian gentry worthy of her aristocratic fancy. In fact, we were a family of rich provincial Jews living in the Pale.

My stepfather owned houses in Slobodka, the city across the Neris where most Jews in the area lived, as well as small tracts of forest and farmland in districts nearby. He bought and sold real estate, held mortgages, and leased property and rented concessions to other Jews. Meir Shavelson, the son of his bookkeeper and chief rent collector, came once a week for five years to tutor me in Hebrew. I called him Reb Shavelson, and he referred to me in the third person as "little boy," speaking in Yiddish. "The little boy will recite the laws concerning leprosy." "Does the little boy recall the whereabouts of the law pertaining to defilement by flux?" He would pinch me and yank my earlobes when I made mistakes but never give me a nod of approval. When I tried to study silently in his presence, he made me sway and mutter. He countered my objection with an explanation from Joshua. " 'The book of the Law shall not depart from your mouth. You shall murmur it day and night. . . .' What is the meaning of 'shall not depart'? Rabbi Shmuel bar Nahmani said . . ." Absorbed in his expositions, his eyes glazed over. He would rock back and forth, rotate a thumb around an index finger, and pick at his thin neck. He marked the end of an argument by rubbing his nose twice in a downward stroke, combing his fingers through his scraggy beard, and staring at me in challenge. He was a yeshiva student, supported by the Jewish community, and as such entitled to share our board. Yet never once in five years did he let even a sip of water pass his lips in our house. He suspected the purity of our kitchen. We were not, for him, real Jews. If Reb Shavelson was what a real Jew was, I didn't want to be one.

I came to the Jewish language easily because of its similarities to German, but I never felt at home in it. When Basya the kitchenmaid lit into Reb Shavelson, once even throwing his uneaten food in his face, most of her low Yiddish was lost on me. Later on, in America, I came across confidence men and ghetto sirens who gained the trust of new immigrants by speaking in their village accents, but I was deaf to the idea of dialect and nuance. I spoke a serviceable German-Jewish and used it only when I had to.

I learned the elements of Hebrew in spite of Reb Shavelson and disliked most everything I read. He drilled me in the liturgy and ritual prayers, the whole of the five books of the Law and related passages among the Prophets, the curt medieval commentary of Rashi. Talmudic studies would presumably come later, but Reb Shavelson and I both knew that once I'd passed through the ceremony of my bar mitzvah, our weekly ordeal would be over. So far as he was concerned, I was an indifferent learner and his making some kind of recognizable Jew out of me was a good deed wasted. He was correct. Hebrew and the land of Israel were nothing to me, English and America everything.

I prayed to God for an English primer to fall like manna into my hands. I entreated Him to transport me to America, yea at an instant, on an eagle's wings. After a while, when nothing happened, I wondered if there were a God at all, otherwise my prayers, the prayers of an orphan in Israel, would surely have been answered. Often I cried myself to sleep. Mishka would want to crawl into bed with me. Sometimes I let him, sometimes I didn't. One summer day, Sophie said, "Your door was open last night. I heard you sniffling. I don't see what you've got to feel sorry about. Think of the poor peasants." I answered that the tsar had freed the serfs. Sophie laughed. "Freed them to do what?" She looked derisively at the tsar's portrait in my gallery of heroes, to which had been added Washington, Jefferson, and Buffalo Bill. "You should take it down," she said, "and put up Herzen or Bakunin in its place." From this, I realized that Sophie had become a secret follower of the revolutionary *narodniki*.

Alexander Ivanovich Herzen and Mikhail Alexandrovich Bakunin were names I heard until then pronounced only with loathing. Another was Prince Pyotr Alexeyevich Kropotkin. For Madame and Vera Andreyevna, their greatest crime as revolutionaries was their contempt for their birthright, since all three were of the nobility. Beyond that, I had only a vague idea of who they were, based on Madame's routine condemnations.

A few days later I had my first instruction in social revolution. Madame entered our schoolroom exultant and began our French lesson with the news that Bakunin was dead. The enemy of God and the tsar had finally got what he deserved, and she hoped his death had not been an easy one. Having said this, she collapsed among our desks. She had caught the full-face impact of a well-aimed Larousse that flew from Sophie's hand. As we dragged Madame from the room, I caught a glimpse of her underclothes. Nina said, "Stop that!" and Sophie, who was holding Madame's head and shoulders, looked up and glared.

We left her outside the room and barricaded ourselves within. Mishka had wormed his way in unseen, and so it was the four of us against the household. Sophie tore the hem of her petticoat in strips. We tied them around our heads and kept what was left over for bandages. Soon there was pounding and shouting at the door. Sophie put her fingers to her lips. "I'll do the talking," she whispered, and lifted her voice in defiant revolutionary song. Nina joined in, and I followed, then Mishka, too, mouthing the "Internationale" and "Marseillaise" in French.

On the other side of the door, Madame shrieked. This is what our lessons had come to. Vera Andreyevna shrieked back at her, and to us she uttered hoarse threats in Russian. Sophie remained silent. Kazys the gardener came, apparently armed with a woodsman's ax, but refused to break down the door. The children were playing, he said. Vera Andreyevna cursed him in gutter Yiddish, to our astonishment. Frieda the housekeeper, Ruth the cook, Basya the kitchenmaid, and Marya the housemaid each pleaded with us to open the door. Sophie answered them politely—by turns in German, in Jewish, in Russian—and said simply that we would discuss matters with Pyotr Mikhailovich and no one else. Intermittent pounding, shouting, and singing followed as the servants drifted away one by one, leaving only Vera Andreyevna and Madame on guard.

While we waited for Pyotr Mikhailovich to appear, Sophie told us about the heroic men and women of the revolution. We were ablaze with stories of Bakunin's escape from Siberian prison to join the exile Herzen in the West, of Prince Kropotkin, who was released half dead from the dungeons of the terrible Peter-Paul Fortress and had only just now escaped from a prisoners' hospital, and of the beautiful Louise Michel on the barricades of Père-Lachaise. "*V narod!*" she cried. To the people! "*V narod!*" we all cried out together. "*Ils ont essayé de me tuer!*" Madame called to Pyotr Mikhailovich, who knew no French. "They tried to kill me! *Assassins! Orphelins diaboliques!*"

There was a long corridor that led from the front parlor, alongside the staircase, to our wing at the back of the house. Through the keyhole I saw the outline of my stepfather's bulky figure grow as he made his way deliberately down the hall against a barrage of voices. Mishka and Nina shouted "Papa! Papa!" and Madame and Vera Andreyevna kept up a furious fire until he reached the schoolroom. Gently Pyotr Mikhailovich knocked on the door: "Children, may I come in?" Sophie answered, "Only you, Papa, nobody else." As he entered, I saw Vera Andreyevna's furious face and Madame's bruised one. They were trying to push in behind. He blocked them without a look and closed the door.

Sophie was controlled but very near tears. She explained to Pyotr Mikhailovich what had happened, and why. He said Bakunin was no friend of ours, even if what he wrote held some truths for Russia. A few misspoken words by Madame didn't justify throwing a book at her head. Sophie said this wasn't the first time our instruction in etiquette and French had been turned into reactionary preaching. Pyotr Mikhailovich was puzzled. He questioned us further about Madame's lessons, passing a bag of sweets around to each of us. "And what of the Declaration of the Rights of Man?" he said at last. "Does Madame forget in what language it was written?"

Our lessons in French and etiquette came to an end. Madame left the household in disgust. Vera Andreyevna extended her annual summer holiday with her relatives in the Polish provinces. In a few weeks, when a new Madame arrived, her duties were to watch over Vera Andreyevna's three boys and be a companion to their mother. She would have nothing at all to do with us. Frieda the housekeeper would see to our needs. In way of punishment, and to keep us at a distance from Vera Andreyevna, we would eat with the servants from now on, except on Sabbath eve and festival days.

IV

Summer Holiday

MY STEPFATHER'S BUSINESS in Slobodka often kept him working until odd hours. In the past, he would send a message home
for Ruth the cook to keep a platter ready for him. Now Pyotr
Mikhailovich joined us and the servants whenever he could. He
loved his food and sniffed the pots with delight when he entered
the kitchen. He began his meal by tossing down a glass of
schnapps and allowed the servants the same. For a man his size
he ate with delicacy, which belied his second and third helpings.
Afterward we sometimes sang. Pyotr Mikhailovich snapped his
fingers and danced slowly when Basya the kitchenmaid warbled
"Chericheribim." Kazys the gardener and Marya the housemaid
sang only one song in their language, a ballad they said was about
a roguish Polish count and a peasant girl who outwitted him.
Kazys' voice was a thin tenor, Marya's soft and nasal, like a nun's
at evensong. Then Sophie would try to lead us all in a rousing
workers' song in German, and I imagined Vera Andreyevna upstairs fuming. The thought of her made me sing all the louder,
while the servants and Pyotr Mikhailovich sat silent.

Vera Andreyevna spent a month every summer with her family in Bialystok. We had the run of the place for a couple of weeks.
For the rest of the time, Pyotr Mikhailovich closed up the house,

giving the servants a holiday. He traveled by coach through the northern provinces with Sophie, Nina, Mishka, and me, putting up at various Jewish inns. We were welcomed with loud laughter and hugs. I supposed my stepfather was among the best-loved men in the world, not that he held the innkeeper's mortgage. Wherever we stayed, Pyotr Mikhailovich placed us in the care of the innkeeper's wife, while he went off to settle local accounts or to sleep in the sun, which he called fishing. In fact, we were on our own. No innkeeper's wife would dare raise a hand to us.

We generally kept to the grounds of the inn, poking into everything. The countryside was strange to us. The peasants and the village Jews took us for Russians from St. Petersburg, with our Western clothing and my stepfather's side-whiskers, and they kept a careful distance.

Once, near Vitebsk, we were at The White Dove. The kitchen prepared a sweet treat for Pyotr Mikhailovich. We children were to surprise him with it as he dozed by the fishing pond stocked for guests, half a verst down the road. We took what Sophie thought was a shortcut, a service path out back behind the dairy and the kitchen garden. It lost itself in a high meadow, and we pushed through the wild grasses and flies in the direction of the road, Sophie leading the way.

After an hour or so, she said, "There it is. I told you so." We came out onto a narrow road. Sophie turned confidently to the left, and we followed her around a bend into the market of a Jewish village. It was late Friday afternoon. The place was frantic with eleventh-hour bargaining before the Sabbath eve, children and chickens flying around women's skirts, peddlers pleading. A few men of the village drifted through the commotion unconcerned, and by their clothing I realized that Sophie had led us into a community of Chassidim. These strange pietists were not often seen in Kovno-Slobodka, where their ignorance and superstition were met with contempt even by the likes of Reb Shavelson. They stood out from other Jews by their odd costume, which predated Napoleon and made a mockery, said Pyotr Mikhailovich, of our strivings toward enlightenment.

A group of boys came up to us, and we stared at each other in suspicion. "Look at their earlocks," Nina whispered in Russian, "down to their shoulders. They look like Red Indians." Sophie explained to them that we were trying to find The White Dove. "We are staying there," she said, "but we are lost." After a pause, she added, "We are Jews." She enunciated each word in her German-Yiddish but confused languages, calling the inn Die Weisse Taube instead of its Yiddish corruption. The boys responded only to Sophie's final words. "You are Jews?"

I answered yes. "We are your brethren," I said. "We come from far. Many days' march. We seek the inn called The White Dove." I remembered from my adventure books how explorers treated with natives. I offered them Pyotr Mikhailovoch's surprise sweets, which I had carried all the way through the tall meadow grass.

"Unclean!" A woman in a flurry of black skirts knocked the wicker box from my hands and shooed the boys away. "What do you want here?" Sophie repeated firmly that we were looking for The White Dove, that we were lost, that we were Jews. The woman snapped, "Tcha!" She pointed down the road opposite to the way we had come. "One verst to the high road. Then another two versts to the right. You'd better hurry to get there before sunset if, as you say, you are Jews." She spat three times. The women who had gathered behind her spat in chorus, as did the boys, who had returned. Mishka spat back and in an instant was on the ground, fighting. Sophie and I pulled him away. He was grinding his teeth and weeping in rage. The women hooted us down the road until we were out of sight of the village.

We trudged along in silence, shaken. Then Sophie said to me, "Maxie, you're an idiot. What a way to talk—'We are your brethren'!" I reminded her who had gotten us lost in the first place. Nina comforted Mishka, telling him a story. "... and the name of the village was Cacadorf. The four brave children walked into the marketplace alone, and the bravest of them all was little Mikhail Petrovich—his brother and sisters called him Mishka the Lion...." Just as we reached the high road, a carriage rolled into sight and stopped a few yards away. The door opened, and a battered Pyotr Mikhailovich lowered himself to the ground and hobbled toward us. "Children! I was so worried!" We ran to him. "Papa! What happened to you!"

On the way back to the inn we learned that he had been jumped and beaten by poachers as he slept by the fishing pond.

He had actually caught three fish—he wasn't sure what kind— and they had taken them, along with his pocket watch and his money, "Just a few kopecks." Then they had stepped on his reading glasses, pushed him in the pond, and run off. "A couple of your worthy peasants, Sophie, having a little fun."

Sophie stared bleakly out the carriage window while I told Pyotr Mikhailovich of our own misadventure, Mishka chiming in to sing his own praises. My stepfather said he thought perhaps we should go home tomorrow. "We have found 'the people,' and it seems they don't much care for us." Sophie said, "It's not my fault, Papa. Please don't tease." He told her he wanted to spare her from false hope. He patted her cheek. She pushed his hand away and once again turned her face to the window, crying. We left for home the next day.

V

Revolutionary Confidences

THE YEAR WE cut short our summer holiday was 1878. On our return, we found the house vandalized. Not much of value had been taken, only a set of silver salt dishes and two pairs of candlesticks. But several mirrors had been shattered, curtains slashed, the larder ransacked of its tins and vodka, and a gold menorah lay twisted on the parlor floor stuck to a pile of stale human excrement.

Pyotr Mikhailovich was alarmed. Earlier that winter, General Trepov, chief of the St. Petersburg police, had been shot, though not killed, by Vera Zasulich, an admitted revolutionist. Sophie was fired up by the news. She and her father had a sharp exchange of words in the kitchen. He told her she would be wise to be discreet about her opinions outside the house. Sophie said that now precisely was the time to speak out. The servants vanished from the table. Nina and Mishka froze.

Pyotr Mikhailovich told Sophie she mustn't put herself, and all of us, in danger. He began to explain. "In times of trouble, it's—" Sophie interrupted, "—'always the Jews.'" Pyotr Mikhailovich countered, "And from you, Sophie, 'always the people.' What do you know of the people? In times of trouble, the people and the government know only one thing: blame the Jews, rich or poor—us, like it or not." Sophie said she didn't like it. Pyotr Mikhailovich replied, "There is no choice." I started to say we could go to America, but both of them shushed me with a wave.

The message on the parlor floor was clear to Pyotr Mikhailovich. At Sophie's prompting, I had removed Tsar Alexander's portrait from my gallery of heroes. No one had noticed. Now I quietly put it back.

My stepfather sent word to the servants to return early if they were able, to set the house aright. No trace of vandalism should remain when Vera Andreyevna came home. "He treats her like a queen," said Sophie in disgust. "She should be down on her knees with everyone else, cleaning up the mess." I pointed out that the servants were doing all the work, while Pyotr Mikhailovich was spending his days across the river in Slobodka and the rest of us were just knocking about. "Speak for yourself," she said. "Right now we've got more important things to do than wander around the woods. You're interested, Maxie, I know you are." Her "we" was a lightly veiled allusion to some secret student group—Sophie had become much more cautious these past months, after all—but I declined her invitation with a shrug. "Idiot," she said, and strode off.

In fact, on my walks I was puzzling over important things myself. Hebrew lessons with Reb Shavelson had killed my belief in God. There was very little at home to sustain that belief to begin with, since we were observant only to the extent required by Pyotr Mikhailovich's circumstances. If he sold up and established a new business outside the Pale, as his wealth and position allowed, all pretense of religion would certainly fall away, though the legal stigma of Jew would remain. Then why not convert? I asked myself. Convert to what, I answered, another holy swindle?

However I turned matters in my mind, America beckoned, the land of freethinkers. I savored the few words from the New World that I knew from novels—*peacemaker, skunk, coyote, squaw, Apache, canoe*—and relished the exotic sounds of its regions: *Massachusetts, Mississippi, Alabama, Texas, Nebraska*! If the family would not emigrate, then the day would come when I would go alone. My connections seemed tenuous: Pyotr Mikhailovich, though legally my stepfather, was only a distant cousin of my long-dead father. My nearest blood relation was my turnip-face half brother, Mishka. With every mouthful of bread I ate, Vera Andreyevna calculated the drain on her boys' inheritance.

Thoughts such as these led to self-pity. To distract myself, I would stretch out under a tree and sink into *The Last of the Mohicans*, my favorite of Cooper's *Leatherstocking Tales*. Now I was Hawkeye, "La Longue Carabine," now young Uncas, guiding the beauteous sisters Alice and Cora through the North American forests, across misty lakes in silent canoes at dawn. The wooded marshland near our house became a lurking place for savages where I blazed a path of escape for the coming time of trouble. While the Cossack-Hurons attack and raid the house, I lead everyone to the abandoned hutches and safety. "Ask no questions. Be quiet and follow me." Sophie and Nina and Mishka come first, then Pyotr Mikhailovich with Vera Andreyevna, Madame, and Nikki, Nakki, and Nokki, and finally the servants, with Kazys the gardener bringing up the rear, carrying his ax. We reach the hutches and, counting heads, discover one of our party missing: Vera Andreyevna! We find her the next morning, scalped but alive and delirious, not far from our refuge. She had crawled after us through the woods, the human devils having left her for dead.

One afternoon I actually marked a path to the hutches, notching a tree every few yards with my pocketknife. When I reached the clearing I was startled to see smoke rising from the hole at the chimney corner. I dropped to the ground and watched, ready to pick up and run back into the woods at the first movement. But all remained still, and after a few minutes I cautiously walked up to the hutches and went in.

The pigsty was strewn with refuse and stank like a privy. I backed out quickly. The other hutch was close and smoky. A rusty spade was propped against the wall by the hearth. A rumpled bedroll lay near the fire, along with a cracked samovar, a dirty wooden bowl and spoon, empty tins and vodka bottles. In the corner opposite, an open gunnysack held a set of silver salt dishes and two pairs of candlesticks. Sophie would object, but this was surely a matter for the police. Pyotr Mikhailovich would be relieved.

I turned to go, gunnysack in hand, and found the entrance blocked. A huge man in ragged military clothes—gaunt and angular, with twisted features and sunken eyes—was squeezing through the narrow doorway. He barked at me in a language I couldn't understand and lunged forward, arms outstretched. I swung the gunnysack and let it fly at his grinning, unshaven face. As he grabbed at it to protect himself, I scooted around him and out.

He followed right behind and caught the tail end of my tunic. I pulled against him. He lost his grip and fell. I bolted into the cover of the woods and scrabbled into the branches of a tree. I had lost him.

I sat catching my breath. I remembered that among Sophie's books, I had recently come across Dostoyevsky's *Memoirs from the House of the Dead*, about prisoners in Siberia. "You can borrow it, if you like, Maxie," said Sophie. "You might learn a few things that will open your eyes a little." The book was nothing at all like *The Count of Monte Cristo*. Now I recalled the writer's description of a child-murderer, a common kind of Russian criminal, he said, who tortured his victims to death.

Something sailed through the leaves just above my head. Something else struck below me against the tree trunk. I looked down, and there he was on the ground, looking up. He hurled a few more stones and then lifted himself into the tree and ponderously began to climb. I retreated higher. Branches broke under him, and by the time he reached my feet, there was scarcely any support for his great weight. He grabbed at my ankle nevertheless. I kicked out. My boot tip caught him in the eye. He covered it with a grimy paw. With my pocketknife, I stabbed his other hand. He dropped, shouting, hit the earth with a grunt, and lay sprawled on his back without moving.

Whatever nerve I had suddenly drained out of me. I had killed a man! I became giddy and clung to the trunk, and when I finally eased my way to the ground, I was sick and retched beside the body at the base of the tree.

I had killed a man, but why must anyone know? I ran back to the hutches to fetch the spade and spent the next two hours digging a pit as deep and long as I could. I rolled the body into it, using the spade as a lever. I threw in the gunnysack and bedroll, filled in the pit, and covered it with branches. Then I headed for home, exhausted, but determined never to say a word about what I had done.

"You look a mess," said Sophie. "What have you been up to?"

She was standing outside the bathhouse, waiting for the coals to heat. "My God, Maxie, you've got blood all over you!" I told her everything, then and there.

Sophie was impressed. She asked me to describe the man again. Was I sure about his wearing a uniform? about his distorted face? Yes. I remembered the buttons on his coat were of tarnished brass, the gold trim faded and filthy. His mouth and jaws looked as though yanked to one side. "Bobelis," said Sophie in a whisper, "Sergeant Bobelis. He had his face shot up in the Crimea. He was with the police for twenty years. A well-known torturer. A Jew-hater. They court-martialed him and broke him to private a year ago. He was supposed to have been selling impounded vodka on the black market. That's what they said. But they'd have sent him to Siberia for that. The real reason was that prisoners were dying under his torture. Instead of forcing false confessions, he killed them. He'd break the bones of women and boys with his bare hands, once he had his way with them. After the court-martial, he disappeared."

I felt faint. Already I was transporting myself to Siberia. Sophie told me not to worry. "Since Trepov, they've got other things on their mind than Bobelis. Maxie, you'd better clean up. Get in the bathhouse. I'll bring you some fresh clothes."

The next day, the two of us went out to the hutches. We buried in the woods Bobelis's wooden bowl and spoon, the cracked samovar and empty bottles and tins, and all other telltale items we found. I showed her where I had dug the pit the day before. "Good," said Sophie, "very well concealed, comrade."

VI

Taking My Stand

THAT FALL, I entered *gimnaziya*. Sophie tried to draw me into her circle, her school and mine being sister institutions that shared some grounds and classes. I resisted. She wondered how I could still be indifferent, hinting at a new understanding between us, and gave me clippings, books, thumbed-over manuscripts, and poorly printed pamphlets, any number of which could have landed us in prison. Wordlessly lifting from my hands a novel of the American West, she would replace it with a revolutionary tract, and then tell me how I ought to respond to it. Of a ten-year-old article by Herzen or Bakunin from the exile journal *Kolokol*: "This should ring some bells." Of Nechayev's *Catechism of a Revolutionary*: "Something to toughen you up." *The Communist Manifesto* would "broaden your historical perspective." Turgenev's *Fathers and Sons* and Chernyshevsky's *What Is to Be Done?* had to be read one right after the other. "They'll tell you who we are and what we are and where we will be going." As far as I was concerned, I was going to America. The revolution was a swamp that would trap and bury me. I pictured myself dead in the woods, like Bobelis.

Among the boys in school, I found others who felt as I did. We formed our own circle and set about learning English. There were four of us, Yuri Kagan, Kalman Grossbard, Sergei Stepanov, and myself. We had no primer and no one to guide us, but each of us had something to contribute.

Yuri and Kalman were first cousins. Their grandfather had actually been to America and come back, having either made or lost a fortune there, trading with the Indians or selling guns to the Texas Rangers—the story was unclear. The old man had left his family an American legacy of two books in English. One, to my disappointment, was neither a novel nor a guidebook, but a King James Bible. The other was a pocket-size handbook, printed in Boston in 1809, entitled *The Young Lady's Accidence: or, a short and easy introduction to English Grammar. Designed principally for the use of young Learners, more especially those of the fair sex, though proper for either*, by Caleb Bingham, A.M.

Sergei's father was a doctor who had received his training in Berlin. Among his books was a long-unused 1847 Flügel's *Wörterbuch*, a German-English dictionary which Dr. Stepanov would never miss.

My contribution to our group was a knowledge of German.

Our method of learning was deliberate. Each of us copied all of *The Young Lady's Accidence*, without understanding what he was copying, in order to preserve the original and work better on our own. Every week, we wrote out several verses of the King James Bible, starting with Genesis, and I would look up the words in Flügel and translate them into Russian for my friends. At home, we would compare the English verses with the versions we understood—I the Hebrew and German, the cousins the Hebrew and Yiddish, Sergei the Russian and Slavonic. At our next meeting, we tried to make sense of our homework and copied out a new set of verses.

The Young Lady's Accidence was well organized for our purposes. Even without a full understanding of the language it was possible to grasp the overall patterns of "Article," "Noun," "Pronoun," and so on. It became clear that English was a simplified kind of German, or Yiddish for that matter, which made things much easier for the cousins and me. It also solved the matter of pronunciation. We confidently assigned German phonetic values to the English alphabet. Sergei knew no German and was furious at our facility. "How do you know this?" he shouted. "You're making it up!" We explained patiently. We needed his dictionary.

Between my studies in school, my own study of English, and Sophie's relentless program, I had no time for Reb Shavelson and his irrelevant instruction. Over the summer, I had grown several inches. I was quite big for my age, as strong as the older boys in school, and my body was already showing early signs of manhood. A Latin and Greek teacher at *gimnaziya* called me Maximus, and the nickname spread. Reb Shavelson, who now came up only to my eyes, no longer dared to pinch me or twist my ears. The one time he tried, I knocked his hand away. He looked at me in astonishment and then shrugged, as if to say, You are nothing to me. After that, my Hebrew lessons drifted, and I went to Pyotr Mikhailovich to bring them to an end. We sat in his study and had a serious discussion over sourballs. He was sympathetic but reminded me of my bar mitzvah, just a few months away. I told him I had no intention of going through with it. "I am an atheist," I declared. "There is no God. Why be a hypocrite?"

Pyotr Mikhailovich explained to me the nature of hypocrisy. It was necessary, he said, to make compromises with the world in order to live safely in it. "I draw the line at religion," I said. "No compromise, never." At that moment, I vowed to myself that I would banish all signs of religion from my life. There would be no hocus-pocus ceremonies in my home—my home in America.

"When I was a boy your age, I read this." He pointed over his shoulder to a book on a shelf behind him. "Spinoza's *Ethics*. I learned from it two essential things. First, that there is no personal God, no being, no entity aware of me, of my life, of my thoughts. But, second, that there is a totality of things, which we might call God or Nature, and the better we understand it the better we can exist in active harmony with it and lead good lives. This remains my philosophy today, Maxie. The world requires difficult, even terrible things of us, but a mind that holds to reason will still be free."

Sophie would have known how to reply. She would have told her father that his so-called philosophy was simply a liberal bourgeois delusion, a rationale for keeping things as they are, at the expense of the workers and peasants. Instead, I said, on the verge of wavering, "If it weren't for Reb Shavelson." Pyotr Mikhailovich said, "So he's the problem, is he?" I answered yes, and also God. "Of course, Maxie," he said, "but we've just settled that."

My stepfather could arrange for the ceremony to be held at any one of the small congregations in Slobodka, instead of the big, ornate synagogue on Jagshto Street in the Old City that we attended. Or perhaps Jagshto Street might provide an auxiliary chamber, such as its small courtroom, just a few people, the quorum, no celebration. While he talked, I thought of myself in a close room hurrying through the prescribed words of prayer and the Law. I pictured the stony faces of the hired quorum and the rabbi, who owed my stepfather rent. Reb Shavelson would be there, looking on amused. I said, "No."

Pyotr Mikhailovich suggested I'd been talking with Sophie. Again I said, "No"—not about this, I hadn't. He shook his head sadly and rose slowly from his chair. "Stay here," he said, and left the room. I sat there ashamed. If I did as he asked, how much would it hurt me? Sophie would roll her eyes and call me an idiot—she would do that anyway. Every day, I went to school and with everyone else sang *Bozhe Tsaria Khrani*, "God Save the Tsar," and so did Sophie. Who was I to stand on principle?

Pyotr Mikhailovich came back carrying a thick book, which he held to his chest as he sat down. "Maxie, when my father found me reading Spinoza, he whipped me. He made me rend my clothes in penance and sit covered with ashes. He destroyed the book. I found another copy. He had his beliefs. I have mine. And now it seems you have yours. I won't have you suffer for them on my account. This book is yours." He held it out to me: a Russian-English dictionary. "A little something I was saving for your bar mitzvah."

Ruth the cook and Basya the kitchenmaid were happy never to see Reb Shavelson's face again, but felt bad for me. They thought I had done something I would always regret. Sophie said she was proud of me. I told her to leave me alone.

VII

The People's Will

AMONG THE YOUNGER faculty at *gimnaziya* were some teachers
of a revolutionary bent. They were careful with their opinions,
but I was sure of one Greek and Latin instructor, a Pole by the
name of Kazimierz Wojcicki. Sophie spoke about him with heated
admiration. When he addressed me in class, I sometimes felt her
looking at me through his eyes. "Don't be an idiot, Maximus.
Demokratia, *aristokratia*, and murder are all class definitions. The
first two determine the rights of ownership and franchise, the last
the right to kill. What does this tell you about the death of
Socrates?"

Men and women like Mr. Wojcicki had gone out to the people
by the hundreds during the legendary summer of 1874. The peasant commune, said Herzen, was the natural seedbed of socialism:
V narod! Rejected by the peasants, driven underground and into
exile, they became martyrs and an inspiration to younger students,
who in turn spread the revolutionary fire among friends. If you
looked for the flames, they were everywhere. They had touched
Sophie while she was still at primary school. The headmistress's
daughter, who taught music, had not returned after the summer
of '74. The mother refused to talk, but the girls in school heard
rumors. Madeleine was in a penal colony near the Arctic Circle.

She had been butchered by peasants. She had drowned crossing the border into Prussia. She had been betrayed to border guards and was imprisoned in Vilna awaiting trial. Finally it came out that Madeleine had run off with her lover and been disowned, but not before the stories about her had made impassioned *narodniki* of some of the girls. The illegal literature they received from older brothers and sisters they passed like love notes from hand to hand. As they became older themselves, they began to meet at one another's houses on the pretext of a birthday or sewing party. At our house, Mishka was their pet, and he'd joyfully burrow his big head into their laps. Otherwise you'd suppose the revolution was mostly a girls' affair. If I happened on them uninvited in the garden, they fell silent. Indoors I could listen through a door. Sophie would lead the discussion, her voice always low and firm. It was difficult to tell the voices of the others apart when they became excited, talking, for example, about love.

One rainy spring afternoon, they were shut up in the schoolroom. There were Sophie and Nina, Fanya Ruttenberg and Chava Goldman, Olga Stepanov, and their little Mishka. Fanya was Nina's best friend from the one-room-schoolhouse days. Chava, a cousin of Fanya's, was living in Königsberg but returned to Kovno every so often to visit family. Olga was my friend Sergei's twin sister.

They were discussing marriage. I had my ear to the door. Sophie declared that, as Chernyshevsky made clear, marriage must be an equal partnership. Only with this understanding, without interference from religion or the state, could such a union become a successful economic unit, a domestic commune. Women and men must choose freely. In Chernyshevsky's book, it was Verochka herself who invited her husband into her room. There was a wave of giggles. I looked through the keyhole and saw Nina's face, flushed and dreamy. "I wonder what it feels like," she said, "kissing a man." Sophie answered, "Chernyshevsky doesn't say precisely. However, Verochka does seem to enjoy caressing."

"Let's try Mishka!" There was a scraping of chairs. Nina's face disappeared from view. I could no longer identify voices. "Sticky; he tastes like candy.... He's so small.... Close your eyes and pretend. It's only a question of size! ... Well, let's pretend I'm the man.... Mmn ... Yes, that's very nice.... Do it again."

In time, the girls were absorbed into a wider circle of revolutionary students—first Sophie, then Nina, Fanya, and Olga. They lost track of Chava, whose family eventually moved to St. Petersburg. Meetings at our house became less common, but inevitably I became a courier between my stepsisters and the boys at *gimnaziya* and their university friends who grimly called themselves the People's Will. I told Sophie I was tired of running messages. "Don't be ridiculous," she said. "We're not asking you to go far out of your way."

This was true. Often after school, I walked across the bridge on Jurbarko that connected the Old City with Slobodka. I made my way through the narrow streets to my stepfather's place of business, a stuffy pair of rooms off a tenement courtyard. There he sat, Pyotr Mikhailovich, in the company of an old Jew in a skullcap, sorting papers. In my stepfather's countinghouse, there was no Spinoza. The man with him was Shneur Shavelson, Reb Meir's father. My job was to help collect rents. I was learning the business. "You won't be going off to America for a while yet, Maxie."

With my pockets stuffed with I.O.U.s, I made the rounds of various shops and in between dropped off copy for a leaflet to an underground printer, picked up a sealed packet from one attic room and delivered it to another. But revolution was far from my mind. I used the time to practice English, translating the signs over the shops and in the windows, even the street signs, calling up the words from memory, noting down those I didn't know. On the day the tsar was assassinated, I was rehearsing the rules of syntax. "Note to Rule V. When the infinitive mode stands as a nominative to a verb, it is said to be absolute; but it is more especially so, when it stands independently of the sentence; thus, *to tell you the truth*, I was not there."

It was the first of March, the time of the ice breakup. Hurrying across the bridge after school, I caught sight of the people gathered below at the river's edge. There looked to be uncommon shouting and waving between groups, against the groans of the ice. Two women stood off together, hugging each other and weeping. Some laughing dockhands swayed in rhythm, singing and holding a bottle high. On the other side of the Neris, along the shore I saw no Jews.

Slobodka was unnaturally quiet, scarcely anyone on the streets.

My stepfather's place of business was locked. Sophie had composed a manifesto that I was supposed to leave with the printer, now hidden in a warehouse basement. When I knocked, there was no answer, but I was certain someone was there. "Open up. It's me, Max Kraft—Maximus." After a few minutes, I left and returned to my stepfather's, only to find it still closed, though the streets were beginning to fill with knots of Jews, whispering and wringing their hands. I headed back across the Jurbarko bridge, through the Old City, and by the time I reached home, I had picked up the story of the bomb assassination of the tsar by the People's Will. Sophie's manifesto I had torn into bits and scattered to the wind.

Vera Andreyevna and Pyotr Mikhailovich were in the parlor when I came home, listening to Madame resign. She would not remain under the same roof with my stepsisters. They were murderers, no better than beasts. "And you," she said, catching sight of me, "you are as bad. We know about you, off by yourself in the woods!" I started, thinking she knew about Bobelis. Vera Andreyevna fixed me with a triumphant smirk. My gentle stepfather rolled his eyes up toward the ceiling in exasperation and slammed his hands on his thighs. "Enough!" Vera Andreyevna paled. "Enough! She may go. Good riddance!" Madame fled upstairs to her packing. Turning to his wife, Pyotr Mikhailovich said, "I will have a few words alone with Maxie." We withdrew to his study.

He asked me if I had seen my sisters anytime that afternoon. I said I had been in Slobodka, but his place of business was closed. He shut his eyes and shook his head, as if to clear his mind: he should have left a note. Had I seen my sisters at all during the day, between classes? I said no and reminded him it was Sunday: school was closed. But in fact, I recalled seeing Sophie and Nina and Mr. Wojcicki pass by in a closed carriage on the bridge. First there was Nina's face, looking out but off to the distance, then Sophie's, looking sharply in my direction, then Mr. Wojcicki's. Then the carriage disappeared, and I continued on to the streets of Slobodka. I wondered why they were together and why they seemed so alarmed at the sight of me.

"So, Maxie," said Pyotr Mikhailovich, "you can swear to me that you know nothing of today's tragedy in St. Petersburg." I said, "Yes." With my hand on *The Young Lady's Accidence*: to tell you the truth, I was not there. He said, "Good. And the same for Sophie and Nina?" I answered that Kovno was a long way from St. Petersburg. "Yes, Maxie," he agreed. "And Siberia is even farther."

VIII

Exiles

SOPHIE AND NINA never came home. They were picked up near the Prussian border with Mr. Wojcicki, trying to row across the Vistula at night. Mr. Wojcicki was shot and killed. Police records identified him as a onetime revolutionist. My stepsisters were assumed to be his confederates. They were returned to Kovno for questioning by the secret police. I thought of Bobelis rotting in the woods nearby. They were held for weeks without charge at the fortresslike prison on a bight of the Neman, which I passed on the way to school. Pyotr Mikhailovich visited his daughters every day. He supposed that so long as he was allowed to see them, they were safe—he was, after all, a man of some local prominence. They were transferred to St. Petersburg overnight without warning on April 5. Two days earlier, the tsar's assassins had been hanged, a young woman named Sophie—Sophie Perovskaya—among them.

Pyotr Mikhailovich rushed off to the capital. He left me, he said, the man of the house, but what did that mean? Vera Andreyevna had gone with her three boys to Bialystok for an extended stay. There were five servants, with only Mishka and me to feed. Meals became irregular. The women's sighs drifted through the empty house. Mishka wanted to know when everyone was coming home. "How should I know?" I answered. "Maybe never." He began to cry. I suggested that he stay in Sophie's and Nina's room and take care of their things for them. He liked that idea, and I helped him move. After seven years, I had a room to myself again.

My stepfather wrote me from St. Petersburg every few days, and I read his letters aloud to the servants and Mishka. Sophie and Nina were in a prison cell crowded with presumed *narodniki* who, like them, were being charged with treasonous conspiracy in the vaguest possible terms. Sophie at seventeen would be tried as an adult. Nina was only fourteen, and Pyotr Mikhailovich hoped to have the case against her dismissed. "But she is so loyal to her sister," he wrote, "that even if they release her I fear they will have to tear her from Sophie's side."

By mid-May, the trial was over. Charges against Nina were withdrawn at the last moment, and she sat next to her father while Sophie and a dozen other very young people were condemned to exile. The real *narodniki* were dead or had fled. Now it was time to teach the children a lesson. Sophie was exiled to Tomsk. Nina insisted on going with her.

Pyotr Mikhailovich returned home looking drawn, his cheeks hollow beneath his side-whiskers, From the south, in the Ukraine and Moldavia, came reports of government-inspired pogroms, in small Jewish villages mass rape of women and girls, many of whom were said to have sickened and gone mad. "I consider myself a broken man," my stepfather said to me one day in his study. He opened his Spinoza at random. " 'Proposition XVIII. Desire born of joy, all things being equal, is stronger than that born of sorrow.' Maxie," he asked, "am I missing something here?" Then he brushed the book from his desk onto the floor.

At *gimnaziya*, pictures of the murdered tsar were shrouded in black crepe, and pictures of the new tsar were hung beside them. We still sang *Bozhe Tsaria Khrani* every day as before, but now without smirking. The teachers made no mention of Mr. Wojcicki's absence or the whereabouts of my stepsisters. Yuri Kagan, Kalman Grossbard, and Sergei Stepanov avoided my eyes. It was understood that our English study group was suspended. Fanya Ruttenberg and Olga Stepanov passed by silently in the hallways. There would be no more messages to run. Every one of us expected to be arrested. None of us was.

Nina wrote periodically. She and Sophie were living in the

household of a wealthy merchant of peasant background named Timofei Timofeyich Yakovlev. They were treated well, even with respect, because of their education and what Yakovlev called their good breeding. Sophie was employed as a tutor for the many children on the estate. Nina first attended the district school and then *gimnaziya*, paying room and board from the money her father sent. They had no direct contact with the political exiles in the area, most of whom lived in extremely primitive conditions, performing the meanest kinds of labor. I learned later that Nina put aside a portion of her monthly allowance from home to buy food, clothing, and medicine for the exiles, with the help of Yakovlev, who was district judge and, apparently, a quiet liberal.

It was hard to read between the lines of Nina's letters. She was wary of the censor. Her penmanship was exquisite and, as she told me years later, she hated the idea of a single word of hers being rudely blacked out by an unknown hand. We were concerned that Sophie never wrote, except for a few words scrawled now and then at the bottom of a page. The truth was, she had fallen into an unshakable gloom. She had arrived at Tomsk pregnant. Her baby, a boy she named Kazimierz, was born in midwinter and died of cholera in midsummer. "He's dead, Nina—Kazimierz is dead," she would say to her sister, by which she meant at the time her baby, Mr. Wojcicki, and the revolution. "Maybe Maxie was right. Perhaps we should have gone to America."

They asked for pictures of the family. There were none to send. Pyotr Mikhailovich hired a photographer, who turned the parlor upside down with his equipment. When my stepfather suggested that the servants be included, the photographer immediately began to pack up. He wouldn't even hear of a separate group portrait. There were tears in his eyes. He spoke with a French accent, but when the newest Madame quieted him down, it turned out he knew very little French. He had come to Russia as a small boy, he said, and had lost his mother tongue. Of the servants, only Madame was allowed to sit for the photographer, and she had joined the household after my stepsisters were arrested. Frieda the housekeeper, Ruth the cook, and Basya the kitchenmaid said afterward that it would not have been proper for them to have had their picture taken with us. Kazys the gardener and Marya the housemaid crossed themselves and said amen. Nevertheless, everyone, servants and family alike, passed the prints around with admiration.

In the final portrait, Vera Andreyevna's three grinning boys are draped on a low chaise in the foreground. They wear knickers, and their hair is parted and slicked. In real life, they were pale and freckled, with light red hair. Here they look dark, like the rest of us.

Above them, in stiff leather armchairs, sit Vera Andreyevna on the left and Pyotr Mikhailovich on the right. Her skirts balloon out from a narrow, corseted waist. Her hair is pulled back and piled high in curls. Pensive and prim, she rests her chin on a single finger. My stepfather sits slumped, a hand inside his jacket, over his heart. There are bags under his eyes, and his face is blank.

I stand towering in the middle of the back row, flanked at arm's length on the right by Mishka and by Madame on the left. My brother is puffed up in his school uniform, his arms crossed and his big head cocky. I sport an Eton jacket and floppy tie, the wisp of a mustache. There is a little smile on my face. I recall thinking as I held my expression: This picture is for my sisters in Siberia.

Madame is dressed in a long-waisted dress that shows as medium gray—it was in the flesh a lush green—with a lacey, bib-like collar. Her hair is thick and braided down the back, her gaze direct and relaxed. She looks the way I remember first seeing her, when Vera Andreyevna returned from Bialystok after the trial. In strode a smart-looking young woman while I was reading on the sofa in the parlor. I hurried to my feet. "You must be Maxim," she said, taking my hand. "*Bonjour, Maxime. Je m'appele Ariane.* 'Good day, Maxim. My name is Ariane.' Lesson for the day. Now come help me with these damn bags," she added in Yiddish.

Forever missing in the back row are Sophie and Nina. In the space on either side of me, where they ought to have been, appear instead pale hangings on the parlor wall. Nina should have been on my right, one hand on Mishka's shoulder, her dark curls in disarray. Sophie on my other side would have on an everyday dress with a loose white collar. Her fair hair tied back, tight-lipped and impatient, she was in my mind's eye in silent suspension between underground meetings.

Pyotr Mikhailovich sent a framed copy of the photograph to his daughters. Another was hung in the parlor. A third he eventually gave to me, and it was the only family I brought with me to America.

Nina wrote back to thank him, though she and Sophie were sorry there was nothing to remember my mother by. She asked Pyotr Mikhailovich to write and tell them about her, and also about their own mother, of whom they had no recollection at all. "How could that be?" he asked one evening at dinner. Ever since my stepsisters' exile, Mishka and I ate with the family and Madame Ariane Lévy in the dining room. Vera Andreyevna was more tolerant of her husband's other children now that there were fewer of them around. "How could that be?" Pyotr Mikhailovich repeated. "I say a prayer for her, for both of them, every year."

This disturbed me. I knew my stepfather, with Shneur Shavelson's connivance, had begun to spend part of each day at synagogue. I had no idea that all along he had been reciting for them the anniversary mourner's prayer. "What was their mother's name?" I asked. Pyotr Mikhailovich looked startled. Vera Andreyevna shifted uncomfortably in her chair and cleared her throat. One of her boys took her hand and said, "If you died, Mama, I'd remember you forever." Madame Ariane said that in Paris the current medical term for memory loss was *l'amnésie*, and it seemed in many cases to be associated more with emotional pain than with organic pathology. Vera Andreyevna excused herself from the table. My stepfather became moody and silent. The boys grew restless, and Madame Ariane took them from the room, leaving Mishka and me alone with Pyotr Mikhailovich, who was poking distractedly at the cake on his plate. "In answer to your question, Maxie," he said, "her name was Clara Diamant."

I was taken aback. Diamant was my father's family name. Pyotr Mikhailovich traced the connections. Clara and my father, Osip, were first cousins. My own mother, Fanya, was a relative of both the Diamants and the Krafts, though her family name was Brauer. They were all descended from a group of German Jews who had settled in Kovno at the turn of the century. It seemed I had blood relations, however distant, after all, Sophie and Nina among them.

Mishka demanded to know why these truths had been hidden

from us. Pyotr Mikhailovich tried to explain. Nothing had deliberately been concealed. Who did we think those people were,
named Diamant and Brauer, who came by every so often on the
holidays to pay their respects? They would have visited more
frequently if they could, but even we should be able to see how
difficult these matters were for Vera Andreyevna. In life, it was
necessary to move forward and not dwell for too long on the past.
The Christians have a saying: Let the dead bury the dead.

"She made us eat in the kitchen," said Mishka. "In our own
home, she's treated us like serfs." My stepfather pushed his plate
away. "It has not been easy for a man," he said. "Maxie, tell your
brother what it is like to lose not one but two wives, not one but
two daughters, to raise seven children in a house of contention,
in a time of trouble. Tell him." He rose from the table and headed
for his study without a further word. Mishka sat expectantly, actually waiting for me to speak. "Lucky us," I said, reaching for
my stepfather's uneaten cake. Then what I told Mishka was: If
he was a good boy and agreed to change the subject, he could
have the larger half.

IX

In Love

THAT SUMMER, PYOTR Mikhailovich took no holiday. He spent his days in Slobodka, looking for a new house, something unobtrusive in among the shops and tenements. He kept his intention to himself. When he went off with Shneur Shavelson and left his place of business in my hands, I supposed it was to attend prayers at some small synagogue nearby. At dinner one evening, he summoned attention by tapping his water glass and announced his plan to move the family across the river. Basya the kitchenmaid was clearing the dishes and let several crash to the floor. Otherwise my stepfather's words met with uncertain silence followed by Vera Andreyevna's stony "Never," to which I added: "Slobodka! Why not America?"

Pyotr Mikhailovich acknowledged there were good reasons for making either move but pointed out that Slobodka was nearer. America was too far from Sophie and Nina. "Never," said Vera Andreyevna. "Not Slobodka, not America. Only St. Petersburg or Moscow." It was not even twenty-five years, my stepfather said, since all restrictions on Jews' living in Kovno had been lifted. Under the new regime, restrictions might well be reimposed. Real-estate prices across the river were already rising in anticipation. The value of the present property here would fall. Now was the time to make the move. "Pyotr Mikhailovich," said Vera

Andreyevna in her most elevated Russian, "any such restrictions would apply only to the common Jew, not a man of your merchant rank." "Vera Andreyevna," said Pyotr Mikhailovich, "what you say is perfectly true. Nevertheless, even rank may be restricted if the holy tsar so decrees. Or perhaps our Little Father will simply bleed me white, until I become one of your common Jews. I repeat: Now is the time to move." Vera Andreyevna answered, "And I repeat: Here, or St. Petersburg, or Moscow."

The family did not move. Vera Andreyevna remained aloof in her suburban villa, while in the streets of Slobodka shops were closing or changing hands as Jewish families began to leave for my America. Fanya Ruttenberg went, followed by her two older brothers, Lev and Fedya, who were denied university admission as Jews and were suddenly ripe for military conscription, a term of twenty-five years. I expected the same lot awaited me. In my gallery of boys' heroes, between Mark Twain and James Fenimore Cooper, hung the picture of the old tsar, but not the new.

Without my stepsisters, the house seemed too quiet. I was surprised to find sometimes that I missed even Mishka's company, now that we had separate rooms. He took his charge seriously, to watch over Sophie's and Nina's things. Much of their clothing had been sent to them. We had burned their illegal literature. But what was left of their possessions Mishka kept in meticulous order. He read their remaining books with devotion and let no one look at them without his permission. If I wanted to reread an episode in *Dead Souls*, there was Mishka watching. "These books aren't yours," I said. "Sophie and Nina used to give them out all the time." He sat with his arms folded and shook his head. "But how would you know?" I added. "That was before you even knew how to read."

It was best to leave Mishka alone with his shrine. I had my *Lady's Accidence* and King James, my schoolwork, my American novels. On sunny days, I sat reading in the garden or found a shady spot in the woods nearby. *The Adventures of Tom Sawyer* was being serialized in one of my favorite magazines. One warm autumn afternoon, as I lay under a tree not far from the abandoned hutches, a shadow came over the page. Softly someone lifted the magazine from my hands. Sophie! I thought. They're back! I twisted around to see my stepsisters' smiling faces.

"*Salut, Maxime!*" It was Madame Ariane, seated on the grass behind my head. "I left the brats with their mother," she said. "A special treat for them. I told her I was feeling a little under the weather." I looked at the sky. The weather looked clear to me. "What a boy you are, Maxim. You don't understand anything. Just a big puppy, you couldn't hurt anything, could you?" She kissed me and pushed me down on the grass. "Could you?" We were perhaps ten yards from where I'd killed Bobelis. "Only in self-defense," I said. She put her fingers over my mouth. "Honorable sir. Keep quiet."

After that day, until warm weather set in again, we visited each other late at night. Ariane devised a system of secret signals. Her napkin ring was in the form of a diving petrel. At dinner's end, the beak pointed toward me meant "Your room," toward her "My room." Laid sideways, her napkin ring indicated "Not tonight."

If I was put off for two days running, I became sullen. The first time Ariane came to me, she said, "I've never done this in a boy's room before." I asked her, cautiously, how many rooms she was comparing. She laughed. "Less than you imagine, Maxim, and more than you really want to know." When she signaled "Not tonight," my heart sank. What if there were at least a room for every city in Europe where she had lived—Brussels, Paris, Berlin, Warsaw, Bialystok, Kovno? The thought sent me into despair. I was sixteen, in love with a twenty-year-old woman, and jealous of her years without me. I wanted her to come away with me to America. She gently waved my plea aside and mentioned Paris. "Yes, yes," I said, "Paris, and then New York."

One night in bed, she told me her full name was Ariane Rahel Lévy-Mendès. The moon shone on my gallery of boys' heroes. Under the eyes of Washington, Jefferson, Lincoln, and the rest, I whispered: "Well, we could go to South America then." She was touched by my sacrifice for love. "It's just a fancy name, Maxim. I'm not Spanish." A great-grandfather Moïse, liberated from the Venetian ghetto, had followed Napoleon to France. He had married into a family of Alsatian Jews and later fallen at Waterloo. His posterity bore his name as if it were a mark of gentility. "My father, Abramo, was a locksmith in Cracow."

I said I thought she'd been born in Paris and lived in Brussels and Berlin and Warsaw. "As a baby, on the way to Cracow. You don't imagine I'd find a position as a French governess if I didn't stretch the truth a little. But we did speak French at home,

Maxim. My parents died of consumption one after another, when I was fifteen. I've taken care of myself ever since, any way I can." I loved her for her frankness. "I'll get you to Paris, Ariane. I promise." She said, "I know that, puppy. One way or another, you will."

Mostly we met in her room, "Madame's room." Lying in her warm bed, I entertained her with stories about her various predecessors. She asked me their names and what they had looked like. "They had no names," I said. "They were all just 'Madame,' and they were old, and ugly, like Vera Andreyevna." Ariane said Vera Andreyevna was only thirty-five and not ugly, simply unhappy. Her marriage to Pyotr Mikhailovich had been arranged by her family through a matchmaker. They thought him a prize catch. It was Vera Andreyevna who thought Pyotr Mikhailovich was old and ugly. "But he's not an unattractive man, your stepfather. If Vera Andreyevna weren't such a stick, she might love him for his money. Maxim, you look shocked."

I felt uneasy with her talk. I was confused by my momentary jealousy of Pyotr Mikhailovich. Ariane sensed what troubled me and began to reminisce about her grandmother Bérénice, her mother's mother, from Strasbourg. "She came to live with us in Cracow as a very old lady. One day, for no reason I can remember, she told me she had been married twice, first to a brilliant Hebrew scholar who had died young, and then to my grandfather, to whom she had been devoted. But her first husband had been her real love. He had been years younger than she, and poor. The marriage had been arranged. When she mentioned their wedding night, I'll never forget how her ancient eyes glowed. 'Ariane,' she said, 'we had only just met. It was like making silent love with a beautiful stranger.' Maxim, sometimes I think we're like them, you and I."

Her comparison was devious though gentle. I was hardly poor. We were hardly captive, except to the danger of discovery. I was simply younger, so far as I could see. But I was willing to be beguiled by Ariane's artful tale of love made timeless in the imagination. In truth, she was saying our time was running out.

I entered my last year at *gimnaziya* in the fall of 1883, knowing that in just a few months we'd be on our way to Paris, and then America. I pictured myself with Ariane openly strolling along the Champs-Élysées, the two of us on the high sea hugging at the rail and laughing.

X

Betrayals

THE DISTANCE THAT had grown around me in school remained. It was begun out of fear of the secret police and continued out of habit. I was surprised one day after classes when Yuri Kagan, Kalman Grossbard, and Sergei Stepanov walked up to me and suggested we renew our study group. I was even a little hopeful. Without me, all three had let their English fade. The cousins were planning to emigrate to Cape Town. Sergei would be attending medical school in Edinburgh. "Why not America?" I asked. They shrugged. They'd be going where their families were willing to send them, and anywhere West was better than here. We decided to meet weekly, just as we had done before—before the assassination, the pogroms, my stepsisters' exile, before Ariane. But we, the four of us together, no longer looked to the same future, so things were not as they had been in the past. Then, we had argued about pronunciation, puzzled over spelling, and talked about bowie knives and Indians and how to protect a wagon train at night. Now we worked stolidly and held our dreams in silence.

Mishka started *gimnaziya* as I was finishing. He was of a new generation of student *narodniki*, more bitter and violent than Sophie's had been. When winter set in, I sometimes caught sight of him and his friends on the frozen river in fierce fights with rival cliques. They made their snowballs with an icy core. They built snow-block breastworks and stocked them with ammunition for strategic advance and retreat. Their leader was a boy named Sasha, recently demoted a full grade for writing an essay entitled "There Is No God." Mishka idolized him and boasted at dinner how he was practically Sasha's right-hand man.

"Sasha?" Pyotr Mikhailovich asked sharply. "What Sasha? Who is his father, what is his family name?" Vera Andreyevna's face tightened. Ariane looked concerned, as if to say, "Yes, tell us Mishka," while turning her napkin in my direction. "The teachers call him Ovsei Osipovich," said Mishka. "He calls himself Alexander." My stepfather pressed again for the family name. "Berkman," Mishka replied.

"Poor Osip's son," said Pyotr Mikhailovich. He knew the family well. He had been to school in Vilna with the boy's father and uncles Nathan and Mark Nathanson. "We were boys together." Now Osip, who had made a fortune in wholesale shoes, was dead. Pyotr Mikhailovich had stayed in his big house in St. Petersburg while awaiting Sophie's trial. His widow had come to settle near her wealthy brother Nathan. "The dictator of Kovno," Mishka laughed. "That's what Sasha calls him." Pyotr Mikhailovich took offense. "He's hardly that. Your Sasha must have heard it from his uncle Mark, the one in exile in Siberia. The boy's mother is ill. She can't control him. And now," he said, looking pointedly at Mishka, "he's apparently run wild."

Ariane appeared after midnight, irritated. "This family of yours, Maxim, what a circus. Vera Andreyevna cracks her whip, the big bear dances, the three trained dogs do their flips and lick her feet. Now she's bullied your stepfather into threatening to send Mishka to boarding school, unless." I asked unless what. "You can't guess? Unless the boy stops running around with his friends 'the assassins.' Or unless he starts learning his Hebrew, which he refuses to do. You'd better talk to him, Maxim. God what a family. I'm glad it's not mine."

I said it wasn't really mine either. Let them send Mishka away. "He's your brother," Ariane reminded me, "your own flesh and blood, even if he is a little prig." Mishka was only a half brother, I said. "And which half is that? Maxim, you can be cold." I told Ariane I loved her alone and cared only for her. "Don't worry about me, puppy," she said, "I'm saving my kopecks."

Mishka sat in his sisters' shrine, his chin out and his arms crossed. With his hair close-cropped, he looked like a fuzzy gourd carved into a glowering face. "I won't," he said. "She just wants us both out of the house, so Nikki, Nakki, and Nokki can take our rooms and she can get away at night from Papa. Everyone knows you're going to America, so I get sent off to school. Or I prepare for a bar mitzvah. I won't do it. You didn't; why should I?" I explained how things were different now. With Sophie and Nina in exile and me about to leave, it would break Pyotr Mikhailovich's heart if Mishka allowed himself to be sent away. "You're just being stubborn," I said. The blood rushed to Mishka's face. "Stubborn! That's something, coming from you. What a hypocrite! I've got principles, even if you don't. What would Sasha say?" I said Sasha wouldn't say anything if Mishka stopped talking to him. Then he wouldn't have to go away to school, or even study Hebrew. "Unless," I added, "you really do want to break your father's heart." Mishka said, "Sasha's my friend. I'll talk to whom I please." "Then it's off to boarding school," I said, and headed out the door. Mishka yelled out. "Maxie!" I turned. He looked at me in confusion. "You mean you really won't stand up for me?" I shrugged and lifted my hands as if helpless in the matter. "Well then," he said, "we'll go to America together, like you promised."

I closed the door and sat down on the bed beside him. "Like I what?" I asked. "Like you promised," he repeated. I said, "And when precisely was this?" Now Mishka was whining. "When I was small, you said we'd go to America. To be with our mama." I said, "That was just a story, Mishka, only children's make-believe." I got up to go. "But you did say it," he said. I nodded. "And you are going to America soon." I nodded again. "Then you're a liar!" he shouted. "And a cheat! Bourgeois scum!" As I shut the door behind me I heard him say evenly, "I'll get you."

After the New Year, Mishka was sent to a Jewish reformist boarding school in Vilna. Pyotr Mikhailovich had wanted to enroll him in an orthodox yeshiva, but Vera Andreyevna objected to that, for reasons of propriety. The whole family and Ariane saw him off at the train station. The more of us there were, the less able he would be to bolt and run. A cheery Vera Andreyevna gave his cheek a peck while her boys tugged at his overcoat. Ariane wished him *bonne chance*. I shook his hand. Pyotr

Mikhailovich threw his arms around his son and rocked back and forth. Mishka stood stone-faced throughout and boarded the train without a word.

In March of that year I turned eighteen. There was little to celebrate. Ariane and I scarcely met anymore at night, with Nikki, Nakki, and Nokki now so close by in what had been my stepsisters', and then Mishka's, room. On the day of my birthday, the servants, except Ariane, who was just Madame to them, held a quiet party in the kitchen. We shared some honey cake and sweet wine and recalled happier times. I read aloud an old letter from a cousin of my mother's in America, which Pyotr Mikhailovich had recently found, wishing her well on her second marriage. Perhaps I had family in America, I said hopefully. Marya the housemaid wept remembering my mother. Frieda the housekeeper was bitter about my stepsisters and startled the others by saying that a government which treats children that way deserves to be overthrown. To which Basya the kitchenmaid added, referring to Vera Andreyevna, that any wife who could treat her stepchildren so ought to be thrown out of the house. Ruth the cook said how thin Pyotr Mikhailovich was becoming, less than a shadow of himself. "Broken heart, broken stomach," said Kazys the gardener.

My stepfather had let his beard grow in below his sidewhiskers. He had given up his candy. He recited morning prayers in his study, attended synagogue three times a day, and began to stoop from the habit of praying. Pyotr Mikhailovich Kraft, the Spinozist and man of enlightenment, had turned into a bent old Jew. I told Ariane as much one afternoon in the garden during my last spring at home. "What an *antisémite* you are, Maxim," she said. I asked her to explain. The word was unfamiliar. "In current scientific parlance it refers to an instinctual racial antipathy to the sons of Shem, be they Hebrews, Bedouin, or of the Levant. It's in the blood. Religion has nothing whatever to do with it." I asked her not to tease me. "Religion is the great scourge of mankind," I said. "You've never disagreed." She answered, "Then we should pity mankind, Maxim—your stepfather included." With her back to the house, she blew me a reassuring kiss. Then, holding herself straight, she said, "Vera Andreyevna sent me to tell you that Mishka has been expelled from boarding school. He will be coming home tomorrow and will be sharing your room."

Mishka returned home sullen and close-mouthed. Whatever had happened to him, he wasn't talking to me about it. He evidently still blamed me for his being sent away. I had nothing to say to him either. I blamed him for coming back. My room was as packed as a secondhand store with my own belongings and Sophie's and Nina's and once again Mishka's. Vera Andreyevna insisted there was no place for storage in the house. My gallery of heroes was no more. In its place stood my stepsisters' bookcase. I had offered the pictures to Vera Andreyevna's boys, but they had covered their walls with colorful prints of famous regiments, Cossacks and Circassians, Hussars and Zouaves. The portraits of Lincoln and the others lay stacked under my bed. Mishka returned Sophie's and Nina's books to their earlier order and resumed guard.

I felt desperate to be alone with Ariane. Through a series of half-understood signals and hurried exchanges, we finally arranged a rendezvous in the woods. It was a bright afternoon toward the end of May. I had just passed my final examinations and felt both anxious and hopeful about the future—so much, I thought, depended on Ariane. Trees were in flower, the air was crisp and sweet. Ariane held my arm as we crossed the clearing around the hutches. At our feet, fallen blossoms tumbled in the breeze. She found a smooth spot a short way into the woods, out of the sun, and spread her wrap. I shook my head. It was where I had buried Bobelis. "It looks like a grave," I said. Ariane looked up. "*Le tombeau d'amour?* How gloomy and romantic, Maxim. You haven't stopped sighing since we met."

We moved on until we came across a small glade half hidden by bramble. There we spent the afternoon. I told her that I was going to America in just a few weeks. Was she coming with me? She reminded me that when she left, it would be for Paris. "Of course. Paris first, then America." Ariane said that those were never her words. I said she would want for nothing. Soon I would be independent and rich. Ariane suggested that Vera Andreyevna would never allow that. I explained. Pyotr Mikhailovich was arranging credit for me abroad, secured against my mother's dowry. According to her marriage contract with my stepfather, the market value of the assets she brought to their union were to be held in trust for her children. Vera Andreyevna disputed Pyotr Mikhailovich's interpretation of market value. She took it to mean simply the value of the principal on the exchange. He took it to mean the value of both the principal and its accumulated investments. I would draw a quarterly allowance of a thousand American dollars until I turned twenty-five. "Unless I marry first." Thereafter, I would come into my full inheritance. "At least a hundred thousand American dollars," I said, "perhaps more." Ariane was braiding a garland of dried grass and wild roses. I waited for her response. She set the wreath on my head and said, "For your *baccalauréat*, Maxim. You'd make a fine-looking pagan."

There was a sudden rustling in the brambles and the sound of cracking twigs. I jumped to my feet and pushed through a narrow opening in the brake. In the distance, scampering in three directions, were Nikki, Nakki, and Nokki. Ariane stood next to me. She said she'd left the boys to play in the garden. Mishka had been there, reading, and offered to keep an eye on them. "Mishka?" I said. "Then he's out there hiding right now. They've probably been trailing us all along." Ariane said she should have known. Her lips were pursed, her mouth drawn down. "I'm sorry, Maxim."

We walked back slowly to the house. Before we reached the garden she took the garland from my head and ran her fingers through my hair, smiling sadly. "You can write me *poste restante*, Poste Générale, Paris. I'll be using my full name. *Au revoir*, puppy." She threw her shoulders back and walked across the garden, to the steady rise of Vera Andreyevna's shouting.

XI

My Journey West

ARIANE'S DEPARTURE DELAYED mine. Pyotr Mikhailovich wanted to give me time to cool down. He was afraid I would follow her. Vera Andreyevna pressed my stepfather to reconsider the terms of my inheritance, lest my mother's legacy fall into the hands of that Lévy woman, the whore. Meanwhile, Mishka and I were banished once again to the kitchen. Mishka was shocked and infuriated. I reminded him how in ancient times there was no distinction made between a turncoat and the bearer of bad tidings—both were run through, or worse. But Mishka admitted to nothing. He was generally silent, ate his meals quickly, and often missed them altogether, slipping off, I supposed, to meet with his nihilist friends. The day would come, said the servants, when Mishka would disappear for good.

Emigration was the constant talk in the kitchen—who had gone and how they had gotten out, who was going next. Yuri Kagan, Kalman Grossbard, and Sergei Stepanov had left by boat. All three had sailed from Riga, their families paying dearly for passports. I wanted to take that route myself, but having a stepsister in political exile raised bureaucratic obstacles, and I was told that for my exit papers there would be at least a year's wait. Reluctantly, I resolved to cross the border illegally, as thousands of other people were doing. This meant traveling lightly, ready to strap my valise to my back. The most common crossing points were along the Prussian and Austro-Hungarian frontiers, where the guards on both sides looked away, for a price. Circumstances were not at all as they had been three years before, when Sophie, Nina, and Mr. Wojcicki had been caught on the Vistula. Illegal emigration was now tacitly encouraged. There was money to be had from it, and it was ridding Russia of its Jews at an unimaginable pace besides. Nevertheless, I felt uneasy about the northern route and made up my mind to travel south to the Ukraine and pass over into Austria, to the railway junction at Brody.

It was mid-August when I finally left. Pyotr Mikhailovich decided to accompany me to the border, as far as Dubno. Vera Andreyevna and her boys were with their relatives in Bialystok. The servants were on their summer holiday, but we had as good as said our farewells at my eighteenth birthday. Only Ruth the cook was staying on, to keep the larder open for Mishka, who came and went as he pleased and was nowhere to be seen at the time. "A stray cat," she called him. On the day before my departure, I posted a letter to Sophie and Nina, saying that I expected to see them some year soon in America, and left another for Mishka, telling him to take care of himself, if only for his sisters' sake. I also wrote Ariane, as I had a dozen times since the end of May, no matter that I had received no word from her in return.

We traveled by coach through the Pale, from the provinces of Kovno, Vilna, and Grodno into Volhynia, a distance of three hundred fifty miles. We stopped three times a day for Pyotr Mikhailovich to pray at the roadside, while the coachman and I stood watch. Every day we put up at a new inn, except on the Sabbath, when we holed up for two nights near a Jewish village outside Kovel. I feigned illness and stayed in my room, reading through my *Lady's Accidence*, while my stepfather walked to the local synagogue. The sight of these villages disturbed me, with their evident filth and ignorance and poverty. I asked Pyotr Mikhailovich precisely what he was praying for. "Precisely this: the salvation of the Jews." I said I was surprised at his narrow view. "No, Maxie, you are mistaken. Believe me, the day the people of Israel can breath free, the world will be safe for everyone. Because until that day comes, the world is safe for no one."

I asked, why the Jews. He answered, why not. I said since God seemed to be taking his time, America appeared to be a faster way to salvation. "For oneself, perhaps yes—but not for the world."

The nearer we came to the border crossing, the thicker the roads were with fugitive Jews. We reached Dubno after ten days. There I changed into a workman's outfit and put on a cloth cap. In my valise, besides my English grammar, I carried the photograph of my family, a good suit and pair of shoes, a change of socks and underclothing, and a sweater that Frieda the housekeeper had knitted for me. Small packets of paper money were sewn into the lining of my jacket. In my money belt, I carried letters of credit and enough gold and silver coin to see me through to New York. On my arrival in America, I was expected to look up my mother's cousin, who, if he still lived, went by the name of Henry Brewer. He had emigrated thirty years earlier and, after living for a time in one of the Southern states, had settled near New York in a village called Harlem. That was all we knew. Nobody had heard from him in years. It was his letter I had read to the servants on my eighteenth birthday, causing Marya the housemaid to weep, and I had it with me now.

After breakfast at the inn, my stepfather and I said good-bye. I thought it best to join the stream of foot travelers unobtrusively rather than be seen descending from a private coach. I began to thank Pyotr Mikhailovich for taking me this far. He brushed my words away and advised me to check through my money and possessions one last time. I asked him please not to linger once I was gone. It was a quiet leave-taking.

I attached myself to a group of a dozen men, from Podolia to the south, who had walked one hundred fifty miles from their village near Mogilev. I came across them at the roadside. One of them had fallen and twisted his ankle slightly, and now the guide they had hired to smuggle them over the border was demanding more money for the supposed inconvenience and danger of bringing the injured man along. The men had little money to spare. I offered to pay the difference and then some if I could join them, and after a bit of haggling they agreed. Toward evening, we left the road and pushed through a meadow to a small grove of crabapple trees. There amid the sharp, sweet smell of fallen fruit, we rested and ate our last meal in Russia, two hard-boiled eggs each and a hunk of dry bread washed down with a few sips of sour kvass.

Around midnight, we rose and made for the border. Under the light of a crescent moon and a wash of stars, we stumbled along singly and in pairs, helping the man with the twisted ankle. Now we were up to our knees in water fording a stream, now hugging the ground at a signal from our guide. I wondered if it was just so much playacting on his part. As the sun came up, one of our group whispered, "When do we reach the border?" Our guide answered out loud, "We crossed an hour ago. You're in Austria now." Soon afterward, we turned onto a road crowded with tired, muddied refugees, and there I parted with my companions.

Brody was chaos. The dusty streets running from the market square to the railway station were jammed with people. It seemed as if whole families, even villages had amassed there. Long queues, for food and shelter, clothing and medicine, tickets and visas, spilled off the plank sidewalks and lost themselves in the crush. There were signs in German and Yiddish, Russian and Polish, Byelorussian and Ukrainian, and something not French which I supposed was Rumanian. There was no talk, only shouting, and always in dialect, but I managed at one point to understand that I was standing in a food line, and there I held my place.

The sign at the head of the line was in Hebrew characters. I paid it no attention. Only as I was about to take my portion of bread did I realize that the words were neither Hebrew nor Yiddish. The letters spelled out what could only be "Alliance Israélite Universelle." *"Merci,"* I said to the woman handing out the bread. *"Où se trouve le directeur de ce bureau-ci?"* She looked up in surprise. I explained that I needed help to go to Paris, where my only living relative, *"ma cousine Ariane,"* now resided. She gave me an address and pointed in the direction of the railway station.

It took me a while to pick my way to the storefront office of the Alliance Israélite. There, too, was a long line, but the people had more the look of anxiety than of hunger. This was where visas could be issued and transportation abroad arranged. After a few hours' wait, I stood before a weary young man with a waxed mustache seated behind a table spread with papers and printed forms. Even though I spoke to him in French, he addressed me in Yiddish. He said that it was not usual for someone in my circumstances to proceed to Paris. I explained that I had lost all my family but one in the pogroms and that she, my cousin, now lived in Paris. We were, I said, educated people. He said that the Alliance was there simply to assist Jews en route to America, no matter who they were. *"Mais naturellement,"* I said, *"d'abord Paris, Amerique ensuite."* Impossible. The very next day he could put me on the Berlin-Antwerp train, with everyone else. That was the closest to Paris he could manage. Of course, I was free to travel entirely on my own, if I so chose. He looked me up and down, amused, and I remembered my clothes and where I was and what I was. After a night in the shelter of the Alliance Israélite Universelle, I boarded the train to Antwerp with some hundreds of other refugees.

XII

The Passage Over

I FOUND MYSELF in the same railway car as my border-crossing companions from Podolia. They shouted out "Max! Max!" and greeted me with hugs. The benches were close and filled the width of the car except for a narrow aisle. My rediscovered friends squeezed together to make room for me, and a bench that would have comfortably seated three people held five. I barely remembered their names. There had been little need for talk among us two days before. Now we recalled our adventure as if it were already legend, forgetting that everyone else around us had a similar story to tell. In our exodus, the railway junction at Brody was at best the other side of a Red Sea.

The train started up with hurrahs, halted a half hour later for no apparent reason, then started up again only to be held at the German border. Once inside Germany, it was stopped miles short of any station. One by one, each car was emptied of its passengers. We were quick-marched to a large barn nearby, which was fitted out for medical inspection. Men were separated from women and children. We were stripped, run through a lukewarm shower, and made to rub ourselves with disinfectant. There was little opportunity for protest. Our papers stamped, we reboarded the train and took our places, stuporous from hunger and humiliation.

At another checkpoint in the middle of nowhere, a customs inspection was made. This time, all passengers, with their baggage, were ordered to stand alongside the train. Uniformed officials stormed through the railway cars seizing anything left behind. There wasn't much. The inspectors outside confiscated a few live goats, chickens, and geese, suspicious medicinal powders and Jewish potions, and some gaudy objects assumed to be stolen goods. People cursed and fought to keep what they had. I stared down at the man who rummaged through my valise and intimidated him with my perfect German. All my money and possessions remained intact. The inspectors seemed disappointed with so little contraband. The actual smuggled wares were us.

With so many delays, the train ride to Berlin, normally a few hours' journey, took a day and a half. Once there, we were quarantined in barracks for two weeks. No Oriental diseases showed themselves, only outbreaks of unrestrained homesickness. In all this time, I became friends with the man in the border-crossing party who had twisted his ankle, Isaac Zilberzweig. We sat next to each other on the train and bunked side by side in the barracks. We were about the same age, but Zak looked considerably older than I. His face was weathered and seamed about the eyes. His tough body was slightly stooped, with his legs bowed at the knees, I supposed from rickets. He said it was from working and praying most of his life. I asked what he prayed for. "Not to work," he answered. He was going to America to become rich. "And you?" he asked. I told him I didn't pray. He laughed and slapped my back and said he didn't either anymore. What he meant was why was I going to America. "Never to have to pray," I answered, "and also to practice English." English? He took it as a joke and laughed again. Who on this train knew English? I told him I did. He became serious and asked how much he could learn between here and New York. He said he'd pay me back for my time when he became rich.

By the time we reached Berlin, we knew the story of each other's life and Zak could count change in English. He came from a poor family, charcoal burners in a village outside Pinsk. He had left home four years before, at the age of fifteen, to escape conscription, and had worked his way south to Podolia as a peddler, an odd jobber, even a roustabout for a Ukrainian circus, until they discovered he was a Jew. Zak poked me in the ribs. "It was the lady bareback rider. You should have seen her face." They beat him and turned him over to the police, who resettled him in a village near Mogilev. Then the army recruiters came to round up their quota, and he left for America.

I told Zak everything about myself except the truth—that is, about my money and how I'd killed Bobelis, and I made out that Ariane had been a French governess in someone else's house. He thought I'd be wasting my time in Paris. "She's set up by now, some rich man's whore." I stiffened and said I'd see for myself. He burst out laughing. "If you want love, Max, you'd be better off going to a marriage broker." Ariane, too, had said something like that.

After we were released from quarantine, Zak was informed that his group would be embarking from Hamburg instead of Antwerp. We promised to look each other up in New York. "You'll be able to find me, Max. I'll be on Wall Street." "Goodbye," we said in English, "we shall see each other again soon, in America."

The journey from Berlin to Antwerp was quick, with no inspection at the Belgian border. Once in Antwerp, I quietly detached myself from the emigrants. In the public bath at the railway station, I changed into my better clothes and then converted my money at the foreign-exchange window into Belgian and French francs and American dollars. In a café outside, I dined on medallions of pork, *pommes frites*, and Trappist beer. I'm no longer a Jew, I said to myself, and smiled to think of Reb Shavelson refusing Ruth the cook's food. I was a long way from Kovno now.

Toward night, I returned to the station. The refugees were still there, waiting listlessly for transport to the docks. I walked past them unrecognized in my suit, purchased a first-class ticket, *wagon-lit*, to Paris, and arrived at the Gare du Nord at dawn, exhausted. The human body is not made for rapid change, and in twenty-four hours I had traveled the breadth of western Europe and gone from barracks inmate to young gentleman. Also I had slept badly, dreaming of Ariane.

I hired a carriage outside the station. The driver knew a pension not far from the Poste Centrale that let rooms by the week.

He asked if this was my first visit to Paris. I said yes. He complimented me on my French and took me on a circuitous route, and charged me for it, to an ancient building near Les Halles. The concierge was delighted to have me and asked only that I pay a week's rent in advance and another for *sûreté*. There would, of course, be an additional charge for meals. I gave her two francs more, and she showed me to a stuffy attic room looking onto a back alley. There I dropped my valise and, tired though I was, found my way to the Poste Centrale just as the doors were opening. A letter was waiting for me from Ariane.

Salut!, she wrote. Welcome to Paris. If I wished to see her, I should leave a letter for her. She would arrange a rendezvous within a day or two. We could could not meet sooner, *hélas*, as she was presently engaged. She was not surprised I had not received her earlier letters. She supposed they had been intercepted by Vera Andreyevna. *Au revoir*. She signed herself Ariane Rahel Lévy-Mendès. I left a brief reply. I ended it as I had all my letters to her—"With eternal love, M."

We met two days later at a sidewalk café on the Champs-Élysées. I arrived early. She arrived late—the woman in a burgundy dress, with matching hat and parasol, who descended from an open carriage just as I was about to leave. *"Bonjour, Maxime,"* she said merrily. *"Je m'appele Ariane.* You look as if you don't recognize me." No, no, I said. She put her hand on mine. "I haven't changed that much in four months, have I?" Her face was powdered, her cheeks blushed with rouge, with a fake mole below her lips. But the voice was Ariane's and the direct gaze.

She asked me about my journey. I told her how I had come through Brody and Antwerp and been quarantined in Berlin. Ariane was sympathetic and said she couldn't imagine me cooped up so long speaking Yiddish. I said I wasn't an *antisémite*. "I didn't say you were," she answered. "That was merely a linguistic observation."

I asked her about herself. Ariane repeated what she had written in her letter two days before: she was presently engaged. When I pressed for an explanation, she laughed. "You don't really want to know." She could have been anything from a registered prostitute to a rich man's whore, and I said so. "Or a governess," said Ariane. "Or the keeper of a millinery shop." She looked me in the eye. "Are you?" I asked. "Am I what, a registered prostitute or a rich man's whore?" Ariane rose from the table. "Maxim," she said, "no more testing. You can't hold on to what was never yours." She hailed a carriage and was gone. If I had called out, what could I have said? You'll come with me to America?

With a guidebook in hand I walked the streets of Paris, taking the tour I had expected to make with Ariane. Her voice was one Baedecker in my mind, Sophie's was another. "The Boulevard Haussmann," said Ariane, "was named for Baron Georges Haussmann, who created the splendid Paris we know today, with its grand vistas and avenues, for Napoleon III." My stepsister said, "Comrade, tens of thousands of people were evicted from their homes. Whole neighborhoods were razed, so that in the event of another revolution the boulevards would provide the emperor's gendarmes with the clear military advantage."

"The Tuileries gardens, Maxim, were laid out by André Lenôtre for Louis XIV. He designed the gardens at Versailles as well."

"The Commune forever! They burned the Tuileries palace only thirteen years ago, comrade. When the government troops entered Paris, in one week twenty thousand people were butchered. Their blood lies under the gravel of these garden paths."

At a bookstall beside the Seine, I bought for one centime a used pamphlet, *Dieu et l'état*, by "Michel Bakounine." As I leafed through it, I heard Ariane say, "The man's arguments are provocative, Maxim, and clever as well. Here on page eleven, where someone's check marks are, he quotes Voltaire, '*Si Dieu n'existait pas, il faudrait l'inventer.*' And here on page twenty-four, 'je retourne la phrase de Voltaire, et je dis que, *si Dieu existait, il faudrait l'abolir.*' "

Sophie said, "Here in the Tomsk district, we'd be shot if that pamphlet were found in our possession. If only we could, we'd take the risk."

In the Bois de Boulogne, I apologized to Ariane for my jealousy. Sophie kept silent, but Nina whispered, "Say so in a letter. She can't have been receiving mail *poste restante* only from you. She'll be in touch with you again in no time."

Two days later, when Ariane had not written back, I left at last for America. I sailed from Le Havre on the steam freighter

Massapeag, an ocean tramp out of New London returning to home port after two years. I booked passage at dockside on the morning of departure, knowing no other way. The captain looked up from counting crates and spoke before I did. "Strapping lad," he said. "I'd take you on if I could, but I've got a full crew aboard." He turned back to his lading.

I was baffled. This was the first time I had been addressed by a born speaker of English, and I had scarcely understood a word. Only by the shake of his head and his turning away did I realize I was not to be allowed on his ship. I said to him, "Sir, thou knowest not yet mine intent. If thou hast room still for a traveler to sail with thee, I am he. I would an habitation make in America." After that my English faltered, and I drew on French and German to explain that I was an *émigré* from *Russland*.

The captain called out excitedly. Two women hurried down the gangway. He looked from them to me and said, " 'And when Saul stood among the people, he was higher than any of the people from his shoulders and upward.' This young Hebrew giant speaks the language of St. Paul." The women cried, "Amen, the kingdom of God is surely at hand. As it is said, 'not until the conversion of the Jews.' " I took all this, what I understood of it, as customary freethinking American banter about religion and the peculiar way these people had of welcoming a stranger on board. In the excitement, I was unable to put into English Bakunin's revision of Voltaire, "If God existed, it would be necessary to abolish him," a sentiment I felt they would enjoy.

The *Massapeag* took a slow route home, six weeks in all, putting in at ports in the Maritime Provinces and New England. My first view of the New World was the Labrador coast, not New York harbor, my first step on American soil at Portland, Maine, not Castle Garden. By the time I landed at the beginning of November, I was hesitant but grammatical in everyday English. To correct my oddities of speech, I spent hours at remote spots on the deck speaking into the wind.

I turned out to be the only paying passenger. I took my meals with the captain-owner of the *Massapeag*, Thomas Mewshaw, and his sisters Martha and Mary. A third sister was watching over the family house near New London. All were unmarried. They called themselves Bible Christians. The sisters sailed with their brother by turns to do missionary work, which consisted of preaching and distributing the English Bible throughout the world. I asked how they could explain away the existence of the Bible in other languages. "At the end of days," said Martha. "Which is now," said Mary. "Amen," said Captain Mewshaw. "At the end of days," repeated Martha, "English is the language in which the Almighty speaks to His elect." She pointed to me, Max Kraft, a Hebrew lad from Russia, who spoke the language of Scripture, as a sign and a prodigy. Mary then declared that I spoke with circumcised lips, an image I found alarming. This was not the first time she had talked about circumcision in my presence. She referred to baptism as circumcision of the soul and the making of converts akin to David's gathering of the foreskins of slain Philistines after battle. She looked at me pointedly after saying such things. As a Hebrew, I presumably had intimate knowledge of the matter.

Tobacco and strong drink were not allowed on the *Massapeag*. I wondered how many new hands knew this when they signed on. On Sundays, a sober crew growled hymns on deck to Mary's zealous pumping on a portable organ, while Martha conducted and urged them with her hands to sing louder. Captain Mewshaw preached the sermon, improvising on a Biblical passage picked on the spot at random, "as the Lord wills." I had to remind myself that the *Massapeag* was not America. Suppose I had returned to Antwerp and sailed with a boatload of Chassidim or Russian Old Believers, how much better would I have felt then?

The books in the captain's small library were Christian inspirational. In the confines of my cabin, I read and reread Bakunin's little atheist pamphlet. At times, I angrily muttered the words aloud, as Reb Shavelson had taught me to mutter Hebrew. One blustery day, I shouted over and over my favorite passage into the wind: "*Si Dieu existait, il faudrait l'abolir*'!"

"Practicing English again, Max?" I turned, startled. It was Mary. "What reading matter is this?" she asked. I held it away from her. "Nothing special," I said. Just then the ship dipped into a trough. I lost my balance and with it my hold on the pamphlet. *Dieu et l'état* sailed up into the wind and dropped into the waves of the gray sea. "God damn it," I said. Mary was shocked. I had taken the Lord's name in vain. She looked young and bewildered, while for three weeks I had been thinking of her as severe and ugly, like Vera Andreyevna. I remembered that Ariane had said Vera Andreyevna was simply unhappy. Now I saw that Mary, flushed and confused, was not much older than Ariane. "I think I'm getting seasick," I said, and went back to my cramped bunk. For the rest of the voyage, I avoided direct conversation with Mary Mewshaw and worked on my English pronunciation in full view of the crew.

I disembarked at New London on Saturday, November 1, 1884. The customs and immigration man who came aboard, apparently an old friend of the captain, quickly looked me up and down. "Strapping lad," he said. "Any diseases?" I answered no. He said I could be on my way then. Without good-byes, I made my escape from the *Massapeag*.

Part Two

I

Real Americans

A WOMAN SEATED beside me on the train to New York introduced me to sandwiches, soda pop, and McIntosh Reds. A uniformed porter stood in the aisle with a tray strapped to him. The
names he gave to the foods meant nothing to me. The woman
explained ham sandwich, sarsaparilla, oranges, and apples. "Yes,
yes," I said, "I know ham and apples." I asked if the porter was
a nigger. She put a finger to her lips. "Negro," she said, and asked
where I came from. Russia, I said. Russia? Was I a Yid? I owned
that I was but added that soon I would be an American. "Then
you'll have to shave off that mustache." It was thin and wispy,
she said, and made me look foreign, as did my clothes. My suit
was cut too trim, the jacket was too long, the lapels were too
narrow. She patted me all over and told me to turn around. "Not
enough padding in the shoulders. The vent in the back is too
long. Turn around again. No, I won't even look at your trousers."
A stiff collar was preferable to my soft one, a bow tie to my floppy
Windsor. I must have a hat.

She left the train at Bridgeport. I thanked her for her advice
and gave her my name. "Max," she laughed, "not exactly red,
white, and blue." I threw open the window and called out to her.
She quickened her steps and entered the station, and I never
learned the name of my first acquaintance in America.

The porter came around again. I asked for another sarsaparilla and discovered a roll of bills was missing from my jacket pocket, twenty-three crisp American dollars. Max, I said to myself, you're an idiot. But I smiled to realize I had just talked to myself in English.

It was brilliant autumn my first whole day in America. The intense colors of the trees stood out against clear blue sky and neat clapboard villages along the railway line. I continued talking to myself. I am here, I said. I have eaten a ham sandwich and an American apple and drunk sarsaparilla. I can think in English. I have been robbed. I remembered this sentence from *The Young Lady's Accidence*: "Wisdom is a defence, and money is a defence; but the excellency of knowledge is, that wisdom giveth life to them who have it." For the first time since leaving Kovno, I felt I might cry. "What a boy he is," said Ariane. "Pay no mind," said Sophie, "he's just feeling sorry for himself." They were both speaking English.

Once in New York, I took a room at a small hotel near the Grand Central Depot. The clerk had a bushy red mustache that drooped in what I supposed was the American fashion. His loose jacket was tan and checkered. He wore a high collar with a crimson bow tie. He asked where I was from. "Germany," I said. "*Sprechen Sie Deutsch, mein Herr?*" he asked. I said, "Of course." "*Sauerkraut*," he said, "*Knackwurst, Bockbier.*" I asked, "Yes, what about them?" "Nothing at all," he said, and dropped his eyes to the registry. Afterward, while I was shaving my upper lip, I realized he was being friendly, telling me the German words he knew, not trying to draw me into conversation in a foreign tongue. So long as I stood on American soil, I would speak only English. Still, when I left the hotel an hour later, I was relieved that the mustached clerk wasn't there.

It was Sunday. Shops were closed, street vendors and churches were doing business, children were out with their governesses promenading along the Croton Reservoir. I thought of Ariane. I walked north up Fifth Avenue to Harlem. Mansions gave way to undeveloped lots and shanties on one side and the walled stretch of Central Park on the other. Upper Harlem's country houses brought to mind my stepfather's villa in Kovno. I imagined my mother's cousin, Henry Brewer, looking like Pyotr Mikhailovich, receiving me in the parlor of my childhood home now removed to St. Nicholas Avenue.

All around me, it seemed, were churches, people flowing in and out of them like fish with the tide. I remembered Bakunin. Alone in my cabin on the *Massapeag*, I had recited his words. The existence of God entails the abdication of human reason and justice and the abnegation of human liberty. Therefore, abolish him. Ariane said we should pity mankind for its empty belief. But Kovno was one thing—this was America. There was nothing pitiable about the size of St. Patrick's Cathedral or that strange edifice near the reservoir, with Moorish towers and cupolas, that turned out to be a reformist synagogue, Temple Emanu-El. I could not dismiss them, as Ariane might have, simply as the cheap medieval fantasies of immigrants. Those were European dreams, I thought. They didn't belong here.

The next day, I walked downtown. As I turned in my key, the red-mustached clerk caught sight of my bare upper lip. He raised his eyebrows in surprise. "*Gott in Himmel*," he said, "you've been schnitzeled." I laughed, happy that I understood his joke. I could see he was pleased. He was smiling and said "So long" as I was leaving. "Oh, no," I answered, "not so long as yours. That's why I shaved mine off."

I made my way to the harbor, a distance as far from my hotel as Harlem, but street maps say nothing about the density of crowds and traffic. Uptown had been a stroll of an hour and a half. Downtown took three times as long. A straight path along Fifth Avenue and Broadway led through the edge of the ghetto. If I closed my eyes, from the voices around me alone I might have been in the streets of Brody or Slobodka. But other sounds pressed in. The clatter of carriages, horses' neighing and blowing, the bell of the horse trolley and the conductor's shouting, in the background at intervals the crash of elevated trains oncoming and receding. Between split seconds of silence came the screeching of gulls. The stink of horse manure and coal smoke cleared, and from the harbor wafted the smell of the sea.

From a peddler of ready-made clothes, I bought a derby, a shirt and two collars, and a purple bow tie. The peddler spoke to me in Yiddish. I answered in English. He carried on the rest of the transaction in something in between. I said I'd wear the hat right there. He wrapped the other items in used brown paper and said it was a pleasure doing business with a real American. I told him to keep the change, all of fifteen cents. He thanked me and half bowed as if I were royalty. I looked down and touched the brim of my derby, my American crown, and strode down Broadway, thinking, When Saul stood among the people, he was higher from his shoulders upward.

At a particularly noisy intersection I realized I was crossing Wall Street. The crush of people and carriages blocked the side streets, some narrow and winding as in the Old City of Kovno, but bounded by buildings with great, ornate stone façades. When Sophie had denounced "the money temples of Wall Street," I pictured columned structures, such as Mr. Wojcicki had described on the Acropolis, but strung loosely atop a Great Wall of China. As I inched forward through a sea of derbies, I found myself scanning hopefully for my friend Zak Zilberzweig. He said I'd find him on Wall Street.

I lingered outside Castle Garden and watched the people emerging bewildered from the immigration station. They paid me, a real American, no attention as I drifted among them. There were plenty of other Americans waiting to meet them and making their presence known. A rough-looking character with a kerchief around his neck went from one group of young men to another recruiting common laborers for a dollar a day. He quickly rounded up a team of six or seven and marched them off to the job, whatever it was. A bespectacled little man hurried about asking in Yiddish, "Are you a tailor? Are you a tailor?" and finding two, hustled them off in a carriage. A man and woman hovered near a large family and then inquired, in the family's accent, if they were by chance from Nemirov. No, the family said, they came from Bar. The couple moved on and in a wholly different accent asked another family if they hailed from Polotzk. Yes, they did. We, too, said the couple. It was a miracle in America! The family broke into tears and placed themselves in the couple's hands. More a confidence trick than a miracle, I thought. A vendor sold maps of New York, soda pop, candy, sausages, fruit, bread, at an extravagant price, everything for twenty-five cents. He came up to me after a while and said, "What's your game, Jack? You're in my space." I said my name was Max and I supposed I could stand where I liked. "Suppose nothing," he said. "Where are you from?" "France," I said. "Well, Max, I suggest you cancan on out of here if you've got no business." I noticed amid the noisy commotion of the immigrants, several Americans watching me in silence, and I left.

Back at the hotel I decided it was time at last to look up my mother's cousin. The clerks at the front desk were helpful and found a number of Henry Brewers listed in the city directory and on the telephone exchange. They explained how to crank the telephone box and ring up the operator to place calls. The red-mustached clerk, Osgood was his name, prompted me through my first attempts and watched merrily while I tried it alone and lapsed into King James English. "Max, not *my greetings, brethren*," he said. "Just, *hello*." A Henry Brewer who lived not in Harlem but at Rhinelander Gardens, in Greenwich Village, recognized my name, Maxim. I was Fanya and Osip's boy. He was glad to know the family was finally coming to America and invited me to tea the next day.

II

A Home

HENRY BREWER OWNED a three-story row house on West Eleventh Street, one of several set well back from the street, with balconies of wrought-iron filigree and gardens in the rear. He and his family stood waiting for me on the veranda as I walked the long front yard and then met me halfway down the stairs. I hadn't expected such a welcome. There was Henry Brewer himself, his wife, Elizabeth, his daughter, Abigail, three of the smallest people I'd seen in America outside the ghetto. He was stocky and clean-shaven except for the tuft of a jaunty little goatee. "Call me Uncle," he said. I noticed he had no accent. Elizabeth was plump and excitable. She hugged me tightly and insisted I call her Aunt Libby. Her English was peculiar. I wondered where she might be from. It came out quickly that she was born in Charleston, in the Carolinas, and her house made her feel almost back home. Abigail, a girl my age, was slight and solemn, with pale red hair. Standing two steps above me, she looked into my face at eye level. Gravely she extended a hand. "Maxim," she said, "you must call me Abby." "Uncle Henry," I said, laughing, "Aunt Libby, Abby—but only if you call me Max." As we entered the front door, I saw in the shadows of the veranda a Negro couple smiling and shaking their heads. Aunt Libby said, "Sally and Sam. I brought them with me from Charleston. They're free now of course," she added, "but when you treat your coloreds right, they stay faithful." She said this in earshot of Sally and Sam. Sophie in my mind asked, "The tsar freed the serfs to do what?"

It was a mild day for the season. We had tea in the garden, Sally serving dainty finger foods and Aunt Libby pouring and straining from a porcelain pot. There was no samovar. I showed them how we drank tea in Kovno, without milk, sucking it through a lump of sugar. Uncle Henry said he'd nearly forgotten—but shouldn't I be drinking from a glass? Aunt Libby took me around the garden, pointing to bare stalks among evergreen shrubs and dry ivy. "These are my azaleas and my rhododendrons," she said, "and these are my magnolias. We had the cuttings sent from home, didn't we, Sally?" Sally said yes ma'am.

Sam came to take away the dishes, clearing his throat all the while and, it seemed to me, grumbling. Afterward Abby and Uncle Henry showed me the house. "I saw you watching Sam," said Abby. I said I was and wondered why he was angry. "He's not angry," Abby answered, "he's mute. That's his way of talking to Sally. Some Simon Legree cut out Sam's tongue when he was a boy, for talking back to a white man. Mama's family found him in the streets and took him in. Only Sally can understand him." I asked Abby who Simon Legree was. A moment later we entered the library, and she handed me a book. "Simon Legree the overseer, you'll find him in here."

"I see you're a booklover," said Uncle Henry. I was running my eyes along the shelves, row upon row, from floor to ceiling, against four walls. There were no windows, but a small turret-like skylight brought late-afternoon sun into the room. In my hands I held *Uncle Tom's Cabin*. On the shelves were books by other writers I had never heard of—Bret Harte, Ralph Waldo Emerson, Walt Whitman, Henry David Thoreau—and all, all of my boy's hero James Fenimore Cooper, leatherbound. I laid Mrs. Stowe's novel down and picked out *The Adventures of Huckleberry Finn*. "You know Mark Twain?" asked Abby. I nodded. "Only in Russian." "This is his newest," she said. "Mama dislikes it. She finds it contrived." I opened up *Leaves of Grass* and read, astonished, "I sing the body electric." There were books by English authors, translations from Greek and Latin, French and German and Italian, even a handful from Russian and Jewish. "Is every-thing in English?" I asked. "Everything," said Uncle Henry. "We're in America now." These might have been my words. I jumped when I heard them.

After being shown the house, I was asked to dinner. I said I didn't want to impose on them further. It was no imposition at all. Carl was coming. It wasn't as if they'd be short of guests. I asked who Carl was. "My fiancé," said Abby. He wasn't due to arrive for a while, however, and Uncle Henry said that would give us time to talk over some practical matters. Sam came around to light the lamps. Uncle Henry and I again went upstairs to the library. There was a patter of rain on the darkening skylight. We sat side by side at a writing table in the center of the room. I explained to my newfound relative Pyotr Mikhailovich's plans re-garding my mother's will and handed him the various documents I had brought with me from Kovno. Among them was Uncle Henry's own letter to my mother. He asked me to translate. After all these years in America, he'd lost most of his Russian. Now, he said, even his German was fading and existed only in outline. "Everything is there except the words." He was looking at the letter he had written fifteen years before.

Uncle Henry suggested that since I was a minor, the bank might want to appoint a trustee until I was old enough legally to manage my own affairs. I asked what bank was that. "My bank," answered Uncle Henry, "the Bank of America." I said I liked the name. "Well then," he said, "you'll come around tomorrow morn-ing with your belongings. We'll stop by my shop on the way." I asked why I needed to bring my belongings. "We're taking you in as our boarder," he said. "The upstairs guest room is yours." It was next to the library. I didn't refuse.

There were many reasons for staying at West Eleventh Street—the comforts of a home, Uncle Henry's help in arranging my finances, simply the time it gave me to accustom myself to living a life in English in a new land. But it was the books more than anything else that captured me. In the library of the Brewers' house, my real American education began, the words I read com-ing no longer through a haze of Russian and German.

Carl Franks arrived damp from the rain and scowling. He hardly acknowledged my presence at first but held forth angrily in the parlor about the weather, about drunken Irishmen in the streets and German agitators, about the elections. I asked what elections he meant. "The presidential elections, Mac. Today is Election Day, or haven't you noticed. You're in America now." He turned to Abby and said under his breath, "Typical greenhorn. I don't see why you want to bother with these people." Abby looked away. Sally announced that dinner was served.

Throughout the meal, Carl Franks continued his harangues and his secret asides to Abby that everyone could hear. I hesitated to speak up to him. I felt it wasn't my place. Everything was fuel for his fury. But what fired it most was Tammany and the Democrats. Uncle Henry mentioned he had closed his place of business early that day, to give his employees time to go to the polls. Carl Franks said, "Several times each. Honest John Kelly knows how to get the votes out for his man." Uncle Henry said he employed only one Irishman, who happened to be a Republican, like Carl Franks, and also a temperance man. All the rest were Russian Jews and Germans, who would vote their conscience. "Then your Russians won't vote at all," Carl Franks said, looking straight at me, "and your Germans will want to blow up the polls." Then he went on about anarchists and unionists and the eight-hour day, when everyone knew that God made them twenty-four. "These people," he said, "they're taking bread from the mouths of native-born Americans, but they don't like to work."

Carl Franks was about the height of my friend Zak, but very soft around the middle and with creamy hands. He didn't appear to me to be someone who liked to work himself, and I said so laughingly to Abby. He lowered his voice and said to me with a half-smile, "If that's meant to be a joke, it's at my expense, and I don't find it amusing." I said he had made a number of remarks at my expense and others' without the excuse of joking. "I've been talking politics," he replied, and turned away, as if to say, What do you know about it? Aunt Libby said, "Well, that will be enough politics for today. Good heavens! Life will go on no matter who wins the election." She told Carl Franks I would be staying with them for a good long while, as a boarder. We should be friends. I was his dear Abby's cousin, after all. The look of hate he gave me reminded me of Mishka guarding his sisters' books.

He left shortly afterward. "No hard feelings," he said.

"None," I answered. Coldly we shook hands. I could see it bothered him to look up at me, as if my size put him at a disadvantage, and perhaps it did. When I said to Abby I was sorry if I had misspoken, she replied, "Small-minded—small-minded and petty is what Carl can be. Sometimes he needs to be told." Not once while they were together did Abby and Carl Franks kiss or show affection, even in greeting.

I said my good-byes before long and took a hack to my hotel. There were no drunken Irishmen or foreign agitators in the quiet streets. The lamplit cobblestones were slick in the soft rain. I puzzled over the nature of formal engagements. I thought of Sophie and Mr. Wojcicki, the runaway lovers in the carriage on the Jurbarko bridge, and tried to imagine Abby and her "fiancé" in their place. I thought of Ariane.

The clerk Osgood was on duty. "The night owl returns to his roost," he said. It was nine-thirty. I told him I'd be leaving the next day. "So it went well with Mr. Brewer?" he asked. "I said yes, I thought I'd be living there for a while. "Keep me in mind, Max." He gave me his card. "Clarence Ward Osgood," it read, "Sales Agent," with a postal box number as the address. I asked him what he sold. "Whatever you've got," he said. "Right now, these." He took out a tin of little blue pills, Dr. Miller's Sal Eupeptic. "But I'm expecting to branch out soon, full-time, perhaps into real estate. Isn't that Brewer's line?" I said I hadn't discussed my uncle's business with him. I thought he had a shop of some kind. "Brewer Realty," he said, "I think that's him." Osgood gave me two of Dr. Miller's Sal Eupeptics. "They'll make you sleep like a baby, Max." Instead I dreamed of the barracks in Berlin and searches by border guards who shouted, but in English not German, like Carl Franks.

III

Routines New and Old

AT DINNER THE first night at home with my new family, we discussed my future. Carl Franks wasn't there. Uncle Henry said that as my financial trustee he felt it his duty to advise me. He suggested I study engineering. The country was growing, the city expanding northward. The doors from Europe were open. Homes had to be built for the new immigrants. He quoted Walt Whitman: "In the labor of engines and trades and the labor of fields I find the developments, And find eternal meanings." I said that in coming to America, I hadn't considered going back to school. Besides, my training at *gimnaziya* had been in the classics. I didn't know the difference between chemistry and physics. The numbers I knew best I learned from my stepfather's account books. Aunt Libby thought that perhaps I might be happier studying architecture, like her brother Elias, who had gone to Rome and now was designing public works in the Argentine. I said I didn't have the ability to draw. Abby asked, "Why does Max have to decide anything just yet? He's only four days off the boat."

Later Uncle Henry explained. The two of us were sitting in the library. Aunt Libby and Abby had left to attend a lecture at the Cooper Union. "Max," he said, "you're something of a daydreamer." I said I had learned English and traveled across Europe to America on my own. "Of course. I didn't say an idler. And I'm a dreamer myself. America is a land for dreams and dreamers, Europe for nightmares." I told him I was troubled by those Old World nightmares I'd seen on Fifth Avenue, St. Patrick's and that synagogue out of *Arabian Nights*. Uncle Henry said everything was in the materials. Renwick, the same man who designed St. Patrick's, also built the row house we were in. "You take the materials and you change them with your dream. Walt Whitman says it. 'The shapes arise! Shapes of factories, arsenals, foundries, markets. The main shapes arise! Shapes of Democracy total, result of centuries.' " He added that he intended to expand Brewer Realty into building construction. He was already negotiating for undeveloped lots uptown in Harlem and even Washington Heights. The shop could use an engineeer with a knowledge of materials, a dreamer.

I entered City College after the New Year. Every morning, I walked across town to the school building at Lexington Avenue and Twenty-third Street. In the afternoon, if there were no classes, I rode the elevated train down to Brewer Realty on Canal and Lafayette. Uncle Henry liked to pore over with me his latest maps and sketches. "Max," he'd say, "I'm thinking of these three lots overlooking the river. There's talk about a new El line coming that way." I'd ask what would happen if he bought and they didn't bring in the El. Uncle Henry would answer quietly, more to himself than to me, "But they will, they will." A few days later he'd be spreading out a new plan.

Uncle Henry's mind was uptown, but Brewer Realty in those days owned only downtown residential and small commercial properties. Often I went out to collect rents in the Irish and Italian neighborhoods below Washington Square and in the ghetto south of Houston Street. I spoke only English. Twice a month I made deposits at the Bank of America, a Greek temple on the corner of William Street and Wall. I always looked for Zak among the crowds. From the bank I walked to the harbor. I waited that winter for the entire bay to freeze over and then in the spring for it to crack open like an earthquake. But the currents were too swift, the waters too wide, not like the Neman and the Neris. That year the Hudson and the East River froze in spots along the shore, for a short time locking aging wooden barges and sailing ships in their slips, while the steamships and tugboats glided on freely. In Kovno, from December into March the only things that moved along the rivers were the children playing or fighting on the ice. "As long as you're making comparisons," said Ariane, "I'll tell you this, Maxim: You've come all this way to America, but you really haven't come very far, have you?" She was right. I was living in New York much as I had as a boy in Kovno, my life a round of school classes, rent-collecting, reading, and studying.

I confided in Abby and she in me. *Gymnaziya*, I told her, was happier than City College. The teachers here were needlessly strict and were especially severe with the immigrants. The American students were aloof and mocking. As a friend of mine used to say, they were anti-Semites. Abby burst out laughing. "Anti-whats?" She had never heard the word before. After I explained, she asked if a Jew could be an anti-Semite. I hesitated, thinking she might mean me: "In some ways yes and in some ways no." "Well," she said, "Carl most certainly is one, and his mother came from Poland!" I showed her the photograph of my family in Kovno. She studied it face by face. "Everybody looks different," she said, "except for the three boys. It doesn't look like a family at all." Then she pointed at Ariane. "Is she the one you fell in love with and followed to Paris?" I admitted it but was puzzled how she knew. I'd never told anyone except Zak. Abby said she guessed it from little things that just now added up. I asked her about her engagement. "Mama wants it," she said. "I don't know what I'm going to do." A friend of hers had finished normal school and was now teaching evening and weekend classes for immigrants. "I'd like that," she said, "but Mama thinks it would offend Carl." I said she wasn't married yet. She looked again at the picture of Ariane and said, "You're right, Max. I'm not married to him yet."

Carl Franks came to dinner once a week and sometimes on weekends. No one was sure what he did betweentimes. He alluded to law and having a license to practice but was not associated with any firm. He mentioned trips to the state capital in Albany, called the Republican leader Thomas Platt "Tom," and talked about blocking the new president, Grover Cleveland, at every turn. As far as I could see, there was no great difference between the two American political parties, and I said so. Both seemed organized on the same principle, self-interest. In choosing one or the other, you tied yourself to the most favorable network of patronage, as in Rome people chose either Pompey or Caesar. Uncle Henry saw some truth in the parallel but said that here we have no hereditary patricians. He saw the political parties as great webs of people, spun by the people for the people. Carl Franks asked between his teeth if I knew of a better way. He said America was the freest nation on earth. Sam stood by growling with a hot, heavy platter of food.

"We all know about the corrupt party machines," said Abby. "Why is it suddenly up to Max to be the reformer?" She added that she in fact knew of a better way. Carl Franks said with a little smile, "Tell us, Abby, what way is that?" "Give the vote to the women." Carl Franks flushed angrily. "Gracious," said Aunt Libby, "I don't care much for politics, but it seems to me that if the women did have their way, there'd be more peace and loving-kindness in this world." I thought of Sophie standing over Bobelis's grave pit. "Very well concealed, comrade," she said.

Aunt Libby always had a good word to say about Carl Franks. His father had been a physician whom she had first consulted years ago for a chronic catarrh that developed when she arrived in New York and she and Uncle Henry lived in a drafty farm-house in Harlem. A German grandfather of Dr. Franks had been at Valley Forge with Washington. A Dutch ancestor was buried in the remnant of the Sephardic cemetery tucked away on Eleventh Street, across the avenue from Uncle Henry's house. Aunt Libby pointed out the stone. She said Dr. Franks had been a dear and generous man. His wife was from Poland, and he even wrote poetry. "What care I, O Israel, whence thou last fled! Our tribes now are one. Rest thy wand'rer's head." When she settled in New York just before the late and terrible War Between the States, it was Dr. Franks who introduced her and Uncle Henry to the liberal reformist community. Naturally she had hopes for a match between her daughter and the late Dr. Franks's son.

Abby said her parents had come North because of the slavery question. "Papa opened a hardware and tinsmith shop in Charleston after he came over from Russia. Some friends who had gone to England began sending him Herzen's *Kolokol*." I said I knew the journal; my stepsister Sophie used to give me old copies of it to read. "He started to lose his customers when he told them that if the Russian tsar could consider emancipating the peasant serfs, we in America could consider freeing our colored serfs. So Mama and Papa had to come north." With Sally and Sam, I said. "That's right. You know how Mama is. But it meant they were freed."

For my nineteenth birthday, Abby and Aunt Libby took me shopping for new clothes. Until then, I'd continued to buy off peddlers' carts. Abby said I was getting a motley look, like a scarecrow. I said I really didn't care and didn't want to be fussed over. Besides, I was still growing—but at six foot three I knew that was a lie. The week before, I had come home wearing a new tan jacket, checkered and bright as autumn leaves, something I thought Clarence Ward Osgood might admire. Abby said, "Max, excuse me, but oh my God." I asked what God had to do with her liking or not liking my jacket.

We spent the afternoon, a Saturday, in the A. T. Stewart Store at Broadway near Astor Place. Across from the Cast-Iron Palace, as it was called, stood Grace Church, another bad dream of Mr. Renwick's. I said it was a pretend church, with make-believe history. Abby wanted to know if I disapproved of it only because it was a church. I said I'd never heard of a Gothic synagogue. "Be serious, Max. What if it weren't a church?" she asked. "What if it were something else?" I said it should be something else. The two buildings should be reversed, a cast-iron church and a marble emporium.

Abby and Aunt Libby took me from shop to shop along the galleries beneath the great skylight in Stewart's. Most of what we bought was sent home, but I found a ready-made chestnut jacket that I put on immediately and a maroon bow tie to match. Aunt Libby said we should be sure to pick up something for Carl. Abby asked why, since it was Max's birthday. She refused to look at the cherrywood boot trees her mother held out for comment. Aunt Libby had them boxed to carry, in case Carl came to call the next day.

Abby suggested we look in on her teacher friend, who was giving English classes at the new German library nearby, the Freie Bibliothek und Lesehall. If we hurried over we might get there before the afternoon session ended. "You'll find this interesting,

Max." I knew I would, considering the peculiar way I'd learned English. But I also went for Abby's sake. She seemed so eager. Aunt Libby arrived breathless a few steps behind us after the four-block walk. In the rear of the library, some twenty-odd chairs and a blackboard had been set up. From the chalkings, I could see this wasn't a class for beginners. There were some lines of poetry written in both German and English, I thought perhaps of Heine's. The teacher was using them to demonstrate points of grammar—just then, the difference between the German separable prefix and the English dangling preposition. "That's just like Blanche," Abby whispered, "bringing poetry into everything."

The girl Blanche broke off her instruction. The class seemed relieved. "We have some visitors," she said. "I hope you don't mind if they sit in for these last few minutes." She motioned in our direction with a long, lean arm. The students turned to look. They were mostly grown men, with mustaches of various shapes and sizes, all trimmed and brushed up in the German style. A handful of women were grouped together in a middle row. Next to them sat Zak. He shouted, "Max!" and scrambled through the chairs. We hugged and punched each other like boys.

Zak and I drew aside to a quiet corner so the class could continue. We talked in excited undertones, in English. I asked him what he was doing, taking classes here in the German library—and on the Sabbath, I joked. He explained that he had a job with long hours, as a cloak-shop presser. Saturday was his only guaranteed time off. "I told them I came over from Berlin. This is not exactly a lie," he laughed. "They believe me." He looked at my chestnut jacket and asked if I worked on Wall Street. I said no, I worked with my uncle and was going to college. He looked questioningly at Abby and Aunt Libby. "If they are your wife and mother-in-law," he said, "they did not come with you from Paris." I saw they were paying more attention to us than the class, which was just ending. I motioned them to come over while quickly explaining to Zak who they were. He combed his fingers through his hair and stepped forward with a broad smile. "Isidore Silver," he said. I wondered what he had done with Isaac Zilberzweig. "My friend Zak," I said. "You've heard me talk about him." I made the introductions. Aunt Libby said it was a pleasure to be sure. "Today is Max's birthday, Mr. Silver," said Abby. "We're going to have a dinner treat. You're welcome to join. Max has told us so much about you, I feel as if you're one of the family already." Zak said he felt honored. "But please, Miss Brewer, call me Zak." She answered, "Call me Abby," and took his arm. Aunt Libby paled. "Good heavens!" she said. "I've lost Carl's boot trees. Where could I have left them?" She rushed out into the street, the box clutched in her hand.

IV

Love Again

EVERY YEAR IN July and August, Uncle Henry rented a country house in upper Harlem or the Bronx. That year, at Aunt Libby's urging, he took a cottage farther out of the city, in Asbury Park on the New Jersey shore. Her intention was to separate Abby and Zak. At three in the afternoon on Fridays, Uncle Henry and I closed Brewer Realty. We took the ferry to Weehawken and from there the train to Asbury Park. I carried a long letter from Zak to Abby. Monday mornings before dawn, we started the return trip, in my pocket Abby's newest letter to Zak. I also had with me sheaves of Blanche Viereck's weekly poetical outpourings.

It turned out that Abby had spoken about me to Blanche and had taken me to the German library to introduce us. Zak wasn't part of anyone's design. Blanche, too, came to my birthday dinner. Aunt Libby was reserved and courteous. The rest of us, including Uncle Henry, had a lively time. A year ago, in Kovno I sat alone with the servants for the last time, in sad remembrance. Now I was speaking and laughing in English, in America!, with people I hadn't even known before. The intimations in Blanche's gaze I thought were clear. I said to Ariane, "I've come pretty far after all."

Zak told the story of how the two of us had met. If it weren't for me, his companions would have left him, with his twisted ankle, on the side of the road. Blanche was thrilled at the romance of our adventure and gripped my arm. After dinner, she played Liszt and Chopin on the parlor spinet, her hair becoming a storm of blond curls. Abby sat comfortably next to Zak in the love seat. She caught my eye and winked. The following day, she wrote to Carl Franks, telling him he needn't call again, their engagement was off. He returned the letter immediately, to Aunt Libby, with a note: "What does this mean?" Aunt Libby confronted her daughter, who said, "It means just what it says. If I marry anyone, it will be someone like Isidore Silver." Uncle Henry asked me, feigning reproach, if I had anything to do with this awkward business. I said no. "I didn't think you did," he answered, "but you know how your aunt is." Then he added, "I never liked Carl Franks anyway."

I met Zak later that week during his lunch break, instead of going directly from school to Brewer Realty. He said orders were slow, there was no hurry for him to get back to the shop. We walked from the ghetto down to the East River slips. It was a mild day for March, and we sat outdoors on an empty pier and had sandwiches and sarsaparilla. Zak wanted to hear all about Abby and her family. When I told him she had broken with her fiancé, Carl Franks, he seemed pleased but reflective. He said, "The mother, your aunt, she will make difficulties." Then he shrugged and grinned, as if to say, What are difficulties to me?

Zak again brought up the family. I said they weren't really close relations. In fact, Henry Brewer's memory of my mother was of a little girl. He had gone abroad, to Zürich, to study medicine. In Switzerland, he fell in with revolutionary exiles of '48. He even once met Herzen. Then he gave up his studies to come to America. He wrote his friends in Europe, "For a Jew, the only revolution possible is here." Zak said, "Rich revolutionists. Max, I knew you were not poor. You never told me you were a prince." I said that when we were in the barracks in Berlin, I was just another refugee. Zak patted my shoulder and smiled: "I did not mean to hurt." I walked him back to the shop where he worked on Essex Street, in a tenement strung with wash along the fire escapes and up the central stairwell. Not it, but the identical building next door was owned by Brewer Realty. Zak gave me a note for Abby and asked did I mind. I said of course not, I was a veteran courier of the People's Will. I heard him laugh as he disappeared among the clotheslines.

Abby wanted to hear everything I knew about Zak. She was impressed with his English, which after only a few months in America had the barest trace of an accent. Blanche told her his German was excellent and was amazed to learn that Zak was a villager from the Ukraine. After Saturday classes at the Freie Bibliothek, the four of us went to one of the cafés in the ghetto. Zak entertained us by placing orders in the waiter's dialect, whatever it might be. I said that when I was a small boy, I used to think of every language as a separate room, with its own furniture and the set of its windows letting in or out just so much light. Zak thought of languages as being like different kinds of musical instruments. When he was a roustabout, the musicians in the circus band jumped from instrument to instrument. They could play on anything new in a few minutes, after testing the tuning and the stops. Blanche asked how well, really, could they play. She was thinking of all her practice time on Liszt and Chopin. "Well enough for a circus," he answered. "The bandmaster used to say: 'For ten kopecks I will play on any instrument you want. For twenty-five kopecks I will play any song you want. For fifty kopecks and the Bolshoi Theater I will perform an opera.' Miss Viereck—Blanche—for ten cents I will speak any language you want. I will even make one up for you. For a quarter I will tell you any story you want. For a half-dollar and a college education, I will write you one of those long poems you like so much." Blanche tried to laugh, understanding this was a joke.

Within a few weeks after that first meeting at the German library, Zak stopped attending classes and spent his Saturdays with Abby. He had been boarding with a family. Now he rented a small, two-room tenement, still in the ghetto, and Abby visited him there. The signs of their intimacy were cozy and unashamed. Blanche was envious. She wondered why we couldn't be as happy. If I had a place of my own, I asked, would she visit? She said no, unless perhaps we were to be married. "Then," I said, "we'll never be like Zak and Abby." Blanche said there was more to it than that. When I asked how she would know, she flushed. "It's you, Max. I can't get to you. You're behind a closed door." "Just a boy in his language room," said Ariane. Blanche squeezed my hands. "Let me in." I said, angrily, "What for?"

Blanche had no idea what she was doing to me, nor I to her, I suppose. We walked through Central Park like the lovers we were not. At the lake, she threw crumbs to the water birds. Some swans and geese battled for the food and beat their wings. Blanche, her eyes bright, quoted some lines about Leda that set me boiling. I'd do anything she asked, even marry. Blanche hugged me tightly. She couldn't marry me, she said sorrowfully, her being a Christian and I a Hebrew. I shouted, "What are you talking about! This is America!" I told her, "Who's closing doors now?"

When I tried not to see her, Blanche began waiting for me after my classes. When I missed school on her account, she wrote me letters and poems that twisted me around so much I had to start seeing her again. Zak said I should go to a brothel; there was nothing to be ashamed of. He gave me a playful poke. I said I already had. He let the matter be.

The first time was in the ghetto, a tenement on Hester Street shared by a dozen young women. "Not what I mean by an urban collective," said Sophie. I learned about the place from a boy in the street passing out printed cards in Yiddish. I spoke English, as always. The transaction was awkward, and I never went back. The second time was a town house near Union Square I heard some American students at City College talk about. The rooms were plush, heavy with drapery and perfume, the services expensive. I might have returned but for a glimpse I had through a partially open door of Carl Franks rioting with half-naked children. It was an alarming picture. Then I remembered that the girl I'd just been with, an American, was herself barely in her teens. There was a third time, one afternoon in the ghetto. A curt housewife alone at home with her baby offered herself in exchange for the rent. I made up the difference to Brewer Realty out of my pocket. For all of this, I put the blame on Blanche.

Summer brought some relief. I made the weekly trip to Asbury Park. Blanche sent me her poems from upstate, in Catskill, where her family owned a house. I responded to her with brief notes, such as Mr. Wojcicki might have made, on what I thought were mistakes in diction and technique. I found her verses extravagant, plaints from the wood nymphs Echo, Peitho, and Callirhoe to a chill Narcissus. She wrote that I was being cruel. After I explained the nymphs and Narcissus to Zak, he said Blanche was writing to herself, not really to me at all. Zak was reminded of a young married woman in his village said to be possessed by a demon, who inflamed her with lecherous stories she told to everyone, even children. She was finally divorced by her husband. He said she was cold and the marriage had never been consummated. "The midwife examined her, Max, and it was true."

Blanche was hurt at first by my comments, then in turn angry, apologetic, and derisive. In her final poem of the summer, she drowned her Narcissus in the pool of his own ignorance, to the wood sprites' tinkling laughter. When we met again in September, we hardly recognized each other. Blanche was fleshy and thick. I was trying to grow an American mustache. We sat in Sachs's Café on Suffolk Street with nothing to say, while all around us young men and women talked heatedly of anarchism, the eight-hour day, and the continuing international war against absolutism. I heard the voices of Sophie and Nina and their friends arguing in the garden. "Open your eyes, Max," said Blanche. "You can at least have the courtesy to look at me."

From a table behind Blanche, a hand waved in my direction. A young woman called out, "Maximus!" I recognized Fanya Ruttenberg, Nina's closest friend, and other faces I thought I knew from Sophie's circle. "Excuse me," I said to Blanche, "I'll be right back." She nodded grimly. Everyone at the table seemed to know me or who I was: a brother of the heroic Sophie Kraft. Speaking Russian and German mixed with Yiddish they asked after my stepsisters. I answered in English that they were still alive and well as far as I knew. Fanya switched over to English. She pointed to two men I realized had to be her older brothers Lev and Fedya. "You remember Leo and Ted." They called her Fanny. She said she had so much she was eager to tell me. I followed her every word. Fanny always could be a spirited talker. Olga Stepanov was with Kropotkin's exile followers in London, and her brother Sergei had dropped his medical studies in Edinburgh to join her. Fanny's cousin Chava Goldman and her sister Helene were planning to emigrate at the end of the year.

Whatever became of my little brother Mishka, the one with the big head? We lost ourselves in talk. She remembered how once in kindergarten I'd come to her rescue and sharpened her pencil, and then beat back an attack by the Russian boys. "But your friend, Max," said Fanny, "weren't you with someone?" I turned around. Blanche was gone.

V

A Ghetto Commune

FANNY AND HER brothers lived in a commune, in a tenement on Allen Street, with several other young Russian Jews recently arrived from the Baltic provinces. The girls had two sewing machines and turned out piecework, which provided most of the income. They did all the cooking. The boys picked up work where they could, but employment for them was hard to find. Their appearance aroused distrust outside their own circles. With their cropped hair, steel-rimmed glasses, and uncertain English, they seemed like the student revolutionaries they still were at heart. Everything was shared in the commune—food, money, clothing, books—except beds. The girls slept in rooms on one side of the tenement flat, the boys on the other. There were cautious manners about the single toilet and bath. Free love was much talked about, as a historical necessity come the inevitable breakdown of domestic slavery. Marriage was a property arrangement, and all property was theft. Meanwhile, Fanny's brothers watched over her the way Mishka had guarded his sisters' books. They called me the Yankee behind my back, because I spoke only English. I said the revolution in America would have to happen in the language of the place. They answered that the workers of the world spoke the international language of the oppressed.

When there was a little extra in their funds, the whole commune might command a table at Sachs's Café. Occasionally the boys alone went farther uptown, out of the ghetto, to Schwab's Saloon on East First Street. There gathered Old World social revolutionaries of all persuasions, arguing in every language except English about taking direct action, the use of political violence, and the fight for the eight-hour day. Comrades in the Midwest and Texas were joining with striking American trade unionists. This raised questions about the compromising nature of reform, as opposed to abolition of the wage system itself and private property. Mitigation could only lead to temporary reconciliation; reconciliation, to the weakening of the revolutionist's hand.

The fiercest proponent of violence was Johann Most, the editor of the anarchist newspaper *Freiheit*. He held forth in Schwab's, surrounded by followers, while he attacked and humiliated anyone who argued with him. The boys from the Allen Street commune sat awestruck. I did not warm to him. His bristling beard covered a twisted face that reminded me of Bobelis. I was troubled by his talk of propaganda by deed, of *Attentate*, and once said so to Fanny's brothers. Most overheard me and asked in German if the young man would stand up and frame his question. The saloon grew silent. As I rose, I felt the disadvantage of my height. "If a bomb explodes under the wrong feet," I asked in English, "in an 'attempt,' for reasons of propaganda, is there more or less blood than if it explodes under the right feet?" Most responded in German. He explained to the room at large what I had said, in case they hadn't understood. I began to sit down. "Stand!" he said. "Who is it who is asking such a question?" But he answered this for himself as I, a self-serving bourgeois sentimentalist, walked out into the street alone, without the boys from the Allen Street commune. I said in my heart to Most, I once killed a man who looked like you.

I stayed away from Allen Street for some weeks. Only later did I learn I had impressed Fanny's brothers by my composure. Johann Most was admired by Jewish radicals, but he was also feared. Many thought his antireligious diatribes went too far. I had read his German pamphlet *The God Plague*. He called the idea of God an imposition of swindlers, of popes and rabbis, whom in the end the people would hang in the church belfries and wonder why they hadn't done it sooner.

Jewish anarchists founded their own Pioneers of Liberty, I thought, in part to get out from under Most's controlling hand. When asked to join, I told Fanny's brothers I'd give them money but that was all. "You're still fighting European battles," I said, "in a foreign language on American soil." They asked what alternative I'd suggest. I said that because I raise questions doesn't mean I have to have answers. In their talk of doing away with property, religion, and the state, of free associations coming together for the common good, they'd forgotten the most basic right of all. "And what is that?" asked Leo or Ted. I answered, "The right to be left alone." After that they called me the Individualist.

I understood I was accepted by the boys at Allen Street only because I was Sophie Kraft's brother. For Sophie's sake, I paid the rent, even though she warned, "Maxie, you can't buy your way out of the revolution." Besides Fanny and her brothers, there were three other boys and two girls in the commune. Their names escape me, except for Zipporah Gelb, who reminded me of a blowzy Ariane. Fanny I thought of as an old friend. Her brothers were so protective of her, anything beyond friendship was unimaginable. When the subject of free love came up, Zipporah gave each boy a hooded glance, for him alone, that said: "Bring on the revolution."

When Zak and Abby married, after New Year of 1886, Fanny and I were to be witnesses before the judge. The commune was scornful, but Leo and Ted came along just the same, to see, they said, how these things were done in America. The other boys were curious to observe the rite of property arrangement. I said Abby's mother was threatening disownment. Zipporah and the remaining girl decided not to be left out of a communal undertaking. I surprised Zak and Abby with a wedding party of nine anarchists. Fanny's eyes filled when Zak slipped a gold ring on Abby's finger and swept her up into his arms. The boys impulsively thumped Zak on the back. The girls hugged Abby. Zipporah said, "I don't know why I'm crying." Afterward I treated everyone to a party at Sachs's Café. Friends joined us from other tables. Someone improvised a mock wedding canopy and sang, "Bridegroom, go to the bride." The whole café seemed to pick up the refrain of "Chericheribim." Zak allowed himself to speak Yiddish. He sang a charcoal-burners' wedding song that made of the long, slow heat of a charcoal fire a happy story of married love, whose embers never ceased to glow. "And so shall it be with the revolution," said Fanny's brothers.

We lingered at Sachs's Café well into the evening, after Zak and Abby had gone to their honeymoon hotel uptown. The conversation turned to free love. Leo and Ted said if Abby was going to be disowned, there was no point to the marriage. She and Zak should simply live together openly. Fanny gave them a sour look. Zipporah said love and marriage rarely have anything to do with each other. Yes, Abby and Zak were in love; everyone could see that. It was an indication of how far we all had yet to go that we wept at the wedding, a secular wedding at that, performed by a state-appointed judge! If you thought about it, she said, we weren't very far from the arranged marriages of our parents. Zak's charcoal-burners' song was pathetic emotionalism. Zipporah fell back in her chair and stared moodily at the boys.

I said I once heard an interesting story concerning arranged marriages. I told them about Ariane's grandmother—without mentioning Ariane by name—how in her old age she remembered the romance of her wedding night, the time she made silent love to a beautiful stranger. The boys were agitated. They said the woman was no better than a whore. Zipporah said, "If we were back in Russia, I could have been made to marry any one of you here." She looked at the boys one by one. I felt a foot rubbing up against my calf. I reached beneath the table and ran a hand upward from the foot as far as it could go, until it became wedged between two crossing knees—and they weren't Zipporah Gelb's at all. They were Fanny's.

In Kovno, there was a moment before the winter ice cracked when everything stood still. Sometimes in my dreams, the moment lasted. I skate along frozen rivers, past groups of silent watchers, past Brody and Paris, into a Sachs's Café on Suffolk Street that is also the garden of my stepfather's house. Fanny is there with her brothers. In the smoky room or sunny garden is everyone I have known or will know, though few are visible and those who are vary. The rest sit at tables in the shadows or are hidden among bushes and trees.

No one speaks, yet I am spoken to and asked to answer. I say, *How shall I do so, seeing my mother died when I was but five?*

There hath been a misunderstanding, I am told. The voice is my own. I reach for Fanny's hand.

The memory of this dream accumulated slowly. Not until I had it for a second or third time did I remember clearly having dreamed it before. After that, it became a sign to me that something was done, quietly and perhaps offhand, which changed my life. A man my size shies away from dramatic gestures. The first occasion of the dream was after Zak and Abby married. Fanny and I were alone together for the first time, in Zak's tenement, late in the afternoon. We lay in bed. One of us said drowsily, "I love you." The other said, perhaps offhand, "I love you, too." Then we slept.

VI

Echoes from the Past

MY NEWEST ATTEMPT at a mustache failed. Fanny watched as I shaved it off, using one of Zak's razors. She said her brothers would kill me. I said they wouldn't touch me so long as I contributed to the Cause by paying their rent. "Besides," I laughed, "they won't recognize me right away without my mustache." Fanny was serious. I told her Leo and Ted reminded me of twins in one of Abby's English children's books, two grouchy brothers named Tweedledum and Tweedledee. "And who do I remind you of?" she asked. I fixed upon the first name that came to mind. "Verochka," I said. "Chernyshevsky's Vera Pavlovna? Oh no, Max. That's your sister Sophie. No. I'm Natasha, in *War and Peace*! Yes ... No ... I am," she whispered, "Dostoyevsky's Lizaveta Nikolayevna," and looked blackly at the floor. I could almost hear the words she was thinking, in whatever language it was that Fanny thought in during those years: *shameless, impulsive, disloyal, attacked by a mob*. When she wasn't in hopeful spirits, Fanny expected disaster. I said, "Don't worry about your brothers. You know what they called them at *gimnaziya*?" She shook her head. "The Oxes." That made Fanny smile.

I took a flat on Allen Street, down the block from the commune, in one of Uncle Henry's properties. He gave me, as a start for a library of my own, his complete set of James Fenimore Cooper. Soon afterward, the Silvers moved into the same building. The three of us, Abby and Zak and I, were at that time unwelcome at West Eleventh Street. For months after the wedding, Aunt Libby was laid up with a lingering catarrh and melancholia. She said she no longer had a daughter. Uncle Henry said she'd come around with the spring weather: "You know how she is." Zak came quietly onto the payroll of Brewer Realty. Fanny drifted away from the commune and moved in with me. Her brothers, as I expected, made no open trouble. They ignored her, on the street, in Sachs's Café, at meetings. I stopped paying their rent. The commune dissolved. Leo and Ted disappeared from the ghetto. Fanny heard they'd gone to Chicago, to stand with the striking McCormick workers in the fight for the eight-hour day. The comrades in New York were evasive when Fanny asked the whereabouts of her brothers. Not that she really cared where they were, she said, after the coldhearted way they'd treated her.

A nationwide general strike was called for May 1. Across the country, a quarter of a million workers demanded the eight-hour day. The newspaper hawkers shouted the headlines. Foreign agitators were blamed. In the ghetto, there was fear of police terror. The radicals said the revolution had come at last to America's shores. Zak shrugged. He said, "Name me one imported revolution." We were all having tea a few days later in Aunt Libby's garden when the news came of the Haymarket Square bombing in Chicago. The magnolias were in blossom. The azaleas were starting to unfold. Abby announced she was going to have a baby at the end of the year. Mother and daughter were reconciled. Uncle Henry left for a few moments and returned looking pale, a newspaper limp in his hands. He toppled into a chair. Fanny was the first to rush over to him. "I'm all right," he said, "but look." The headlines blazoned an anarchist massacre, wild carnage among police and demonstrators, with casualties in the hundreds. "My God! My brothers!" said Fanny. She searched through the paper for their names among the dead and wounded. As it turned out, Leo and Ted were not in Chicago at all. They were in Cincinnati, where the strike was peaceful and died away, as it did in New York. In the ghetto that evening, I heard two men talking. One said, "To think we traveled so far—for this! Strikes, bombs, revolution." The other said, "But in America no one blames the Jews. They blame the Germans."   .

Not long after this, I received a letter from Pyotr Mikhailovich, postmarked Slobodka. He addressed me, in German, as his dearest son, the last of his living children he could write to and call his own. Vera Andreyevna had left him and gone back with her boys to her family in Bialystok. Mishka had run off at last. Sophie's exile had been extended for another seven years, this time for concealing forbidden literature said by the police to have been smuggled to her by Nina. The two of them had been transferred east, beyond Lake Baikal. The authorities would not tell him where. "Maxie, who without God in their hearts returns from the Valley of the Shadow of Death? My daughters are lost to me forever."

The troubles started, he wrote, just after my departure. New laws concerning Jews began to be enforced rigorously. Old laws were rediscovered. Marya the housemaid and Kazys the gardener had to leave. A decree of 1820 forbade Jews from having Christian servants. Jews were no longer allowed to own property outside the cities. Pyotr Mikhailovich had to sell his village holdings at a great loss. To raise money, he auctioned off the villa in Kovno with its surrounding land and moved to Slobodka. It was then that Mishka disappeared and Vera Andreyevna deserted him. Of the servants, only Ruth the cook remained with him now.

The wooded marshland behind the old house was divided into lots by builders. Near two abandoned hovels workmen uncovered an unmarked grave. The skeleton was wrapped in what remained of a worm-eaten military coat. An inquest determined the death to have occurred seven to ten years earlier, caused by a violent snapping of the neck and spine. Parts of the jaw were wired together. The police concluded the dead man to be a certain Jurgis Bobelis, a onetime sergeant especially hated by local revolutionists during the reign of the late tsar. Pyotr Mikhailovich spent a week in prison, under interrogation. Suspicion fell on Sophie. He told his inquisitors she was only a girl at the time of Bobelis's death. How could she have done away with a man his size? An investigator was sent to Tomsk to question Sophie. Shortly afterward, the case was closed, unsolved. But Sophie was found to have illegal writings in her possession and was banished with Nina to Transbaikalia.

He concluded: "Now I would be as our forebears, my wealth the clothes on my back, the Books of the Law, and a bag of jewels. I am ready to go where God wills. Your loving father, Pyotr Mikhailovich Kraft." He added in a postscript that what remained of my inheritance, after the forced sale of property, was being transferred in its entirety to America. Converting from rubles, it should amount to some twelve thousand dollars, over and above the six thousand already sent. He commended my mother's cousin, Hirsch Kalmanovich Brauer, for his care on my behalf.

I showed the letter to Uncle Henry. He told me the money was expected, by way of the Rothschild bank in Paris. "Pyotr Mikhailovich," he said, "has become a mournful old Jew." I remembered telling Ariane as much, it seemed centuries ago. Now that I was with Fanny, I scarcely thought of Ariane. Her voice was gone from my mind. "Yes," said Uncle Henry, "a mournful old Jew, and he may be younger than I am. He has a lot to be mournful about. Europe crushes us."

Fanny wept over my stepfather's letter. She called it a low groan from hell. Pyotr Mikhailovich was as good as dead. As if Sophie, then a thirteen-year-old girl, could have had anything to do with killing that torturer Bobelis! And yet Sophie, Nina, even Mishka were doomed. I told her she was right. Sophie only helped cover up Bobelis's grave pit and get rid of the evidence. Fanny was puzzled. "What are you saying, Max? That the People's Will did it?" "No," I said, "I did."

"You!" she cried. We were sitting in our tiny parlor on Allen Street. "Yes," I said, "with my pocketknife." I held it out in my hand. It was the same one I'd used to sharpen Fanny's pencil, in kindergarten. She asked me please to put it away. Her face grew weary as I told her the story. She put her hands over her ears. "I don't want to hear any more," she said. Then she shouted: "I didn't come to America to make a revolution! I came here to be safe!" That's when we decided to marry and in time move uptown out of the ghetto. I'd have been happy to go sooner but was uncertain of my finances and prospects. I wondered if Uncle Henry still hoped I would come into the business now that I was worth so little. He was shocked when I said so. "Eighteen thousand is a considerable sum. But the money's not important. The future is in you and Zak. 'The past and present wilt—I have fill'd them, emptied them, And proceed to fill the next fold of the future!' Walt Whitman." I suggested it was time for me to draw a salary, as Zak did, and not live off a quarterly allowance as I had been doing. I added: "In the fall, I won't be going back to school." Uncle Henry started to object. He stopped when I said Fanny and I were getting married. He understood a family man has to pay his own way.

We were married in the parlor on West Eleventh Street. Aunt Libby wanted a reformist rabbi to perform the ceremony. I said no. Fanny, to my surprise, seemed let down. "Good gracious," said Aunt Libby, "with no wedding canopy, how will you feel really and truly married?" At Zak's suggestion, we raised a canopy but were married under it by a judge. Zak and Abby invited some neighbors from our building on Allen Street. Fanny's brothers refused to come at first, then brought the whole of the former commune. Uncle Henry hired a little Jewish band. Zak sang the charcoal-burners' marriage song, which, although regressive, had everyone weeping. Zipporah Gelb said, "After all, why not? It's an authentic song of the people." Sally and Sam served food from a buffet. The boys from the former commune ate hungrily of the food taken from the workers' mouths, most especially the smoked salmon, cold asparagus, and imported caviar.

We danced and sang until the early-morning hours. The next day, Fanny and I left on a river cruise up the Hudson as far as Glens Falls. From there we looped back slowly through the Adirondacks. Fanny said the countryside was the most beautiful she'd ever seen. Before coming to America she'd never been out of the province of Kovno. I told her that ever since I was a boy and read Cooper's *Leatherstocking Tales*, I'd dreamed of coming here. On the way home after two weeks, we put money down on some lakefront acreage between Liberty and Woodville, in the hills just south of the Catskills. I asked Fanny what we should call it. She suggested taking the title of one of Cooper's books. Our place by Stump Lake we named The Pioneers.

VII

No Family Now

AT THE VERY end of August came the great earthquake of 1886 that leveled most of Charleston. Aunt Libby was taken with a fever. She lay in bed for days at a summer cottage in the Bronx, mistaking each of her visitors for someone else. Uncle Henry thought she was having one of her episodes. She often took on that way, with rheums and nervous prostration, after distressing news. Aunt Libby had no family to speak of left in the South, but in her, he said, the inward eyes of memory and imagination were strong. Everyone understood how Aunt Libby was. Only Zak had misgivings. Looking him full in the face, she called him Papa. He said to Abby, "Tell your father we've got to find a physician." There was no telephone. Sam readied the carriage and drove Zak and me from house to house in Throgs Neck, inquiring after a doctor. We returned after dark with a Dr. Monck, who was retired and at first recommended leeching, but Aunt Libby was too far gone for that. He said she had an advanced brain fever and couldn't last the night. He sponged her off and made her comfortable. Aunt Libby said to him, "How nice to see you again, Judge." Uncle Henry and Sally sat up all night at her bedside. At sunup she opened her eyes and stopped breathing.

Abby miscarried in her sixth month. Fanny was with her at

Allen Street. The baby would have been a girl. It would have been named Elizabeth, after Abby's mother. Fanny said it seemed hard enough just to bring a baby into this world, so how do we think we can ever make a revolution? We were in our little parlor, in the spot we called the Oriental corner, decorated with beaded pillows and a Persian throw rug. Fanny's brothers had just gone. They'd come to tell us about the Haymarket trial. Five comrades were sentenced to be hanged. The remaining three were given long prison terms, one for fifteen years, the other two for life. There was no evidence that any of them had thrown the bomb. All but two were Germans.

Leo and Ted were annoyed at what they thought was our indifference. I said we'd been caught up in other matters—the double tragedy of Aunt Libby's death and Abby's losing her baby. Fanny's brothers said, with no real concern, they hadn't been aware. "And why weren't you?" asked Fanny. "When it comes to what happens in my life, why aren't you aware?" They sat, stolid, side by side on our sofa. They'd been away, raising money for the Haymarket comrades' defense, in Ohio, Pennsylvania, and upstate New York. In Rochester, they'd visited with cousins Lena and Helene Zodikow and their half sister, Chava Goldman. Lena was married to a man named Cominsky. All three sisters gave to the defense fund, but the parents nothing. Helene and Chava each contributed a dollar out of their factory wages of two and a half dollars a week. "You've seen Chava?" said Fanny. "How does she look?" Chava was calling herself Emma now, they said. She looked the way she always had, like Fanny, except with lighter and straighter hair, and she was shorter by a few inches. The two could be sisters. "We were like sisters, too," said Fanny. "Nina Kraft and Chava Goldman were the sisters I never had."

Leo and Ted urged us to join the new anarchist group, the Pioneers of Liberty. That's when I told them I'd give them money, but how could they ask me, the Yankee, I joked, to join a Yiddish-speaking association? When they left Fanny said, "Oxes!" She thought they were trying to use us. "Use us," I asked, "in what way?" She said, "They know we own a place near Liberty named The Pioneers. They'll want it for themselves." We had to call it something, since we were planning to rent out cottages on the lakefront and build a manor for summer boarders.

Then and there, we changed the name of our property at Stump Lake to The Pathfinder.

Before the year's end, Uncle Henry decided to sell the house on West Eleventh Street. Aunt Libby's presence was in every room. He said he couldn't remain in the past. With the profits from the sale, he would capitalize Brewer Realty and turn it over to Zak and me, while he traveled. "Travel?" asked Abby. "Papa, travel where?" "America!" said Uncle Henry. " 'On journeys through the States we start'!" He would keep a journal and write letters to Abby. Perhaps, he suggested, they might even be publishable. Zak caught my eye and laughed. Fanny wondered why. She asked me later if it was the idea of Uncle Henry writing a book. I said, no, it was Zak's excitement at running a company. He was impatient with plans for the business. He wanted to sell off the downtown property and build uptown and in the Bronx. Uncle Henry had the vision but wouldn't let go of his tenements. Brewer Realty had a dozen buildings. If we sold them one by one, we could keep up income while we bought new lots and started construction. In three to five years, Fanny and I could move uptown.

Fanny said that was too long a wait, unless I enjoyed the sight of the whores on Allen Street. The ghetto's red-light district was right outside the front door. "I'm tired of this place," she said. "I'm tired of my brothers. Look." She handed me a letter. It was from her parents in Kovno but addressed to Leo and Ted—that is, Lev and Fedya—as if they were living with us. Fanny had written her family when she and I married. She sent them money to emigrate. Now they were writing her brothers, not Fanny, to say they were going instead to Shavl, the town where they'd been born. They had read about the revolution in America. They urged Lev and Fedya to watch over their little Fanya, to see she didn't become involved with the nihilists. They feared she'd made the mistake of her life marrying a brother of that terrorist Sophie Kraft. "They will die in Shavl," said Fanny, "and I don't care." She threw the letter into the garbage. "I have no family now."

We moved uptown to a brick row house, on East One Hundred Third Street, in the spring of 1887. Zak and Abby decided to stay in the ghetto for the time being but moved to Suffolk Street, away from the prostitution. Zak wanted to be near the business. Abby enrolled in the teachers' education course at New

York University. She hoped soon to be fluent in Jewish, which would help her in her intended work. She found the language colorful and expressive. I said it was a mongrel jargon that had no grammar. Abby thought I was going too far. Every language had a grammar. As someone said—she'd forgotten who—in words lie the history of the race. I said yes, the history we'd rather not remember. By then, Zak and I had lost all traces of our accents. Fanny still had trouble with her *r*'s, which she pronounced with a burr. Her short *a*'s came out as short *e*'s—she called me "Mex." When she became excited, her *w*'s turned into *v*'s. Our rule for ourselves was to speak only English in the house. At the Silvers', or any other place, when Fanny fell into Yiddish she sounded provincial. If she had to speak like a European, I preferred her German, which was precise and serviceable, or her rich and literary Russian. As for me, no words of my own except English ones passed my lips.

At Abby's suggestion, Fanny worked without pay two evenings a week at the Aguilar Free Library on East One Hundred Tenth Street. She said she needed to keep busy but found the idea of teaching English to immigrants unappealing. I thought perhaps we might have children soon. "What for," she asked, "in a world like this?" She was sure that what happened to Abby, or worse, would happen to her. For her twentieth birthday, I bought her a pony-chaise. She kept it at a stable a few blocks away and took it out for a long fast trot at least twice a day. She did this, she said, to get away from Sally and Sam. They had come with us after Uncle Henry started on his travels. Fanny objected. They frightened her, Sam especially. She said if they could they'd slit our throats. "They're not Gypsies," I said. "They've been with the family all their lives." "Exactly," said Fanny. She relented after talking with Abby, who expected to take Sally and Sam back again when she and Zak moved away from the ghetto.

Uncle Henry sent postcards with stereoscopic pictures of America's grand views. Twice a week, he wrote Abby long letters. She read them to us every weekend, when she and Zak came to visit or we went to their place on Suffolk Street. He talked about the landmarks he had seen. He misquoted Walt Whitman. He never said a word about himself beyond "I am well." Abby was worried. "He's thinking of Mama all the time," she said. "I can tell."

The first leg of his planned railroad route took him to the city of Washington, from there to Charleston and then southwest to New Orleans. From New Orleans he intended to steam up the Mississippi to St. Louis and then ride along what had been the Santa Fe Trail. He was hoping to see buffalo, but never got far enough west. A doctor for the Santa Fe Railroad wrote that, stepping out for air at Big Bend, where the Arkansas River curves, he collapsed in the Kansas summer heat and suffered heart failure. We had his iced body sent back to New York and buried him next to Aunt Libby, in a family plot on Long Island. After the funeral, in the black mourners' carriage, Fanny said through her tears, "Now we don't have to read those awful letters anymore." She said this in Yiddish, her gestures and intonation indicating a joke. Abby took a moment to make out what had been said and then broke into wild laughter. Zak and the rest of us joined in, gasping and slapping our thighs. Later Fanny said to me, "You see, Max, Yiddish has its uses."

On November 11, four Haymarket men were hanged. A fifth, Louis Lingg, killed himself in prison the day before, with a cigar packed with nitroglycerin. I sat in the offices of Brewer Realty reading about the executions and hearing Sophie's voice. "Maxie," she said, " 'If you attack us with cannon, we will reply with dynamite.' These are the words of the heroic Lingg. We will make of this black day a beginning. Remember Bakunin: 'The passion for destruction is also a creative passion!' " Abby came by to see Zak. She looked haggard. He was out collecting back rents. I pointed to the headlines. She looked at them blankly and said, "I have no family now." I thought of my stepsisters, by then likely dead of hunger and malaria. I thought of Mishka, liable to blow himself to pieces, like Lingg, in some useless *Attentat*, and of the families of the dead anarchists in Chicago. I imagined Pyotr Mikhailovich, robbed of a bag of jewels, his fragile Jew's body beaten bloody and thrown in the fields for the crows. I remembered my real father's frozen stare as he lay on the floor with his back broken. I recalled my mother's last, soft smile. I said to Abby, perhaps inadequately, "I know how you feel." She whispered, "I know you do." On her American face at that moment was the dazed look of a new immigrant. "I'm like the rest of you now," she said, in Jewish.

VIII

Our Fight Against God

I WAS PROUD to go out driving with Fanny in her pony-chaise. We'd sit together under the sun hood, Fanny holding the reins. She'd click her tongue at Queenie, her little bay filly, and say, "Once around the park, Max?" On Sundays, we liked to stop for refreshment at the Dairy near the south end of Central Park. We watched the milch cows grazing and the children, escaped from their nannies, hiding among them. Other days, she might take us up through Harlem to inspect unsold lots, and then along Riverside Drive into Washington Heights, with its mansions overlooking the Hudson. I said about the mansions that one day soon they'd have to go. Fanny suggested that her brothers would be glad to help, all I had to do was supply the dynamite.

Before long, the Silvers bought a brownstone on East One Hundred Fifth Street. We were neighbors again. In a year or so, Zak said, we'd be moving the business uptown to us. We began sending someone else out to make rent collections. Zak promised Abby he'd speak Yiddish with her at home. "But not in your house, Max—not to worry." I said he could speak to me in whatever language he chose. I would answer in English. "I was joking," he laughed. Fanny was relieved to be rid of Sally and Sam. She didn't care for Sally's cooking or the way Sam stood by clearing his throat while we ate. Then Abby began to have second thoughts about Sally and Sam. She wouldn't be treated like a child by them, out of habit. She didn't want her new home to be a ghost of the old. As it turned out, Sally and Sam had second thoughts of their own. They had saved some money—four hundred dollars—and decided to go west to Washington Territory and work for themselves. Zak's offer of another four hundred dollars they refused with dignity. Abby pressed the matter. Sally said, "Child, we're on our own."

We received a letter from Shavl for Fanny's brothers, forwarded from our old Allen Street address. I said to Fanny as she was about to throw it away that I'd give it to them myself. We still had business in the ghetto, where I was likely to find them. Fanny shrugged. "Suit yourself," she said. "I don't know why you'd want to bother." For the next several weeks, she asked me if I'd delivered the letter yet. I carried it with me most everywhere, but there was no sign of Leo and Ted. She thought perhaps I wasn't looking hard enough. Oughtn't I ask around for them. I said I had. I'd even stopped by the *Freiheit* offices on William Street, where Johann Most's followers, even reluctant ones, braving Most, often spent their time going through revolutionary publications sent from all over. Fanny became jumpy. "But what do they say about my brothers?" No one had seen them for months.

I found them at last one afternoon in Sachs's Café. It turned out they'd been in London. They'd seen my old friend Sergei Stepanov and his sister Olga, who were active in the Russian circle around Kropotkin. From them, they heard a rumor that Sophie and Nina had escaped, but just how, or where they were now, no one seemed to know. Fanny's brothers had gone abroad as go-betweens for the New York and London Jewish groups. Some of the London comrades were now coming here to help the Pioneers start a journal. I wondered where Leo and Ted had gotten the money for such traveling. "From you and Fanny, of course," they said. Turning to a companion, they added in German: "They've got so much they forget where they spend it." I understood from this that Fanny, without telling me, had been supporting her brothers, and with them the Cause. I said, "Glad to be of service."

This was late fall of '88. The young man with Fanny's brothers looked familiar. I was introduced to him as Sophie Kraft's brother. The fellow looked me up and down and then said in Russian, "Oh, the other brother." He said this with a suggestion of a smile, as if he were remembering an old joke. It was Sasha Berkman, Mishka's idol, who'd been punished in *gimnaziya* for his essay "There Is No God." Now he was working as a typesetter for *Freiheit*. Fanny's brothers wondered if he had an interest in the new journal. Sasha was noncommittal. He reflectively devoured an extra-large steak, bought, I had no doubt, with my money. I told him, in English, that I'd admired him for the bravery of his schoolboy atheism. He seemed pleased and gave a gentlemanly nod between swallows. He said, in careful English, "It was to be done." I quoted Bakunin, *"Si Dieu existait, il faudrait l'abolir."* He answered in Yiddish, "Neither God nor master."

I told Fanny I'd finally seen her brothers and given them the letter from Shavl. She asked, "Well, what did they say?" I said they barely glanced at the letter and put it aside. They were with a comrade from Kovno, Sasha Berkman—Fanny wouldn't know him; he'd come with his family to Kovno after she had emigrated. Her brothers were talking to Sasha about some new journal. They'd been to London and back for the Pioneers. "To London?" asked Fanny. "Yes," I said, "with the money you gave them." Fanny colored but said nothing. I told her about Sophie's and Nina's possible escape from Transbaikalia. That excited her. Perhaps they'd make their way here, she said. I told her that sometimes I heard Sophie's voice telling me what to do, what to think. Fanny laughed. "Just like in Kovno, even after all these years." I said it was Sophie's voice that pulled me into Sachs's Café, that tied me somehow to the revolution. "No," I corrected myself, "not the revolution, but the revolutionists, whom we've known all our lives." "Yes," said Fanny, "my brothers."

The Pioneers of Liberty launched their weekly, *Truth*, in February. It lasted until midsummer, when it ran out of funds, for which Fanny and I weren't to blame. I might read Yiddish even if I wouldn't speak it, and the contents of *Truth* were lively enough. A novel of Emile Zola's was serialized. A special edition in March marked the eighteenth anniversary of the Paris Commune. It brought to mind the great schoolroom uprising in my stepfather's house and Sophie with a band around her head. "You anarchists," said Zak, "even as children, looking for heroic scenes and martyrdom." In the pages of *Truth*, there were also poems I didn't care for, especially by a David Edelstadt. "The moans of all the sufferers, Echo in my heart," and so on. I told Fanny that if I'd ever showed rhymes so poor to Mr. Wojcicki, nihilist or not, he'd have had me expelled from *gimnaziya*, or in any case demoted, like Sasha Berkman. Fanny thought maybe not. "Revolutionists love their own blood and thunder, even if they hate that of everyone else." Abby said, "Max just thinks poetry and Yiddish are in open contradiction."

Sasha didn't become active on the new journal, nor did Fanny's brothers, except in the physical sense of tying, loading, and delivering the weekly issues of *Truth*. Leo and Ted were uncomplaining draft animals for the Cause. They were willing to do anything for the sake of the revolution, and ready, said Fanny, to travel anywhere on our money. On Friday nights, they attended the discussion group at the Pioneers' club on Orchard Street and sat silent through hours of impassioned argument. At that time, Jewish anarchists and socialists were trying to work together. The only matter they seemed to agree upon was the nonexistence of God. Fanny and I would return home long after midnight, overwrought and exhausted, but still smiling over some new parody of the daily Hebrew prayers. Some evenings, the whole shabby hall resounded in mock liturgy. Those were the only times Fanny's brothers opened their mouths in public. I rarely talked myself. Fanny said if I insisted on speaking only English at the Pioneers', to a room full of excited greenhorns, I could just as well get a point across shouting in Chinese. I would have said that though I found their satirical prayers amusing, perhaps they were protesting too much. So long as they derided the Jewish god they remained Jews. Here in America, we could all simply turn our backs on religion. No longer was there "Jew" stamped on an internal passport that made any of us a second-class citizen. Then several voices would have shot back at me that religion was not simply a private matter of conscience. God and the state were still hand in glove. Both must be destroyed with propaganda, by word or by deed.

We went down to Orchard Street, though not every Friday, regardless of our misgivings. I said to myself, They know me as Sophie Kraft's brother—very well, I'll go for Sophie's sake. These meetings, open and noisy, were inconceivable in Russia. For Sophie, if she was still living, the Pioneers' club would be a kind of paradise. Sasha Berkman usually came with his cousin Modest Aronstam, an artist whom everyone called Modska or, sometimes, the Twin. Sasha chose his words carefully, I supposed at first because, as with me, Yiddish was not his mother tongue. His arguments, never personally vicious, always cut to the heart of a matter. He took for a model Chernyshevsky's stoic hero Rakhmetov. I understood this was his self-determined revolutionist's bearing. His economy of speech and gesture suggested a dynamiter in sure control of his fuse. He was not tall. His features were thick. He wore glasses. His body looked as tough as hardwood, ready if need be to ram through a prison wall.

Fanny and I spent most of that August at our place at Stump Lake. We had running water brought to The Pathfinder cottages and the foundation laid for the manor house. We returned to the city in September to find the Pioneers of Liberty in battle with all but the socialists over plans for a Yom Kippur ball, on the holiest day of the year for observant Jews. For the orthodox, it was a time of no work, of fasting, contrition, and self-denial. Staging a fete on that Day of Atonement, it was felt, was brilliant propaganda by deed. At the Pioneers', everyone was for it. It wasn't often that anarchists might implement a direct action and at the same time have a little fun. As Zak said, when it came to fasting, contrition, and self-denial, revolutionists themselves were pretty much inclined to year-round observance.

A young man rose to his feet and assumed a posture for religious debate, twirling earlocks that were no longer there and stabbing a forefinger into the air. "Lest we forget," he said, "the Talmud itself provides justification for our ball." He cited a passage where a certain Rabbi Simon ben Gamaliel said that in ancient Israel, on the Day of Atonement, the people of Jerusalem donned clean white clothes, and the young men and women went out into the vineyard for merrymaking. Shouts went up: "We don't need that kind of justification!" Sasha was there with Modska the Twin. Between them sat a small blonde girl, wild with excitement, whose voice was among the loudest. At the sight of her Fanny started. Wasn't that her cousin Emma? We turned to Fanny's brothers and pointed questioningly at the girl. Yes, they said, it was their cousin, come from Rochester. She'd arrived a month ago and fallen in with Sasha.

We ate late that night at Sachs's Café, Fanny and I and her

brothers, Emma with Sasha and Modska. The bill was of course paid by me. Emma did most of the talking, in German. She had come to New York on August 15, she said. On that very day, she met Sasha and Johann Most and joined the Cause. Rochester was deadly, and more than once she had attempted to break away from her family. She even tried marriage, to a man named Kershner, a weakling. Emma flushed. Sasha gave a little smile. It was Haymarket, she said, that set her afire. She threw a woman guest out of her father's house for calling the Haymarket martyrs "murderers"! The great injustice made her an anarchist, for now and ever. Fanny recalled to her the meetings of Sophie's circle, how as children they discussed Herzen, Marx, and Chernyshevsky. "I remember Max hanging about," said Emma. "He used to peek at us through the keyhole." After supper, as we parted, Fanny and Emma hugged and kissed the air beside each other's cheek. During the hack ride home, Fanny sat tensed, her arms folded. "She's changed," said Fanny. Yes, I said, we're none of us children anymore. "That's not what I mean, Max. You wouldn't take your eyes off her." I said if I didn't that was because Emma was talking, while the rest of us were eating. "You hardly touched your food," said Fanny.

The Silvers said they'd go with us to the Yom Kippur ball, even though Abby thought it was childish. She and Zak had joined the Ethical Culture Society and attended weekly lectures. "Reformism without God," Zak called it, but he enjoyed the formality and show. I thought it was an empty shell, and said so: What was the point of making an institution of nonbelief? Abby felt that people needed something, some ceremony, however slight. I said, "Not I." Fanny said that I'd always been that way, even as a boy in Kovno. Zak said what he remembered most about his childhood was going hungry. What he'd liked about the holidays and Sabbaths was the extra food. He didn't care if it came from charity. Fasting on the Day of Atonement was cruel. Once one of his sisters collapsed from hunger and thirst in the village synagogue, at the back of the women's gallery. The women gave her smelling salts but no water. They held her propped up against the wall for the next several hours, until sundown, when the service was over. It was with that memory he was going to the Yom Kippur ball. The four of us were then agreed: In America, people aren't obliged by any law to starve themselves for the sake of heaven.

The year 5650 since the creation of the world began in late September with furious denunciations of the upcoming Yom Kippur ball. The depraved revelers should be ostracized. Rumors were spread that the ball was canceled. The Pioneers countered with a flier: "The orthodox and reform religious swindlers have set afloat a rotten, filthy lie, to the effect that the ball which we have been planning to hold on the great festival of the slaughter of fowl (Yom Kippur) in Clarendon Hall, 114–118 East 13th Street, has been called off." On the day of the ball, however, the owner of Clarendon Hall went back on his agreement. Hundreds of people gathered on East Thirteenth Street to protest and from there to march to the socialists' Fourth Street Labor Lyceum, whose doors were opened for the celebration. We sang the "Marseillaise" and the revolutionary songs of my childhood, the ones Sophie used to lead in the kitchen after dinner. Sympathizers hung out of windows and waved. Some demonstrators yelled out in English, "Join us!" From one town house several women yelled back in Yiddish, "We can't! We're working today!" The demonstrators cried, "Good for you!" The house was the brothel where I'd seen Carl Franks.

The Pioneers of Liberty distributed free cigarettes, coffee, and sandwiches. Emma and Zipporah Gelb were among the women in charge of the trays. When the march to the Labor Lyceum began, everyone puffed away on cigarettes, even if they'd never smoked before in their lives. Fanny and Abby were exhilarated, giddy from tobacco and shouting slogans. Zak and I carried signs. His said in Jewish, "Neither God nor master!"; mine in English, "Down with superstition!" Fanny bit into her sandwich. "It's good, Max," she said, "what is it?" I said it was ham and cheese. Fanny turned ashen. After all her years in America, she still kept shy of pork and shellfish and dairy foods mixed with meat. She pushed to the edge of the crowd and sat down on the curb. "I'll be all right," she said, and became violently ill. Abby put an arm around her and said, "I'll take you home." Zak and I gave our signs away. We walked with Fanny and Abby to Union Square and saw them into a hack. "Don't be long, boys," said Abby.

Zak and I caught up with the tail end of the marchers. Behind us trailed small groups of orthodox toughs, flinging pebbles and piping taunts in Yiddish. They closed in without a standoff as we reached the Labor Lyceum. There were perhaps a dozen of us left outside the hall with a gang three times as big at our heels. The doors of the Lyceum broke open and out charged Sasha, leading a group of our boys. My size made me a clear target for the ghetto punks. A flying bottle caught me full in the face. I was thrown up against a wall. Zak came bobbing like a porpoise through the brawl and peeled off my attackers from behind, cracking their heads together. Sasha held the high ground on the Lyceum steps. He laid about him like a tree become animate, beating back assault after assault with steady arm blows. Then Fanny's brothers appeared from a side alley, in a flank attack that routed the defenders of God. The girls inside made heroes of us, Emma, Zipporah Gelb, and others. They sponged and bandaged our small wounds. Emma gave Sasha a great hug and kiss. "You, too, Max," she said. I kissed her back. My head ached from the fight. I was confused. For the moment, I thought she was Fanny.

Meanwhile, the speakers pounded away at religion. Johann Most delivered the keynote, dubbed Kol Nidre, the name of the central liturgical prayer on Yom Kippur. He extolled the benefits of fasting for fat capitalists and moneylenders. His diatribe made some people uneasy. Why talk of moneylenders, not bankers? What was he insinuating? Someone said, "Kol Nidre, and he's not even a Jew!" After the speeches, the real ball began. Over a thousand people were packed into the Labor Lyceum, but everywhere I turned I saw Emma kicking up her heels. She whirled by and said, "I'll save a dance for you, Max!" But I grew dizzy and sat on the floor amid the dancers, until Zak helped me up and piloted me out the doors.

At home in our parlor, Fanny and Abby were playing cards and drinking hot cocoa. They jumped up from their chairs at the sight of us both, bandaged and slightly bloody. Zak described the fight. "Heroes," said Abby. "Zak, be a coward next time." Looking me over, Fanny asked, "On your shirt, Max, is that blood?" I looked down. I thought maybe a little but had difficulty saying so. I tried to speak Fanny's name but couldn't. Blood gushed from my nose. I blacked out.

IX

Lovers' Quarrels

IT TOOK ME weeks to recover from my concussion. At home one day, I was amused to read in the newspaper of the wedding at Grace Episcopal Church of Miss Blanche Louise Viereck, daughter of Judge Felix Adolphus Viereck and Mrs. Philippa Haan Viereck of Brooklyn and Catskill, to Mr. Carl Benedict Franks, Esq., of New York and Albany, son of the late Dr. Solomon Elias Franks and Mrs. Nathalie Lowe Franks. Abby was furious. Zak said, "All those middle names." In his village near Pinsk, a middle name was something thrown at you in the street or schoolroom that stuck. "I won't tell you what they called me. It's one reason I left." Abby wouldn't laugh. I remembered Carl Franks's remarks about immigrants and said Blanche wouldn't be teaching at the Freie Bibliothek after this. "No," said Abby, in Jewish, "they've gone over to the other side." When she lost her parents, Abby received notes of sympathy from her uncle Elias in the Argentine, whom she'd never met, and nothing from Blanche Viereck or Carl Franks. She could understand about him, but Blanche had once been her closest friend. "They deserve each other then," said Fanny, "this Blanche and the convert." This nun and the satyr, I said to myself.

Fanny's brothers and cousin Emma came to call. Fanny was

out taking Queenie for a trot, even though it was bitter winter. I made them hot cocoa. We hadn't yet found anyone to Fanny's satisfaction to replace Sally and Sam. Emma looked over the house with appreciation and said Sasha wouldn't approve of such comfort. I said I didn't think it was required to wear a hair shirt for the Cause. Alexander Herzen and Friedrich Engels made no apologies for their money, nor would I. If I could give it away, it had to come from somewhere. Emma said she did need funds for her first speaking tour, to Rochester, Buffalo, and Cleveland. Johann Most had taken her under his wing and trained her, and now he was sending her out on her own. Out from under the gargoyle's wing, I thought, and said, "Will ten dollars do?" Emma said, in German, "Very generous of you, Mr. Kraft," and gave me a kiss.

Fanny walked in the room. "You here?" she said. Her brothers asked if they could store a few things with us. Fanny asked, "What things?" They pointed to two battered leather bags. "What's in them," asked Fanny, "dynamite?" Emma laughed. "Don't be foolish, dearie." We kept the bags, in return for a promise from Fanny's brothers to write to the family in Shavl. "You'll give them a post-office address," said Fanny, "and tell them to send you letters there." Fanny said after Emma and her brothers left, "On your cheek, Max—a cocoa kiss," and made as if to slap the spot.

Zak was happy to be running the business. He brought me papers to sign, checks to endorse, and blueprints to consider. All the ghetto properties were now sold. We had several contiguous lots under construction in Harlem, two undeveloped ones in Washington Heights with a view of the Hudson, and three more out of the city, in the Bronx. In January of 1890, we became Silver & Kraft, Inc., Realty & Construction, with offices on East One Hundred Tenth Street, just off the park. I could walk to work. From the office windows, I could watch Fanny drive up in her pony-chaise with a hot boxed lunch for Zak and me. There was hardly a reason to go downtown anymore. Once my dizzy spells passed, I did go occasionally to Friday-night meetings at the Pioneers'. Fanny refused. I told her I had to, for Sophie. Fanny asked if this would go on forever. I said no, just until I knew for sure whether my stepsisters were alive or dead. "Do what you like then, Max," she said, "only don't bring those people around here." She meant by this her cousin Emma and especially her brothers. Zak one evening had picked the locks on their leather bags. He used a pin to show a trick he'd learned from the Great Prostak himself, an illusionist in the Ukrainian circus where Zak had been a roustabout. "You'll never guess what's in here," he said. "Don't tell me," Abby laughed, "old shoes? Hebrew prayer books?" Fanny peeked over Zak's shoulder. "My God!" she screamed. "Dynamite! Get it out of here!"

It was simply large bottles of the basic ingredients, along with vials and burners, casings and clockworks. Nothing was mixed. The chemicals were inert. "I don't care," said Fanny. "Get rid of it all. Now." Zak and I scattered the contents of the bags in Central Park, the way Sophie and I had once done with Bobelis's things after I'd buried him. "They lied to us," said Fanny. "My own brothers and cousin. Suppose it was prepared? How could they? Risking our lives for their revolution."

I returned the emptied bags to Fanny's brothers during a break in the next Friday-night meeting at the Pioneers'. Emma was there, back from her speaking tour. She stood by tight-lipped while I explained how I'd disposed of the explosives. I said none of them had been truthful. They had put Fanny and me in danger without our knowledge and consent. Fanny's brothers answered that what I'd thrown away was perfectly harmless and I knew it—who was being honest now? I owed them money for it. "Owe you?" I said. "You bought it with my money in the first place."

The meeting resumed, and Emma walked away without a word. She took her place between Sasha and Modska the Twin. Zipporah Gelb drifted by me and under her breath said something in English I couldn't catch, about bedfellows or benchfellows. The discussion turned to the continuing fight for the eight-hour day. Emma rose to her feet. She said that on her recent tour, speaking to German workers upstate and in Ohio, she began to reconsider the unionist position. A murmur went up. Emma faced a clique of Johann Most's followers. She lashed out, as she had learned to do from Most. By not joining the struggle for improved labor conditions, they were mocking the workers chained to the block—the older ones especially, who felt they might not live to see the revolution. Shouts went up. "Deserter!" "Peukert!"

Josef Peukert was Johann Most's rival among German anarchists. His Autonomie group, based in London, had recently set up in New York. Most charged that Peukert had at one time betrayed a comrade to the German police. While I was ill, a meeting was called by Jewish socialists and anarchists to reconcile their differences. Sasha threw his own anarchist camp into confusion by demanding an investigation of the accusation against Peukert. The meeting ended in chaos after several days. I knew something of the events from the Yiddish newspapers Abby and Fanny shared and left lying about to tease me. Now, while Emma spoke, Zipporah Gelb, beside me, whispered details. Johann Most was known to be in love with Emma. He was rumored to have proposed marriage and wept when she turned him down. He was jealous of Sasha and after the business about Peukert was heard to call him an arrogant young Jew. I glanced at Emma and whispered back to Zipporah Gelb, "You mean it's all just another lovers' quarrel." She pulled back to look at me and laughed. "I never said that."

I left the Pioneers' that night thinking of Sophie. It was for her sake I'd gone to these meetings. For her I'd given money, for her kept up with Fanny's brothers, when Fanny herself seemed willing to cut all family connections. I imagined Sophie rising amid the Friday-night squawking, silencing the hall with one quiet word, in Russian: "Enough." Among the Yiddish journals Abby read was the weekly *Morning Star*, a short-lived successor to the short-lived *Truth*. It lasted long enough to serialize Chernyshevky's *What Is to Be Done?* Fanny said something was lost in the translation. "Yes," I said, "the revolution." I heard Sophie's voice, instructing her friends in the garden back of Pyotr Mikhailovich's villa. I told Fanny I wouldn't be going to the Pioneers' club anymore. It wasn't Sophie's place.

That summer, Fanny and I began renting out the lakeside cottages at The Pathfinder. Fanny insisted on advertising only in the Yiddish newspapers. She wanted to know the kind of people we'd be getting. In the area around Stump Lake, there were settlements of White Russians, Ukrainians, and Poles. We saw them stomp into the general store in Woodville in their great boots and eat black bread and whole herrings out of a barrel, washing it all down with kvass or vodka straight from the bottle. They terrified

Fanny. She said she hadn't come to America to die in a pogrom. We hired a Jewish couple named Kretchmer to manage the place and run the kitchen and dining room, in the one completed wing of the manor house. The cottages filled quickly. Word got out among the Pioneers' that Fanny and Max Kraft owned The Pathfinder. Our property at Stump Lake became an anarchist retreat. Fanny's brothers came to stay for a week. They apologized to Fanny and promised, "No dynamite." I told Zak I'd stopped going downtown to the Pioneers' meetings on Orchard Street, so Orchard Street came upstate to me. Now we knew the kind of people we'd be getting.

Cousin Emma wrote, in German—to me, not Fanny—saying she'd heard the food was excellent at The Pathfinder, especially the stuffed whitefish, her own specialty. However, she was too busy to get away. "Who invited her," said Fanny. Emma was supporting the new Dress and Cloakmakers' Union in a weeks' long strike. I sent her ten dollars for the strike fund. She wrote back to thank me. The money would keep one man on the picket lines for a week, instead of slaving in a sweatshop fourteen hours a day. The strike ended successfully at the end of July. After that, it was months before I heard from her again. She and Sasha, with Modska and two other young women, had started a commune in New Haven. I'd be a welcome guest, anytime. I sent them twenty dollars. I showed Emma's letter to Fanny. "I notice she writes only to you," she said, "your dear Emma." Zak, who was working at a correspondence course in engineering, thought the strain between Fanny and Emma was the same as a bad bond between bricks. If you had two the same size and shape and simply laid them lengthwise, the bond wouldn't take. The two cousins looked alike. They talked alike. "If you put them in the same room and stand them side by side," he said, "they will not take."

We passed up the second Yom Kippur ball, out in Brooklyn, and held our own celebration at Delmonico's. Fanny tasted a shrimp and liked it. She suggested we should do this every year. Abby toasted Silver & Kraft. That week we had opened our first apartment houses in Harlem for rental, the Abigail Arms and the Frances Arms. Zak and I raised our glasses: "To the ladies, our muses." Our tenants were mostly immigrants in their first move uptown, beginning to prosper. For them, the revolution meant nothing except news of street agitation, fearful assassinations, and bombs. There was Ida Sussman, who came by our offices every month to count out her rent in coins and comment on whatever news caught her eye. On May 2, 1891, it happened to be an account of a workers' rally the day before at Union Square. An unknown young woman waving a red flag had addressed the crowd in German from the back of an open delivery wagon while the police were leading it away. "Crazy girl," said Ida Sussman in Yiddish. "These people talk, talk, talk. Speeches don't pay the rent, do they, Mr. Kraft." Not these speeches, I said. The woman on the delivery wagon was Emma, back from New Haven. I saw her myself, hoisted up by Sasha and Modska. I'd been browsing along Ladies' Mile for a gift for Fanny, for our fifth wedding anniversary. The route ran from A. T. Stewart's to Madison Square and cut through Union Square, where I walked into international labor's third May Day rally. Emma waved her red flag, looking from afar like Fanny standing up in her pony-chaise. I waved back with my hat. "Max," said Sophie's voice, "you know which side you're on." Soon after, Emma wrote to say she was no longer in New Haven. She and Sasha were living on Forsyth Street, in the ghetto. I sent her a little something for the Cause, equal in amount to Ida Sussman's rent.

In June, we opened the manor house at The Pathfinder. There were twelve guest rooms in addition to the lakeside cottages and a suite for Fanny and me. Fanny decided to stay for the entire summer. The city was hot. She had stopped working as a volunteer at the library. She was bored. I could come up on weekends. I said she knew that would be difficult, with all the new construction Zak and I had under way. "Then come up when you can, Max," she said. "If you get lonely, you can go downtown and visit your friends." I said I hadn't talked to Emma since the night I'd returned the leather bags. In fact, the last time I'd seen her was at a distance, over a month ago at Union Square, addressing a crowd—the day I'd bought Fanny her diamond brooch. "Whoever mentioned Emma?" said Fanny.

Zak saw no problem. "One of you has to be there, the other here. That's business." He persuaded Abby to go up for some of the time to be with Fanny. Zak and I worked seven days a week while they were gone. We survived on an American diet of ham sandwiches, sarsaparilla, and apples. At summer's end, we had two new row houses and another small apartment house, the Sophia, near completion. I said we'd have a good year not to atone for at Delmonico's.

Came the end of August, I got away at last to The Pathfinder. I knew most of the guests from the Pioneers' club. Fanny's brothers shared a cottage with Zipporah Gelb, but on what terms no one could say. There were discussion groups on Friday evenings. Sunday and Wednesday were the nights for an American barbeque. Later, around the dying fire, everyone sang European workers' and revolutionary songs. After we closed for the season in September, Fanny said at Delmonico's, "We must have cousin Emma up." Zak caught my eye, winked, and toasted the revolution, which will make all things possible. Fanny tried not to laugh. Once again, I wondered how much or what the revolution might mean to us if we didn't know the revolutionists. Even Sophie's voice couldn't answer that.

Next I heard, Emma was in Massachusetts. She wrote me, in German, first from Springfield, and then from Worcester. She and Sasha and Modska had opened a lunchroom and ice-cream parlor. It would seem to go against their principles to engage in any kind of business, but they had broken completely with Johann Most and had no source of funds beyond their own labors. Their earnings would be set aside for their return to Russia. They determined it was there, she wrote, and not America, that they might work most effectively for the Cause, among people whose languages they spoke and whose aspirations for freedom were their own.

I was astonished. I told Fanny I couldn't send them money. Fanny had fallen out again with her brothers. "Good," she said, "it's about time you cut her off. What a family!" I didn't want Fanny to misunderstand. I said I might still give them money for the Cause, here, in America—but to go back to Russia, never. Maybe I should talk to them. "Go ahead, Max," Fanny snapped. "But what about me?" I asked what about her. "Last summer," said Fanny, "you left me alone for ten weeks." I raised my voice. I said that was cockeyed. It was she, Fanny, who had insisted on spending the summer upstate. "You didn't try very hard to stop me, did you, Max!" she shouted, and marched out of the room.

I packed my bag, confused, and took the first train out from the Grand Central Depot to Worcester.

I found the little restaurant with no trouble. It was toward evening when I arrived, on a cool day early in April. Business was good, the place nearly filled. I slipped into an empty chair at a corner table. Emma herself came to take my order. With my face in the menu I said, "A ham sandwich on rye bread, please, and a sarsaparilla." They had no sarsaparilla, she answered, would I care for coffee instead. It was the first time I'd heard Emma speak English. Her accent was thicker than Fanny's. I said a cup of coffee would be fine, and looked up from the menu. Her face, usually serious, even severe, opened into a smile. "Max! What a surprise! What brings you here?" she asked in German. I said I'd just come for a friendly visit, and to talk her out of going back to Russia. The smile on Emma's face froze.

Emma, Sasha, and Modska rented rooms from a family in a house nearby. Our arguing began civilly in the lunchroom after the last customer had left. It continued heatedly through the night in their cramped quarters. Its end found me alone at dawn at the railway station, waiting for the next train to New York.

Sasha asked why, precisely, they ought not to return to Russia. I said I couldn't answer precisely without falling into a trap. I reminded him that I, too, had studied Greek and knew the tricks of sophistry. I wouldn't let him win an argument on words alone. Sasha was impatient. I was still the "other brother," the big joke who hung around and peeked through keyholes. I rehearsed my credentials. Was Sasha's uncle Mark Nathanson in exile in Siberia? Sasha looked at me sharply: this was not common knowledge. So, too, I said, were my sisters, Sophie and Nina. Sophie's lover, Mr. Wojcicki, was shot and killed in his escape from Russia. My brother Mishka had disappeared into the revolutionary underground. Back in Kovno, I used to run messages for the People's Will. All this had been when we were children. Recently, when the bones of Sergeant Jurgis Bobelis were unearthed, it was my stepfather, Pyotr Mikhailovich, who was held for questioning by the tsarist police—and because of that, Sophie and Nina were removed to a harsher place of exile, a virtual sentence of death. Sasha momentarily looked pained. He recalled that my stepfather stayed with his own family in St. Petersburg at the time of

Sophie's trial. "He was a kind man," said Sasha. "He disagreed with my father—he'd read Herzen and Chernyshevsky." I said yes, those were Sophie's books. Then I added: "It was I who killed Bobelis," and briefly told the story.

Sasha would not be impressed. My deed was thoughtless and unplanned, not the act of a revolutionist. My loyalties, he said, were to family and friends who had joined the Cause, not the revolution for its own sake. How could I presume to tell them, whose only thought was to live—or die!—for the Cause, what actions to take? The revolution has no room for liberal sentimentalists. Sasha just then sounded like Johann Most, and I told him so. After that, we shook off all politeness.

Yes, I said, I associated myself with them because of Sophie. What of it? My contributions were in good money, my martyr's blood as red as theirs if I should stand in the way of a bullet or bomb in an inadvertent *Attentat*. Sasha drew himself up. Propaganda by deed, he said, is never inadvertent. As for the blood of a chance bystander, the revolution is the great end that justifies the violent means. Violence without motive is an empty gesture at best—at worst, it is murder.

"Next you'll be telling me," I said, "that God is on the side of the revolution." No, their narrow view was Old World. An uprising of workers and peasants? What did they know of workers and peasants anyway? Who were they to accuse me of sentimentality? America was new, different, and fertile ground for change. Russia was primitive, barren, and had no place for them. What could they effect there, as Jews? And what could they effect here, as foreigners? In Russia, they would be excluded by law and tradition. In America, they were excluding themselves. Revolution was made in the language of the place, or not at all.

They disagreed, though Emma and Modska less so then Sasha, or so it seemed to me. Was I saying there was a true revolutionary tradition in America? It was a middle-class tradition, hardly revolutionary, made to protect property and blind to the social question of poverty and wage-slavery. I called America fertile ground? On the contrary, it needed copious manuring. In Russia, the peasants had a long history of communal sharing. In America, every farmer plowed his stony field alone. Even what passed here as a kind of anarchism was merely militant bourgeois reformism. Here there was no literature to nourish the revolution, let alone the mind. Who was the American Pushkin, who the Gogol, Turgenev, Chernyshevsky?

I countered with Whitman, Twain, Hawthorne, and Thoreau. I told them about Uncle Henry's library. "Five thousand books," I said, "all in English." Nearly half were now in my own study, the rest with our friends the Silvers. I suggested they look them over before they wrote off America and returned to the black hole of Europe.

Emma fiercely asked who was I to talk about America. I had scarcely been out of the city of New York since I'd arrived there—what? seven or eight years ago. She had lived upstate and traveled as far as the Canadian border and to the Midwest. She had worked side by side with workers in the factories and talked with them on her speaking tours. "Immigrant workers," I said. "Greenhorn Americans. What languages did you speak to them in? German. Yiddish. Maybe a little Russian." The workers of the world, said Emma, all speak the language of the exploited. "That," I replied, "is simply rhetoric. I've heard that one mouthed by Fanny's brothers."

We talked in tightening circles, until Modska said it was time we got some sleep. There were only two beds and a sofa that was much too short for me. I wondered how they managed their ménage. On their bookshelves, I noticed, in German, *The Science of Revolutionary Warfare*, Johann Most's notorious book on the making of bombs. Had they really broken with that man, or, as I had joked to Zipporah Gelb, was their revolution just another lovers' quarrel? I left in disgust and caught behind me the sound of their sleepy laughter, I supposed at my expense, as the sun rose and lighted my way to the Worcester station. On the train, I dreamed again of skating around the world on the Neman and into Sachs's Café. Fanny is crying helplessly. Her brothers sit unmoved on either side of her, their faces featureless blanks. She holds a broken pencil in her hand. I take it from her and whittle a sharp new point. She rewards me with a smile. A voice, my own, says *There hath been a misunderstanding*. I reach for Fanny's hand.

X

Attentat!

FANNY WAS IN the parlor when I came home, not alone crying but holding a Sunday afternoon party with some of our women tenants and their friends. They were playing cards, all corseted and in their feathers and finery, chattering in Yiddish. Abby was there and Ida Sussman, our tenant in the Frances Arms. Most of the rest were unknown to me, including a maid serving coffee and finger foods, whose name they called out continually. "Daisy! More coffee! Daisy! A little seltzer!" Fanny asked what I thought of her, the little American girl. "She's from Boston," she said proudly, "a real gem," and hurried back to the card table without a word about my return. Ida Sussman said, "Mr. Kraft, what a heroine your wife is, a regular Molly Pitcher!" Cheers went up. They sang "For she's a jolly good fellow." Abby came over and explained. She said Fanny's friends thought I'd been away on business. After I walked out, Fanny took Queenie for a furious trot up Riverside Drive. In Washington Heights, she was overtaken by a runaway carriage, a one-horse cabriolet. The driver had fallen off his rear perch. The lone passenger, a woman, was screaming for help. Fanny without a second thought urged Queenie on. The pony-chaise crowded the carriage to the side of the road. Fanny reached out and grabbed the trailing reins. The cabriolet came to a quiet stop. "The horse," said Abby, "bent over to chew the grass, as if nothing had happened."

The woman in the carriage was unhurt. She admired Queenie's pluck and offered to buy her. Fanny said the pony wasn't for sale, but after today perhaps the woman's horse might be. "Never my Betsy," the woman answered. "Never my Queenie either," said Fanny. A strolling policeman came by and offered to drive the woman home. "You seem to know horses, Mrs. Kraft," she said, and gave Fanny her card. "You might appreciate our stable. Do call." Abby said I'd never guess who the woman was: Mrs. Winifred Ault Baker, the wife of Harry Neal Baker, the "Cracker King." I said yes, I knew Baker's Famous Breakfast Biscuits. "Well," said Abby, "he also maintains one of the largest private stables in the city." Fanny was to pay a visit the following Sunday, at four o'clock in the afternoon. Just then, Fanny joined us. She took my arm. "Four o'clock, high-tea time," she said. "Just like they serve in Emma's famous lunchroom. Right, Max?"

Fanny had placed a notice for a domestic in the want column of the New York *Sun*. Daisy answered it in person and was waiting at our front door after Fanny's encounter with Mrs. Baker. Fanny felt expansive and hired her on the spot. The girl's full name was Daisy Osgood. "Osgood," I said. "You aren't by chance related to a Clarence Ward Osgood? A salesman." She was not. But I thought of the man and his luxuriant mustache. I told Fanny perhaps I might try growing one again, in part as a reminder of my break with Emma and her comrades. "Good," said Fanny, "that way you won't forget."

One week later, Fanny said, "Your mustache, Max—you can shave it off." She was sitting in the parlor, in the darkened Oriental corner, her hat and coat still on, looking, I thought, a little ill. I asked what Mrs. Baker had served with tea to make her sick. Fanny said, "Nothing. What tea? There was no tea, and no Mrs. Baker either. Mrs. Baker sailed for Europe three days ago. She left word that if a certain Mrs. Kraft, a Jewess, should come calling, to show her the horses." Fanny flung her handbag across the room. "Max, I never set foot in the house! A groom came, a boy, and took me through the stalls. That's all." Then she added under her breath: "I'm sorry you threw out my brothers' dynamite." I asked if she was serious. She certainly was. One stick would blow out the foundation of the Baker mansion and tumble it into the Hudson. "I don't mean about the dynamite," I said, half joking. "I mean about shaving off my mustache." Fanny waved my words away and asked me just to get her what she needed from her brothers. "Maxie," said Sophie in my mind, "an act of pure vengeance is not a revolutionary *Attentat*." Her voice wasn't entirely her own, but had an edge, like Sasha's.

I looked halfheartedly for Fanny's brothers. Fortunately they were nowhere to be found. They could have been any place in the country, agitating for the Cause, tensions among workers were so high. Zak said not to take Fanny so exactly at her word. Abby agreed. "You know how she is, Max." It turned out that Fanny's brothers had gone back to Russia. A letter arrived from Kovno late in June. Leo and Ted had become Lev and Fedya again. They wrote somewhat guardedly, in German, because of the tsarist police. We were not to be surprised at their leaving. As the saying goes, the goat goes to the pasture, not the pasture to the goat. They would return to America at such a time as there was more work in their field. Right now, the Baltic provinces held better prospects. "Tell Max," they said, "that friends say the cats are in Vladivostok and have picked up the stray kitten." I understood from this that Sophie and Nina had followed Bakunin's escape route east along the Amur to the Pacific coast and were living underground, with comrades—and apparently Mishka was with them. Fanny's brothers also wrote that Pyotr Mikhailovich was dead. His heart had given out after a rigorous fast. His ex-wife had got hold of what remained of his property and sold it off. The letter closed, as it had opened, with formal regards. There was an indirect greeting from Fanny's parents in Shavl. "They could have told me they were leaving," said Fanny. She was sorry about the old man, my stepfather. I said yes, he gave me everything. I might have wound up in an orphanage in Slobodka. "Or in Vladivostok, in hiding," said Fanny. "Max, forget the dynamite." I told her not to worry, it had already slipped my mind. Fanny said there'd be more than enough killing soon, at Homestead.

A strike at Andrew Carnegie's steelworks in Homestead, Pennsylvania, looked more like a war. Some newspapers even said it was revolution. Zak said the fight was about money, not revolution: what else should Americans fight for? Carnegie himself was in Scotland and left matters to his plant manager, Henry Clay Frick. The workers determined to bargain for a new contract that provided higher wages for greater output. Frick would not bargain. He would cut wages instead and countered with a lockout. The workers struck on June 28. Frick evicted families from the company houses—widows, children, pregnant women. He raised a fence three miles long around the steelworks. It was topped with barbed wire and studded with loopholes for snipers. At night, electric searchlights beamed from watchtowers twelve feet high. Frick hired three hundred Pinkerton guards to protect, he said, the nonunion workers he intended to bring in. The guards came up the Monongahela River in barges at dawn on July 6. Between them and the fenced-in mill were hundreds of armed strikers and their families. Both sides opened fire. The Pinkertons tried to force their way through. The strikers tried to drive them back with guns and sink the barges with firebrands and dynamite. The Pinkertons broke through the strikers' lines and ran a six-hundred-yard gauntlet to the mill, clubbed and kicked all the way. The battle on July 6 left sixteen dead on both sides and half the Pinkertons injured. The governor of Pennsylvania called in the militia. It was clear which side the state was on. Frick with his private army had broken the strike, with the government's help.

The Kretchmers, who managed The Pathfinder, telephoned from Stump Lake. The place was suddenly empty. Reservations for July were canceled. What should they do? It was this business at Homestead, they said. "Mr. Kraft, these people with their ideas, they're not reliable." They meant by this our anarchist clientele. "What you want are good Jewish families, nice people, observant, like we used to get when we ran our own place in Chernigov." I told them to close down, clear out, and leave the keys with the night watchman. Zak said Fanny's brothers were missing a great opportunity in America with Homestead. He was impressed by the bold revolutionary actions being taken. Fanny was puzzled: What actions? "Canceling vacations," he said, "for the Cause." All the revolutionary talk, anarchist, socialist, Marxist, seemed like so much hollow thunder to me. I wondered why I'd ever thought to go to Worcester. Where was Emma? Where were Sasha and

Modska? The time for deeds was now, and they were letting it pass.

Fanny and I spent a few days at The Pathfinder straightening accounts. We hired caretakers to keep squatters out until such time as we'd reopen. Fanny was anxious about the White Russians, Poles, and Ukrainians nearby and a troop of Gypsies with a dancing bear that we passed on the road to the village. I was more worried about skunks and rats. Fanny said that when we reopened we'd be more careful. No more anarchists. We were finished with that. I reminded her that she'd advertised in the Yiddish papers. Fanny was the one who was concerned about the kind of people we'd be getting. She laughed and said in Yiddish, "You're right, Max. When we open again, just for you—no Jews." Fanny was in high spirits, I supposed because she was rid of her brothers at last.

We returned to the city by boat on a Saturday in mid-July. Daisy met us at the pier. We sent our baggage home with her and said we'd be eating out. It was such a cool night for summer. "We'll buy ices from a vendor, Max," said Fanny, "and drink champagne at an outdoor café." We strolled along the south side of Union Square. Fanny said that, after dark, you'd think this part of Ladies' Mile was a regular red-light district. All the women looked so garish, they might as well be streetwalkers. "They are streetwalkers," I said. "Not that one," Fanny whispered. "My God, Max, she looks just like cousin Emma." I said it couldn't be Emma, she never got herself up that way, with bright makeup and in high heels. Besides, she was still in Worcester, so far as I knew. "No, Max, I'm sure it's her." I hurried over to the woman. "You look familiar," I said. She looked up at me in alarm and stepped back out of the lamplight. I stepped forward to get a clear view of her face. She fled into the shadows. I told Fanny it couldn't have been Emma, she would have recognized me. Fanny said not in the poor light, especially with my mustache. I asked why Emma would ever want to dress up like a whore. "What a question, Max," said Fanny, taking my arm. "To raise money for the Cause, of course."

Not long after that cool evening, a heat wave swept the east. In New York, before the month was up, more than six hundred people died. Horses dropped in the streets, tying up traffic. It was too hot to take Queenie out. Fanny said we should have stayed longer upstate. We'd been having such a lovely time. It was crazy heat, she said, you could see it in people's eyes. It was late afternoon. We were walking slowly through the park and sipping lemonade. Feverish men and women sat fanning themselves on benches, staring at us silently as we passed. "Don't look back," said Fanny. "You never know what they'll do." We stopped to buy an afternoon newspaper at the kiosk on East One Hundred Tenth Street, just outside the park. The headlines made Fanny gasp. At a glance, four words told us of disaster: "FRICK"—"ASSASSINATION ATTEMPT"—"BERGMAN." Sasha had made an *Attentat*, and failed.

The newspaper accounts were confused. They had gotten Sasha's name wrong. The police, they said, were looking for an accomplice, a certain Bakhmetov. We supposed Sasha had assumed the name at some point, it sounded so close to Chernyshevsky's Rakhmetov. We knew that whatever Sasha had done, he'd have done it alone. This much was clear: he had gone to Pittsburgh, talked his way into Henry Clay Frick's private office, and there shot the man three times and stabbed him more than once in a struggle. Frick was likely to live. Sasha was arrested on the spot. A nitroglycerin capsule was pried out of his mouth. Asked what it was, he said candy. Evidently Sasha intended suicide, by blowing his own head off like the Haymarket martyr Louis Lingg. Fanny said it must have been the heat that drove him to it.

Within the next several days, the Pittsburgh police arrested two comrades, Henry Bauer and also Carl Nold, with whom Sasha was said to have stayed before the *Attentat*. In New York, a search was on for Emma. Fanny was terrified the police would come for us. Emma wasn't really a close cousin, she said. They had only a great-grandfather in common. "Let's go back to the country, Max," she said. The police raided the apartment where Emma was now living but found no incriminating evidence. I thought of that long night in Worcester weeks earlier. I'd argued against a return to Russia. If my words meant anything, they had led in some measure to Sasha's blunder. Zak said to put the thought out of my mind. It wasn't my fault Sasha was such a poor shot.

The American newspapers, no great friends of Frick, condemned Sasha. The anarchists and socialists did likewise. Johann

Most pretended at first not to know who this "Bergman" was. He then attacked Sasha in the pages of *Freiheit*. He implied the *Attentat* against Frick was sham, a setup to gain public favor for Frick. Berkman, he wrote, had used a toy pistol.

Emma virtually alone defended Sasha. She eulogized him in *Der Anarchist*, the newspaper put out by Josef Peukert's Autonomie group, Johann Most's hated rivals. She organized a protest meeting. I sent money and enclosed a note, in English, "For Sasha's defense—in remembrance of Worcester." Fanny made plans for us to go up to Stump Lake. A railway strike in mid-August tied up all travel in the state. One hundred fifty cars were burned in Buffalo. The militia was called in, just as at Homestead. "What country are we living in?" asked Fanny. Ida Sussman, counting out her September rent, said, "Mr. Kraft, if you ask me, we should take all the leaders—the union leaders, the business leaders, the politicians—and put them together in a room to fight and kill each other. Then, no more leaders—who needs them?" I said to her, "Why Ida, you're an anarchist." She answered that she was nothing of the kind. She didn't believe in violence.

Johann Most renewed his attack. In a "Reflections on *Attentate*" he hedged his position on propaganda by deed. Emma responded in *Der Anarchist*. She called him a traitor and a coward. Most went silent. Meanwhile, Sasha was tried and, of course, convicted. I was incensed. I remembered standing alone in Schwab's Saloon, all eyes upon me, while Johann Most scorched me as a bourgeois sentimentalist for doubting his word. Sasha's act was useless, foolish bravado, but Most the fire-eater was hardly the one to call it so. I determined to say it to his face at his next lecture. Zak tried to talk me out of it, then he said he'd go with me, to cover my rear. Seeing they couldn't stop us, Fanny and Abby insisted on coming, too, as a better shield. Comrades didn't hit women, at least not in public. "No heroics," they added. "This isn't a Yom Kippur ball."

It was supposed to be a routine talk of Most's, in his usual downtown hall, but everyone expected more than the usual thumping. Months had gone by since Emma's challenge in *Der Anarchist*. Most would be addressing an excitable crowd. We took seats in a middle row near the center aisle. I was close enough to the podium to be heard but near enough to the door, Zak noticed, to make a fast retreat. I intended to confront Most as he began. He rose to speak. I whispered to myself, Now.

There was a tumult in the front row. Emma was on her feet, shouting. She charged Most to prove his insinuations against Alexander Berkman. The hall fell silent. Most dismissed the interruption. He would not respond to the demands of a hysterical woman. At that, Emma flew at Most. From under her cloak she drew a horsewhip and beat him with it around the head and shoulders. He staggered halfway to his knees. She broke the whip and flung the pieces in his face. The audience was in a roar. Emma strode up the aisle and out the door, protected by Modska and some other boys. It was the final touch to her lovers' quarrel and, as Zak said, splendid propaganda by deed.

Part Three

I

Posterity

SASHA'S FATE STIRRED up terrible memories. Fanny said it was like living again through the black days after the tsar's assassination. At *gimnaziya*, the students were almost mute with anxiety as word spread among them of Mr. Wojcicki's death and my stepsisters' imprisonment. When Sophie was sentenced, Fanny and her friends wept in the hallways and had to pretend they were still grieving for the tsar. I recalled that at the time of the trial, Pyotr Mikhailovich stayed with Sasha's family in St. Petersburg. I said it was no wonder we were grim with foreboding. Sasha had brought the shadow of the People's Will to our door and the hand of Russia to our throats.

At his trial in mid-September, Sasha had spoken in his own defense. He didn't deny his attempt on Frick's life but intended to explain the high motive behind it. He had prepared his speech in German. The court interpreter was blind and unable to read Sasha's words. The judge cut the apologia short. The jury deliberated swiftly and found Sasha guilty on several charges, only one of which, to my mind, was sure—his assault on Frick. For the failed assassination, Sasha should have received a prison term of seven years. He was doomed instead to twenty-two. Even Johann Most assailed the severity of the punishment, though who could say to what end. Surely he didn't want Emma back. Sasha was sent to the Western Penitentiary of Pennsylvania in Allegheny City. He would be released, if he survived, in 1914—an old man of forty-three, I thought, nearly Johann Most's age. I supposed the Cause had finished itself off at one blow.

Fanny was relieved. Her brothers were gone, back to Russia perhaps for good. Emma's cause would now be Sasha. We'd have some peace in our lives. She said she was going to have a child. I asked her when she'd changed her mind. "My mind has nothing to do with it, Max," she laughed. Fanny put her hand flat against her midriff. "I'm pregnant." We were sitting in the Oriental corner. The bellpull was a length of woven cloth depicting Paradise. There were birds, beasts, fruit trees, flowers, and no children. The scene was like the hush I imagined that follows revolution, before the aftermath has begun. Perhaps we were in our own Paradise now. Sophie's voice said to remember where Sasha was; in that hell, there were no children either. I reminded myself we were in neither place. This was America, of our own making. We were going to have an American child, Fanny and I, who would grow up speaking English, without the curse of Europe. We celebrated at Delmonico's with Zak and Abby and afterward drank champagne riding in an open carriage in the park under a harvest moon. I'd never seen Fanny so happy. In her exuberance, she said to Abby, "I'll have six children! Three for us, and three for you and Zak!" Zak started forward but quickly sat back, trying to take Fanny's words in good part. Abby smiled thinly in the moonlight.

The Silvers couldn't have children because of the peculiar shape, the doctors said, of Abby's womb. Zak was concerned for her sake but had no real interest for himself in children. He said money was a kinder posterity. It didn't talk back and was more reliable in sickness and old age. Zak rarely talked about his family. He was one of seven children, most of whom died young in a cholera epidemic that also took their mother. He liked to say, "If my father had a hundred dollars for every one of us, he'd have been the richest man in the village." At Delmonico's that evening, Abby suggested he send his father the money now. If he wanted, he could bring the family over. Zak said the only way they'd see the money was if he carried it there himself in coin. His village was a few miles outside Pinsk. Every mile traveled was a century further into the past. When he left twelve years before, he'd stepped out of the Middle Ages, and he wasn't going back. "Never," he said. Fanny and I agreed, "Never." Abby looked at us, the immigrants, almost as if to say, I don't really understand you people.

We had nothing to go back to. Fanny's family had as good as written her off. She was finished with them herself and, she insisted, the revolution as well. Zak's village was likely to have been ravaged in the pogroms, his family butchered or long gone from there. For myself, the Kovno of my memories was no more. Even if all this were not so, none of us would return. I told Abby that her father called Europe a land of nightmares. "Europe," she said, "isn't the question." Fanny said, if there was a question at all it was, what were we talking about. "I'm going to have a child," she said, "and it's not going to be any ghetto sheeny, some seamstress or peddler." Abby said, "I'll remind you that my papa was a peddler when he first came to America." Fanny replied, "Exactly."

Fanny's labor began later and lasted longer than expected. She thought she was going to die. When she cried out "Max! Max!" I heard my mother's voice screaming "Osip! Osip!" I told Fanny she had brought new life into the world. She looked at me, exhausted, and said, "Why did you let me?" We had a modern physician who understood the contagious nature of childbed fever and the use of hygiene over incense and amulets. After our Joseph was born, he gladly performed the circumcision as we requested, with medical exactitude and no rites of the desert tent. The prepuce, Dr. Schapira explained, was excess flesh, an unwholesome carrier of disease. "Poor little thing," Daisy our housekeeper said. She and Abby took care of the baby for a couple of weeks, while Fanny regained her strength and peace of mind. Afterward Fanny thanked them and apologized for her moods to Abby. She didn't know what had gotten in to her these past few months. Abby said, "Never mind, dear. We're all one family, and there's one more of us now." They were sitting in the Oriental corner. Fanny held the baby and kissed the top of his head. "Joey," she said. "Joseph Peter. Little Maximus. He takes after his big handsome papa." Daisy said he'd be a regular heartbreaker. Fanny sighed.

"Don't say that, Daisy. The first to be broken is always the mother's heart."

Zak said that in Russia babies were strictly women's business. He was glad to have me back with him on the job. The stock market had plunged, banks were calling in loans, and we could be in trouble. Ida Sussman tearfully counted out her June rent in pennies. Six months ago, her husband, Jake, had his own shop with a dozen workers, turning out men's coats. Now that was all gone. He was spending his days lying around the house or at synagogue, praying. "Prayers don't put soup on the table, do they, Mr. Kraft." I said not that I'd heard of lately.

In July, we cut off the payroll and let our workmen go. We had the telephone removed from our offices. Zak and I started going out to collect rents ourselves again. Mainly we brought back I.O.U.s. We sold our undeveloped lots in the Bronx and Washington Heights at a loss in order to maintain our properties in Harlem. Fanny said to sell Queenie and the pony-chaise. The Silvers invited us to move in with them. Their brownstone on East One Hundred Fifth Street was larger than our row house, which Fanny and I merely rented. Reluctantly we accepted. I thought of Sophie. She said, "I'm not feeling sorry for you two. Think of the workers thrown out of their homes into the street." We reminded ourselves that counting the baby, Daisy, and the Silvers own house help, we'd be seven people under a very ample roof. The merged library, ours and the Silvers', would be far larger than Uncle Henry's ever was. Besides, by giving up the row house we could hold on to our place at Stump Lake, which we hoped to reopen one day. Fanny wondered now if that day would ever come. She said she wasn't getting rid of a stick of furniture. Abby said, "Of course, who was expecting otherwise, dear?" I had only one concern. Zak laughed: "Not Yiddish!" I said, "Yes. Please, not around the baby."

We moved in September. Sitting in the Silvers' parlor, we held a council of war. Zak said the business could survive the slump if we raised a few thousand dollars more. He pointed to the unpacked crates and boxes Fanny and I had brought with us—what hadn't been sent to storage. Fanny braced herself to protect our possessions. "I don't mean all this valuable lumber," he joked. Fanny relaxed. "I mean cold cash. Like this." He held up a filled sock and poured out its contents on top of a crate. "Fifty-seven double eagles. One thousand four hundred dollars in coin of the realm." He'd been putting them by for a few years, exchanging loose bills for gold every month. He called it the hoarding instinct of the race and looked at us one by one, smiling boyishly. It turned out we each had a small cache of gold dollars hidden somewhere, even Abby, who flushed as she produced a silk purse secreted in the upholstery of Zak's favorite chair.

We counted almost three thousand dollars piled in little columns on the crate. "Beautiful," said Zak. He told a story about his uncle Asher, a crazy hermit who lived alone in the marshes beyond the village. No one knew how he made his living. It was rumored he had buried treasure under the dirt floor of his shack. One day while he was out scavenging, or whatever he did for work, thieves came and, sure enough, dug up a strongbox and stole it away. Uncle Asher wailed and rent his clothes, but inside he was laughing. The strongbox was a decoy and held nothing but worthless stones. Three feet below, at the same spot, the real treasure lay hidden. "Of course," said Zak, "we only found this out later. The thieves came back, enraged, and murdered him." Fanny asked what was in the other box. "More stones. I told you, he was crazy."

The money we came up with, I noted, was likely half a year's payroll for Jake Sussman's shop. Zak said he and I could more than double it in a month. Abby asked how. Zak mimed a throw of dice. "Not gambling, Zak!" she said. "I won't let you. It can't be that bad." I told Abby it was. She looked defeated. She didn't doubt Zak, but I supposed a sober word from me about money was telling. I've heard it laughed about me that Max Kraft believes he can live off the air itself, like an uncle Asher.

Fanny was excited. She said why stop at double or triple when we could make enough money to buy back the sold properties. Zak shook his head. That would be stretching the risk too far. A gambling house needs small winners. It was good business to keep the customers' hopes up. The idea, he said, was for us to turn house strategy to our own advantage. He and I would each start with a stake of five hundred dollars. By making safe bets, taking the least risk, we should easily increase our stakes by five percent over the course of an evening, without attracting attention. "What happens if you lose," asked Abby. "We leave," Zak answered. "We leave when we've won or lost our five percent. But we're working with odds, remember." He pulled out a Hoyle's manual from his pocket. "And here the odds are." Then Zak told about Levchenko, the bear trainer in the Ukrainian circus. The man had several wives, in various districts from Lvov to Odessa. He rolled his own cigarettes using dark Turkish tobacco and boasted they were made from camel dung. He liked to wrestle, stripped to the waist, with his bears. He drank a bottle of vodka a day. But Levchenko would not gamble. He said it was a sin to take risks with the good fortune God had placed in your hands. His dream was to own a circus of his own, but everyone knew he never would—Levchenko was afraid of going bankrupt. I said to Zak I'd never gambled in my life either. "Max," he said, "not to worry. You've been playing careful odds since the day you were born."

II

My American Friend

THE SILVERS' HOUSE help was Alice Ward, a relative of our
Daisy. She had come down from Boston just before the slump
and for some days shared Daisy's room. With a new baby in the
house and Fanny still in a poor way, Alice at once made herself
useful to us. Abby hired her shortly afterward, replacing a maid
of theirs called Lulu, under whose mattress were discovered several pieces of missing dinner silver. I said to the girls, Daisy
Osgood and Alice Ward, that when I first came to America nine
years ago, I knew a Clarence Ward Osgood. "He was a hotel
clerk and something of a salesman on the side. He sold liver pills."
I said this looking directly at Daisy, who had previously denied
any connection with Osgood. Now she dropped her eyes to the
floor. Alice blanched and owned he was their uncle. "I thought
so," I said. "He came around the other day, on the excuse of
looking you up. He'd heard you both worked for us and thought
it might mean at the shop. He needs work himself. We might
take him on." Daisy almost in tears said, "Oh, don't!" and apologized for lying. She'd been afraid I'd let her go if I knew the
man was a near relation. Osgood was a good-for-nothing, the
family black sheep. "A bum," said Alice.

Osgood had walked in while Zak and I were practicing card

games at our worktable, cleared of useless blueprints, the open
Hoyle's manual close by. We recognized each other at once. He'd
gotten paunchy but his handlebars were as grand and red as I
remembered and his hound's-tooth jacket as bright. He wore his
derby raffishly tilted back. "Max Kraft, I presume," he said. "Not
Dr. Livingstone," I answered. "Osgood, meet my partner, Zak."
They nodded. I asked Osgood if he still sold those little pills. He
grinned. "No more. The maker's gone out of business. Besides, I
found out what's in them. Now I keep them just for myself, for
special occasions." He looked over my shoulder at my hand, then
at the cards face up on the table, and inquired what game I
thought I was playing. I said I thought it was stud poker. "I like
those mustachios of yours, Max," he said, "but your hand is a
calamity. Allow me." He took over my cards and beat Zak several
games running. After that, the three of us played, and Osgood
again won hand after hand. "If you boys were playing for money,"
he said, "Silver & Kraft would be Osgood & Company now." He
offered to coach us in the ways of American gambling, since we
clearly could use a few tips. Zak agreed but said we couldn't put
him directly on a payroll. Perhaps a stake for himself would
do—say, fifty dollars for starters. "In eagles," said Osgood. Zak
said of course. Osgood pocketed the money without counting.
Then he asked after the girls. He hadn't come here for himself,
he said, but simply to hunt up his old friend Max Kraft and to
check on the welfare of his nieces Daisy and Alice, the fairest
blossoms on the family tree. I explained that they were house
domestics. "Safe at home?" said Osgood. "In good health, I suppose," he added carelessly. I answered, "To be sure." Osgood rose
to go. The coins clinked in his jacket. He looked well pleased. It
was settled that he'd be back the next afternoon. "Be ready for
it, boys," he said. "Blackjack's the game—twenty-one to you."

Zak said he purposely let Osgood win. We needed the experience of his kind of bluffing. The man had a certain style. He
knew the gambling parlance. "He's got the lingo, and he'll get us
into the dens." I said Osgood would run through his stake in no
time. Zak shrugged. We wouldn't need him for very long.

Ida Sussman wanted to know who the American was that
came around every afternoon. She liked to drop by the shop to
get away from her husband, Jake, who had stopped praying and

started sleeping all day instead. I said Osgood was my oldest American friend. "Well, you certainly make some funny ones, that's all I can say, Mr. Kraft." She opened a newspaper on the front desk and pointed to a story about Emma, who had just been sentenced to a year's imprisonment on Blackwells Island for incitement to riot. Two months earlier, in August, she had addressed a crowd of unemployed workers and told them to demonstrate in front of the houses of the rich and demand jobs. If no jobs were forthcoming, they should demand bread. If bread were not given freely, they should take it for themselves. Ida pondered the notion of direct action. "Can you imagine Jake doing a thing like that?" Then she asked if it was true what they said in her building, that I knew this Goldman woman. I didn't deny it. We came from the same town in Russia, I explained. She and my wife and sisters had been friendly as girls. Emma Goldman, in fact, was a cousin, a very distant one, of my wife. "Of Mrs. Kraft!" said Ida. "What kind of families do you two come from?" I thought of Fanny's brothers storing dynamite at our house. I thought of Sophie, Nina, and Mishka, of their life underground, and wondered where they might now be. I said to Ida that we came from interesting families, in their own way.

It was more than a year since Sasha's trial. I'd had a brief thank you for money I sent in his behalf, initialed "EG," on a calling card. The address, 51 First Street, was of Schwab's Saloon. I supposed by this that Emma had taken over the chair of Johann Most. She'd be no more charitable than he to troubling questioners. Her name seemed always in the newspapers. She was Red Emma now. Fanny refused to read the stories. She said that part of our lives was over. When I told her Emma was going to prison, Fanny asked, "What did you expect?" Abby thought that so long as Sasha was suffering, Emma would want to suffer with him somehow in the same way. "Yes," said Fanny, "and make everyone else suffer, too."

Ida Sussman thought Zak and I and the American were simply idling our time with cards and dice while business was bad. She wished Jake would interest himself in something, too, anything at all. We said he was welcome to join us, but she shook her head. Jake didn't approve of games. Zak asked Ida, "What about yourself?" She drew up a chair, and we became a foursome.

Our practice sessions lasted perhaps three weeks. We played only poker, twenty-one, and craps, what Osgood called the necessaries, using chips, with one of us in the role of "house." Ida was a sharp player. Her best game was twenty-one. When the time came to gamble in earnest, we'd be sorry to have to leave her behind. Where we were going, said Osgood, was no place for a lady. Ida spit. Zak was dealer. "Hit me," she said to him. "Hit me again." Turning to me she added: "I never said I was a lady, did I, Mr. Kraft," and raked in her chips. Zak laughed. He said to Ida, "You remind me of Maria Shustova, the tightrope walker." Ida cut him off. "Don't tell me, Mr. Silver, please. But I'd like to know why a woman shouldn't have the same chance as anyone to earn a dollar. When I pay the rent, my money's as good as Jake's. If I don't pay, you turn us both out into the street." Zak and I said, "Never." We offered to stake Ida to twenty-five dollars. She glanced at Osgood, who was frowning. "Make it fifty," she said, "the same as him."

Zak's calculation of the risk proved near the mark. We each won our five percent more often than we lost it. By year's end, our original combined stake of a thousand dollars was more than tripled. The mortgages on our Harlem properties and lost rents were covered for a year. We had our telephone reinstalled. Ida ran her fifty dollars up to three hundred. She carefully paid us back her original stake and three months' rent, which left her with well over two hundred dollars. By then, Jake had disappeared. He had forbidden Ida to go out in the evenings. Was she a good Jewish housewife or a gentile whore? Ida reminded him they'd been together five years and had known each other as children—what did he think he'd been married to up until now? He wouldn't answer. He just rolled over on the couch, said Ida, like a good Jewish husband. Now what was she going to do, be a lady gambler for the rest of her life? Zak told her not to worry. We had a place for her at the shop. She could work the switchboard and keep the books. "Our own queen of diamonds and accomplice in crime," said Zak. Ida flushed. "Thank you, Mr. Silver," she said. But behind closed doors, she called him Isidore.

Osgood lost everything within the first week. We carried him for a while after that, advancing him a few dollars at a time, to Ida's disgust. She never called him by name and referred to him only as the American. I said to her there were all kinds of Americans. She'd been here long enough to know he wasn't typical. He gave a bad name to the rest. "If you say so, Mr. Kraft," said Ida. "All I know is, he'd sell the roof over your head for a whiskey and tell you the fresh air was good for you."

Osgood's game was craps, and his drink was rye. He took us to gambling joints all around the city and in drunken bravado quickly abandoned himself to the dice. Zak told him not to swallow, just touch the glass to his lips. The house made as much money on drinks as it did on the betting. Osgood paid no attention. We left him every night slumped in a corner, dead to the world and drooling, or worse. Nevertheless, he'd turn up at the shop late the following afternoon, ready for another round. Wherever we went, Zak introduced Ida as his sister, who was just there to look. She dressed demurely in a shirtwaist suit. We'd buy her a sherry, which she pretended to sip, with a wince. After watching the players at twenty-one, she'd hesitantly venture a hand, then another, and in a guileless manner many more. No one took Ida quite seriously, as Zak supposed when he devised her strategy, and she walked off with the game.

The gambling houses to which Osgood led us were mostly situated among the brothels, theaters, and dance halls near Broadway north of Madison Square, in brownstones near Union Square, and once even in the ghetto. When we reached where we were going, Osgood liked to call out, "Familiar to you, Max?" Sometimes it felt that way. In a plush card room on Thirteenth Street, I found myself in a large poker game across from Carl Franks. He didn't recognize me with my mustache. "Do I know you?" he said. I answered no. "Then stop looking at me, mister," he said, "and play cards." I bluffed him up to fifty dollars and won with two pairs. Carl Franks stormed away from the table. Zak thought I played too riskily. We'd agreed to avoid betting feuds. "That was Carl Franks," I said. Zak seemed amused. "That pig?" He smiled. Here in the flesh was Abby's onetime fiancé and the man who'd married Blanche Viereck—Zak's rival and, in an odd way, mine. Then Zak turned savage. He said if I'd only let him know, he'd have left Carl Franks with nothing in the world but his skin and blubber. Maybe we could coax the man into another game. We looked in the other rooms, but Carl Franks was gone.

At the blackjack table, a group of men was fussing over helpless little Ida. Osgood was already face down on a banquette along a wall in the dicing room.

In a tenement basement on Allen Street, Zak and Ida gambled in Yiddish. Ida came off badly. There in the ghetto no one was fooled by her manner. Osgood was uncomfortable. He didn't speak the language, and I wasn't the one to help him. There was nothing to drink except slivovitz and beer, and not much of either. Osgood had heard of the place only by accident and thought we'd be happy to be with our own element. I wondered aloud what element was that. Then I told Osgood we wouldn't be needing his services anymore, and walked away from his whining reply. I left shortly afterward. The street was alive with prostitutes calling out from doorways. Gangs of children shouted, darting in among the horses and pushcarts that moved slowly along the cobblestones in the evening half-light. It was filthy underfoot. I'd forgotten how the ghetto stank.

Turning onto Grand Street, I ran into Modska the Twin. I hadn't spoken to him since Worcester. He scarcely knew me on account of my mustache. Modska was wary, until I told him I could have thrashed Johann Most for what he'd said about Sasha after the *Attentat*, but Emma had got there first. Modska said he'd been able to keep in touch with Sasha through the sub-rosa prison mail, and with Emma on Blackwells Island quite openly. Sasha was desperate to escape, in spite of a planned appeal. Emma seemed almost happy. She shared her food packages with less fortunate prisoners, wrote letters for them, and was helping in the sick ward. "She asks after you," said Modska. "She's heard about your sisters." "My sisters? What about them?" I said. That's when I learned that Sophie and Nina had escaped Siberia and were somewhere in America.

III

From Underground

LATE ONE MORNING, shortly after the New Year, Fanny rang me up at the shop. Business was still slow. Zak and Ida worked on the accounts. I was reading Bakunin's *God and the State*, which I'd never thought to reread in English until I happened across a copy in a bookshop. "If God existed, it would be necessary to abolish him." The sentiment had fire in any language. When I picked up the telephone receiver, I half expected the argument to continue on the other end. Fanny's choking voice said instead, "Max, come home quick." I heard a woman crying. I shouted into the telephone, "Is it the baby?" But Fanny had rung off.

I rushed home past Osgood, who'd been lingering by the shop all morning looking for a chance to talk to Zak or me. He asked what was the hurry. When I didn't answer, he followed at my heels down the streets, up the doorstep, and into the parlor. Three strange Russians rose abruptly to their feet, two women in worn, old-fashioned clothes and a lean, feverish-looking man. "Maxie!" the women cried, and held out their arms. We embraced, my sisters and I, and Mishka, too, after thirteen years.

We stepped back to look at one another. All the time of our separation, in my mind's eye we remained children. Sophie's re-current voice was an adolescent girl's. Now her fair hair had small clouds of ashy gray. Nina's cheeks were high and hollow, her eyes no longer dreamy. Mishka had hardly grown. His big head barely reached my shoulders. His face was taut, the skin weather-beaten. My sisters and brother had lost their youth to exile.

Osgood was witness to our reunion. Fanny, speaking Russian, was constrained to introduce him as a friend of the family. My sisters said to him, in careful English, that they were pleased to meet him. Osgood bowed and said he was honored. He had heard so much about them from their brother, he lied, and put himself forward as my oldest American friend. He said this with his eyes fixed on Nina. She returned his stare without blinking, smiling softly, until he dropped his gaze. "Osgood," she said slowly, and he blushed. Nina mused in French that he was a droll American type. Mishka watched them, tight-lipped. The years contracted, and I saw him as a boy guarding his sisters' books.

Zak and Ida hurried in, out of breath. They had heard me shout into the receiver and found I had left the door to the shop wide open. Zak handed me *God and the State*. Apparently it had fallen out of my pocket into the street. Sophie took the booklet out of my hands, inspected it, and returned it with an approving nod. "So, Maxie," she said in Russian, "you're still thinking about our great Cause." I answered in English that yes, I was thinking. She asked when would I begin to act. I said perhaps when the revolution comes. "Perhaps," said Sophie, smiling. "We shall wait." Fanny laughed nervously. She said that in America, things were different from the way they were in Russia. "Of course, Fanya," said Sophie. "In America, the people starve in English. In Russia, there are so many more languages in which to starve, even forbidden ones."

Ida was awestruck. Like Osgood, she understood only part of what was said, since she knew no Russian. Even Zak seemed restrained. Village Jews, I thought. I remembered our summer expeditions with Pyotr Mikhailovich and how the provincials kept at a distance. It never occurred to me before that Zak or Ida actually could have been one of those shy, dirty children who came to beg Sabbath scraps from the innkeeper's wife.

When Abby arrived, Ida left, saying she had to mind the shop. She told me, "I came here a Jewish girl from Turov. These people—excuse me, Mr. Kraft, your family—are from some other

place I don't understand." Fanny said, "Ida, I'm from there also."
Ida objected. "Mrs. Kraft, you're already an American." Abby
came in with a big smile. She had finished her studies and was
now teaching English to new immigrants, at the Educational
Alliance in the ghetto. She greeted her relatives from Russia in
Yiddish. Sophie said in Russian that Abby needn't speak Jewish
jargon. Nina and she were amused by how everyone in America
expected them to talk Yiddish. It was hardly the language of use
in Siberia. Even as children, they'd simply picked it up in the
kitchen. Nina said, "Perhaps cousin Abigail would prefer us to
speak German." Abby didn't understand a word of what had been
said and seemed crushed when Zak explained. When I suggested
we all speak English, everyone laughed but agreed to try. "Dear
Maxie and his English," said Nina. Sophie recalled how as a boy
I was always running off somewhere to study the language or to
read some American trash. "And yet," I smiled, "here we all are
at last, in America." Sophie said, "Yes, for now." From this, I
understood that her heart was still in Russia, as Emma's and
Sasha's had been. I supposed she'd return at the first opportunity,
and said so. "If the revolutionary situation permits," she replied.
"We shall wait, and work, and we shall see. Meanwhile, we shall
stay."

Daisy and Alice brought in the baby. Nina took Joey on her
lap and fussed over him. She called him her little macaroon and
said didn't he look just the way Mishka did at the same age. I
said I didn't think so. Mishka went over to study the baby's face.
He determined there was no resemblance to himself whatsoever,
at any age. "He looks like Max," said Fanny. "Who else should
he look like?" Sophie suggested, "Perhaps somewhat like you,
Fanya, or Maxie's mother." She peered down and declared, "No,
the father precisely." Nina after reflection agreed.

Fanny told the girls to take the baby away and prepare re-
freshments. Zak thought our guests might care to see the library,
which was adjacent to the parlor. "Christ almighty!" said Osgood.
"Look at all those books! Which shelf has the Sears and Roebuck
catalog, Max?" Sophie and Nina slowly paced along the book-
lined walls, running their palms over the spines. Sophie pursed
and unpursed her lips, nodding and then shaking her head. Nina
grew tearful. She said it reminded her of Papa's study, except

everything seemed to be in English. Sophie said that wasn't quite so. She stood in front of a dozen books in Yiddish that Abby had bought, among them *The Communist Manifesto*. "In jargon," said Sophie, as if amused.

Daisy came to say a light lunch was ready. In the passageway between the library and parlor hung a few pictures. There was a miniature of Aunt Libby, looking slim and girlish, and an oil of Abby as a child holding a rag doll. The rest were photographs: three studio wedding portraits—of Zak and Abby, Uncle Henry and Aunt Libby, Fanny and me—and the family grouping in Pyotr Mikhailovich's villa taken it seemed so long ago. Nina, catching sight of her father's figure, began to cry. Mishka turned away. Nina said they lost their copy when she and her sister were transported from Tomsk to Transbaikalia. "Then at least we thought we'd lost no more than a photograph," she said. "Now here is the picture again. But what was behind it is gone." Sophie added: "Soon the revolution will sweep away every trace of that pathetic bourgeois life that was Papa's, leaving only this." I wondered how they'd heard of their father's death. Sophie said, "I shall explain."

Daisy and Alice set up food trays around the parlor. As we ate, Sophie and Nina together told their story of exile and escape, speaking English correctly but cautiously, lacking words. Eventually they lapsed completely into Russian. Zak quietly conveyed the gist of what they said to Abby.

Sophie recalled Mr. Wojcicki. She said the two of them were intimate, even though she was only a girl of sixteen and Kazimierz a man nearing thirty. In Latin class, she had been deeply moved by his dramatic accounts of the brothers Gracchi and the slaves' revolt under Spartacus. He had noticed her intense interest. Little by little, she was drawn into his set of university students and nihilist intellectuals. Sophie was encouraged to continue her circle of *gimnaziya* students. "You, Maxie, were now and then the liaison between the two groups." I claimed I'd been a blind courier. Sophie disagreed. "You were sympathetic. You knew what you were about. You could have joined us anytime you wished."

Organization was loose. What connected the revolutionary groups in Russia was a certain harmony of spirit. "The self-discipline of autonomy," she said, "not the reins of authority." Thus the news of the tsar's assassination came as a thunderclap. Their memories of that day were vivid. Sophie and Nina were at Kazimierz's flat in Slobodka. They were copying out "The Spirit of Revolt," which Kropotkin had recently published in his *Le Révolté*. The journal had been smuggled in from Switzerland. Kazimierz made translations of the tract into Russian and into Polish, the forbidden language, and intended to print them that week at the underground press. Instead, he fled to the Prussian border in anticipation of raids by the secret police. Nina refused to return home alone. "And I would not part from Kazimierz," said Sophie, "nor he from me."

I said I'd seen them going over the Jurbarko bridge. They admitted they'd seen me, too, but couldn't stop or let themselves be hailed, not even by me. "Your trusted courier," I said. Sophie was firm: "Especially so." Kazimierz was cautious. They changed carriages several times and crossed the border on foot at night. He avoided the most direct route west, to Königsberg. Instead, they headed southwest, intending to loop north again once they crossed the Vistula, well into Prussia. They were betrayed nevertheless. They hadn't understood the complicity among the guards and peasants on both sides of the border. Under ordinary circumstances, they'd have escaped. But in the wake of the tsar's assassination, there was a bounty to be paid for returning fugitives to Russia. The Pole who rented them a rowboat, after counting his money, shot Kazimierz in the back of the head. This was near Marienburg. Under the full moon, the estuary and Bay of Danzig lay open to view.

Sophie and Nina, with Mr. Wojcicki's body, were returned to Kovno. At checkpoint after checkpoint, first in Prussia and then in their home province, they watched what they supposed were shares of the reward change hands. "Such misdirected cooperation among the masses," said Sophie, "when turned to revolutionary purposes, will shake the earth." Her composure was chilling. Abby looked at her in alarm. Then Sophie added: "Don't imagine I thought this at the time. Not at all. I was sixteen. Kazimierz was dead. I remember wishing I could hold my breath and die." She considered breaking away from the guards so she, too, could be shot and killed. Nina's presence alone prevented her. Sophie understood in time that she'd been saved not for herself but for the Cause. "I am nothing," said Sophie. She sat high in her chair with her chin up. "Nothing," she repeated. "The revolution is everything."

Nina was afraid she and her sister would be used badly by the guards. The Germans who took them to the border tried to make coarse jokes in a dialect the girls could barely understand, but were cowed by the body bag on the floor of the carriage. "They thought we were some kind of witches," said Nina. The Russian guards were abrupt. They angrily prodded them with rifle butts and called them Jewess assassins. The jailors at the prison in Kovno were civil, presumably on Pyotr Mikhailovich's account. The girls had expected to be tortured by the likes of a Jurgis Bobelis. Sophie and Nina were put in a stark but clean cell of their own, where their father visited them every day. He brought them clothes and food, always with a little candy, and what he said was good news but was, in fact, no news at all. He assured them his influence and connections would protect them.

Without warning, late one night they were roused from sleep and sent to St. Petersburg. They were packed into a small prison cell with a half-dozen other young women, none of them much older than themselves. There was hardly room to lie down and just one slop bucket to share. Sophie was frequently nauseous. She supposed it was from the closeness of the air. Then she realized she was pregnant. The women congratulated her. Sophie said, "The life growing inside me came from Kazimierz. I felt as if I were carrying the revolution itself."

Pyotr Mikhailvich followed Sophie and Nina to St. Petersburg. He was not allowed to see them together. His visits to the Litovsky prison, first with one daughter and then the other, were limited to a few minutes. They had to talk across a distance of several feet, separated by bars, in a room noisy with other prisoners and visitors. When for privacy they began to speak German, the guards shouted, "Russian!" In the circumstances, it was impossible for Sophie to tell her father of her condition. I said if she had, she'd have broken his heart. "That is what Nina imagined," said Sophie, "but I had no secrets from Papa." I asked if that included her revolutionist work. Sophie said Papa understood her views. What she didn't tell him were matters that involved other people. "He never knew," she said, "that you killed that man Bobelis." Zak started at this remark. Abby, after she understood it, turned pale. Years before, I'd shown them Pyotr Mikhailovich's letter that made mention of the police torturer's exhumed remains, but without bringing myself into it. Abby whispered, "My God." Sophie took no notice. In the visitors' room in prison, she said, only the most urgent concerns could be made known. Pyotr Mikhailovich was anxiously working to have the charges against Nina dismissed and Sophie shown leniency. He succeeded on both accounts, but to no purpose. Sophie would continue in the revolutionary struggle no matter where, and Nina was determined to share her sister's fate. The last view they had of Pyotr Mikhailovich, he was standing on the platform at the St. Petersburg station toward dawn, straining impossibly for a glimpse of his daughters. They could see him in the distance, between the heads of other young exiles who had crowded to the windows of the guarded railway car.

Nina said she found a strange providence in the fact that Papa while in St. Petersburg had stayed with the family of Alexander Berkman, who would soon afterward become Mishka's friend. She'd been following Sasha's recent case and wondered how much of an example Sophie might have been to him. I said her reputation among the comrades from the Baltic provinces was considerable. In fact, it was through Sasha's cousin Modska and Emma Goldman I'd learned that Nina and Sophie were in America. Nina laughed. Who'd have supposed that this Red Emma was her plump little friend Chava? Was it true that she was Berkman's lover? I nodded. "A strange providence," Nina reflected again. Sophie thought it was nothing of the kind. She invoked Kropotkin: There are times when revolution becomes an imperative necessity. The forces of history, she said, will create in such periods an inevitable like-mindedness at all levels of society, everywhere. "Comrades will always recognize each other, even here, in America." I suggested we might call that the providence of history. Nina said that was what she meant all along.

After the trial, Sophie and Nina were transported to the exile-forwarding compound in Moscow, and from there to Tyumen, beyond the Urals. From Tyumen to Tomsk was a river voyage of ten days. On the prison barge, among the convoy of three hundred convicts and volunteer settlers, Sophie was the only political exile, and she and her sister were carefully segregated from the rest. On their journey east, they were treated with increasing sympathy, even respect, the farther they traveled from Russia proper. As the grip of St. Petersburg loosened, said Sophie, so rose the spirit of liberty and cooperation—in a word, the makings of a natural society: of anarchism. The contempt of provincial officials for the law, their web of bribery and petty corruption, what were these but a perverted mutualism, misdirected self-interest as yet unaware of the collective might of the commune? Fanny, beside me, sighed wearily. "Yes, Fanya," said Sophie, "I know it is sad. Papa used to ask what I knew of the people. In this, he was right. I knew nothing. Social revolution will come about only when the bourgeoisie joins with the people. There is the dray, and there is the dray horse. Separate, they are useless. Our task is to harness the one to the other." I said this was the first kind word about the bourgeoisie I'd heard in years. Sophie said even people with the best intentions can be blinded by the prejudices of their class. Kropotkin's great "Appeal to the Young" was a clarion call to the bourgeoisie and workers to come together for humanity's sake, an antidote to the Marxists' narrow summons. I told her I hadn't read the piece. No matter, she'd lend me a copy. She said she knew where my heart lay and mentioned Herzen, the Englishman Robert Owen, and even Engels as examples of men of means who put their wealth at the disposal of social change, if not revolution. Nina smiled sweetly. "To their names, Maxie," she said, I supposed with humor, "Sophie means to add yours."

Zak started to laugh. "Revolution on credit! Forgive me," he said, "but all this reminds me of Reb Feivel the bootmaker in my village." Reb Feivel as a young man had left to go to America to make his fortune, having been rejected as a suitor by the rabbi's youngest daughter. Ten years later he returned a wealthy man— he had a sewing machine. He set up what he called an American shop. One man cut the soles, another the tops, a third did the cobbling. Reb Feivel alone stitched on the machine. Everyone in the village wanted new American boots, but few had the money to pay. Reb Feivel said that was all right, he'd extend them credit. Credit? said the rabbi. You mean usury! No, said Reb Feivel, I mean credit, American credit: the villagers would pay him for their boots in monthly installments over a period of one or two years, without interest. Reb Feivel, of course, quietly figured interest into the price of the boots, but their cost was still less than the Russian boots of his rivals. Soon all the village had American boots and, on Reb Feivel's advice, was living on credit. The butcher felt rich. Suddenly everyone was ordering meat, for which he overcharged, and paying him for it in installments. He had a fortune coming to him. The beggars danced in the streets, looking forward to happy tomorrows when their promised handouts came due. Then, after two years, Reb Feivel eloped with the rabbi's daughter and returned to America. The American boots started to fall apart, and the old bootmakers required full payment for repairs. There was no money left to spare. People couldn't pay the butcher's high prices, on any terms. When the beggars demanded their due, they were knocked down into the mud. "No one was rich anymore," said Zak, "and Reb Feivel was to blame. The rabbi cursed him for a thief who stole his daughter and with her the villagers' credit."

I supposed Sophie would be angered by Zak's story. To my surprise, she thought it over seriously. Perhaps she intended to enroll Zak, too, among the patrons of the Cause. She said she found his phrase "revolution on credit" not entirely irrelevant. The *mutualisme* of M. Proudhon, the conception of the People's Bank, rested on the organization of credit on a cooperative basis. It is not the capitalists' gold or the Marxists' surplus value of labor but the humanitarian spirit itself that adds worth even to the most precious commodity. That is why when we speak of a gift of love, we know it bears greater value than that same gift given thoughtlessly. As for Zak's villagers, they trusted in Reb Feivel's word alone to make their own revolution on credit. "It is a pity," she said, "they did not trust in themselves. But how could they, those Jews, with their wizened God and suffocating Law and their impossible jargon."

Abby asked what Yiddish had to do with the matter. "I was born and raised a Jewess in America," she said. "The Jewish language is more foreign to me than to any of you, but I've heard it spoken eloquently, and that in behalf of your 'Cause.'" She read in the Jewish newspapers articles and literature few

American papers would print. She saw in the ghetto every day working men and women struggling for their lives in a new land, and in their hands, in Jewish, Dostoyevsky, Tolstoy, Goethe, Anatole France. She taught these people English, and some of them were better read, in their own language, than she in hers. "You seemed before," said Abby, "looking at the *Manifesto* in Jewish, about to laugh. Are there not Jews, too, among your workers of the world?"

Sophie graciously accepted everything Abby said, and then added: "But of course, dear, what you say simply points to the inadequacies of the language. It borrows its grammar and half its words from one dead language, a medieval German. Its alphabet and the rest of its vocabulary it takes from Hebrew, another dead language. When Chava Goldman speaks, as you say, eloquently in jargon in our behalf, I would suppose the girl is in fact speaking a corrupted German."

Abby objected. Sophie was resolute. I remembered her standing up to the women in the Chassidic village, even as her Yiddish failed her and in her mouth turned into German. "I would remind you," she said, "we were discussing village Jews, whose understanding of the world is limited by a deficient patois rough-hewn over centuries of humiliation, poverty, and superstition." I couldn't have put it better, and said so. Abby rose to leave the room. Zak somehow dissuaded her. "Mr. Silver," said Sophie, "you know what I say is true. There can be no revolution for the Jews until they unbuild their own fences of religion and language." Among the settlers in Siberia, who spoke only Russian, a new breed of free Jew walked unashamed. In Tomsk, she and Nina lived in the household of Timofei Timofeyich Yakovlev. At his dinner table, it was not unusual to be seated next to a guest, perhaps a tall peasant with a straight back, named Kahanov or Davidovich. "From this you will understand," Nina put in, "our life there, though hard, was not all toil and deprivation."

IV

From Underground—Continued

MISHKA SO FAR said nothing. He'd never been talkative, but his silence now was grim and, I supposed, a little cagey. Osgood sat clear of Mishka. He sprawled his legs as if he were in a saloon. He was all eyes for Nina and managed to inch his chair close to hers. Nina acknowledged him with an occasional unhurried smile. She said, in Russian, that Timofei Timofeyich Yakovlev drunk was like this clownish American sober. Either way, Yakovlev was pliable. Nina reached over and touched Osgood's arm. His face flamed red. "Yes," she said, "very much like Timofei Timofeyich."

Several families lived on Yakovlev's estate, free peasants in origin like Timofei Timofeyich himself. For their younger children, he kept a one-room schoolhouse. Sophie was made their teacher. She also tutored those of the older children who attended the district school and were likely to go on to the local *gimnaziya* and university. A district judge, Yakovlev could ignore the imperial rule that forbade political exiles to teach. Siberia didn't seem quite so bleak as Sophie and Nina had imagined. Those first years might have been tolerable were it not for the tragedies that haunted Sophie, her lover's murder and her baby's death. When she came due, she thought of her labor as the pangs of the revolution. It was December. The solstice, the midwife said, was an auspicious time for giving birth. Sophie named her baby Kazimierz. When people began to whisper about the father, Sophie let it be known that he'd been killed in an accident on the Vistula shortly after the two of them had married secretly and eloped. "This was no lie," she said. "Kazimierz Wojcicki and I were truly married in our hearts." They had no use for the so-called sanctions of the state and its church lackeys, nor the state for them, an apostate Catholic and an unbelieving Jewess.

The baby had his father's features in miniature. Sophie cooed at him in Latin, *rebello*, *rebellas*, *rebellat*, and he seemed to understand. Timofey Timofeyich, a widower with no children, proposed to adopt him. Sophie rejected the idea. The boy could grow up without a father, but he must know who and what his father was and so carry on in his place. I recalled Mr. Wojcicki's description of a funeral procession in ancient Rome, in which the living paraded in the masks of their ancestors. I thought, What a terrible burden. A Brutus frees Rome from the Tarquins: ergo, a Brutus must free Rome from Caesar. What mask must a Maximus wear, the Kovno landlord's sorrowing visage or the astonished face of the roofer with a broken back? This Maximus chose neither. He came to America instead.

Sophie's baby died that summer of cholera. After she buried him, nothing seemed to matter. Grief drained her of hope. There would be no revolution in her lifetime, or, if there were, she wouldn't care. She even thought of me and wondered if I might have been right about going to America, such was her despair. Timofei Timofeyich was kind. He relieved Sophie of her teaching and tutoring and gave her French novels, but she couldn't bring herself to read. She spent months in bed, her face turned to the wall.

Nina entered *gimnaziya*. One day, she placed at Sophie's bedside two pamphlets of Kropotkin's, in Russian, painstakingly copied by hand. One was "The Spirit of Revolt," the very piece they'd been copying themselves the day the tsar was assassinated. The other was "An Appeal to the Young." Sophie wouldn't look. What did she want with these? She told her sister to take the pamphlets back to wherever she got them. Nina refused. If Sophie wouldn't read them, then Nina would, aloud. The sound of

Kropotkin's words shocked Sophie out of her lethargy. "I was alive again," she said, "not for my own sake but for the revolution." I imagined Sophie marching to a dirgelike "Internationale," holding to her face the death mask of Kazimierz Wojcicki.

The source of the pamphlets was a nihilist circle at *gimnaziya* with which Nina had made cautious contact. She was purposefully shy with her schoolmates. When pressed about herself, she hinted at German ancestry and being parentless. She'd been taken in by the district judge, Yakovlev, whom she suggested had at one time been associated in commerce with her father, a merchant from the Baltic provinces. Timofei Timofeyich's family fortune had been made in the central Siberian river trade. The school officials knew Nina's true circumstances and her relation to the exile Sophie Kraft, but said nothing. Nina tried not to provoke them. A classmate of hers named Sonya Rashin grew friendly in spite of Nina's reserve and repeatedly invited her home. Nina put off accepting, until one day Sonya let slip an oblique reference to Chernyshevsky. A group of girls was discussing marriage and named the handsomest young men each of them knew. Sonya turned to Nina and said wasn't it sickening, as if all the world had to offer for women were men and babies. It was for women themselves to resolve the women's question. When her schooling was finished, Sonya intended to form a women's collective, and the men could go sniffing elsewhere for their fun. Nina understood that Sonya was in love with her older brother, Georgi, and was confused. "When I brought up free love," Nina laughed, "the girl blushed to her toes."

Georgi was an engineering student at the university and belonged to a revolutionist group. Through him, Sonya and her friends obtained the literature that in the end caused Sophie and Nina to be sent to Transbaikalia, where their life would be hard work. In Tomsk, Sophie's exile was privileged. Less fortunate political outcasts lived in ramshackle camps. They grew their own food and, like serfs, performed the dreariest labor. It was months before Nina told Sonya and Georgi about her sister, fearing the exposure. "By then," said Nina, "Georgi was in love with me— Sonya, too, without knowing it—and they would do anything I asked." She added: "Timofei Timofeyich was also not a little smitten."

Sophie, after her reawakening, made plans for escape. She would not wait five years in Tomsk, only to be denied a passport. She intended to go to Switzerland or England. Nina, traveling legally, would eventually follow. Meanwhile, Sophie resumed her teaching and tutoring. She indoctrinated her pupils with the idea of social revolution in everything but the name. Nina easily persuaded Timofei Timofeyich to use part of her monthly allowance to help the political exiles in their squalor. Besides being in love, Yakovlev was something of a reformist. She also put aside, from her pocket, money for Sophie's escape.

Among the student revolutionists, Sophie's legend grew. It was unwise for her to meet with them directly. They knew her through short, telling critiques on the literature they funneled her way. Sophie said she took no credit for them. The voice was not hers at all but Kazimierz Wojcicki's, and she often signed his initials. Apparently, he was in Sophie's head for years, much the way Sophie was in mine. I thought how remarkable was the authority we gave to an inner voice, and said so. Sophie wasn't offended. "Maxie," she said, "there is no other authority."

Sophie's seclusion added to the romance of the situation for Sonya and Georgi. On the rare occasions they came to dinner, when Sophie was present all three sat speechless. Afterward Sonya and Georgi told their comrades of Sophie's brilliant, tactical self-effacement. The brother and sister were more sentimentalist than revolutionary, but this was not to Sophie's or Nina's disadvantage. Nina's gift, as Sophie called it, kept Sonya and Georgi afire. Nina smiled at Osgood to demonstrate her gift. Once again, the man flushed crimson.

Correspondence with Pyotr Mikhailovich was difficult. I said I remembered Nina's early letters, before I left for America. They suggested more than they gave. "Yes, because of the censors," said Nina. "But Papa's letters became strange, filled with religious argumentation, as if we cared about that." He told them he was writing, in Hebrew, a commentary on Job that would reconcile Spinoza with orthodoxy, and included passages from it translated into a barely intelligible German. From this they understood their father had become devout. I said yes, he turned into an old Jew. Sophie and Nina shook their heads, perplexed. Mishka worked his jaw muscles, I supposed in angry remembrance. Only at the end of Pyotr Mikhailovich's letters, sometimes in an abrupt post-script, was there any word of home. The bits of news were disconnected from one letter to the next. The new Madame had been let go. Which Madame was that? Mishka was no longer at boarding school. Why and where had he been sent? Maxie was safely in America. When had he left? Finally Pyotr Mikhailovich wrote that the villa was sold. Sophie and Nina realized then that even if they wished to finish out the term of exile and return to Kovno, there would be no home waiting. They had no family now.

Through Georgi's comrades, Sophie expected to obtain a false passport, and Nina, too, as a precaution. They would keep the forged papers under the floorboards of their room, along with the money for escape. It was early spring of 1886, while they were waiting for the passports, that an investigator from the secret police came to question Sophie about the death years before of Jurgis Bobelis. She of course knew nothing of the matter. How could she, being only a girl at the time? Bobelis? Who was he? The investigator seemed satisfied with her answers and owned that his presence in Tomsk was senseless, a bureaucratic bungle. Being there, he felt like a character out of Gogol. They discussed literature. The man was a devotee of Turgenev. Sophie still told him nothing about Bobelis, or me, and they parted friends. The next day, while Sophie was teaching and Nina was at *gimnaziya*, he returned and ransacked their room. In Sophie's mattress he found the dreaded conspirator Nechayev's *Catechism of a Revolutionary*, copied in Nina's distinctive hand. There was some irony in the discovery, since Sophie had a growing uneasiness with Nechayev's clandestine severity.

Timofei Timofeyich was angry and aggrieved. He stood amid the rubble of the room and asked Sophie and Nina how they could have betrayed him. He had seen their dossiers and taken pity on them. If he had daughters, he'd asked himself, mightn't they, too, have been caught up in the struggles of the day? He received them into his home. He saved Sophie from the deadening fate of the friendless exile. He arranged for Nina to remain with her sister. For all this, they repaid him by endangering him and his entire household.

A police guard was posted inside the door. Timofei Timofeyich ordered him out of the room. He said this was still his house, he was still district judge, the girls were still under his jurisdiction. The man left. Timofei Timofeyich locked the door behind him and turned to Sophie and Nina, his face dark and twisted with emotion. "If he was drunk," said Nina, "who knew what he might do? We separated, one on either side of him, so he couldn't rush at us both at once." Timofey Timofeyich lurched toward Nina. She backed off. He grabbed at her skirts, fell to his knees, and confessed he was the unhappiest man in the world. He wept noisily to think of losing Nina, as if she were his to lose! As if he, not they, were about to be imprisoned and afterward transported who knew where! The guard pounded on the door. An escort was waiting. Timofei Timofeyich rose to his feet and called out that he was almost finished. He stood by meekly as Sophie and Nina each packed a small valise, and he turned away when they told him to. While Nina changed her clothes, Sophie smoothly removed the escape money from under the floorboards and hid it in the lining of her bag. Timofei Timofeyich unlocked the door. The guard rubbed his hands together and said with a wink that it must have been a good thrashing, just what these bitches deserved.

Sophie and Nina spent a few nights at the exile-forwarding prison in Tomsk and the next several weeks on the wearying march east beyond Lake Baikal to Chita. They were attached to a mixed party of soldiers' wives going out to join their husbands, political exiles, and criminals in shackles. Travel was by foot along the muddy, narrow Siberian Post Road. They slept at night in vermin-infested post-house barracks. Once Sophie and Nina knew where they were being sent, their spirits rose. Chita was a venerable place of exile, to which the Decembrist revolutionaries sixty years earlier had been banished. Bakunin in Transbaikalia had traveled the Amur to its mouth and from there sailed to America. They determined to do the same, no matter the means.

In Chita, they learned they were to be separated. Nina was ordered back to Irkutsk, in East Siberia. An assistant district chief named Hlebka hinted she could make it worth his while to have the order rescinded. Otherwise, if they must stay together, the man joked, Sophie and Nina might sign on with the next boatload of women, criminal exiles, about to leave for the lower Amur. There was a settlement of released convicts near Blagoveshchensk, and the women had volunteered to marry the men unseen in return for their own freedom. "Blagoveshchensk was on our route of escape, halfway downriver to the sea," said Nina. "Hlebka was repulsive, soft and fat, with greasy Cossack mustachios. We of course chose the settlers." I said they went at last to the people. Sophie answered, "*V narod*, precisely."

Volkova was barely a year old. In that time, the men had cut many acres of forest and built a cookhouse and a dormitory cabin in which they had waited out the winter. They had survived on beets, potatoes, cabbage, stale bread, and kvass, and smelled it. Now, with spring, the cleared land could be prepared for sowing. On the barge with the women came a cage of chickens and a flock of goats. The goats and chickens were to be held in common; not so the women, who would be assigned by lot. There were forty men and only twenty-eight women. Sophie and Nina were given away, respectively, to an Estonian ax-murderer and an Armenian extortionist from Odessa. The men who drew blank lots grew angry and sullen, as did some of the others at the first sight of their intended wives.

Sophie seized control. She told the women to stay together and then framed, with their consent, a list of demands. One: The women would not cohabit with their new husbands until private dwellings were built for each couple. Two: Until such dwellings were built, the women would sleep apart from the men, in their own quarters in the dormitory cabin. Three: The women would not cook for, mix with, let alone cohabit with the men until such time as the men bathed. Four: For those new couples inclined to religious belief and observance, their unions would not be deemed in effect until consecrated by a priestly representative of the Orthodox church at Blagoveshchensk. This last was not at all of Sophie's making, but she understood it would lend force to the other demands in the minds of the men, who might turn violent.

By this means, it was months before all the marriages were consummated. The settlers and their allotted brides gained time for changing the chance arrangements. Some balked at marriage altogether, such as Ivar the ax-murderer, who found the women's presence, Sophie's especially, dismaying. No one dared claim Sophie. She made her views on traditional marriage clear. From being chief spokeswoman she became chief of Volkova, the

Madame Hetman as she was called, possibly, I thought, with some affection. Nina lived with her Armenian. "My little Arshag," she said, "with his soft brown eyes." He said one day he hoped to go to America, there to dwell under his own fig tree and vine. When the time came for escape, she'd have taken him along if she could. She added: "But Arshag dreamed of ease in a Garden of Eden, not the work of the revolution."

Abby asked who were these women convicts? What had they done to become slaves to men who were criminals like themselves and no better than they were? Sophie answered that it was true the women had arrived as chattel, but by removing themselves at once from the men and setting forth their demands, they established their equality. Yes, they were convicted exiles, but the laws had broken them more than they the laws. An illiterate worker in a textile mill in St. Petersburg one day coughed up blood. She left the factory and took in laundry to earn her bread. She found a string of pearls in her washing and sold it. Perhaps now she could get medical treatment. Instead, she was exiled as a thief. Another girl in like circumstances turned to prostitution. She stabbed her procurer to death after he cheated and beat her once too often. "I could go on," said Sophie, "but as you say, dear cousin, our women were no worse than our men." Law was society's mirror, not its protector. It preserved people only for the sake of their property. Simply put, criminality was whatever endangered so-called legitimate ownership. When at last the revolution abolished private property as such, crime would become obsolete.

"No," said Fanny. Memories of Russia often troubled her. Sometimes at night when she awoke from a bad dream, she reminded herself aloud, in English, that she was in America. She said to Sophie that it wasn't simply a question of definition. A nightmare lived in every human heart, a blackness we could never change and never understand. Sophie brushed the idea aside. "If I believed that, Fanya," she said, "I would have put a pistol to my head by now." Zak cleared his throat to catch my eye, and winked. He was ready to hand her the gun.

Sophie continued. "As Maxie pointed out, we went to the people at last. I assure you, as a fact: all the criminal exiles were victims of ill-conceived laws." Abby asked how Ivar the ax-murderer was a helpless victim. Sophie answered that "helpless" was never her word. Ivar had been a pig farmer on a small estate. The end of serfdom brought him freedom and an allotment of land that was good for raising flax but bad for pigs. He could not meet his redemption payments for his land and was forced to sell out and move to the capital, Tallinn. There, unable to find work, he became a lost man. Ivar's sickness was one that could be cured. His story was multiplied by as many settlers as they had at their commune near the Amur. They organized themselves, under Sophie's guidance, as a successful anarchist collective: everyone an equal worker, everyone an equal owner of the means of production, everyone an equal sharer in its yield. As for supposed crime, there was virtually none. The shame of public opinion proved a strong check against willful deviance, which was called to account by a wall of silence.

Zak asked how Sophie and Nina could have brought themselves to leave this utopia. He said this with a straight face. Sophie replied that after four and half years, her work there was done. The commune could carry on without her. Volkova was a germ of the revolution in the East. Technically she and Nina had gained their freedom by joining the settlement. In point of fact, once word got out that they had left, the shadow of the secret police would always be near. They needed to move swiftly and quietly. They had five hundred rubles in escape money, two hundred fifty American dollars—enough, they hoped, to pay for passage on a riverboat to Nikolayevsk, false passports, and the voyage out to America. Sophie and Nina routinely went by cart to Blagoveshchensk, with Arshag driving, to trade for supplies. They could trust Arshag to delay his return to the settlement for a few days to cover their disappearance.

The arrival of Mishka hastened their plan. Nina was the first to recognize him at the boat landing. Sophie was bargaining over shipments of seed and cement. Arshag said to Nina he didn't like the way that man over there was looking at her, the one near the gangplank of the stern-wheeler. "I raised my eyes," said Nina, "and when I saw him, I knew him at once. My blood jumped." She must have cried out. Sophie turned toward her and followed her line of sight to the landing. Even she gasped. Mishka put his finger to his lips. I looked over at him now. He stood at the parlor window, his back to the room, signaling I supposed a kind of modesty.

Boat traffic on the Amur was heavy that year. Work had begun in the East on the Trans-Siberian Railway. Mishka was a stoker on a paddle-wheel steamer that carried supplies from Pokrovka at the head of the river to Khabarovsk, the northern terminus of the Ussuri line, which would eventually reach south to the seaport of Vladivostok. The leg from Blagoveshchensk to Khabarovsk took only a few days. Sophie and Nina could stow away in the hold on the last trip out in November, before the Amur froze over, slowing immediate pursuit. The Ussuri would still be navigable south to Lake Khanka. From there, the post road led directly to Vladivostok, though travel was arduous. Nina said, "We told Mishka we had made the march from Tomsk to Chita. How could this be worse?" Mishka had the names of comrades in Vladivostok who could arrange for false passports and hide the three of them until they booked passage abroad. Such was Mishka's plan. It hinged only on money. Steerage to America might be as high as sixty dollars for each of them. Mishka hinted the sum could be raised. All property was theft. For a revolutionist, the concept of thievery, the theft of a theft, was absurd. Sophie and Nina were relieved to learn their escape money was sufficient.

Zak was impatient. He wanted to know how Mishka had come to find his sisters in Blagoveshchensk in the first place. When had he left Kovno? How had he made his way east? "I ask," he said, "because I know something of such things." He reminded us that he had run away from home at the age of fifteen. "Yes," said Nina, "Mishka's age exactly."

The story of the search was quickly told. Details were wanting in Nina's Russian. Mishka didn't expand on his adventures—Mishka, this calculated mystery that was my brother, brave Mishka the Lion in the Chassidic village, Mishka the snitch. I thought, The little boy has learned not to be boastful or complaining. Nechayev wrote that the revolutionist was doomed, a man with no sentiments, no attachments, no name; his only thought, his one passion: the revolution. Our housemaids, Daisy and Alice, stared at Mishka, dumbstruck. They edged closer to Zak the better to overhear his retelling of Nina's account.

Life for Mishka in Kovno was suffocating. Pytor Mikhailovich had sold the villa and moved to a small flat in Slobodka above his place of business. With Shneur Shavelson, he studied and prayed and meditated over skewered stacks of promissory notes. Ruth the cook came twice a week to prepare meals that could be eaten hot or cold and left silently when her work was done. Mishka stopped going to school and learned to live in the streets. He still hung about with Sasha Berkman's group, but most of them were determined to leave for America. Mishka meant to travel in the opposite direction. From Nina's letters, he knew the names of his sisters' friends, Sonya and Georgi Rashin, and of the district judge Yakovlev. It was possible to obtain false identification papers. Zak asked how. Mishka wouldn't say. With a Christian name, he'd be safe from the army recruiters who kidnapped lone Jews, and able as well to escape the confines of the Pale. I asked what new name he went by. Mishka wouldn't say. It was possible to find work, no questions asked, laying the rail lines that crossed White Russia and the Ukraine to the Urals. It was possible to volunteer for settlement in Siberia and then simply disappear from the convoy when it reached Tomsk, only to discover that the people one was seeking had been transported two years before, sent to East Siberia or even somewhere beyond Lake Baikal. From whom did Mishka learn this? Nina said she believed from Sonya Rashin—Mishka would never really say. I'd have supposed Mishka would be more trusting of his sisters, and said so. Sophie replied, "Mishka came to find us, Maxie. He did, and now we are here. There is rhetoric, and there are deeds. Revolution is not made simply by words but by the ideas of those words translated into action." I looked at Mishka, the translator, and, remembering Chernyshevsky in Yiddish, thought again how much of the revolution could be lost in translation.

Cutting through the evasions, the plausible story of Mishka's search was this. He arrived in Tomsk to find his sisters gone, Yakovlev a recluse relieved of his duties, Georgi Rashin away on a mining survey in the north, and Sonya restless with plans to study medicine abroad. She gave Mishka the names of comrades in Krasnoyarsk and Irkutsk who would know Sophie by reputation and perhaps have information about her and Nina's whereabouts. Mishka slowly worked his way eastward, living for a time on roots and berries and the bread and kvass the villagers left out at night for escaped convicts and exiles on the march. The comrades in Krasnoyarsk had been arrested. Those in Irkutsk had a contact in the district administration, a clerk who located the names of Sophie and Nina Kraft on a transporation list to Chita. Mishka found work in the river trade, as a dockhand, a bargeman, a stoker, and reached Chita in the spring of 1890. A friend of the administrative clerk in Irkutsk turned out to be a personal aide to assistant district chief Hlebka. This aide, Boris Ecks, remembered Sophie and Nina very well—who could forget Hlebka's grand humiliation at the hands of the anarchist who spurned him, choosing volunteer marriage and resettlement over the assistant district chief's bed? Mishka continued on to Sretensk, to Pokrovka, to the boat landing at Blagoveshchensk that day in midsummer when Sophie and Nina were bartering for supplies. Before the end of the year, they would reach Vladivostok together as planned. There they would live underground for several months, with the help of friends of Boris Ecks, before crossing the Pacific.

It was while they were waiting in Vladivostok, said Sophie, that they learned of Pyotr Mikhailovich's death. Word reached them from Lev and Fedya Ruttenberg in Kovno. Fanny said, "Not my brothers!" She was hoping never to hear of them again. Nina explained. During all the years in Volkova, they received no letters from Papa. They realized after a while that their own letters to him and any of Papa's to them were confiscated by the secret police. Very likely, Pyotr Mikhailovich had no idea where his daughters were or if they were even alive. Now, through the friends of Boris Ecks, they wrote to Papa, to let him know they were safe, with Mishka, and soon to leave for America.

Zak asked how the letter was sent that it could find its way to Fanny's brothers, of all people. Nina laughed. By underground express, or so the friends of Boris Ecks called it. Documents of all kinds passed from one revolutionary group to another and so made their way across Russia in a matter of months, even weeks if a courier happened to be on a freighter to Odessa. Fanny's brothers had been in Kazimierz Wojcicki's circle. Evidently, its remnant was regrouping. "This gave us heart," said Sophie. "One day soon, we, too, might return home to Kovno." Fanny said if they felt that way from the start, perhaps they should have stayed in Russia—for all that Russia had given them. She enumerated: prison, hiding, exile, death. Zak said a circus he'd been with once had passed through a Jewish village after an Easter pogrom. He recalled bloated bodies under a blue sky, flies, dried blood on the wildflowers. "And you'd return," he said, "to that." Sophie shook her head. "Not to that, Mr. Silver, but its end, to assist in the deathblow."

On the boat to San Francisco, they picked up some English by reading back issues of American papers. They learned of the war at Homestead and Alexander Berkman's *Attentat* and imprisonment. They wondered that this Red Emma was the Chava Goldman they knew as a girl, Fanya Ruttenberg's cousin—Fanya, now their brother Maxie's wife, so the Ruttenberg brothers had written. The nearer they sailed to America, the more it took shape in their minds as a familiar place, not Russia but with known people and common fields of battle. I asked why they hadn't written me as soon as they landed. "The habit of caution," said Nina. They traveled under the family name Borov, which the immigration officials took down as Borough. They found the name a useful cover. I said in America there were no secret police. They had broken no laws so far as I knew and couldn't be deported. There was no need for disguise.

Mishka, for the first time, laughed, a single ironic bark. He said Sasha—or should he say Bakhmetov?—will appreciate the humor of my remarks. I understood from this that he must be in touch with Sasha sub rosa, planning no doubt an escape. The boy who for Sophie's and Nina's sake doggedly found his way to Blagoveshchensk would blow out the penitentiary walls for Sasha.

By then I had no desire to know what they had been doing these many months since they disembarked. I knew enough of the answer already. They had tunneled across the New World as it were through the Old World underground. If I asked what were their first impressions of America, Sophie would pronounce upon the state of revolutionary consciousness among the workers she could not have met. Nina would look at Osgood and suggest how in America the eternal boy in every man is strangely manifest. And Mishka wouldn't say.

V

Mishka

OSGOOD TOOK TO hanging about outside the shop or near the house. Ida shooed him away when she saw him, nosing at the door like a stray dog, as she said. Daisy and Alice peeked at him through the curtains and met him in the street in hurried talk. Fanny forbade them to speak with him when they were wheeling the baby. She was afraid he'd steal Joey away. A man like that was like a Gypsy, capable of anything to get what he wanted. I said Osgood wanted only one thing. We couldn't give it to him or pay him to go away. Osgood was in love, and the woman he was in love with was Nina. He supposed he could get to her through me. He insisted his intentions were honorable. Nina was the kind of woman, he said, who would make an honest man of him. I told him his honor and honesty were of no consequence, nor was I in the matter. Nina could speak for herself. Osgood drew himself up. He stroked his big mustache. He begged to differ. "I am led to believe otherwise," he said. "In point of fact, I am told she looks to you as the head of the family." He had heard this from Daisy and Alice, who had it on the authority of Mishka. Osgood and his nieces appeared to be living in a dime romance. Osgood and Nina, an impoverished Russian heiress, were the crossed lovers. I apparently was the girl's deceitful stepbrother, possessor of what remained of the family fortune. Daisy and Alice glanced at me coldly as they went about their chores.

Sophie and Nina had no fixed address. They wrote or telephoned for money. I usually sent the small bills they asked for to a post-office box in Brooklyn under the name Borough or to another, in the Bowery, under the name Kraft. Now and then, we met at Schwab's Saloon, where they felt at home amid the mix of foreign tongues. Mishka never came with them but worried me instead through Osgood and Daisy and Alice. I wondered to what purpose. Zak said, "Like those sisters of yours, for your money—but in his case, all of it." The revolutionist, Nechayev wrote, must trap the capitalist into becoming his slave. He must blackmail his liberal sympathizers, allowing them no route for escape. Zak and I were playing cards at the worktable in the back of the shop. Ida was at the telephone up front, out of hearing. I reminded him that we were not only in business together, but also lived under the same roof. Whatever I had was his and the other way around. "Comrade!" he laughed. He stopped smiling when I said it would be no joke if Mishka found out about him and Ida. He said quietly, "Ida's going to have a baby. She says it's Jake's." I asked why Mishka would believe it, if he had any suspicions at all about the two of them. "It's Jake's for sure, Max," he said. "I've counted the months."

One evening in April, Abby brought home the farewell issue of yet another anarchist weekly, the Jewish *Free Workers' Voice*. She handed it to me without a word, her silent pronouncement, I supposed on the fate of my sisters' Cause in America. Abby still blamed me for her own disappointment in Sophie and Nina. I said, looking at the headline, "Another death knell for Yiddish." Later, in the library, when I turned the pages, a sealed note fell out. It was from Mishka, put there no doubt by Daisy or Alice. He wrote curtly, in German. We must speak. I was to meet him at Sachs's Café, at four o'clock in the afternoon, on any of the next three days. He would be waiting.

I went on the third day, a quarter past the appointed hour. Going into the café was like walking into my dream. It was years since I'd been there, not since I'd been injured at the Yom Kippur ball. Half-familiar faces turned my way, but who would know me with my mustache? A woman—was it Zipporah Gelb?—

almost smiled. I searched for people who weren't there and then found Mishka at the rear, staring into an empty tea glass. "You are late," he said in Russian. After months of not hearing from him, what could be the urgency? Surely it wasn't the revolution fast drawing nigh, I said. My words puzzled him. I explained the phrase "fast drawing nigh" and suggested he start tuning his ear better to English. "When the revolution does come," I said, "you'll want to know it's here." He switched to German. The workers of the world, he said, all understood the language of revolt. "And what language, precisly, is that?" I asked. Mishka aimed his fore-finger between my eyes. "Precisely this," he said, and mimicked the crack of a gun. Then he added, his finger still pointed at my head: "You owe me money." Zak was right.

If we'd been children, I'd have grabbed Mishka's finger and twisted it until he cried. Instead, I waved his hand aside and asked what money he was talking about. "Mama's," he answered, "what was held in trust for us. You took it all, Maxie, both our shares. Now give me mine." I told him he couldn't buy enough dynamite to blow up the Western Penitentiary, where Sasha was, if that was his intention. I wouldn't let him waste the money. I reminded Mishka that Pyotr Mikhailovich had lost virtually everything be-fore he died, that only a small part of Mama's legacy had come to me, that Mishka's share in any case would have been less than mine, since it couldn't have included what had been passed on from Mama's first husband, Osip Diamant, my real father, and that Mishka had forfeited all his claims in his own father's mind by running away from home. In short, I owed him nothing. Mishka of course disagreed. As I rose to leave he said to my back, "Your friend Silver can be careless. His wife would be unhappy to learn." You punk, I thought, we're wise to you already. But I said nothing. "Wise to you": Mishka wouldn't understand the expression.

Nevertheless, I went directly from Sachs's Café to the shop to find Zak. He heard me out and said not to worry, Abby knows. "What?" I asked. "About you and Ida?" Zak shook his head. No, he'd told her about Ida having Jake's kid. Now Abby was out-raged over Ida's plight. Her work in the ghetto brought her case after case of abandoned women and their fatherless children struggling to stay alive in a sea of English. She could perhaps have Jake traced if he was still in the country. Otherwise she insisted Zak keep Ida on the payroll. I asked what Ida had to say about all this. Zak answered with a pinched smile. "She says I should keep her on the payroll and keep away from her bed, and that Jake should go rot wherever he is."

Zak avoided mention of Ida around the house, especially with Daisy and Alice reporting back, through Osgood, to Mishka. Dinner conversation was muted, with one of the girls, all eyes and ears, standing by, while the other glided noiselessly in and out of the kitchen. Fanny said she didn't know why, but somehow they'd become a worse presence than Sally and Sam. East One Hundred Fifth Street was a nest of secrets and nurtured silences. Fanny and Abby refused to discuss Sophie and Nina or Mishka. How could I, then, explain anything about Daisy's and Alice's shadowy behavior without admitting to have been seeing my sisters, without raising Ida's name, without recalling Mishka's threatening hand?

Sophie and Nina would hear no ill of Mishka. I'd always been jealous of him, Nina teased. Sophie said the Cause had no room for personal rivalries. Marx had the soul of a German burgher. His pettiness destroyed the First International, and the lesson was well taken. I thought, By whom, the followers of Most? I asked what of Nechayev. "Exactly so," said Sophie, as if I had proved her point. Nechayev had done a great service by arguing *in extremis*. I reminded Sophie that *in extremis* was not necessarily *ad absurdum*. An *Attentat* was no bloodless theory that somehow got laughed away. She said Nechayev, unlike Marx, was no mere theoretician. He had lived in the end a martyr, and, from all anyone knew, died one as well, after years of solitary confinement in the Peter-Paul Fortress. "As will Sasha," I said, "in the Western Penitentiary, Mishka or no Mishka."

I handed them a packet of dollar bills and half eagles, but asked myself why. Nina took it and leaned across the table at Schwab's to kiss my cheek. She said, as if reading my mind, that she knew I was giving the money for them to live on, not for the Cause. "Dear Maxie," she smiled. She was speaking Russian. "Do you remember this song of Papa's?" Nina hummed a Jewish tune whose nonsense lyrics, a kind of Hebrew gibberish, we all used to giggle at around the kitchen table, while Pyotr Mikhailovich stomped and waved his handkerchief in imitation of a tipsy

Chassid. We giggled again now. Nina said it was still a favorite song of Mishka's. "Maxie, don't forget, he's the only brother you have." Half brother, I thought, but couldn't bring myself to say so.

Zak received an anonymous letter at the shop, slipped under the door. The words were cut from newspaper print and pasted in the following order: "To Isidore Silver, adulterer. We know who is the real father of Mrs. Jacob Sussman's child. 1,000 double eagles will keep rumors from your wife. In the hollow of the great beech near the Dairy. By 6:00 p.m. tomorrow, June 15. Come alone and leave alone. We will be watching." The letter closed with the picture of a dripping dagger. "Not a penny," said Zak, "not for such bad melodrama. Circus clowns could do better." Two days later, at breakfast, Daisy handed Abby an envelope. Abby read what was inside. She paled and through her teeth asked where it came from. Daisy said she found it on the stoop. "Nonsense," said Abby. "It smells of the sachet you keep in your room." She rose and struck the girl across the face, quickly, several times, until her mouth bled. Alice ran in from the kitchen and began to scream. Within the hour, both girls with all their belongings were gone. That was the night the shop and everything in it burned.

The police poked at the rubble and came to the house with empty questions. Fanny froze at the sight of their uniforms. She said under her breath, "Say nothing to the Cossacks." None of us did. Abby thought it was useless to press the matter, we knew what to expect. The police were in Tammany's pocket, and the immigrant greenhorn suffered the worse for it. There was in fact little we could say. We'd thrown out the blackmail letters in disgust. Zak didn't care to raise the subject of Ida, nor I of my sisters. The word "anarchist" was prominent in the newspapers. There seemed to be an endless run of *Attentate* in France. A bomb was thrown into the Chamber of Deputies, another into a café at the Gare St.-Lazare. Sadi Carnot, the president himself, was stabbed to death by an Italian, who shouted as he thrust home, "*Vive la Révolution! Vive l'Anarchie!*" With every reported incident, the American papers brought up the name of Alexander Berkman, the would-be assassin of Henry Clay Frick, and his cohort Red Emma. If the police had the slightest hint of a connection with those two, said Zak, we might as well kiss our insurance payout good-bye. I hadn't realized there was a policy on the shop. "Twenty-five thousand," said Zak. He'd taken it out while I was laid up with my concussion. He clapped me on the shoulder. "No more gambling houses, Max." Presumably our rental properties, the Abigail Arms and the Frances Arms, were insured too. Zak smiled in his boyish way, as if to say, Not to worry.

I searched for Mishka in the ghetto and found him in Sachs's Café, at the same table as before, I supposed his regular place. Zipporah Gelb was with him. This time, she recognized me, Maximus, immediately. After the fire, I shaved off my mustache. "Get rid of it, Max," Fanny said. "Whenever I look at you now, I think of Osgood." Zipporah said I'd been missed. Me or my money, I wondered. Mishka dismissed her with a slight jerk of his head. She left and joined friends to sulk at a table nearby. I told Mishka, "This has got to stop." He broke into a grin. "What has got to stop?" "The letters," I said, "the fire." What letters, what fire? Mishka's mask of innocence was transparent as glass. Behind his grin was the hard face of the schemer making a deal. I was ready to bargain, too. I turned away from the thought that Mishka might not be lying entirely, that Zak was too pleased with what he called the payout, that I, Maximus, was everyone's fool.

I established my ground. "Mishka," I said, "in plain English, I can't give you what isn't mine to give or yours to get." He countered, in German, "Maxie, do you think I want anything for myself?" Then I, equivocally: "No more than Sophie and Nina." Then he, in kind: "Precisely." "Be precise, then." "For Sasha." "Very good, for Sasha. Precisely what for Sasha?" "An escape tunnel." "More practical than dynamite." "Precisely." "His sentence is on appeal. Why not wait for the outcome?" "The appeal will be denied. The tunnel will take time." "How long." "Two years, three years." "And the expense?" "Three hundred a month, for equipment, a hiding place near the prison, bribe money, and two men for the job." "You will show me your plans as they proceed." "Of course, Maxie. Every month, on my word as a brother." I said to myself, Nechayev's word. Nevertheless, we shook hands, the way Americans do, looking, I thought, well pleased. Zipporah Gelb came over and sat herself down. "So," she said in Yiddish, "friends again or not?"

I am skating again on the frozen rivers of the world. I slide into a Sachs's Café that is the garden of my stepfather's villa. At a table with Mishka, hugging his arm, sits Mlle Ariane Rahel Lévy-Mendès. *Il n'est pas mal du tout, votre frère*, she says without moving her lips, and kisses his cheek. Beneath a fancy feathered hat her dress is ripped at the bodice, like Liberté at the barricades, her bared torso bloody. It was she who threw the bomb in the Gare St.-Lazare. *Vive la Révolution! Vive l'Anarchie!* The whole café is restless. I hear Daisy and Alice shrieking. Comes the shout, *Why sittest thou alone? Be thou here with us, Max!* I say, *How shall I do so, seeing my mother died when I was but five years of age?* Mishka murmurs thunderously, *He that is not with me is against me. Thou slanderest thine own mother's son.* I say, *There hath been a misunderstanding*, and reach for Fanny's hand.

VI

Planning an Escape

SILVER & KRAFT temporarily set up shop in the Frances Arms.
With the insurance money, we were able to buy back our unde-
veloped lots in the Bronx and Washington Heights for less than
we'd sold them the year before. Ida continued to keep the books.
Every morning, she eased herself down the stairs from her apartment. In my presence, she made a show of indifference to Zak.
Her baby came in midsummer, delivered at home by a midwife.
Ida was back in the shop the same week. "Business is business,
Mr. Kraft," she said. "In Russia, the peasant women drop their
babies in the field like calves without missing a stroke of work."
At first, she kept the baby in the shop. Zak said that wasn't done
in America. Ida wasn't a peasant, the shop wasn't a bazaar. He
suggested a nursemaid. "You pay for one, Mr. Silver," she said,
"and I'll be happy." I looked at the baby for a resemblance to
Jake or Zak and saw none. Ida said he was his own little man.
She named him Barnard, accent on the second syllable, in memory
of her father, Baruch Fogelman, a carter. He'd been hanged and
disemboweled at the roadside near Turov in the pogroms. I suggested Benedict as more accurate, thinking of Spinoza. Ida said
no. Benedict wasn't American. It was a Christian name, from the
old country. Barnard was class.

After Daisy and Alice left, Fanny went through a series of cooks and housemaids. She said whoever was looking after Joey could take care of little Barney as well. Ida was agreeable, so long as the expense wasn't hers. The baby was picked up in the morning, returned at night, and betweentimes Ida went off with Zak to help him, he said, find new offices. I was alone in the shop when Sophie and Nina came by. They were on their way to a meeting with an Italian anarchist group in Harlem, on behalf of the Russian Progressive Union. Evidently they were finding a niche in the New World. Sophie said the Gruppo Cafiero was held in high regard by Kropotkin himself. I recalled that Carlo Cafiero was a translator of *Dieu et l'état* and told my sisters of my voyage on the *Massapeag* and how my Bakunin disappeared in the waves. Sophie wondered if I wouldn't be spending my entire life at sea, my best intentions sinking. I gave her money for the Cafiero group. "Money isn't always enough, Maxie," said Sophie. She expected me to be at the celebration for Emma's release from Blackwells. Nina said, "Fanya must come. It will be our Kovno circle again."

Fanny was unwilling. The welcome would be like the Yom Kippur ball, with fighting in the streets, in the hall if that repulsive Johann Most were there. Why should any of us go? We were done with these people. She didn't know about Mishka's escape tunnel and the gifts to my sisters. Zak said if I went, he'd have to go, too. Otherwise, he joked, the peddlers of the revolution would wring every penny from me before the evening was over. Abby said it seemed to be an important occasion, with respectable people, held in a proper theater not a hired hall. I said that, though Sophie and Nina would never admit to it, they were shy and anxious about seeing Chava Goldman again and wanted me there for the introductions. Fanny looked at us one by one, her face clouded. "This once," she said, "I'll go."

A grand theater in the Bowery, the Thalia, had been rented for an evening in mid-August. That took more money than the Pioneers of Liberty and the Autonomie group were likely to raise, even with the help of the Italians and the Russian Progressive Union. Presiding was Voltairine de Cleyre, an American anarchist, from Philadelphia. Fanny hadn't thought there were any real American anarchists, only Germans in disguise. "Not at all," said Abby. "Look around, dear. I told you there'd be respectable people."

My sisters found me with no trouble—Maximus, always a head above the crowd. I asked offhand after Mishka, expecting an excusing reply: Mishka prefers to keep in the background and avoids being seen in public circumstances. Instead Nina pointed a few rows in front of us. "There he is," she said, in German, "the hart and the hinds." On one side of Mishka sat Zipporah Gelb. On the other were Daisy and Alice. Nina whispered that she'd been worried about Mishka. She was afraid his years of self-control, underground and in Siberia, had killed his natural urges. What a shame that would have been, for such a pretty boy, though who knew what he saw in that Gelb woman. Daisy and Alice peered around Mishka's big head at Zipporah. Zipporah smiled at them sweetly and tousled Mishka's bristly hair. The girls turned away quickly, caught sight of me behind them, and stared stonily at the stage. Osgood presumably was at that moment in Allegheny City, scouting out likely spots to begin the tunnel, so Mishka last informed me. He told me, too, that his own occasional appearances with women, in whom he had no intrinsic interest, were to dissociate himself from Osgood in distant Allegheny City, should that fool somehow get himself caught. I suggested he'd be wise in that case to drop Daisy and Alice. "Never fear, comrade," said Mishka, in German.

The footlights went up. There on stage were the usual speakers, except Most, together with Voltairine de Cleyre and a beautiful girl no one around us could identify. Voltairine de Cleyre was succinct. She defended the words that led to Emma's imprisonment. The unemployed workers should ask for work. If there were no work, they should ask for bread. If no bread were given, they should take it, as their sacred right. Emma stood up. The audience and everyone onstage rose with her. She looked small and weak. She opened her mouth to speak, but no words came out. She staggered, seemed to be losing her balance, and was led solicitously offstage by a large man with a thick mustache, upturned in the European fashion, to the rising murmur of the crowd. I thought I heard Sophie say, in Russian, "So that is the fiery Red Emma." It was explained that Miss Goldman felt unwell and would address the theater later.

The girl no one knew spoke next. Maria Roda was her name. She was sixteen years old, fresh from Italy, an intimate of the martyred Sante Caserio, who two months before had stabbed to death the president of France. The operatic intensity of her voice and gestures made the audience forget Emma's collapse. Though not many people in the theater could follow her Italian, they cheered the names of Sante Caserio and Alexander Berkman. Fanny was restless, "Max," she whispered, "it's the same nonsense in any language. Murder is murder." I heard Sophie say to Nina, "Yes, we, too, were once sixteen."

The exuberant response to Maria Roda's aria drew Emma quick-stepping back onstage. Once again the audience rose to greet her. Nina laughed. "*Regardez la jalouse.*" Emma was on fire. She'd just finished a term in prison, she said, for talking. If the government intended to go after women for talking, it will have to start with mothers, wives, sisters, and sweethearts—but it will never stop women from talking. No! It was not little Emma Goldman who was jailed, but the right of free speech. Emma addressed the audience in German and English. She rolled her *r*'s like a politician but otherwise had lost her accent. Afterward Zak said to Fanny, "That goes to show, the best way to turn anarchists into real Americans is to send them to jail."

When the speeches were done, Fanny felt a migraine coming on and had to go home. Abby said she would take her. They'd miss the gathering at Schwab's of the inner circle of comrades and friends, but Fanny held the right side of her head, grimacing, and said, "Our regrets." It was not a small crowd. Maria Roda was protected by an escort of Italians who greeted my sisters warmly. At Emma's side was the man with the European mustache. She was surrounded by American admirers and the German regulars at the saloon. The ghetto radicals watched both groups from tables of their own. Voltairine de Cleyre sat among them, talking with Modska the Twin, I was surprised to hear, in Yiddish. Zak prodded my shoulder and said to me in his village dialect, "So, Max, Abby ain't the only one what learned to love the mama tongue." Modska and Voltairine de Cleyre were discussing Sasha. With Emma's release from prison, the cruel perversity of his twenty-two-year sentence was on everyone's mind. Modska said, "Imagine Sasha slaving in a mat shop. We'll get him out one way or another, even if we have to tunnel our way through." I thought, So he's in on it, too. I gave him a knowing look and let my eyes move toward Mishka and back again. "Your brother," said Modska. I nodded. "I know him by sight, of course," he said, coolheaded, "but we've never met formally," and turned back to the conversation with Voltairine de Cleyre. However many people were involved in the escape plan, it was only wise for them not to acknowledge one another in public.

A Russian contingent arrived. Sophie and Nina broke away from the Italians to join the newcomers and called me over. I should escort the two of them to Emma's table for a moment before the toasts began, I was told. I looked for Mishka to come with us, but he was gone. Zipporah Gelb was with her ghetto friends. Daisy and Alice sat close together at a table apart, silent castaways amid a flood of foreign voices. Mishka had made his presence known and then left. I supposed he told Zipporah and the girls to stay, so that the impression of his being there would linger. He might even now be on his way to Allegheny City, while everyone would recall him at Emma's welcome and afterward for the whole time at the party at Schwab's.

Zak was at my side all the while. I asked him if he didn't trust me. "Not with this crowd," he said. "We all have our weaknesses." He was watching Zipporah Gelb approach us as he said this. I quickly reminded him that she was now one of Mishka's marionettes. Zipporah linked her arms with ours and said she hoped we boys wouldn't mind but, so long as we were going over to Emma, she'd come, too. Nina said to Sophie, "*Je n'y comprends rien, cette salope-ci et notre Mishka. Regarde ses sourcils.*" It was true Zipporah's eyes were heavily painted. Most of the women radicals on principle wore no makeup; their faces were as scrubbed as those of nuns, though Nina, I suspected, applied a pale powder to her high cheekbones to dull their rougelike glow. Sophie said we should be quick about it now because once the toasting started it would be endless.

Emma waved when she saw me. Her mustachioed friend, I'd learned by then, was Edward Brady, an Austrian anarchist who had served ten years in prison. He was reserved with me until he saw I was with Sophie and Nina, whom he seemed to know. Emma looked at them in half-recognition and then shouted their names. "And the boy?" she asked, meaning Mishka. Zipporah said he'd stepped out for a moment. Like Daisy and Alice, she must provide him cover. Her job done, Zipporah slipped away. My sisters and Emma hugged. They spoke in German of their mutual admiration and of Sasha's sacrifice, while Emma's lover looked on. Nina said how wonderful if we actually formed our group again. The only missing member was Olga Stepanov, who was in London with Kropotkin. Emma said, "To be sure." Someone at another table tapped a glass to gain the room's attention. "Don't be a stranger, Max," Emma said as we turned away. She and my sisters hugged again and kissed the air. A Russian sprang to his feet, his drink held high. He called out, "Emma, Sasha, Sante, *v narod!*" as Zak and I reached the street door.

Our childhood circle was not revived. In my mind's eye, I imagined the impossible, Sophie and Emma conversing amiably in the parlor at East One Hundred Fifth Street. It is teatime. Nina and Olga Stepanov, over from London, have finished a game of chess and are putting the board away so that Fanny can set out the tea service. Mishka jokes, "What, no samovar?" He and I have been going over the details of Sasha's recent, still-secret escape. "Let's not tell the ladies," says he with a wink. "It will be more of a surprise when he walks in." Emma good-humoredly suggests a contradiction in Sophie's liaison with the Russian and Italian radicals and her advocating cooperation with the bourgeoisie. Sophie laughs. "Emma, dear, how funny you are! It is only an apparent contradiction." Cooperation does not mean compromise, so long as one's dealings are with sympathetic individuals. She rejects the Marxist polarities that equate one entire class with the state and another with the revolution. "The state," says Sophie, "embodies nothing but itself and exists only for self-perpetuation. It will destroy whatever threatens it, irrespective of class." Emma admires Sophie's concision. "Your words," she says, "always cut to the meat of the matter. How could I have thought we disagreed?" Just then comes a knock at the door. A resonant voice says, "May I?" It is Sasha! Emma flies into his arms. In another reverie, the gathering is on the property at Stump Lake. Sasha, torn and bleeding, staggers out from the surrounding trees and collapses at Emma's feet. "Astonishing," says Mishka, "he walked all the way! Where the devil was Osgood with the hay wagon?"

In my daydreaming, I was like that boy again who once imagined Cossack-Hurons in the woods behind his stepfather's villa. In my fancies, everyone spoke English, an element of truth once unimaginable among Sophie's circle in Kovno. I remembered my arguments with Fanny's brothers and the boys of the Allen Street commune. The revolution in America would happen in the language of the place. After her release from Blackwell's, Emma went over to English, with German her occasional expedient. To Jewish audiences, she made it known she would not speak jargon. My sisters resisted America, but after Sophie received a long letter from Kropotkin, in English, they acquired a seeming British accent, picked up who knew where. Kropotkin wrote: "It is people such as you, my dear Sophia Petrovna—willing without fanfare to yield up their youth, their prospects, their very lives to our great Cause—that are the heart and soul of the revolution." Sophie said it was only a matter of time before she and Nina heeded the call from London. "Let them," said Fanny. As for Mishka, he took to wearing a battered plug hat and began to talk like a New York street tough. He dropped the name Borough—except, he said, in Allegheny City—and became plain Mike Kraft.

Zak said English had nothing to do with the revolution, which was after all only a possibility. English was inevitable. A hundred years from now, everyone would be speaking it, the size of the British Empire, past and future, assured it. We were sitting in the parlor. Abby said if what Zak suggested were true, the world would be the poorer for it. Fanny shrugged. "Languages die, like people," she said. "Why be sentimental? You go to a country, you speak the language. It's as simple as that." Abby didn't think the matter was simple at all. There should be no shame in speaking Jewish. She looked at me as she said this. I reminded her that at Emma's welcome, it was she, Abby, who had taken note of what she'd called the respectable people, and she hadn't meant by that the Jewish tailors and Italian gardeners in the audience, never mind Sophie and Nina with their elegant Russian and all those Germans. Why, I asked, wouldn't Abby let us be Americans? She fell back in her chair and gasped. "How am I stopping you?" she said.

I recalled for her the language rooms of my childhood. Abby was a visitor in the Yiddish room. So had I been. So was Fanny. Zak opened the door to leave it years ago, on the train from Brody to Berlin. I told her she seemed to want to lock us in a place we didn't wish to be and where we didn't belong. "Max," she said, "you can't believe that," and left the parlor. Fanny and Zak went after her. They'd be telling her, I supposed, not to worry, she knew how Max was. I wondered how it was that people agreed and disagreed among themselves at the same time. Zak and Ida argued in English and made up in Yiddish, perhaps because they could both speak a common village cant, while Zak's English was superior to hers. If I relaxed my stand on English, I might assign for myself a humor to each language room: to German, melancholy; to English, phlegm; to French, hot blood; to Russian, choler. I might joke in Yiddish, dispute in Hebrew, and when I met with Mishka to talk about the tunnel, we would, naturally, conspire in the international language of revolt.

Abby returned to the parlor alone. She regretted our sharp words. Family should never quarrel, she said. Except for her uncle in the Argentine, she and I were each other's closest blood relation. I was of course right, to all intents, why else would she be teaching English in the ghetto? She admitted her work might occasionally distort her perspective. "But you, Max," she said, "how contemptuous you are!" I doubted I was any more so than my sisters, or cousin Emma, but let the matter pass. For the sake of family peace, I would be like my unbending brother and not always reveal my heart.

Mishka and I met every month as agreed. He'd taken a room in a boardinghouse in Brooklyn, almost in the shadow of the great bridge. It was late spring. Through his window, with a view of a redbrick warehouse wall, drifted the low rattle of the carriage traffic to and from New York, the periodic crash of the elevated train and whistle of the departing ferry, the cries of gulls. In the middle of the room, under a dangling electric lightbulb, was an opened gate-leg table. I gave Mishka an envelope with his monthly allotment. He spread out his plans, then rolled them up again when Mrs. Schultze, his landlady, brought in a tray of ham sandwiches and sarsaparilla. She looked as if she were going to join us. "Not now," he said, waved her away, and once more laid out his sketch of the Western Penitentiary and its surroundings. I'd seen pictures of the prison. From a distance, it might be a royal palace or parliamentary building. I noted the irony in the architecture. Mishka thought it was just a dirty trick. I supposed by this he meant a camouflage. Mishka said, "Yeah, that's what I mean all right."

The high west wall of the prison compound faced the Ohio River, the three other sides the streets of Allegheny City. A little box marked "A" was the three-story house Osgood had rented two blocks east of the north wall. He had turned the place into a small hotel where visitors of inmates might stay. Daisy and Alice were with him, to cook and clean, as well as a general handyman, Boris Vye by name, who belonged to the Russian Progressive Union.

The cellblocks were on the river side. Outbuildings and work-shops filled a portion of the courtyard where the prisoners took their exercise. I said I'd understood from Modska the Twin that Sasha was working in the mat shop, which was nicely placed at the northeast corner of the compound. Mishka marked the spot with a "B." He said that rather than dig directly from the hotel to the mat shop, point A to point B, Osgood and Boris Vye would tunnel among the sewage lines in the area and up into the court-yard. There would be several routes for escape, and consequently several false trails for pursuit. Osgood had obtained a plan of the mains from a drinking pal who worked in the sewers. Sasha might as easily emerge in the hotel basement as in the yard of one of the abandoned homes near the south wall, along what Mishka called Stoylin Street, written Sterling on his sketch. The empty houses had been seized by the banks, with whole families dispossessed, and could be bought or rented cheaply. Mishka drew a new box and marked it "C." I said I was good for the money.

Mishka's plans were as thorough as could be for the moment. Just where and how Sasha entered the tunnel would be considered when the time neared for his escape. Meanwhile, Mishka ex-plained, we were watching Sasha's daily routine, his hours in the mat shop, when he returned to his cell. Sasha—Prisoner A7— was on the ground floor—Range K—of the South Block, in Cell 6. I asked what happened if he were transferred to another shop. What if he were moved to a new cell, or put in solitary? Mishka said we had our spies on the inside and, he added, plenty of time. I said yes, nearly twenty years to go. I wondered who "we" were but didn't ask, knowing Mishka wouldn't say. Instead

I noted Osgood's diligence, managing a hotel by day and digging in the sewers by night. He wouldn't be doing all that work for the money, or for the revolution either, so it would have to be for love, with Nina the object of his heart's desire. Mishka allowed himself a thin smile and didn't deny that was the case. The ferry blew a warning whistle. It was getting on toward dark. I told Mishka to continue spending my money wisely. Mrs. Schultze came to take away the tray with the empty plates and sarsaparilla bottles, lingered, and quietly shut the door behind me as I left.

On the ferry back to New York, I came across Modska. He was returning from the offices of the *Brooklyn Eagle*, where he had sold some drawings. I knew he was an artist but had never seen his work. In tacit complicity, we made no reference to Sasha and the escape tunnel and talked, instead, about art. We walked from the ferry terminal to Sachs's Café. Fanny was upstate, with Ida and the children, checking on the property at Stump Lake. I'd asked Abby to tell the cook not to expect me for dinner. Modska showed me his pen-and-inks. His delicate lines showed a fine eye for detail. "That's where all the beauty lies," he said, "in the details."

In his portfolio was a flawless sketch of Emma in a combative posture, raising high not a horsewhip but her pince-nez. Looking at it I suggested, laughing, that truth was beauty, and beauty truth—perhaps that was all we needed to know. Modska agreed. He couldn't have put it better himself. As an artist and an anarchist, that was his position exactly. Then he added, searching for his words in English but finding them finally in German: "Unless it reconciles opposites, how else should art be redemptive?" I asked in what sense he supposed art was so. He said, "In the revolutionary sense, of course. The people's needs and aspirations in the end will decide what should best survive." I couldn't agree more, I said, but thought, Who shall it be: Michelangelo or Modest Aronstam? Nevertheless, I complimented him on his likeness of Emma, and meant it. Modska was pleased. He confessed that once, years ago, he'd tried to paint her au natural. She was a restless model. He lost his concentration and spoiled the picture. To do her justice, one must capture Emma in action. "But no one," he said, smiling sadly, "no one can capture Emma." Soon she'd be leaving for Europe.

Europe! I reminded Modska of that night in Worcester when we'd argued so bitterly until dawn. After Homestead, the issue of America seemed settled. Emma's whip hand signaled the end for German. Her English now was nearly as good as mine. Modska said I misunderstood. She was only going for a short while, to study in Vienna, continuing the nursing and midwife training she'd begun in the hospital at Blackwells. He'd be supporting her efforts with the sales of his art. I said I'd never give anyone money to leave America, not Emma, not my sisters, not even Johann Most, not for any reason. Modska was surprised at my vehemence. I was thinking of the desperate crowds in Brody, the barracks in Berlin, the emigrants awaiting steerage at the Antwerp station, everyone pushing westward. Having come to America, to reverse direction seemed a terrible betrayal of realities, worse than a betrayal of dreams. "She'll be back, Max," said Modska. I asked what that fellow Brady thought. He said Ed Brady was all for Emma's going. "To tell you the truth," he added, "I don't mind her being away from him for a while." Neither of us mentioned Sasha. Zipporah Gelb sidled past with barely a nod and took a table in the back with friends. I understood her coolness toward us as part of the bond of silence concerning Sasha's escape.

VII

Undone

FANNY HOPED EMMA would never return from Europe. She said the Cause was just a sponge for my money. Business was turning around. People were coming up to the mountains again in the summer. Stump Lake was a better investment for the future than the revolution. If we didn't make our property a permanent camp soon, the Gypsies across the lake would. The place was in shambles in spite of the caretakers, with signs of squatters. She and Ida called in the sheriff to drive off a tramp from the woods nearby, a drunkard with a filthy red beard. Ida thought it was Osgood. I said that was impossible, but couldn't reveal he was digging tunnels in the Allegheny City sewers. "Then how do you explain, Mr. Kraft," said Ida, "that we haven't seen that bum here at the shop for months, and before we couldn't get rid of him." I told her, a half-truth, that most likely Mishka had sent Osgood on some fool's errand, his nieces with him. "If you say so, Mr. Kraft," said Ida. "But if that wasn't Osgood we saw, it could have been his brother." I suggested that all these back-alley drunks looked alike to her from a distance. Zak said the man was probably just a Gypsy. "What Gypsy?" said Ida. "There were no Gypsies." On the other side of the lake were the remains of a peddlers' cart and a broken-down trailer-caravan. Fanny had made of them a Gypsy band, Ida couldn't understand how.

I doubted we could have the property ready in time for summer guests. Zak agreed. Abby had her own ideas about Stump
Lake. We should keep it open all year round. Fanny asked what
business it was of theirs. They'd never even seen the property. We
were at the park Dairy. I'd bought Fanny a new carriage, a two-
seater surrey drawn by a pranceful roan called Princess. We had
taken the children for the afternoon. Joey walked uncertainly
through the grass. He stopped to pick a dandelion and brought
it back to Barney, who was crawling at our feet. Barney ate the
flower. Fanny said she was going to have another baby; could I
forgive her? "Forgive you for what?" I asked, smiling. Fanny said,
"For bringing death into the world." She spread her arms as she
spoke and took in the blue sky, the children dashing around the
Dairy, the milch cows kneeling among the greenery and gold-
enrod, and beyond them the hollow beech where Zak was to have
dropped his blackmail. I said she hadn't killed anyone that I knew
of. "Don't joke with me, Max," she said. "If I could get rid of
this thing, I would." I doubted if Dr. Schapira, the sanitary cir-
cumciser, would be of help. Perhaps cousin Emma, as a nurse,
might know a way, if we could get to her before she set off for
Europe. Fanny said she'd rather try a hot bath, castor oil, and a
fall down a long flight of stairs. Emma had renounced having
children, for the sake of the Cause. Fanny wouldn't be lectured
to on a private matter. Then she said, "Max, if you want me to
have the baby ..." I said I wanted her to be happy. "Oh, that,"
said Fanny, "what does that have to do with anything? It comes.
It goes."

Abby said, "Of course you'll have the baby, dear." There were
no sure alternatives, otherwise the ghetto orphanages wouldn't be
so full. It wasn't only the fathers who died or disappeared to
escape poverty and squalor. "Look," she said later, gesturing. We
were sitting in the parlor after dinner. "Look at all you can give
a child. Think of what that child might give in turn to the world."
Fanny looked at me, as if to say, Now see who's lecturing. Zak
recalled an old baba in the marshes outside his village. When a
girl or an unhappy young wife was in a predicament, she might
vanish for a couple of days, and the women would whisper among
themselves that she'd gone to the baba. Even the rabbi's wife,
already a middle-aged woman with grown children, was thought
to have visited the marshes, but then gave birth to twins. After

that, they had a saying if the roof fell in, or the goat died, or a boy was dragged off to the army: "Who's been seeing the baba?" Fanny said not to worry, the only one she knew was on her way to Vienna.

Fanny's term was difficult. Her legs and face swelled. She was weak and dizzy. Her skin was scaly and dry. Dr. Schapira detected diabetes but assured us it was temporary. He told Fanny to drink sixteen glasses of water a day, eat plenty of red meat, and avoid fruit and sweets. Once the baby was born, her body would revert to its normal, healthy condition. Fanny scarcely believed it. She wouldn't look at herself and had all the mirrors covered, as in a house of mourning. I remembered Pyotr Mikhailovich's villa after my mother died. When I lifted aside the cloth to shave, who's face would I see? Every day I greeted myself with a bright American good morning! and a big, false smile. Stump Lake lost its urgency. Let the squatters have it for another few months. I kept my meetings with Mishka brief and gave him what money he needed. It was heading into winter. The tunneling was ahead of schedule. Sasha would make his escape by this time next year. I was glad to hear it but impatient with details, my mind ever on Fanny.

Sophie and Nina were less confident than Dr. Schapira. In Volkova, there had been no doctor. My sisters had nursed the women through all their discomforts and been midwives at dozens of births. Fanny needed daily care, and they would give it. To my surprise, Fanny welcomed their company. The three of them improved their English by reading aloud novels from our library by Dickens and Twain. There was little talk of revolution. Sophie insisted she never forced her opinions on anyone. Nina said Fanny's thinking was in the balance now. When she was well again, she'd remember this time as a happy interlude and come round to the Cause again.

Fanny's pains began during a snowstorm on a February afternoon and lasted through to the following morning. The telephone lines were down. There was no way to contact Dr. Schapira. Fanny groaned through clenched teeth, "Max, who said the second one was easier?" Sophie and Nina arrived caked in snow. The trolleys weren't running. There were no carriages in the streets. They'd walked for an hour, from a meeting with the

Cafiero group just a few blocks away. Sophie immediately organized the household. The cook was set to boiling pots of water. Everything must be sterile. Joey's nurse should keep the boy out of earshot of his mother. Abby was to bring fresh sheets and rags to the bedroom and carry out the wet and bloodied ones to be boiled. She was to fetch coffee and sandwiches for Sophie and Nina, cool water for Fanny, and whatever else was needed at the lying-in. Zak and I, the men, were to stay away. We sat up all night in the library. Zak explained his newest plan for Silver & Kraft. He was trying to distract me from Abby's footsteps running up and down the stairs and Fanny's cries. The lots we were able to buy back so cheaply a year ago were hot properties, now that all of the Bronx was annexed to the city. The speculators' eyes were far uptown. We'd be smart to sell at a profit and put our money where it belonged, in our pockets and in the real construction that was starting up again, in Harlem and on either side of the park. Fanny's voice came distantly through the walls. Whatever she was calling, I heard it as "Osip! Osip!"

At dawn, there was a sudden stillness in the household. It was like that moment in Kovno before the ice cracked on the frozen rivers. Zak and I rushed upstairs. Abby and my sisters huddled at Fanny's bedside, their backs to the door, in what seemed a struggle. There was a squeal, followed by relaxed laughter. Nina turned and saw Zak and me in the doorway. "No men allowed yet," she said, grinning. "It's a girl." Fanny was exhausted and slept for hours. Late in the day, the male contingent of East One Hundred Fifth Street was invited in. Zak and I entered the bedroom with Joey between us, each holding him by a hand. Fanny sat up in bed, the baby in her arms, her hair in a long, thick braid. Already the puffiness seemed gone from her face. "Joseph," she said, "this is your sister, Elizabeth." I lifted the boy to the tiny, crimson face. "Kiss," I said. Fanny smiled up at me. "Maximus," she said, "you won't believe me, but I've been thinking about Stump Lake."

Abby was pleased the baby was named after her mother. She understood it as a way of apology for Fanny's recent dark moods. Sophie was disappointed. She had drawn up a list of heroines of the revolution and supposed Fanny would choose from among them. I told Sophie I'd never thought of her as a sentimentalist.

"Sentiment has nothing to do with it," she said. "I happen to think Louise Michel Kraft is a strong name." I thought, Another Roman mask on the long march of the revolution. Nina said, "They can save it for the next child." I said of course, knowing there was not likely to be one. After the streets were cleared of snow, Dr. Schapira made his call. He said mother and daughter were doing fine and that my sisters had assisted remarkably well under the circumstances. However, he wouldn't advise Fanny to carry another baby to a full term if she could help it. We asked him what he suggested. "That you be careful," he said, without explaining precisely what he meant.

Fanny was grateful to my sisters. They became regular visitors. Zak and Abby began to find them tolerable. If Mishka were with them, it would be a different matter. At dinner one evening, Fanny proposed they manage the property at Stump Lake. Sophie said it went against their principles to engage in business, like bourgeois socialists. I said it was an opportunity for them to save for their move to London—a quiet reminder that I would not give them, or anyone else, money to live abroad. Abby said TB was epidemic in the ghetto, and sanatoriums upstate had no room for guests. Stump Lake would be a service to a patient's family and friends. "Emma," said Fanny, "opened that ice-cream parlor of hers, before the *Attentat*, so she and Sasha could go back to Russia." Then she added, a little mischievously, I thought: "Max can tell you all about it." Sophie asked exactly when we intended to reopen the place. Fanny said sometime in the fall. We didn't mention Zak's real-estate deals, which would raise the necessary capital. "You understand," said Sophie, "this isn't for ourselves, but for the Cause."

As Mishka predicted, Sasha's appeal was denied. It was urgent that all efforts in his behalf should center on the tunnel. After his escape, Sasha would go underground and slip quietly out of the country. I told Mishka I couldn't have any part in that. It wasn't in our agreement. "We'll see," he said. The table in his room was covered by the plans, much elaborated over the year before, with arrows and dotted and solid lines marking sewer mains, entrance and exit points, and routes false and true. Mishka traced the likeliest paths with his finger. Sasha would emerge in the cellar of the hotel or, if that proved too dangerous, alongside the privy of a house off Sterling Street. Mishka picked a day in late October. In the week before the escape, Boris Vye would plant faked clues above and below ground. I said I understood how Sasha would come out of the tunnel, but how would he get in? Mishka put his thumb over the arrow next to the mat shop. He said, "This here's the storage bin for matting." It had a false bottom that concealed an opening into the sewers. An excuse would be found for Sasha to linger in the shop at the end of the day, toward dusk. The guard there was another drinking pal of Osgood's, name of Charlie Mack. The man had six children and a sick wife and would do anything for money. "How pitiful," I said. Mishka dropped his street accent. He said, in Russian, the revolution had no pity. What helped it succeed was right, what stood in its way was unforgivable. In my mind, as he said this, I heard his boy's voice in controlled fury piping, "I'll get you."

He switched back to English and opened a small ledger in which he kept a record of his expenses for the escape. The entries were cryptic, in the guise of household costs, but I recognized how my money had been spent. I told Mishka he'd have made a good businessman. He didn't appreciate the joke. "I'm getting out of here until after the break," he said. Mrs. Schultze was crowding him with questions, always poking around his room. She might be a spy for the police. I asked him where he'd be hiding out. Mishka wouldn't say. Instead, he tapped the ledger and let me know he needed his next three months' allotment in advance. I said I couldn't say no to someone who kept so scrupulous a reckoning.

That summer, Stump Lake again lay idle. Zak and I scouted new lots while we waited for the sales to close on the old properties uptown. Fanny took the children and their nurse to Asbury Park. I went down every weekend, sometimes with Ida and her boy, sometimes with Zak and Abby, never all of them at once. I wondered how long Zak could keep up his intrigue. He said not to worry, things weren't what they seemed. Ida had ideas. All she needed was the cash to get started. When Ida was out of the shop, running her millinery, she'd drift away on her own. In the meantime, nobody was about to say or do anything foolish. "Let's hope not," I said. I was thinking of Mishka. One intrigue, it seemed, was always sure to breed another.

It was mid-October when Fanny and I finally went to Stump Lake. She said, "Let's make it a special trip, Max." We took a boat up the Hudson, the way we used to, and left the children home with their nurse and Abby. The long wall of the Palisades was topped with color, an autumn icing on a giant cake. The sky was as clear and blue as when I left the *Massapeag* and rode the train down through New England. I told Fanny we had to see America. She said, "We already are." I meant all of it. Fanny said, "Whatever for?" We weren't discoverers. We went to a place to live—Stump Lake was ours—and maybe take in the scenery along the way.

The establishment where we had reservations claimed to have no room when the clerk heard Fanny's accent. He was courteous and offered to send on our baggage to wherever we might be lodging. Fanny was outraged. She remembered being shown the stables by Mrs. Winifred Ault Baker's groom. She asked me how much of the country I wanted to discover now. "Look what happened to Uncle Henry," she said. "He went to see America, and died." We stayed at a boardinghouse near our property. Fanny had to talk for both of us. I couldn't bear the Yiddish chatter and wouldn't, of course, respond to anyone except in English. Fanny thought I couldn't very well stand on principle after being tossed out of an American hotel. I said, quoting a village saying of Zak's, "If my enemy calls me a dog, am I then a dog?" Fanny answered, "And if you are a dog, why wish to be a cat?"

We hired a buggy and drove over to Stump Lake. Fanny was relieved to find no trace of the Gypsy wagons across from our property. The manor house and cottages needed minor repairs and refurbishing, no more than a month's work. Evidently the caretakers had been able to keep new squatters away. We spent the next few days drawing up a checklist for Sophie and Nina. I ordered whatever supplies possible through the General Store, while Fanny waited in the buggy. She wouldn't go in because of the peasants from the old country sitting around the pickled herring barrel, drinking kvass at ten in the morning. "Pigs," she said, "and we have the hotel doors slammed in our faces."

The day we were to leave, one of the sheriff's men came to the boardinghouse. They were holding a man who claimed to work for me. He was picked up, drunk, the night before, trying to trespass on our land. Fanny and I went off to the county jail in the deputy's wagon. Some of the boardinghouse guests held their heads in their hands, others rent their clothes in mourning, thinking we were being deported under some new law they hadn't heard of concerning the Jews.

Osgood was sleeping it off in the lockup. Fanny turned away at the sight. The sheriff's man asked, "You know this stiff?" I said no. I wanted to get into the cell and kick Osgood awake. It was the end of October. I'd like to have shouted, How could you have run out on us now? but was afraid to reveal a word about the escape. Fanny didn't contradict me. She asked the deputy if this was the man they'd chased away the year before. The deputy couldn't say for sure. After a while, all these country drunks looked the same. He said they couldn't hold the bum without charges, whoever he was. When he was sober, they'd throw him out of town.

I told Fanny we wanted nothing to do with Osgood. She wondered how he even found our property. Once Sophie and Nina settled in, he'd never go away. They certainly wouldn't call in the sheriff's man. I said not to worry, my sisters could take care of themselves. Osgood was nothing next to an Estonian ax-murderer and the other innocents at Volkova. The Palisades were duller on the boat trip back. The newspapers on board carried no story about the escape from prison of the anarchist Berkman, the man who tried to murder Henry Clay Frick. Perhaps I'd misjudged Osgood; the plan had failed, Sasha had been caught, and Osgood had fled. Or the authorities had suppressed the news, the police were quietly on the trail of Sasha and the conspirators, and the detectives would be waiting in the parlor when Fanny and I got home.

By mid-November, there was still no word from Allegheny City, and no police at the door. Sophie and Nina got up a crew of Italians, all from the Gruppo Cafiero, and left by train for Stump Lake. I told my sisters about Osgood. "If he shows up again," said Sophie, "he'll work like everyone else." I asked what if he refused to work. Nina laughed. "He'll work," she said. "That's a man who will do anything I say. From each according to his abilities." But by the announced opening of Kraft's Hotel and Guesthouses in December, Osgood hadn't reappeared, and neither had Mishka. It was time to break the silence.

I sought out Modska and found him at Schwab's Saloon. He

was sitting with Zipporah Gelb. They hailed me as I came through the door. Zipporah was all smiles. "Max," she said, "I don't blame you anymore about your brother." Blame me? "For running off," she said, "with those two stupid American girls." She meant Daisy and Alice. I didn't know anything about it. Zipporah looked at me in disbelief. I cautiously suggested Mishka's absence, and the girls', too, had to do with that business in Allegheny City. Modska, always so amiable, snapped, "What business are you talking about? Sasha's appeal was thrown out on a technicality." Emma was back from Vienna. She and Modska were agreed: Only direct action could save Sasha now. "Yes," I said, "the tunnel." He answered, "Exactly." I said, "Well, I was talking about Mishka." He answered, "What does Mishka have to do with it? We've got to start raising money for the escape." I asked, "You don't know?" Modska said, "Know about what?" A whisper died on my lips: *"You don't know about Mishka's plan."* My blood ran cold. There was no plan—no hotel near the prison, no guard named Charlie Mack, no house on Sterling Street, no Boris Vye. I'd had only Mishka's word for it and the evidence of his sketches and false ledger. P. T. Barnum himself couldn't have conned me better.

VIII

Heart-to-Heart

IDA LEFT THE shop and opened a fancy-hat store on the Boulevard, as upper Broadway was called. She moved out of the Frances Arms to an apartment near her store, where, she said, Barnard, by observing the clientele, could learn to be a gentleman. Silver & Kraft acquired a loose string of lots within walking distance of Sussman's Millinery. Zak and Ida weren't drifting very far apart. Zak said, What could he do? Ida had a mind of her own and the money to back it. I asked whose money. "We have our terms," said Zak. "Ida understands her obligations. She isn't like that red crowd of yours." I didn't argue the point. Now that business was expanding, we needed more space. I insisted we keep the shop close to home. Zak didn't argue either. We rented offices at the old address at One Hundred Tenth Street, which had been rebuilt since the fire. Zak's strategy was to buy sliver lots among blocks of row-house development and then to hold out against the big realtors for a fat profit. To these same realtors we announced ourselves as building contractors and took on whatever jobs they had. Zak liked to spend his days at the construction sites. He said it had nothing to do with being near Ida's store; he just got edgy too long indoors. If we were building in the ghetto, where Abby worked, he'd be there, too. Watching Zak run excitedly along the planking, his hat in one hand and his cane in the other, I had to believe him. He might wave to me to follow, but I rarely would. The boards seemed too thin to hold the weight of Maximus and too narrow for his feet.

I kept the books and managed the Frances Arms and the Abigail Arms, hired the work crew and watched the payroll. Our foreman, Marco Tullio Pacifici, had the most splendid mustache I ever saw, enfolding his entire lower lip. On his lunch break, he studied *La Divina Commedia* and *Dio e lo Stato*. I asked whom he preferred, Dante or Bakunin. "Like so and like so," he said through his mustache. "A revolutionist should not be an ignorant man." With the rest of the crew, he read and debated the Italian-American newspapers, chiefly the Cafiero group's *L'Anarchico* and *La Questione Sociale*. Zak was disgusted that our men were a gang of reds. I said not to worry, they were workingmen not dynamiters. All they asked was a fair wage and an eight-hour day. These same men had done fine work at Stump Lake and finished the job ahead of time. Zak relented, with reservations. He supposed they'd have to be good men to brave Sophie's hetmanship, but they'd better not try any direct action on the job.

One afternoon, we saw Marco swing up onto an overhead beam from a standing position and race over the girders to free one of the crew who'd gotten a leg caught over the side of the hoist. Zak said to Marco, "You moved like an acrobat." Marco answered, "I am an acrobat." In the old country, he'd been a high-wire artist, of the famed family troupe I Magnifici Pacifici. They toured all of Italy and Sicily, the Balkans, and the Tyrol. He watched his family, one by one, fall to their deaths, at private exhibitions for rich patrons who enjoined them to perform without a net. His twin brother, Quinto Tullio, his mama, his papa, his sister Emilia were all dead, for the amusement of the bosses. "My life on the tightrope," he said, "I see that it is—what is the word in English—a *metafora* of the life of the worker. I can no longer pretend I am so high above the masses. I shall fall next. And so I come to America. Here, I change the tightrope for the pick and shovel. It is not so dangerous. And I work for the revolution, that never again should men live or die for the amusement of others. *Evviva l'anarchia*."

Zak and Marco took to trading circus stories. They often

stayed late at the job or sat in the shop with some of the crew, passing around a bottle of wine. Zak said he was pulling away from Ida. It wasn't long before he felt easy in Italian. The men said he was all right for a boss. Pretty soon he'd come over to their side. In his heart, Signore Zak was a workingman, one of the people. About me they were uncertain. They called me a bourgeois socialist. Zak assured them I was all right, too. Wasn't I Sophie's brother? At this, said Zak, the men rolled their eyes. Then he told them I'd been a courier for the People's Will in Russia and had even killed a man, a notorious torturer for the secret police, using the very knife I carried in my pocket to this day. That won them over, with reservations, since I was the man with the payroll and, unlike Zak, wouldn't speak Italian. Zak said not to worry, just give the crew a little more time. I thanked him for speaking up for me to our gang of reds.

Abby was troubled about Zak but wouldn't say why. She couldn't talk freely at home and asked to meet me in the ghetto. I supposed it had to do with Ida, but didn't say so. I suggested Sachs's Café, for old times' sake. Abby took an afternoon off from work, so she and I, as she said, could have a heart-to-heart. We sat in the rear, with Mishka's regular table, now empty, in view. I hadn't seen him for months, nor had anyone else I knew of, not Sophie and Nina, not even our waiter, who said Mishka was no longer welcome, having disappeared after running up a large bill. The manager of Sachs's came over. He asked if it was true I was Mishka's brother, referring to him as Mike. "And if I am?" I answered. The manager said then I, too, was *persona non grata*, unless I cared to settle my brother's account. I determined to leave. Abby took my arm. We proceeded slowly to the door just as Modska, Zipporah Gelb, and Emma were sitting down. I was surprised to see Emma, thinking from the newspapers that she was rallying crowds in the Midwest. I nodded to their table in greeting. They turned away. Abby looked at me, and said, "What was that all about? I thought these people were your friends." I explained that I'd refused their recent requests for money. Abby said, "Quite right, and it was about time, too—as if revolution were worthy of charity!" I didn't mention that the money was needed for Sasha's real and unpretended escape.

We lunched at Delmonico's and afterward hired a carriage to

take us through Central Park. It was a crisp spring day. Abby tried to talk about anything but Zak. The sight of blossoming magnolias brought to mind her mother's garden. I said, "Zak loved Aunt Libby's garden." Abby noted that I'd always mentioned but never actually described the garden of my stepfather's villa. I said I had no memory for plants. Sophie and Nina could recall the garden better than I. "But Zak," I said, "can tell you all the dialect names for flowers." Abby found it curious that so many Jewish anarchists hailed from the Baltic provinces. I laughed, "Zak must have a good theory about that. We should ask him." I had our driver let us off at the Ramble. Abby became reflective among its dark and intricate paths. She wondered aloud about what had happened to Sally and Sam. There'd never been a word from them since they'd left for Washington Territory. "Zak and I," I said, "were asking ourselves the same thing just the other day." Abby stopped and turned up to me a suddenly weary face. "Max," she said, "I don't think I can love him anymore." First it was the gambling that took him away from home, and the selling of properties, then the fire, then the rebuying and the reselling, now the construction jobs and the time he spent after hours with the crew. "The crew, Max! I come home to Fanny and you and the children. I love you all dearly, but where is my husband? Out drinking with peasants who'd slit his throat or have him shot first thing, should their precious revolution ever come. No, Max, I don't think I can love him anymore." We found a bench to sit on. Abby covered her eyes and wept. In all this, she made no mention of Ida.

When I first entered the language room of English, as a boy in Kovno, my *Lady's Accidence* taught me to distinguish between the indicative mode and the potential mode of expression. I remarked on the difference to Abby. In the indicative, thou lovest, or dost love; in the potential, thou mayest, canst, must, mightest, wouldst, couldst, shouldst love. Through her tears, she said to me, "Don't get pedantic with me now, Max." I answered I was simply responding to her own words. She hadn't said she doesn't love Zak, indicative, but merely the potential: she doesn't think she can love him anymore. I assumed, therefore, that she loveth still, or doth love. Abby, beginning to smile, admitted this was so. Then all she had to do, I pointed out, was eliminate the worst potential.

She said how was that possible? Zak was uninterested in her educational work in the ghetto. At night, he came home late, tight and exhausted. They had no time to talk, and perhaps, she added, weeping again, nothing even left between them to talk about. At least Fanny and I had the children. I suggested that she and Zak had the shop. "The shop, Max?" said Abby. "How is that any business of mine?" I reminded her that it was built largely on her father's legacy. Silver & Kraft was as much hers as mine or Zak's. Abby stood up abruptly and walked back and forth in front of the bench. Was I telling her that Isidore Silver had married her for her money? I said that had been Carl Franks's intention, and where would she be if it had been him she'd married? Abby looked grim. "He did marry me for my money," she said. "Don't deny it. He married me for my money, and I knew it all along."

Abby strode away from the bench and out of the Ramble. I caught up to her and said the money wasn't everything. She asked what else there was. I remembered Zak and Abby's easy intimacy in his little tenement in the ghetto. Abby blushed, as if reading my mind. "That was a long time ago," she said. "Things aren't that way anymore." I thought, No, not since Ida, but of course didn't say so. Abby slowed her pace and kept her eyes down. After a long silence, she looked up and said, "Max, what now?" By then, we were near the north end of the park, at the edge of the Meer. At our feet, a gaggle of waterfowl fought over something invisible. I said Abby should come into the shop. She was astonished. Impossible! Was I suggesting she give up her position at the Alliance? I said yes, if that eliminated the worst potential. Abby hesitatingly allowed that I might, perhaps, have an interesting idea after all, but what on earth would she do? She knew hardly anything about the business. "Well," I said, "what you don't understand, Zak will be happy, more than happy, I'd say charmed and delighted to explain." One of the fighting birds rose up and with flapping wings scooted across the water, triumphant, an unseen prize in its bill. We were a few minutes' walk from the shop. Abby determined to go over and have a look. She was sure the place could use tidying.

IX

Confrontations

MY SISTERS WERE sparing with the telephone. Sophie sent
a letter every month from Stump Lake, with an appended summary of accounts in Nina's clear hand, unwittingly suggestive of
Mishka's false ledger. She wrote in June to say Kropotkin was
coming to America in the fall. The itinerary wasn't yet set, but
she would be traveling some of the way with the Cause's great
philosopher. I was paying her expenses. She would keep me informed. The letter closed with a description of an encounter with
Osgood. The man was in an alcoholic delirium. Sophie was familiar with the symptoms from the earliest days of Volkova, before the men had learned to follow the will of the collective.
Guests discovered him one night at the old Gypsy camp across
the lake, building a bonfire under a can of beans. Sophie and
Nina went to investigate. When Osgood saw Nina, he called her
his goddess, his fair one, and, meaning to fall at her feet, fell
instead into the fire. He cried he was being roasted for his sins.
They dragged him out. Osgood insisted on making to Nina what
he called his confession, a jumble of blubberings about his saintly
mother, lost opportunities for riches, the explosives and the girls.
They asked what explosives, what girls. He stared at them wide-
eyed and then at the flames. "The Russian!" he said, and passed
out. It was as if he had said *the Devil!*

They put him in a guesthouse for the night. In the morning he was gone, and with him the bedding. Sophie dismissed Osgood's ravings, but Nina worried that they had to do with Mishka—perhaps he was injured, or dead: how else explain his silence? I showed the letter to Zak one evening in the library. He said how many Russians did Osgood know. The devil was Mishka for sure, but he supposed my brother was too clever to fuss with dynamite himself. I said he'd likely decoyed Daisy and Alice. I imagined aloud a remote site alongside an ocean dune on a blustery day. Mishka is determined to effect an *Attentat* of his own, to finish the one Sasha started, this time by razing Henry Clay Frick's mansion in Pittsburgh while Frick is home in bed. The girls kneel to set the detonation caps on a test explosive, while Mishka and Osgood watch at a distance. A gust of wind knocks one of the girls off balance. They fumble the wires, and that is the end of Daisy and Alice. Osgood runs off and goes into hiding from Mishka. "And Mishka," I said, "goes into hiding from the police and," I added, "from me." I went on to tell how I'd been bilked of several thousand dollars, to lend credence to my fiction.

Zak laughed until he choked. He calculated that Mishka had gotten out of me precisely the money he claimed as his inheritance. Who'd have thought the punk would be so scrupulous? As for Daisy and Alice, I'd told a good story, but he'd seen the girls streetwalking along Ladies' Mile not two weeks ago. They even made advances, until they recognized Zak and fled. We could guess they were working for Mishka. I reminded Zak of the explosives. He said it must have been fireworks in Osgood's degenerated brain. I wrote as much to my sisters, agreeing with Sophie about the insignificance of Osgood's jabber, but in my heart not quite believing this was so.

Abby took to the shop as though she'd been there all her life. Our tenants trusted her and invited her in for a glass of tea and gossip when she collected rents. She helped them with their English, they corrected her Yiddish, and it was much like teaching in the ghetto, except there were no formal lessons and no classrooms. Zak said she spoke Yiddish now like a housewife, not like a schoolmarm, and meant this as a compliment. The crew thought she was grand and spoke to her in Italian, even though she barely understood the language. She sat around the shop, taking her share of wine, and had to admit talking revolution this way was more exciting than social work. Marco explained that was because the social question could not be answered by reform. To be a social worker was to be like a village *strega*, who bound open sores with herbs, without first cleaning out the pus. He said how sad the discovery that the contagion remained, and how inspiring to learn its cause. Liberty, equality, fraternity—yes!—if by this was meant not only political but also economic and social liberation. The French Revolution was political—the witch's poultice of liberty—its beneficiary the bourgeoisie. The answer to the social question was the social revolution. Equality and fraternity would be secured when the workingman controlled the means of production. The men raised their fists in salute and drank to *la rivoluzione sociale*. Zak and I brought up our arms halfway. They drank to *la Signora Silver*. Abby, sitting close to Zak, looked bright and happy. Then we all drank to *il filosofo anarchico*, Pyotr Alekseyevich Kropotkin.

By then, Kropotkin's tour was all arranged. While in New York, he'd be staying nearby, at an apartment of a comrade on East Ninety-sixth Street, and Sophie, of course, would be with us. Sophie promised an introduction but admonished that his schedule was tight. Nina was expected down from Stump Lake only on the occasion of Kropotkin's main public appearances here, at the end of October and again in late November; otherwise, she'd attend to the business of Kraft's Hotel and Guesthouses alone. Tickets to Kropotkin's first lecture were being sold at Schwab's Saloon. Zak said we should pay for the crew's seats. They were the best men we'd ever had. If Kropotkin had anything to do with it, so be it. His generous philosophy was a far cry from that of those ghetto fire-breathers Zak was protecting me from all these years.

Zipporah Gelb was dispensing the tickets at Schwab's. She had a black eye and puffy cheek and wouldn't look at me directly. I asked for a dozen tickets. She snapped in Yiddish, "What are you, Rothschild, buying up the house? Leave a few seats for the workers, if you please." I paid her four dollars and told her for whom I was purchasing the extra tickets. "So, it's a good deed?" she said. "Then you don't mind if I keep the change, for charity." I asked what charity. "Sasha," she hissed. In her anger, Zipporah forgot herself and turned to me squarely with her swollen face. I said to keep the change. I'd even add a few dollars to it. The reason I hadn't given money for Sasha before, when asked, had to do with Mishka. "Him!" said Zipporah, and quickly put a hand over her cheek and eye. I explained, in a low voice, without going into details, that Mishka had led me to believe it was he who was plotting Sasha's escape. He'd gotten quite a bit of money for it from me, before he disappeared. "Well," she said in English, "he's back now, and this is what he gave me," meaning her bruises. Then she leaned back and laughed. "Aren't we a pair of suckers, Max. Mr. Moneybags and Miss Lovesick."

She called over a Russian girl to relieve her. The two of us took a quiet table at the back. Zipporah said she'd been powerfully drawn to Mishka. After years of listening to the bickering at every meeting of the Pioneers of Liberty, to the venom between rival followers of Most and Peukert, to the denunciations among anarchists and Marxists and socialists—after all that, Mishka came quietly on the scene with the revolution etched into his face and the smell of Siberia on him. She drew in a deep breath. He was the image of the *narodniki* of her childhood. Her oldest brother, Leonid, was studying chemistry at the teachers' seminary in Vilna in '81. He was exiled to Irkutsk and died of typhus on the march. She didn't know where he was buried. I asked why Leonid had been arrested. The police claimed to have found materials for explosives in his room, but Zipporah supposed they were the kinds of things any chemistry student might have, otherwise he'd have been hanged. "Not the kinds of things," I said, "that Mishka has." Zipporah looked at me for a while before answering. "So, you know about that." I nodded, pretending. Then I said what I didn't know was how our latter-day Nechayev managed to give her such a shiner. "He punched me, Max. How else?" She added: "Luckily, I got away. He meant to kill me."

Zipporah used to visit Mishka in his room in Brooklyn. The German landlady hated her and always tried to bump and trip her on the stairs. One evening, the woman refused to let Zipporah in. She said "Mike" had run off, vanished, owing back rent. Zipporah struggled with her in the vestibule, knocked her down, and raced up to Mishka's room. It was empty, the only trace of him some charred scraps of paper around the gas log in the fireplace, bits of a sketch and a tally. That was a year ago. "I could cry, remembering," said Zipporah, but didn't. Behind Mishka's reserve she'd believed there was strength and passion, not a brittle heart, a heart of ice. I agreed that Mishka was no Berkman, but wondered aloud what comrade would accept the truth of him coming from me, his brother. Zipporah said there was one such comrade, sitting with me now—that, at least, was a beginning.

I told her what Mishka was like as a boy, cosseted by his sisters, pigheaded, touchy, vengeful. Zipporah said some people didn't change much. I said I thought no one changed at all. We became better at being who we were while disguising it more. Zipporah said surely I couldn't mean social conditions were irrelevant. I said I didn't see how a general condition determined individual peculiarities. The poor Jews crammed into the tenements of Slobodka and the peasants in the countryside didn't form Mishka's character. Zipporah insisted, "Not directly they didn't." I conceded the point. She admitted it was no concern of hers anymore why Mishka was a liar, a pimp, probably a murderer, and, worst of all, a danger to the Cause. "Then," I said, "by his own revolutionary logic, you should kill him." Zipporah smiled tightly. The thought had crossed her mind.

Three days ago, she had seen those two American cows of Mishka's near Washington Square, tricked out like whores. It was early morning. Zipporah was on her way to work, at a shirtwaist factory in a loft off the Square. Daisy and Alice looked as though they'd been up all night. Zipporah followed them to a tenement in the Irish slum close by. The name Borough was scratched onto one of the mailboxes in the entranceway. Daisy and Alice came out of the building after a few minutes and walked away sleepily, arm in arm. Zipporah said, "I thought for a moment, stupidly, that this was my chance." "Your chance for what?" I asked. Zipporah said she supposed for love.

Mishka, when he heard her voice, opened his door without smiling and motioned her to come in, as though there had been no lapse of time since they'd seen each other, as though this were still his room in Brooklyn. Then she remembered the girls streetwalking and glimpsed behind Mishka a neat arrangement of chemical apparatus and an open book propped up against a tin of crackers. Zipporah recognized Johann Most's manual, *The Science of Revolutionary Warfare*. She asked Mishka in Russian if he were planning to blow up Grant's Tomb. He said that would be, as a matter of fact, a fitting mockery of the so-called free union of American states. She questioned the value of the act of a self-appointed anarchist. He said what other kind of anarchist can there truly be. Destruction becomes pure art in the hands of such an individual. Zipporah thought at first he might be ridiculing her. Not once did he show surprise at seeing her. Not once did he inquire how she'd found out where he lived. She asked him where he'd been for the past year. Mishka wouldn't say. He hinted at a web that stretched across the continent, woven from a single strand.

Zipporah flared up. She reminded Mishka that the Cause had no use for a revolutionary elite. The concept was discredited long ago and existed only in bourgeois fantasies. Mishka said such fantasies can seem real enough to a prisoner of the tsarist Third Section. She told him defensive tactics were one thing, conspiracy another. For a would-be conspirator, he was a fool. Mishka's face darkened. Zipporah hammered at him. "And why not, Max," she said, throwing her head back, once again unmindful of her black eye, "he left me, without a word." She called him an amateur and pointed to his equipment, in full view of the door for all to see. Was he so experienced a chemist that he would not demolish the tenement and the innocent people who lived there? He couldn't leave a clearer trail for the police than by sending those idiot girls out to the streets, ostensibly, no doubt, for the good of the Cause! As if the revolution were somehow beyond all morality. Besides, Mishka wasn't so accomplished a lover that they wouldn't turn on him before long. At that, he grabbed her by the throat, and when she struggled free, he hit her.

The crew was pleased to have tickets to Kropotkin's lectures, but Marco was disturbed by the story I told about Mishka. He and Zak and I were pacing off a lot across from the Frances Arms and the Abigail Arms, one we'd managed to hold on to over the years and were able at last to develop. Marco said, "This is a terrible man. Excuse me, Signore Kraft, if I say this thing about your brother." I explained he was only a half brother. That was enough of a brother, said Marco, to forbid violence against him. My mother's blood ran in both our veins. Nevertheless, a way must be found to dissociate him from us. Zak suggested nothing could be simpler: buy him off. If Mishka held anything dear, it seemed to be ready cash. Marco grieved that this was so. My sisters would have to open their eyes and harden their hearts. Zak said so far as Sophie was concerned, not to worry.

We paid a couple of street boys twenty-five cents to watch for a week the comings and goings of Mishka and of the girls. Mishka left the tenement regularly every morning at ten, to buy food off a pushcart or mail a letter, and always to walk slowly along the north side of Washington Square, studying the row houses there. I thought he might choose one of them as the target of his *Attentat*. It was not lost on me that these expensive homes were in sight of the sweatshops in the cast-iron buildings rising to the east of the Square. Zipporah Gelb, by following Daisy and Alice, would have lost a day's wages if I hadn't recompensed her for her bruises. We learned that the girls were Mishka's only visitors. They came by around midnight and again in the early-morning hours. Once, they stayed the night. We determined that I should confront Mishka just after he returned from his walk. It was early October. Kropotkin's first lecture was in two weeks, and we wanted Mishka out of the way before Sophie and Nina came down from Stump Lake.

Zak and Marco hid in the shadows of the stairwell. They were ready to make a disturbance in the hallway if things turned ugly behind Mishka's door, to leap on him if he tried to run out of the tenement, or if need be to help me force an entry. Mishka recognized my voice and opened immediately. "Maxie," he said, and kissed me in the Russian manner for the first time since Sophie and Nina fled with Kazimierz Wojcicki and Mishka became the guardian dog of his sisters' books. He drew me into the kitchen, where his chemical apparatus was, and speaking in German offered me a glass of tea. I reminded him to use English with me. He said, "Yeah, okay," like an American, his face guileless. I understood he wasn't intending to explain his disappearance to me any more than he had to Zipporah Gelb. As to what preceded it, no explanation was necessary. I wasn't there to ask for my money back but to offer him more, to disappear indefinitely. We talked around the matter. I recalled how, when we were children, on certain Sabbath holidays the entire household was constrained by a semblance of piety. Toward sundown, Vera

Andreyevna would sigh aloud, "If there were only a little light, someone could read." She'd leave the room. One of the Christian servants, Kazys the gardener or Marya the housemaid, would light a reading lamp. Vera Andreyevna would return and without a word pick up her French novel. In this way, the beds were made, meals were served, and the villa remained tidy. Mishka said what hypocritical crap. I agreed. Sophie and I complained as much to Pyotr Mikhailovich at every possible occasion. Mishka could think what he liked about America, but here at least we weren't compelled to be religious hypocrites, even if we weren't welcome in the homes along the north side of Washington Square. Mishka said, "Right. Your good English don't mean nothing." We glanced at his bomb devices. "Nevertheless," I said, putting a twist on my stepfather's sentiments, "what is hypocrisy but another name for the ends justifying the means?" As I said this, I placed a purse of double eagles beside a Bunsen burner. The coins gave out their distinctive clink. On the kitchen table lay a well-thumbed journal. I picked it up. It was called *Free Society* and was published in San Francisco. What I took to be local addresses were written in the margins and blank spaces, transcribed in Cyrillic characters, as if in cipher. "You've been in San Francisco?" I asked. Mishka wouldn't say. He was looking at the little bag of gold. Suddenly, he reached out and pocketed it and asked what was the deal.

Our two street boys reported that Daisy and Alice came by that night, twice the next day, and afterward not at all, having realized Mishka was gone. I wondered whether they felt freed or abandoned. The boys followed them, on a lark, to a boarding-house on East Eighteenth Street. Daisy and Alice leaned on each other like old ladies, dazed, and ignored catcalls and propositions.

Mishka took with him a single valise. It was in our agreement that he leave his apparatus with me. He silently watched as I dismantled his equipment and wrapped it, chemicals, wiring, and all, in butcher paper. I had no illusions that Mishka would stand entirely by his word, but he certainly wouldn't have time here for his *Attentat*. I couldn't let it trouble me what he might do elsewhere, so long as it was west of the Rocky Mountains, according to our terms. When I learned of Michael Borough's whereabouts, a second allotment of cash would be forwarded by express, C.O.D., to ensure delivery to him alone. Further payments would follow, so long as Mishka stayed away. Mishka declared in Russian that the revolution had no physical boundaries. The disinterested revolutionist penetrated every level of society to work his destruction. He understood who had sent me to him. The greatest enemies of the revolution were among the revolutionists themselves. They feared him because they feared death. Therefore, I should let it be known that sentence had been passed on this bourgeois filth, the execution merely delayed, for reasons of expediency. He patted the coins in his pocket. Behind his threats I once again heard his child's voice: "I'll get you."

Zak and I disposed of the chemicals in Central Park, as we'd done years before with the explosives Fanny's brothers had left in my safekeeping. Marco watched mournfully. He regretted the waste of materials that could be used properly to the Cause's advantage. He didn't mean by this gross violence, but a purely symbolic act, by which he understood the significance of propaganda by deed. I asked what effect this act should have. Marco said to provoke. I said, such an *Attentat* wasn't symbolic at all, no matter the just motive behind it, since its immediate intent was violent. If hypocrisy was another name for the ends justifying the means, what then was an *Attentat*. That night, I skated again into the Sachs's Café that was my stepfather's villa. Osgood, the headwaiter, lets me through the door. The rosebushes in the yard are the bookcases in my sister's room. I reach to pick a big white Chernyshevsky blossom. Mishka tries to push my hand away, but is unable to lift his arms and writhes as if chained to his chair. My sisters sit on either side of him. Sophie's face is made of white marble, her blank eyes lidless. Nina weeps, even though a voice, my own, says, *Nothing hath changed. We knew he killed his mother, but forgat. There hath been a misunderstanding.*

X

What We Believed

KROPOTKIN WAS IN Canada for weeks before coming to the United States. He crossed the border at Buffalo because Johann Most was living there, if not expressly hiding from cousin Emma then, I supposed, in some shame. Kropotkin had previously canceled a visit to America on account of the war between the Most and Peukert factions over Sasha. The meeting in Buffalo was intended as a reconciliation. The two men shook hands, made complimentary statements, and afterward the arguing resumed. Fanny said what did we expect. She was happy to see Sophie and Nina but was not interested in Kropotkin anymore. As a girl, she believed in the revolution because it was coming tomorrow, the promise of our lifetime. She said we'd heard it all before. There was still a tsar in Russia. Nothing had changed. It was the evening before Kropotkin's first lecture. Fanny and I were with my sisters in the parlor before dinner, waiting for Zak and Abby, who were working late at the shop. Nina gave Fanny a pitying look and asked what kind of world did she want to leave for her children. Fanny said the world wasn't hers to leave. The best legacy, she understood now, was American dollars. "How pathetic," said Nina, and Fanny, to her surprise, agreed. Pathetic, yes, but no less true for that.

Sophie said we mustn't lose heart. We must hold our vision in mind, like a rise of mountains in the distance that can only be reached one step at a time, even if it takes a hundred years, even a millennium. Fanny said none of us will be here either way, nor will our children. How could Sophie speak of the future with such certainty when tomorrow itself was unsure. Sophie answered, "I must. If I have doubts, I throw them into the flames, as we used to do in Volkova." It was a chilly night. We had a low fire going in the parlor hearth. Sophie threw the remains of her cordial on the coals in obvious ceremony, a gesture that demanded everyone follow suit. Fanny sighed. She understood there was no avoiding the next day's lecture and excused herself to look in on the children. Nina said she wouldn't be surprised if Mishka showed up tomorrow. She felt it in her blood, just as she had that day at Blagoveshchensk when she recognized him at the dock. I said intuition didn't strike me as a reliable instrument of revolution. In point of fact, Mishka right now was likely to be in some far place on the other side of the continent, like Seattle. That name was the first to come to mind. Nina wouldn't hear of it. "Seattle," she said, "impossible. When? What for?" I didn't think Mishka would be on his way to the Klondike, but why he might choose to be there, precisely, he of course would never say. "Mishka doesn't need to declare his intentions," said Sophie. "Wherever he is, there quickens the Cause." I suggested that Mishka's purposes weren't so pure. Nina said neither were mine in belittling him. "Maxie, you haven't had a good word to say about him since Vera Andreyevna made the two of you share the same room as boys." I said surely she didn't mean to reduce the matter to a nursery squabble. Mishka was lower than a common criminal. Nechayev rotting to death in the Peter-Paul Fortress never betrayed his revolutionist's principles. "Your Mishka," I said, "has no principles."

Nina rose in anger. Sophie, the judge of Volkova, told her sister to sit down and hear me out. To me she said, "You will allow me some questions." Her remarks were exacting. I detailed Mishka's scheming and blackmail from the burning of the shop to the sham escape from the Western Penitentiary to Zipporah Gelb's black eye. I tried to avoid mentioning Ida by name, but Sophie coolly, and then Nina warmly, probed Zak's affair. I insisted that an unthinking peccadillo shouldn't sidetrack the argument from Mishka's brutality. Sophie said she was hardly one to take a moral stand on the subject of sex. I replied that Mishka's evident pimping and battery were not beyond revolutionist judgment. Marco in any case didn't think so and called Mishka a terrible man, a danger to us all. Nina was right in supposing Osgood's alcoholic ranting pointed to Mishka. The devil was a rogue assassin cut off from the Cause.

My mention of Osgood was telling. The silence in the parlor was like that moment in Kovno before the winter ice cracked and you could skate around the world. Perhaps my sisters were on the march from Tomsk to Chita, on the riverboat as stowaways escaping from Volkova, or underground in Vladivostok with Mishka, awaiting passage to America. Sophie said, "We will say nothing of this for now to the comrades." She spoke distantly, almost to herself. Nina pressed a hand over her heart, catching her breath. She struggled for words in English, found them in Russian, and choked in midphrase, whispering Nechayev's catechism: The revolutionist must blot out all tender feelings of family, friendship, and love. Sophie spoke up, this time with some force. "If what you say is true, Maxie, you are as accountable as Mishka for any irresponsible deed of his that harms the Cause. You shall inform me of his address when you learn it. Meanwhile, I repeat, not a word to the comrades." I said I'd be happy to oblige, so long as the two of them remained mum about Zak and Ida. Sophie accepted the proviso with a dismissive wave, as if to say the affair was of no revolutionary concern. I dismissed my culpability as well. If Zipporah Gelb had gone back to Mishka with a gun and shot him, it would have spared us all a deal of trouble. In fact, so said Zipporah. I surely was not my brother's keeper. I'd sent him West on the promise of money. There, he'd do us the least damage. Mishka's exact whereabouts would be found in a letter, addressed to me at Stump Lake, from Michael Borough. Nina had only to watch for it in the next weeks, while Sophie was traveling with Kropotkin.

All through the lecture, in spite of myself, I looked for Mishka. Zipporah was sitting on my left. She said to relax, he wouldn't dare show his face around here again while she was alive, knowing what she'd do to him. And it wasn't only her.

Daisy and Alice would tear Mishka to pieces. Zipporah had rescued the girls from their boardinghouse and taken them to her tenement, the former Allen Street commune. The three of them were now bosom friends and worked together in the same sweatshop off Washington Square. I asked what they knew of Osgood. He was dead, for all they cared. Daisy and Alice were finished with men.

Fanny whispered to us to be quiet; as long as she had to be at the lecture, at least let her listen. The American newspapers called Kropotkin the "Prince," a title he'd given up twenty years before, when he escaped Russia. Chickering Hall was no seedy meeting room, of the kind reserved for Johann Most, but a respectable auditorium on lower Fifth Avenue worthy of visiting nobility. Most of the well-turned-out audience hadn't bought tickets from Zipporah Gelb. Here and there were small groups of glowering workingmen, such as Marco and the crew. Guarding either end of the dais were Justus Schwab, the burly saloon keeper himself, and Ed Brady, sitting in for Emma, who was again on tour. Opposite them, in the front row, sat my sisters, got up for the occasion in red blouses and red men's neckties. Zipporah raised her eyebrows. "How chic!" she commented, in Yiddish.

Kropotkin spoke on "Socialism and Its Modern Development." He was a disarming figure, though his accent was thick, his words often jumbled. Fragile spectacles nested between his bald head and shaggy beard. His argument was heartfelt and was received with great applause by the gentry whose privilege he promised, however gently, to destroy. He convinced them that the socialism he intended, based on natural law, was simply a kind of sharing for species survival. I felt Fanny trembling beside me. Amid the clapping, she was crying. She said, "If only it were true!" How mournful it was to hear everything she once believed in, how sad Kropotkin was so kind. She felt nauseous. One of her headaches was coming on. I hurried her out of the hall, Zak and Abby following behind. As we left, I turned and saw my sisters in their fiery dress rise up and shout "V narod!" Among the audience, few picked up the cry.

Fanny recovered on the carriage ride home. All she needed was fresh air. Abby said if that was the case, why not turn back. She was deeply moved by Kropotkin and had hoped to exchange a few words with him. I reminded her that Sophie had promised us a private meeting. Fanny said she couldn't face that crowd again with its chatter. Talk wasn't going to change the human heart anymore than bombs. She recalled an incident when she was a little girl in Shavl, before her family moved to Kovno. Her father was a linen manufacturer. In the spring, he went out with the flax merchants to inspect the early crops and make his bid for a share of the fall harvest. That year, when her father drove to the storehouse to collect his flax, he took Fanny and her brothers with him. "We sat in the wagon," she said, "waiting and waiting for Papa. Then the storehouse door opened at last. What the workmen dragged out weren't bales of flax, but Papa, bleeding." They dumped him in the wagon and yelled in broken Russian, "Jew, the price is good in America, then go to America!" That was the first time, said Fanny, she'd heard the word "America." Her terrified brothers drove the empty wagon home. There she heard another new word, "pogrom."

Abby said, "We know these stories, dear. What do they have to do with Kropotkin's lecture?" "Don't be impatient," said Fanny, "just listen. Understand, this is my earliest remembrance." The year her father was beaten, farm prices had fallen because of the American grain trade. Peasants and workers blamed the secret world government of Jews. There were pogroms in Odessa. Jewish shops and storehouses were sacked and burned. In other parts of Russia, Jews were cheated, as Fanny's father was, in retaliation for forcing prices down, and for hoarding, and for killing Christ. Fanny understood almost nothing of this at the time, except for the fear that drove the family from Shavl to Kovno, where there were more Jews and safety, they thought, in numbers. After a while, her brothers introduced her to the word "revolution." "And then," said Fanny, "the tsar was assassinated. Things got worse, not better, the pogroms the bloodiest in two hundred years. I remembered America, where the price was good. My brothers followed me, to escape conscription." America, pogrom, revolution—everything Fanny knew in this life was covered by these words. She leaned her head wearily against the carriage window and added: "When I left Kovno, Papa recited the prayer for the dead."

Abby tried to probe the connection between Fanny's recollections and Kropotkin, in the same way she deliberated in the shop with Marco and the crew. Fanny would have none of it. Abby said, "You're cutting yourself off from the future." Fanny answered, "No one can do that. The future is what we get. The science, so-called, of revolution has yet to foretell what is to be, let alone put food on a poor man's plate or save a Jew from butchery. Talking won't change the truth."

There was a cold supper waiting at home. Fanny had no appetite. Her headache wasn't gone, after all, and she left to lie down. Abby said, "Well, you two haven't said much. Am I the only member of the family with convictions? Me? The American?" She laughed bitterly. After that, she said, "My papa met Alexander Herzen. He was proud of that, and so am I." I said, "Uncle Henry believed in America, and so did I." Abby asked what precisely I meant by that. America, I explained, was a promise of possibilities I could embrace. Kropotkin's revolution, and my sisters', was a dream I could entertain. Mishka's revolution was no revolution at all, but a brutal fact, like a pogrom or the supposed acts of God. Abby asked, "Where's the poetry in that, Max? My papa believed in more than dry possibilities." I answered that she'd cornered me into being precise. I could, if she liked, recite long passages from Whitman. In the early morning, when mist hung low over Stump Lake, where was I but in a novel by Cooper? More to the point, I knew the Bill of Rights by heart. The boys in the Allen Street commune used to call me the Individualist because I insisted that the most basic right was to be left alone. They also called me the Yankee because I would speak only English. Wasn't there a kind of poetry in the idea of a language everyone could understand? I'd always said the revolution must happen in the language of the place. Then Zak said, quietly, "America is the revolution. Otherwise, how could I be sitting here, safe and comfortable as I am? In the village I came from, how I live now was beyond all possibilities. It wasn't a promise. It wasn't even a dream."

My sisters had never separated before, not as children, not in prison, not on the march in Siberia or underground. Now Sophie was traveling with Kropotkin in America. Nina was heartsick, but of course didn't say so. Sophie wasn't going into exile. She'd be away for only a few weeks. Nina returned from the train station after seeing her sister off, her eyes dull. At dinner, she had nothing to say about last evening's lecture and had no interest in the newspapers' friendly accounts of Kropotkin. Abby suggested camomile tea with valerian, her mama's own recipe. Nina said no thank you, all she needed before returning to Stump Lake was a good night's sleep, meaning that she wouldn't get one. Sophie was to write every day. Nina was anxious to be there when the first letter arrived. "And Mishka's," I reminded her. It was as if I'd cut her with a whip. She jerked her head back, buried her face in her napkin, and grieved.

Fanny took Nina to the guest room and put her to bed. She convinced her to stay on an extra day. After that, Fanny would go with her to Stump Lake. Nina brightened. She said to bring the children. Fanny and Nina could teach them how to gather nuts and late mushrooms in the woods, the way they did in Kovno as girls. I'd liked to have gone, too, but work was about to start on the lot across from the Frances Arms and the Abigail Arms. That week, we'd be breaking ground for the new building and adding to the crew. Besides, Nina wouldn't forgive me for Mishka—as if I were the one who faked the name of revolutionist to mask my dirty work. Zak said not to worry, Nina needed more time to fathom the depths of her baby brother's treacheries. Sophie wouldn't be so sentimental. She'd wear Nina down even from a distance with her daily letters. There was a revolutionist's cate-chism but no red prayer for the dead.

The crew was restless. The men felt they ought to have a stake in Silver & Kraft's plans. They said the new building was a collective endeavor and voted to name it the Sante Arms, after the Italian who had stabbed to death the president of France. Zak joked, "Why not the Sante Daggers." Marco didn't laugh. We'd promised to call the building the Costanza Court, after Marco's wife, still in Italy but soon to join him in America. He regretted the crew's attending Kropotkin's lecture. "They look around and are offended by the rich Americans. Then they see that these people also believe in our revolution, and so they say now is our time. They will take direct action and make an example for other workers in America in their trades. I tell them, you cannot do this thing to Signore Zak and Signore Kraft. They answer, Step aside. If you, Marco Tullio Pacifici, stand in our way, you know what to expect." We were in the shop the evening of the day Nina, with Fanny and the children, left for Stump Lake. Abby didn't understand how Zak found any humor in the situation. "Picture it," he said. "What will happen tomorrow when the crew shows up at the job, on an empty lot without even a tool shanty, and none of us is there?" Abby answered they'd come here to the shop. "Exactly," said Zak, "hats in hand, after standing out in the open all morning with nothing to do. We open some wine. We discuss their demands. We talk about their revolution, as always. The day after tomorrow, we get back to work."

The men showed up as Zak expected, but hardly irresolute or hatless. They were cold and wet with rain, which dripped off the rims of their bowlers. A new face looked angrier than the rest. An agitator, I thought. It turned out to be a relative of one of the crew. He'd arrived on the job with the promise of work and instead came up against what he growled was a lockout. Zak said what lockout, there was nothing to lock. He spoke to the new man and his cousin in their own Apulian dialect. They corrected his pronunciation. He thanked them and said it was important to be proper in respect of another man's speech. "*Prego*," they said, bowing slightly. Marco looked at them in contempt and walked to the back of the shop.

At Abby's invitation, the crew filed inside. Seeing open bottles of wine on the benches along the walls, the men removed their hats and took out bread and sausage and cheese from under their coats. Marco sat apart, staring at an open book. The men ate and talked about the weather. Marco turned a page. The men said if the rain stopped soon, the soil on the lot would be easy for diggng, but if the rain kept up, there would be heavy mud. Marco turned another page and said loudly, without looking up, "What concern is it of yours?" One of the Apulians called out, "The building is ours! *Viva Sante!*" Marco was on him immediately. Abby screamed. The other Apulian tried to jump into the fight. Zak and I held him off with upturned chairs. The crew watched silently. They'd side with the winner. Zak was shouting, "*Basta! Basta!*" I heard myself doing the same. It was the first time since I'd set foot in America that I'd spoken a foreign word.

Marco got to his feet. The Apulian lay dazed on the floor, and two of the crew dragged him away. "Tomorrow," said Marco, "we work on the Costanza, rain or no. You"—he pointed to the uninjured Apulian—"take your friend and go home." Then he added: "This is not the way. This is not Kropotkin. This is not the meaning of *mutualità*." The crew hung their heads. I wondered what they'd be doing if Marco had lost. He turned away from them and went back to his book. The men put on their coats and wet hats and rewrapped their food. Abby said it was all right to take the wine. "*Grazie*," they said. "Tomorrow. *Ciao*."

After the crew left, Marco shut himself in the water closet. I looked at his book, lying open on the worktable. It was Dante's *Divine Comedy*, in an English translation. I remembered Chernyshevsky in Yiddish and thinking how the revolution, the revolution of my youth, was lost in translation. For Marco Tullio Pacifici, what in a translation of Dante was gained? I heard him in the privy reasoning with himself. Occasionally he swore and pounded the wall. Finally he wept. When he emerged, he said calmly, "Perhaps I am a foolish man. In my heart, yes, I believe in the revolution. In my head, no, I do not think it is possible here, now. No more can I live today only for the sake of a future tomorrow. But inside, a voice shall whisper always, '*Evviva l'anarchia*.'"

XI

Devils and Angels

FANNY TELEPHONED EVERY day from Stump Lake. From her I had details of Sophie's letters. Nina wouldn't talk to me as yet, and found the telephone coarse besides, fit only for emergencies. Sophie was pleased to be speaking Russian so much of the time. She held that in no other language, and in no mind more than Pyotr Alexeyevich Kropotkin's, were the science, passion, and humanity of revolution so perfectly combined. His first engagement after New York was in Philadelphia. There he surprised Sophie by conversing with his hosts in Yiddish, even with the American, Voltairine de Cleyre. He teased Sophie that he spoke her ancestral jargon better than she. She teased him back: "Yes, dear comrade, but my German is so much better than yours." Kropotkin enjoyed agreeable banter. He threw up his hands and replied, "True enough, Sophia Petrovna, but our English, yours and mine, will always be hopeless!" Sophie wrote that Maxie ought to be amused.

On that same occasion, Kropotkin brought up the subject of Emma, whom he'd met two years before, while she was in England. He understood she was a relative of Sophie's. A remote one, Sophie explained. They'd had some acquaintance as girls. Emma was a cousin several times removed of the wife of Sophie's stepbrother, Max Kraft. A few comrades nearby nodded, wrote

Sophie. Maxie should know that even in Philadelphia he was known for his generosity to the Cause.

Kropotkin lowered his voice. "Then I can tell you that, though I admire Miss Goldman greatly, I fear she is loose and overconcerned with the sex question." He spoke this in confidence. Voltairine de Cleyre didn't fully agree. The women's question and the sex question went hand in glove. "Nevertheless," she added, "Emma Goldman's self-gratification while Alexander Berkman remains in prison seems willful, does it not? To say nothing of the drain on her valuable energy. I, too, speak in confidence." They held a brief silence in contemplation of Sasha's long martyrdom. Voltairine de Cleyre was decided that, one way or another, his sentence must be cut short. Kropotkin recalled his own confinement in the Peter-Paul Fortress. His terrifying escape from a military prisoners' hospital was brought about through meticulous planning from the outside. Voltairine de Cleyre said the point was well taken. Sophie wrote that this was not a discussion that could continue in a crowded room. Certain ugly occurrences gnawed at her heart. She would speak of them with Pyotr Alexeyevich alone, or with no one at all.

This was Sophie's first allusion to Mishka in her letters. Afterward she was unwavering and direct. Whatever she wrote, it came back somehow to Mishka. Kropotkin's tour took them to Boston for two weeks' stay. On the long train ride from Philadelphia, Sophie told the story of her and Nina's exile and escape and their life in America. Kropotkin was deeply interested in the organization and workings of Volkova. About Mishka, he was by turns sorrowful and aghast. "Our unhappy Russia!" he said. "Tormenting the best of her children, driving them to exile and despair! In the West, a Dostoyevsky and a Nechayev will seem the one a mystic, the other a criminal. They are more like twins contending in the womb of the motherland, their struggle the pangs of the revolution. But those who struggle with one another all too often lose sight of the true goal. I fear your brother, dear Sophia Petrovna, is of that desperate lot." So wrote Sophie to Nina.

Over the telephone, I told Fanny I could hardly raise Mishka even to so low a level as Nechayev, a man who'd murder his fellow comrades. Fanny answered that she wouldn't drag

Dostoyevsky down. At the Allen Street commune, she and Zipporah Gelb read *The Possessed*, in Russian, as a study in bourgeois reaction. Instead, the book opened her eyes at last. Ever since, she'd been trying to get away from all the empty talk of revolution, and the lies, the cruelties, the self-deception. Now here she was at Stump Lake, a go-between for me and my lunatic sisters. "And why, Max?" she said. "Because I'm like you, a sentimentalist with a soft heart. Only you won't show it. You just give them all the money they ask for, whenever they want."

Kropotkin's understanding of Mishka began to lift Nina's spirits. She took the children for little walks in the woods, to forage for winter like the brave peasants in Russia. If Mishka was among the damaged fruit of revolution, Sophie and Nina had no reason to blame themselves. History had swept them into exile, far from home. History was lapping at the ground beneath Pyotr Mikhailovich's villa even as they fled across the Prussian border with Kazimierz Wojcicki. Nina was hesitant to admit it but she saw a certain tragic splendor in history's great tide. Fanny told me history apparently halted at the steps of the general store in Woodville. The White Russians, Ukrainians, and Poles who sat day and night around the herring barrel were scum to Nina. They were traitors to their brothers still suffering under the tsar. Fanny thought what else would they be but scum, since they were peasants, but to Nina she didn't say so.

Sophie reported the substance of Kropotkin's lectures in Boston. "Siberia, the Land of Exile" stirred memories of Tomsk and Volkova and Mishka's odyssey. Kropotkin confessed afterward that thoughts of Sophie's younger brother troubled him. That as a boy, Mishka had endured so much, and now he was lost to the Cause! His inner being was no longer afire, but hardened and contracted into cold rock. So spoke the geologist in Kropotkin. Sophie and Nina would be wise to break all ties to Mishka, however painful this might be. Nor should they hold their stepbrother Max answerable in any wise for a man who betrayed the trust of his comrades. "Sophia Petrovna," he said, "we must have our angels." Sophie was surprised to hear Kropotkin turn the subject so abruptly to religion. She failed to see what a heavenly host and the situation of her brothers had in common. Kropotkin was perplexed. Then, laughing merrily, wrote Sophie, he explained what he meant by angels. They were what Americans called the backers of stage plays. The Cause, too, needed such supporters. If their hands and hearts were not tainted, then neither was their money. Alexander Herzen's great wealth came from his family's Russian estates. Max Kraft, he said, was one of our American angels. He intended this as a compliment. Sophie thought Maxie would want to know.

If I was an angel, we already knew who the devil was. Nina couldn't read Mishka's name in Sophie's letters without pain. Absent, he still had his sisters in his nets, even though they were separated, and they were wrestling their way loose. Fanny wasn't able to help, not my sisters, not in the workings of Kraft's Hotel and Guesthouses. The small staff ran the place with perfect efficiency. Sophie had instructed them in mutualism, and they lived collectively in fear of her. Fanny felt useless and decided to come home. I told her to consider her duty done. Fanny said she'd be back in the city in two days. For tomorrow, Nina planned a Russian picnic, whatever that might be, at the Gypsy camp. The children could hardly wait.

We called it the Gypsy camp, but there were no longer traces of any band. Marco and his men had built a dock and an arbor in from the shoreline, with a view across the water of our cottages sloping up the lawn to the manor house. Guests could walk a path around the lake to the Gypsy camp or row the distance of a half-mile. Stump Lake was round, "Our giant silver dollar in the Catskills," Fanny liked to say. Nina took the oars. "Now we're crossing Lake Baikal," she said to the children. Fanny laid an outdoor table under the arbor. A Russian picnic was cold grass soup, black bread, and sausage, none of which the children touched. Fanny nibbled to be polite but said she didn't remember eating these things as a girl, not in her house in Kovno. Nina hadn't eaten such food either. She learned to cook in Volkova. There, she told the children, you ate what the communal kitchen served or you didn't eat at all. Joey said he wasn't hungry and went exploring with his sister out behind the arbor. They returned while Nina was reading aloud Sophie's newest letter. They stood by quietly until she finished a vignette of Kropotkin visiting a cooperative dining room for needy students at Harvard. Nina looked at the children: "Yes, my macaroons?" Joey said, "We found the Gypsy's grave."

Fanny telephoned me at the shop from the county sheriff's

office. I'd have to come up at once. They'd found the body of a murdered man buried in a shallow pit in the woods near the Gypsy camp. Sophie had to leave Kropotkin's tour and was on her way from Boston. We might have to close the hotel. Some of the guests were already packing. I asked how she knew the man was murdered. Fanny said his skull was split from behind. She couldn't talk now. The sheriff was in the next room. Then she whispered in a trembling voice: "It was Osgood."

Abby went with me to Stump Lake, to take the children home. They were bewildered by the confusion at the hotel and, we could only suppose, by their discovery, about which they were strangely silent. Abby spoke to Nina before we left. Joey and Elizabeth had found the body only partly exposed, lying face down covered by dirt and leaves. Fanny had insisted on calling the police. What if the children did talk? If there were an inquest, Fanny made it clear that she and I would swear we didn't recognize the deceased. I imagined having to look at photographs of a decomposed Osgood. The sheriff's deputy would confirm that he'd jailed the man two years before, and at that time, too, neither Mr. nor Mrs. Kraft could identify him. Nina said under no circumstances would she and Sophie violate their principles. They would refuse to answer any questions put to them.

When Abby and I arrived at Stump Lake, Sophie was already there. Nina took us all to the grave site, a slight hollow amid a clearing in the lakeside shrubbery. I thought, I did a better job as a boy burying Bobelis, but didn't say so. Abby murmured, "Horrible, horrible. Who could have done such a thing?" My sisters exchanged a glance. Sophie said, "Maxie, we must talk." She handed me an envelope. It was a letter, already opened, from Mishka, postmarked Paris. He'd taken my money and gone abroad.

Mishka's letter was brief and addressed to Sophie and Nina as much as it was to me. It referred to a recent visit to Stump Lake. Evidently he'd gone here before going to France, and left abruptly. There had been an argument of some kind—with whom, he wouldn't say, though I already guessed—but on account of it he "varmoosed." Mishka wrote in Russian, with a scattering of crude English badly spelled, I thought perhaps in mockery. He expected that I, Maxie, would cough up the promised "nikkels." "This ain't no threat, brother, just a warning." My sisters watched as I read the letter, then stuffed it in my pocket and stared down at the hole into which Mishka had tumbled Osgood's body.

Sophie and Nina wanted to discuss the matter with me alone. I asked why. There was no point protecting Mishka in the present company. Sophie lifted her chin: "Very well." She and Nina denied previous knowledge of the murder. A gust of wind spun the leaves in the hollow at our feet. Abby said, "Mishka?" Fanny pressed her fingers to her temples. "Enough," she said. "Don't tell me. I don't want to hear. Max, my head!" I rowed her back to the hotel. My sisters and Abby took the path around the lake. Fanny talked to herself. It sounded like a little song: "They knew, they knew, and now we'll be deported." I told Fanny not to worry, no one was going to say a word, we were all agreed—not to the police, not to Ida or Daisy and Alice, who wouldn't mourn for Osgood in any case. Fanny shook her head and repeated her refrain. No law that I knew of could send us back to Russia. We were American citizens in good health. Fanny said they could always pass a law when they needed one. "You're Max Kraft, the murderer's brother? Here's your ticket to Riga. *Do svidanye.*"

The police inquiry, in the end, was perfunctory. A nameless bum, a drunk who habitually trespassed on the Kraft property, slipped and cracked his head open and rolled into a natural depression in the ground. So reported the sheriff's office, and that is what I announced to our remaining guests in the common room of the manor house. Abby by then had taken the children home. We had no fear now that one of them might blurt out to a surprised guest that their mother and aunt had screamed "Osgood!" when they saw the dead Gypsy. Fanny was herself again. She said that, much as she cared for my sisters, they were really to blame. They never should have allowed Osgood to haunt the place. They ought to have called in the sheriff. They ought to have told us weeks ago about Mishka. They should have known better than to believe he was simply going out into the night to have a talk with a poor old friend. My sisters were prepared to take Osgood in again, sober him up Volkova fashion, and join him to the commune, as they called the hotel staff. Dead, he was one less witness to Mishka's dirty work.

Fanny and I had an Oriental corner in our suite at Stump Lake, which served as our parlor. There we sat with my sisters to tell them the time had come for them to leave. Fanny was prepared to be hard. Sophie said, "You are much too exacting, Fanya. You mustn't torture yourself about the children. In another month, they won't even remember what they saw." Nina recalled the incident when we were young and wandered into a village of Chassidim on Sabbath eve. It was outside Minsk. Sophie corrected her: Vitebsk. Nina said of course. Her point was how small and brave Mishka was, trying to protect us from *les primitifs*, those frightful women and filthy boys. It was the same Mishka who'd gone out that night a month ago, her lionheart come once more to the rescue. She looked tearful. "Don't think," she said, "I am blinded by sentimentalism. I know what he has done. I understand what we have to do, for the Cause." Sophie waited stone-faced until Nina finished crying, and then said we must think of Mishka as a man in quarantine wanting proper medicine. I asked, "What medicine is that?" Sophie said, "The revolution." Fanny said it was as likely to kill him as cure him. Sophie answered: "We cannot believe that. No one is excluded from the promise of revolution. As Comrade Kropotkin so often says, revolutions must be made of hope, not despair." She added: "Pyotr Alexeyevich returns to England at the end of the month. He has asked again that Nina and I go with him, and this time we will accept." They'd put aside enough money to meet the expense. They wouldn't ask me for what I wouldn't give. Sophie knew my foolish ideas about staying in America, come what may—as if this were some kind of heaven, she laughed, and all of Europe a hell. My sisters were confident they were leaving the hotel and guesthouses in good order, just as they had the other commune at Volkova. Nina reached out and held Fanny's hands. "Don't be sorry, dear," she said. "England isn't so far away, practically a stone's throw."

We said nothing more about Mishka. The French police were known to keep an anarchist album of hundreds of photographs. I supposed Mishka's picture would soon be among them. He'd be deported from France before long. If anyone was going back to Russia, it was he. Let my sisters in London stand up for him if they had a change of heart. None of them would get help from me.

Fanny was elated, though not unconcerned about the future of Stump Lake. On the train home, she burst into fits of laughter. Did I see the look on the faces of the staff when they heard my sisters were leaving? She recalled the famous day at *gimnaziya* when the history master turned his back to the class and revealed split pants. So far as Fanny was concerned, with her brothers in Shavl and both Mishka and my sisters soon to be abroad, the revolution was over and finished. Under her breath, she gave an American cheer like the ones that rose from the staff quarters the night before. I said there was always cousin Emma. Fanny said, "Emma Goldman isn't the revolution. Emma is Emma." She added: "Not that I care to see her, but you know, Max, she's already an American."

Zak was relieved I was back. The two of us sat in the library after dinner. He and Marco had let the rest of the crew go, after another confrontation. The men were told to throw tarpaulins over a pyramid of leaking mortar sacks. They voted to take their lunch break first, in spite of impending rain. Zak and Marco covered the sacks themselves and then fired the men on the spot. Work on the Costanza Court was at a standstill. I said we could assemble a new crew in a couple of days. The builders with whom we subcontracted could send idled workmen to the shop for Marco to look over. Hiring wasn't the problem, said Zak. Marco felt torn between honor and the revolution he was no longer sure of. A few words from me would give him heart. Marco respected me in these matters, because of how I stood up to Mishka and my sisters. "Stood up to them?" I laughed. "One took my money. The others quit. All of them lied."

From where Zak sat, he could see through to the parlor. He looked toward it uneasily, though no one was there. Fanny and Abby were with the children. "Max," he said, "Ida's giving up the hat store." I didn't think he was seeing Ida, not since Abby came into the shop. I remembered the long walk I took with her in the park. I asked Zak how he could risk the house and the business this way, everything we had in America. He might as well be building bombs in the kitchen, like Mishka.

Zak shook his head. "That isn't how it is." Ida was coughing up blood. She was afraid for her Barnard. If she died, he'd be sent to a Hebrew orphanage and become just another ghetto kid. There'd be no more Fauntleroy suits and curls for him. I said we could look for Jake Sussman. Barney was Sussman's boy. "Maybe yes, maybe no," said Zak. "Ida's not so sure, now that she's got TB." Zak told her to give up the shop and move to the mountains. In his village, the cure for consumption was a year in the hills beyond the marshes, on a diet of egg bread, bone marrow, and kvass. I said the doctors in the sanatoriums upstate prescribed much the same: plenty of rich food and fresh air. That was Zak's thinking, too. Ida didn't know how she'd support herself. She'd said to Zak, "They don't need fancy hats in the mountains, do they, Isidore."

We heard Fanny and Abby coming through the parlor. The children were quiet. They had to be lulled to sleep with bedtime rhymes because they were afraid of having bad dreams again of Gypsies coming to get them. Abby recited for them, "Elizabeth and Joey are fast asleep. The clocks go tick, tock, tack. All is peaceful in our house. Papa's in with Uncle Zak." She thought Sophie might be very wrong about the children forgetting what they saw at the Gypsy camp, the poor dears. Fanny said the only sufferings of consequence for Sophie were those of workers and peasants and supposed martyrs for the Cause. The nightmares of children who weren't actually starving didn't matter. The staff at Stump Lake worked fourteen hours a day, because Sophie had got it into her head that she was directing a social experiment, not a hotel in the Catskills. She'd made a mess of it, with Osgood's murder and the near closing of the place. Who'd want to manage the hotel now? I answered, "Ida Sussman." I explained that she had a touch of TB and was moving upstate for the air. "Terrible!" Abby cried out. "How awful for the woman! Abandoned by her husband, left to raise a child alone, and now this." She insisted we find a position for Ida at Stump Lake. Zak said, a little mischievously, maybe Fanny needed time to mull it over, though he didn't think we'd find a better head for business than Ida's, unless it were that of Fanny herself. "You flatter me," said Fanny. "I've never run a business in my life, have I, Mr. Silver. I'll talk to Ida Sussman tomorrow."

My sisters came down from Stump Lake with all their belongings in two carpetbags and a steamer trunk. Nina was apologetic. They were stocking up for leaner times ahead, with no support from brother Maxie. Otherwise, they'd be content with the rags on their backs. They were sailing toward the end of the month on the same boat as Kropotkin, the R.M.S. *Majestic*. I said they could be forgiven a change of clothes. They weren't traveling steerage. Even a Royal Mail Steamship was likely to maintain a certain code of dress: for example, no red blouses and red men's neckties at the captain's table. Sophie wasn't amused. She and Nina intended to wear the outfit again at Kropotkin's final appearance, at the Great Hall of Cooper Union, where they were to be seated on the platform. Because there were several speaking engagements, we'd scarcely see my sisters at the house during their last few days in America, except to lay their heads. That was fine with Fanny. Did they expect we'd be trailing behind them to every lecture? Besides, the children behaved strangely when Sophie and Nina were around. They played a game of gathering poison mushrooms in the forest. Joey said to his sister, "You be the witch, and I'll be the Gypsy who dies." Sophie was aloof, and Nina with her, as though they had no part in the disasters at Stump Lake. It was all the same to them whether or not we attended the lectures. Our private meeting with Kropotkin was another matter. "You shan't disappoint me, Maxie," said Sophie. "You shall be there on time." The way she spoke, I was again her reluctant courier in Kovno, Maximus, with his ridiculous English grammar in his hands while the revolution rose up all around.

Kropotkin was staying at the apartment of another American angel, John Edelmann by name, not ten blocks from our house. Edelmann was an architect and stood higher on the heavenly ladder than the angel Max, the builder, or so I gathered from the disdainful look he gave when I handed him my card, unless he'd overheard some pointed remark pass between my sisters. Zak and Marco were with me. It was late afternoon. We'd been hiring new men and had come directly from the shop. Abby very much wanted to be there, but stayed home to nurse Fanny through a migraine, her worst ever, that had irrupted at the doorstep with blinding flashes. Marco was uneasy. He'd learned that some of the old crew were calling him *Marco traditore*. He'd put the revolution behind him and was now out of place. Zak said not at all. This was the last chance Sophie and Nina had to get money out of me. To protect Max from his sisters, he joked, it might take the two of them.

We saw Sophie and Nina before they saw us. They were already in their red getup, like two children, I thought, dressed for a costume party. Kropotkin sat at a small writing table at the far end of the living room, riffling through a jumble of papers. My sisters led us over. Sophie said we were not to take up much of Pyotr Alexeyevich's time. He had just returned from a meeting of working comrades in Paterson and was preparing for this evening's lecture. I reminded Sophie that the reason we came was, precisely, to take up the man's time, and at her invitation. Before she could snap a reply, Kropotkin looked up, inquiringly. Nina made the introductions. "Ah," said Kropotkin, "Max Kraft himself, a pleasure." He rose and extended his hand, first to me, then to comrade Silver and comrade Pacifici. His lecture that night was titled "The Great Social Problems of Our Century," but he'd worried over his thoughts enough. By now, they would come out as they would. I didn't tell him we wouldn't be at the Great Hall, to watch my sisters on stage in their revolutionary pride. I posed Fanny's thought, that a nightmare lived in the human heart, an unknowable and unyielding blackness, and suggested these were simply other names for our social problems. Kropotkin responded in words that might have been Sophie's: "If we believed that, comrade, there could be no revolution."

My sisters marched over, Sophie tapping her wristwatch, reminding Pyotr Alexeyevich that time was short. "Even a libertarian isn't entirely at liberty," he said, smiling. "I have my orders. We shall continue our discussion on my next visit to America, Maxim Petrovich." He thanked me for my generosity to the Cause and again shook hands with comrade Silver and comrade Pacifici, while Sophie gathered up his lecture papers. Edelmann brusquely showed us to the door. On the street, Marco recognized two comrades from the Cafiero group coming toward us, heading no doubt to Edelmann's apartment. Marco was relieved to have been there first. He tried to speak to them. They spat on the pavement at his feet and walked on. "The blackness in the human heart," said Marco. "No, my friends, this revolution of theirs, I do not think it is possible."

My sisters and Kropotkin sailed for England the next day. Fanny was weak from her migraine but understood that in seeing Sophie and Nina off, she discharged her final obligation to the

Cause. "Note the date, Max," and I did: November 23, 1897. Nina dropped her reserve. She hugged the children, who stood tensely in the foyer as the carriage waited, and said, "You won't forget your Auntie Nina, will you, my little sugarplums?" Joey mumbled no, while Elizabeth cried. Sophie said to hurry along, they mustn't make Pyotr Alexeyevich anxious they'd miss the boat. In the carriage, she read aloud a newspaper account of Kropotkin's triumphant valediction in the Great Hall. Where nearly twoscore years ago Abraham Lincoln had addressed the slavery question, a Russian prince now rang in the coming socialist era to a full house of five thousand cheering workers. "How foolish," she said, "'a Russian prince.'" Nevertheless, we ought after all to have known we should attend. She fixed us with a look one by one: Zak, Abby, Fanny, me. Abby said, "No one here is a mind reader, my dear. If you wished us to go, you should have said so." Sophie answered that it was not for herself she was speaking. Our absence could be seen as a reproach to the Cause. Nina dropped her eyes, I supposed in disagreement. These were the last words of consequence among us before my sisters and their baggage were aboard ship. Passengers were lined along the railing, calling out their good-byes to the well-wishers on the pier below. Fanny asked what we were waiting for. I said I thought I saw my sisters waving. Fanny laughed in disbelief. I pointed, and there they were, the size of toy soldiers, pointing back. Kropotkin stood with them, also peering in our direction. Nina was gesturing wildly, standing on her toes. Abby said how sad that they should be reaching out to us now. Fanny shouted, "Max!" She pulled at my coat sleeve to draw my attention to a figure a few feet away. To our left, holding up a cloth sign that said, in red Russian characters, "Bon Voyage Comrades," was Mishka. He looked at us quickly and pulled his banner down. At that moment, the *Majestic* sounded its departing blast. Nina twisted frantically as the boat pulled away, stretching her arms out to the dock where Mishka had vanished into the crowd.

Part Four

I

An Exchange of Letters

ZIPPORAH GELB TELEPHONED me at the shop. "He's back," she said. It was a month since we'd seen Mishka on the dock. I was beginning to doubt our senses. This was the first I heard that he'd shown himself again. I asked how she was certain. If I saw her face, she said, I wouldn't ask such a question. She'd been laid up for days. We must meet. I suggested Schwab's. Zipporah said it was too public. I should allow her a little vanity. At the shop was better. She came that day, wearing a veil, which she never removed. Through the net, I made out Zipporah's lips enormously swollen and bandages covering one eye and the cheekbone under the other. "I won't tell you how the rest of me looks," she said. Mishka had come at her from the shadows of the stairwell as she was entering her tenement flat. He pushed her inside from behind and said not to scream, he had a knife. He looked around for Daisy and Alice. Their names were on the mailbox. Zipporah lied and said they'd gone back to their family in Boston. In fact, she told me, they were out shopping for Christmas. She shrugged apologetically. It was an American custom, nothing to do with religion. They even wanted to bring home a Christmas tree, an actual *Tannenbaum*, if I could imagine that on Allen Street. Zipporah grunted. "Don't make me laugh, Max. It hurts. I feel like I'm living in a bad novel by Dostoyevsky, the one he threw away." Then she began to cry, holding her sides in pain.

I recalled for her Kropotkin's words to Sophie, about Dostoyevsky and Nechayev contending in the womb of revolution. Mishka was of their same doomed lot. Zipporah blew her nose behind her veil. She said, "What are you, trying to make me laugh again? The comrades know he's scum. If Kropotkin said that about Mishka, I'm no anarchist, or your precious sisters made it up." I handed her a letter, written two weeks before, from Nina. She read it, then commented: "It isn't possible he could be in two places at once."

Nina's letter was in English. "Dearest brother," she wrote. "Our voyage was uneventful; by and large, it was a kind of holiday. Pyotr Alexeyevich was exhausted from his tour, though pleased with it overall and hopeful for your country. I cannot say the same for Sophie; touching America, she is bitter and unforgiving, without saying precisely why, merely that it is an *incoherent place*. I feel I must apologize for her recent severe demeanor and, perforce, for my own; though certainly the events of the last several weeks were telling on the nerves; how else explain the apparition to my eyes of Mishka at the pier, just as our ship was leaving its berth? He held a farewell sign aloft whilst standing, Maxie, it seemed at your very side; but Sophie and Pyotr Alexeyevich saw nothing; and, truth to say, the phantasm was there and gone in an instant. Sophie insists that such a display on Mishka's part is contrary to his *secretive nature*. Still, the sight, however imaginary, has troubled me; how deeply I dare not say. Pyotr Alexeyevich suggests (counter to his previous advice) that I write Mishka in Paris. I have done so, *poste restante*, and await his reply, which will settle my mind. Meantime, dear Maxie, I ask if you have heard aught of our brother (for brother he is, despite all) or even (though I think it scarcely possible) *seen him*.

"We are settled here at Bromley, a suburb of London proper, in a cottage not far from Pyotr Alexeyevich. Parts of Bromley remind me of our neighborhood district as children, and parts of London itself of Kovno; though doubtless in my memory I have reversed the matter and put Papa's villa and the Old City on the *grander scale*. Even so, not since Sophie's trial have I felt so close to home.

"Brother dear, send my love to Fanya; hug your sweet children and kiss them for their auntie. From Sophie, of course, *the same*. Fond regards to our cousins the Silvers, thanking them &c. for their hospitality. Affectionately, your loving sister, Nina.

"Postcript. I have just now received word from Mishka; three words, to be exact: *'Courage! La Cause!'* To these I add three more: *'Une affaire finie.'*—N."

Zipporah repeated her assertion. It wasn't possible for Mishka to beat her black and blue on Allen Street and at the same time write my hoity-toity sisters from Paris. In her opinion, Mishka's message was a trick, sent by someone else to make Sophie and Nina think he was in France, while that son of a bitch—I should pardon her language—was here in New York. I said that was my thinking as well, the plain English included. Nevertheless we might suppose Mishka had been in France. There was time for him to have returned to bid my sisters bon voyage, gone back to Paris, answered Nina's letter, and then come to New York once more. "In order to do what, Max?" Zipporah said. "Attack me?" We agreed that whatever his purposes, wherever his prowling, Mishka wouldn't say. Even when he wrote my sisters and me at Stump Lake, I realized, it was the postmark that bespoke Paris, nothing in his words.

After he beat her, Mishka left Zipporah on the kitchen floor and ransacked the other rooms. He slit the mattresses, looking for money that wasn't there. He stole the costume jewelry, emptied the penny jar, and, as he left, kicked Zipporah in the stomach and stuffed a sealed envelope, addressed to me, in her blouse. "I'd have shot him if I could," she said. "Next time, this." From her purse she drew an ivory-handled derringer. "Your peacemaker," I said, remembering the dime-novel expression. She answered in Jewish. If that was what they called it, then R.I.P. Zipporah handed me Mishka's letter, opened. She didn't believe she owed him any confidentiality. I wasn't to think she was Mishka's post-man. She'd have burned the letter in the stove if she weren't concerned for my safety. She added: "He meant me to read it. It's his way."

Mishka wrote on printed stationery with a letterhead re-peated in several languages but no address: "International Revo-lutionary Order/Central Council." His words were the usual hash of Russian, some German, and street English, with now a drop of bungled French. The gist of the letter, his demand for money, was by turns couched in threats, slogans, and mushy sentiments about how we shared a room as boys. I took only the threats seriously. I remembered the fire at the shop and that wreck Osgood in his leafy grave, while there sat Zipporah, with her veiled and battered face, watching me read.

Salaud! A certain party once before, in his bourgeois arrogance, had ignored the people's appeal for aid. The Central Council considered his debt outstanding and would call it in, at a specified time of the Council's choosing, or exact retribution if settlement was not made. "Ain't no welshing on no deals, Maxie. Ask your American pal what happens if you try and beat it." So wrote Mishka. Zipporah assumed that I, not Zak, was the certain party, as if I'd never given to the Cause—I, the angel Max. Somehow, Kropotkin's tag for me had gotten around. She wondered who my American friend might be. What Americans did I know besides that drunk Osgood, the girls' uncle? Nobody had seen him for a couple of years. I thought, Mishka's point, exactly, but didn't say so.

I asked Zipporah what she knew of the International Revolutionary Order. "Never heard of it," she said. But when I suggested it was another of Mishka's schemes, she hesitated to admit that was the case. She'd make inquiries about the group among the comrades, even if those who knew of Mishka were now calling him a pariah, perhaps an informer. "Max," she said, "do we throw out a bag of fruit because of one worm in one apple?" She coughed and, groaning, held her hands against her ribs. Whatever the International Revolutionary Order was, Mishka as its spokesman sounded like a landlord demanding back rent. Perhaps it was in the blood. He went on to say that in his last communication, he made it clear that our agreement remained in force, yet where were "them promised nuggits?" It didn't matter, did it, whether he was out West, in Paris, or even back in Kovno, so long as he kept his word *à avoir des absences*. Because I, Maxie, hadn't kept mine, he felt free to come and go as he pleased, as the bearer of this letter well knew. The revolution, he reminded me, recognized no borders. I should remit to M. Michael Borough, Poste Générale, Paris. Wherever he, Mishka, was, the Central Council would let him know of its arrival within days. *RSVP.* At the bottom of the page in red, in place of a signature, was scrawled in Russian: "The Man at the Dock?"

I offered Zipporah a few dollars to cover her time laid up from her beating. She said she couldn't take money for that; I should allow her some pride. "For the the doctor's bill, then," I said, "and of course, for the Cause." Zipporah put the money in her purse. "Also," she added, "for the gun," and left the shop. A few moments later, Fanny and Abby came by in the surrey with a holiday punch for the new crew. Zak thought it would be propaganda by good deed if we knocked off early the day before Christmas and made cheer for the men by giving out a bonus of a day's wages. We didn't want another strike at the Costanza Court. I climbed in the back of the carriage, the pay envelopes in one pocket and Mishka's blackmail note in the other. I intended to talk to Zak about the letter, later, at home. Fanny asked, half joking, "Who was the mysterious woman in the veil?" I said it was Zipporah Gelb. She'd had an accident and bruised her face. "Falling off the barricades," said Fanny, "or out of someone's bed?" "No," I said, "running into Mishka. That's what she came to tell me." The surrey swerved and pulled up at the curb. Fanny and Abby turned, waiting tensely for an explanation. I said not to worry, Zipporah simply confirmed what we already knew. Mishka was back, yes, but not for long. The comrades were suspicious of him. Some thought he was an *agent provocateur*. How could he play his game if everyone was wise to his designing? If he and Zipporah had a fight, it wasn't their first. She was the kind of woman who invited trouble. It took two to quarrel or make a proper swindle. Mishka knew how to pick his prey. Fanny and Abby couldn't agree more, and we drove on to the Costanza Court. I said nothing about Mishka's letter, wondering how best this time to buy him off.

The new crew was pleased by the unexpected Christmas treat. The men had raised a wood truss over the foundation as a cover for the winter. Under the loose timberwork, they sang carols. Marco and Abby joined in, knowing most of the words. Fanny hesitated at the unfamiliar verses. Zak bluffed with irritating bravado, rejoicing in virgin mother and holy child. I of course was silent, having drawn the line between myself and the idea of God long ago, the day I declared to Pyotr Mikhailovich, "No compromise, never." Zipporah Gelb said about Christmas in America that religion had no part in it. I didn't think this was completely true. Where people held to the empty form of superstition, they were likely to supply the content. Once more Bakunin's words came to mind, "If God existed, it would be necessary to abolish him," and immediately after that, Sophie's voice returned to my head. "Maxie," she said, "you're a fine one to suggest no compromise." I told Sophie rational understanding should never be mistaken for compromise, the absolute for the relative. "Mere bourgeois sophistry," she said. "You argue the way Papa did." Zak asked if I was trying to sing carols after all or just talking to myself. I admitted to neither. Here was I, thinking of how to hold Mishka at bay for the sake of a certain party. I didn't care to be needled by Sophie's voice and by that certain party himself. I took my leave at the outbreak of a *Gloria in excelsis deo* and walked back to the shop. What Zak might think about Mishka's hush money didn't matter, not if it came out of my pocket, not if in one breath he might say "Never a penny!" and in the next sing "Angels we have heard on high." I wrote M. Borough in Paris words to the following effect:

"As per the verbal agreement of October last, Monsieur will be pleased to find a remittance of $300 in his name, c/o the offices of American Express, two weeks from the present date. The Central Council should be advised that a certain party, having acknowledged his previous debt, authorizes partial payment to be included in the aforementioned and subsequent remittances; Monsieur will kindly forward $100 to the Central Council toward the settlement of this account. Further remittances will follow, in the first week of each quarter: $200 for Monsieur, $100 for the Central Council. We trust this arrangement will be considered satisfactory."

I read over my words with misgiving. This game could go on as long as Mishka lived. If I ignored him, the comrades in America would get after him soon enough, or so Zipporah Gelb implied. Besides, I couldn't send money abroad to this half brother of mine anymore than to my sisters. I posted my letter directly into the coal stove at the back of the shop and tossed in Mishka's after it. Sophie's voice said, "Well done, comrade. Pyotr Alexeyevich would approve. We must stand firm and trust that in time poor Mishka will recover from his illness." I told her she needn't worry herself over him long. Zipporah's derringer was likely to provide the fastest, surest cure.

II

Our Repast

IDA, WITHOUT ASKING, set up a proper Jewish dining room at Kraft's Hotel and Guesthouses. Her accounts were bloated with expenses for multiple sets of new table and kitchen ware and inspection fees for the attendant rabbi at a sanatorium nearby. The Kretchmers, our first managers, had prepared food in the Jewish manner, but without the official hocus-pocus. At my insistence, they served some American dishes. Barbecued beef and beans was the great favorite of our anarchist and social revolutionary clientele, who were hearty eaters of meat. My sisters preferred Russian and German cooking, on a European plan. The guests were free to take meals elsewhere, and most of them did.

When Fanny and I realized what Ida had done, we hurried up to Stump Lake. We didn't want our name associated with religious observance of any kind, even out of sight in a smoky kitchen. We arrived half-frozen, long after dark, on a bitter night in January. Ida sat us down in the empty dining room. She carried in steaming bowls of dumpling soup, followed by plates of braised chicken, stuffed cabbage, and sweet carrot stew, and a dessert of noodle pudding. Fanny was ravenous and thought it was the best meal she ever had. Ida watched happily as we ate, then poured us all plum brandy. She said in America you could have a Sabbath dinner every day of the week, but only at Kraft's Hotel also after midnight. Fanny put her foot on mine and pressed, as if to say, Max, you can't bring up the business of the kitchen now.

A winter storm kept us at Stump Lake, confined to the hotel grounds until the roads and railways were cleared. Some of the guests tobogganed down the slope from the manor house. Others skated near the shore of the lake. Most played cards and ate. They all told Fanny and me that Ida's new kitchen was the best advertising the hotel could have. Morris the cook, who'd outlasted my sisters' Catskill collective, said the secret was all in the ingredients, strictly readied and blessed according to custom. For such things, there were no substitutes. You didn't improve a recipe by voting. A kitchen wasn't a commune. "Forgive me, Mr. Kraft," he added, "but when I say, 'Quick, the salt,' that's the only mutual aid I need."

Ida's boy, with his long blond curls, was everyone's pet but mine. The guests called him Barnard in his mother's presence and little Barney behind her back. They gave him candy and showed him tricks. He liked to bury his face in the ladies' laps, the way Mishka used to among Sophie's circle of girls in Kovno. Me, he eyed at a distance and shrank from my hand when the guests passed him around, from one to the next, to fuss over. The women said poor little Barney was shy of me because he didn't have a father to call his own. Fanny thought I of all people, orphaned myself, should understand the boy. With his Fauntleroy suits and tiny evil eyes he could turn liquid in an instant, I knew him for the prettified weasel he was, but didn't say so. I told Fanny instead that our Joey was a gentler boy, and she had to agree.

Ida liked to say her Barnard would make his way in the world with his charm and looks. If he had brains, so much the better for seeing after his mother. I said Ida could take care of herself and everyone else at the same time. The hotel had never run more smoothly. We were going over accounts in the Oriental corner. Ida curtsied. "Thank you, Mr. Kraft," she said. The kitchen was the reason why. This was a family hotel, which meant preparing and serving the meals as you would at home, only bigger, better, and on time. Fanny took the opportunity to comment on the religious rigmarole and the cost of four sets of dinner ware and kitchen utensils. With pencil and paper, Ida calculated how many months it would take to amortize the expense. After that, it was all profit, so long as the dining room kept the hotel filled, which it most certainly would. "Certified Jewish kitchen, and on the American plan," she said proudly. "What greenhorn could resist?" Then she added: "For myself, I don't care. If Barnard wants milk with his corned-beef sandwich, I give it, for his bones. We don't need to stand on principle, do we, Mrs. Kraft. But business is business, and good business is best business." Fanny accepted the necessities of the trade. We'd always said religion and commerce went hand in glove. The hotel was ours, but it wasn't home. We oughtn't to drive guests away just because I wanted ham-and-cheese sandwich and sarsaparilla listed on the luncheon menu. What we ate outside the dining room was our own affair.

The roads were plowed out after a few days. Ida took us to the station in the hotel sleigh. Fanny sat with Barney in the back, not, as I suggested, to throw him to the wolves, but to keep him from falling out. The jiggle of the horses' bells carried over Ida's words. Looking straight ahead, she said to me, "How is Isidore? Does he mention my name anymore?" I told her we all held her in the highest regard. She smiled sadly and said, "That wasn't my question, was it, Mr. Kraft." She clicked her tongue at the horses. With the backs of her hands she wiped her eyes, which were smarting, she said, from the wind.

There was a letter at home from the immigration authorities at Ellis Island. They were holding in detention a woman who had arrived with no money and had given my name. A representative from the Hebrew Immigrant Aid Society telephoned the house on her behalf, but because of the storm no one could get through to me at Stump Lake. I said I didn't know a Bertha Gittelman. Zak thought I couldn't be sure. Strange things happened to names as people passed through immigration. He reminded me that when I first met him, on the road to Brody, he was Isaac Zilberzweig. I took the ferry to Ellis Island. The man from the Aid Society thanked me for coming. Many people who'd been through there refused to return. It was difficult to hear him. The man was short. The din of thousands of immigrants' voices came between us, even in a restricted corridor off the main hall. I shouted down at him that, as a matter of fact, this was my first visit to the island. I had landed on these shores from France as a first-class passenger, and in the Castle Garden years besides. He shouted back what I took to be a surprised apology. "*Pardonnez-moi!*" Quite naturally, he'd supposed I was of the same origin as this Bertha Gittelman.

Detainees were interviewed in a small room, across a wooden barrier. I recognized Basya the kitchenmaid at once, a little woman in peasant skirts, wearing a babushka. "Maxie!" she cried out. She reached over the partition to touch me, but was restrained by a matron on guard. The man from the Aid Society said, "You know her then?" I explained that she'd been employed in my father's house. "And that would be, no doubt, before Monsieur emigrated West," he asked. I said exactly so, in our villa in Kovno. This information was repeated in a hearing room before a weary immigration official. I gave the date of my arrival at New London fourteen years earlier and offered to produce the citizenship papers Uncle Henry had arranged. All that proved necessary was that I stand as guarantor, as the official put it, for Bertha Gittelman, to assure them she would not become a public charge and so liable for deportation. I said I would, and Basya the kitchenmaid departed from Ellis Island, gripping my arm with one hand and, with the other, a small bundle. The man from the Hebrew Immigrant Aid Society bid me a ceremonious adieu in French, and Basya, in Yiddish, good luck in America. She asked me, in Russian, if all Americans were like that, or was he, perhaps, a little strange.

Not once on the way to East One Hundred Fifth Street did Basya-Bertha Gittelman let go of my arm or her belongings. I remembered the passengers on the train from Brody to Berlin struggling with the customs officials beside the railway cars in the flat German countryside. Not once did she stop talking. I hadn't remembered her as being so voluble. My memory of Basya the kitchenmaid was jumbled with the other servants and with childhood images that went back so far they played silently in my mind. I responded to her effusions with occasional English words whose meanings were made clear with the point of a finger: "Statue of Liberty," "ferryboat," "carriage," and, finally, "home." When Basya asked if I was married, I said: "Fanya Ruttenberg." She remembered the girl she called, in German, Nina's little friend. Did we have children? I nodded and said their names. She, too, was married, and pronounced her husband's name as if I might know him: "Selig Gittelman, the garment maker on Rivington Street." I shook my head. She searched my face in bewilderment. He'd sent her the money to join him. She was robbed in steerage. It seemed hardly possible that Selig Gittelman, a good Jewish husband, could disappear without a word. Into the Russian army, yes, or in Siberia, but not here, said Basya, not here in America.

She talked on and on in the languages and accent of the Jews of Kovno. She switched from Russian to German to Yiddish in midsentence, grabbing, it seemed, at the words to keep up with her story. When we reached home, she told it over again, not in the quiet of the parlor, but bustling around the house, poking into closets and drawers and behind the drapery, nosing around the kitchen, while the rest of us, the children included, followed in her wake. On the return from Stump Lake, Fanny had once more without warning dismissed the help, both the cook and the nursemaid. Basya clearly sensed the void. "The servant of servants," said Zak. There'd be no firing her. She'd never leave us except for her husband, if she could find him. I wondered if she'd bother to look for him now. Fanny thought not. Wherever Selig Gittelman was, it was the place certain good Jewish husbands belonged. Let him stay there, with Ida's Jake for company. Basya was the kind of help we'd always needed: cook, nurse, and housekeeper all in one, who understood her place. That evening, since Basya would only serve but not sit at the dining-room table, we ate in the kitchen. Afterward, Basya sang "Chericheribim" and Zak danced waving a handkerchief, the way Pyotr Mikhailovich used to do. Basya said, "My first night in America, and I could be in Kovno!" Abby felt she understood at last what life was like for us in Russia. Everyone but me was speaking Yiddish, even in front of the children, who were allowed for the occasion to stay up late. I said in this house, in America, in New York, on East One Hundred Fifth Street in Manhattan, the language we used was English. Abby translated for Basya, who laughed: "Maxie and his English!" In Kovno, in my stepfather's villa, upstairs was Russian and German and Vera Andreyevna's French, downstairs was Yiddish. Then she added: "When I sit in my kitchen, I speak what I like."

Basya was astonished to learn that my sisters had escaped Siberia, and even more that they'd come to America and then left.

Those girls, she said, would never be content, with all their nihilist nonsense and no mother to take them in hand. Mishka she dismissed in disgust. He was a sneak and a thief who'd run off and broken his father's heart. All the servants knew he wasn't worth such sorrow. After Pyotr Mikhailovich sold his villa, Basya went to join Vera Andreyevna's new household in Bialystok, no longer, she thought, as a kitchenmaid but the cook at last. And so it was, for a short time, until Vera Andreyevna took up with a Russian officer, a Captain Vasilev, and married him. Vera Andreyevna became Madame Vasileva, a Christian!—Basya spit three times— and hired a French chef. Basya was a kitchenmaid again, but now had to touch strange foods. God knows, she wasn't a religious fuss. Those rules about milk and meat, the shoulds and the shouldn'ts, weren't good for much. From the looks of our kitchen, she saw we felt the same. But the French were like pigs, they'd eat anything. Vasilev received a promotion. Selig Gittelman, a master tailor, came to measure and fit the captain, now a major, for his new wardrobe of uniforms. Often he'd work long hours there in the house. Basya brought him a little nourishment, not French slops, which he wouldn't taste, but the same noodle soup and chopped herring she made for herself.

Selig was a philosopher. He believed in evolution and the survival of the fittest. Life was a struggle, every man's hand lifted against another. Basya's cooking, he said, made him fit for survival. As it was in the kitchen, thus also in nature. A man's best weapon was his brains, a woman's her protective instinct of the hearth. These together ensured the survival of the species. Competition was a biological necessity. Basya the kitchenmaid and Selig Gittelman, by combining their means and know-how, would prevail. There was a fortune to be made in America from Selig's skill with the scissors and needle. In the twenty years Basya lived and worked in Pyotr Mikhailovich's villa, she'd spent almost nothing on herself. Her ready money was considerable, enough to pay for Selig's emigration and the start-up of his American enterprise. He knew about these matters from his cousin Moritz, who set up as a shirtwaist maker and couldn't sew a buttonhole. If Moritz was now wealthy, how much the more so a master tailor like Selig. This was beyond commonsense wisdom. This was the principle of natural selection. Selig would precede Basya to America and later send her the money to join him. Meantime, she would

continue as kitchenmaid in Vera Andreyevna's house and care for
Selig's mother, who was dim-sighted and crooked with age. That
was nine years ago. Selig wrote every month of his success. After
three years, he sent for her. Selig's mother had become bedridden,
like a baby, and Basya was unable to leave. Selig's letters stopped
coming regularly, and only last year did his mother die. Basya
informed her husband that she was finally on her way to America,
but received no reply. If, God forbid, anything had happened to
him—she again spit three times—to Selig Gittelman, the garment
maker on Rivington Street, why surely there would have been an
important notice in the newspaper. Zak told her, in perfect Kovno
Yiddish, not to worry; it wasn't unusual over the years for a husband and wife to lose touch, even in their own home, so how much
the more between here and Bialystok. Everything was possible in
America, but until her Selig appeared, Basya should find this
kitchen her hearth and this house her refuge and place of rest.

Basya's ways in the kitchen were the same as Ruth the cook's
in Kovno. On East One Hundred Fifth Street, I was served the
dishes from my stepfather's villa. I said if I had to eat the food
of my childhood, this was how I liked it prepared. Fanny thought
the stuffed fish and the dumplings were better than Ida's. Basya
kept no recipes. Fanny followed her around the kitchen, mea-
suring handfuls of meal and pinches of spice, and sent the resulting notes to Ida to try out on the hotel guests. The stuffed
fish met with approval, the dumplings not, lacking what Morris
the cook at Stump Lake called heft. Basya shrugged. "This
Morris," she said, "he must be a Galician. They make dumplings
like lead." Her roasts and stews were tender and juicy, better than
in Kovno, I supposed because of the quality of American meat.
Basya disagreed and admitted to having learned a little something
from Vera Andreyevna's French chef. Nevertheless, banned from
her kitchen were snails, frogs, the flesh of pigs, crawling, slimy
creatures from the sea, and any cheese that smelled, she said, like
a privy. If we wanted carrion, we should go elsewhere, and so on
occasion we did, to Delmonico's or Lüchow's or Paddy's Clam
House, and to the shop for a ham-and-cheese sandwich and
saraparilla.

To the nursery Basya brought tales of ogres, goblins, and
Gypsies that she and Marya the housemaid had once told me. The
children somehow understood her mishmash of speech but talked

to her, with tiny dignity, only in English. They mentioned the Gypsy's grave. Basya thought they were asking for an American story about Gypsies. Joey and Elizabeth instead told her about their finding Osgood's body. Basya barely understood a word, her English being scant and the children's account unclear. Fanny said to pay them no mind. In America, children were allowed to say what they liked, but that didn't mean you always had to listen. Basya said it wasn't so different in Kovno, where Sophie held forth in the kitchen to the servants and her bored father about the will of the people.

Whenever Basya passed between the library and the parlor, she looked away from the group portrait with my sisters absent taken in Kovno, I supposed because of the memories it raised. Zak, for all his stories about his village, almost never mentioned the family he left there. Fanny no longer mentioned her brothers or her parents in Shavl. One day, I found the photograph of the family Kraft hanging with its face to the wall. I turned it around, and behind me heard Basya say in Jewish, "No." She'd have taken the picture down, no doubt, if I hadn't been standing in her way. She pointed through me toward the wall, as if I weren't there. "Abomination," she said. "Her. Him. And him. And him." She spat three times. By the movement of her finger close to my chest, I understood she meant Vera Andreyevna and her boys, Nikki, Nakki, and Nokki—that is, Nikolai, Boris, and Vasily. They'd taken the name Vasilev and blotted out the name Kraft. They'd become Christians, heathens who prayed on their knees to statues. Who was there to recite remembrance for Pyotr Mikhailovich? They weren't fit to appear alongside him. I said that at the time the portrait was made, none of that had happened. "Tcha!" said Basya. I asked why she remained all those years in the Vasilev house if it was so hateful. "And where should I have gone?" she answered. Selig was in America. She had no money, except to feed herself and her mother-in-law. I said Vera Andreyevna and her boys were no great loss to the family. Every time I looked at the photograph now at my back, I made my own remembrance of my stepfather. Then I added: "I carry his name," and set the picture right.

"Tcha," said Basya, this time less harshly. She'd let the picture hang but wasn't finished talking. She jabbed a finger at each of Vera Andreyevna's boys. This one went to military school and

joined a Cossack regiment. That one became a government lawyer, a prosecutor for the police. The other entered the seminary
to be a priest. It was not for nothing Basya turned away from
their faces. She looked at me as if to scold: "Well, Maxie, what
do you say to that?" I said nothing. I listened as Sophie's voice
explained why it was not surprising that in their own way, like
Mishka, these other half brothers of hers should be caught up in
the revolutionary struggle, even in the defense of tsarism. In a
time of troubles, everyone must choose a side. This one was a
killer for the regime, that one an advocate, the other an apologist.
They were sworn to a catechism as pitiless as Nechayev's. They
must sever family ties and deny the name Kraft. As if the Jews,
irrelevant as such to the revolution, were a threat of any kind to
the reigning Imperial Majesty, Lord, Autocrat, et cetera, of all
the Russias! "Maxie," Sophie said, "being an angel isn't always
enough. What side are you on?"

Basya scuttled off to another part of the house. Sophie went
silent. To both of them I might have made the same reply: I didn't
come to America to concern myself with a Russian revolution. I
stood for a while looking at my family seventeen years past, in
another world, so I mused, and then at Ariane, who looked directly back. I noticed for the first time a wry smile at play around
her mouth. "What a family!" she might have said. "How strange
and sad! The possibilities are terrible, Maxim, if you think about
them. Imagine your sisters smuggling themselves into Russia, arrested as revolutionary spies, tortured, prosecuted, and condemned
to hang by their own half brother, the lawyer Boris Vasilev. In
the carriage with them at dawn, as they are conveyed to the place
of execution, is Father Vasily Vasilev, mercilessly proffering conversion at the brink of death. Or imagine the revolution won.
Mishka's Central Council supplants the secret Third Section of
the old regime. Summary justice replaces the knout. Hauled before Mishka is Hetman Nikolai Vasilev of the Ural Cossacks. Half
brother eyes half brother. Mishka tilts his spectacles to sharpen
their focus. 'Take him away,' he says, 'and shoot him.' Now imagine yourself, puppy. You have your library, your home, your business, your country property, Basya the housekeeper and Morris
the cook to prepare Pyotr Mikhailovich's favorite dishes wherever
you are, *cuisine à la juive*. No, Maxim, fourteen years in America
and you still haven't gone very far from Kovno."

III

Cornered Again

LETTERS FROM BROMLEY held no clues as to Mishka's actual whereabouts. Nina never mentioned him. She was pointedly silent touching *une affaire finie*. She wrote instead of domestic matters: the garden she'd planted, Sophie's frequent excursions into London proper, which disrupted the kitchen, Pyotr Alexeyevich's health—all artfully penned and phrased. Sophie occasionally added brusque words of enlightenment. America's war with Spain was imperialism with the sugar coat of liberation. We didn't suppose it was anything else but supported the war all the same. Zak said she'd have put it better if she wrote, "You shall not crucify mankind on a cross of cane." I suggested the war was the final contest in the greater struggle that began with the Anglo-Saxon defeat of the Armada. Abby believed it went far deeper than that for us, otherwise why should we, come yesterday to English, feel as we did. Spaniards burning the farms of Cuban peasants, herding them into unspeakable *concentrados*, awakened racial memories in every Jew. We carried in our blood the ancient experience of torture, expulsion, and *autos-da-fé*. Marco answered, "I don't say no. I am a Neapolitan. Whatever shall stand to break the Spanish Church, *così sia*, so be it." He considered the war with patient gravity. If the fighting didn't end quickly, Marco's wife and little daughter would arrive in America before the Costanza Court was built. Zak and Marco and even I worked alongside what day labor we could find amid the war cries. Fanny refused to hear about the killing or buy Joey the Rough Rider suit he longed for. At dinner, she stopped her ears with her fingers. We shouldn't talk, just get it over with and win.

The crew was back to complement by the summer's end. None of the men saw action or came closer to Cuba than the Florida swamps. We lost only one man, to yellow fever. Carl Franks was another such casualty. There was a hero's obituary in the newspapers. He'd held an honorary commission in the state militia and was compelled by moral duty, so it was reported, to take up arms against the Spanish outrage. Abby wrote a note of sympathy to the widow, the poetess Blanche Viereck Franks, and received an extravagant reply with a poem on the latter-day Cincinnatus, called from the plow to the battle field, only to per- ish before his task was done, "While yet the swarthy host, in vain, Rejoic'd in his demise." Blanche was going to Italy, there to grieve among the weeping willow and mourning cypress. "Poor Blanche," said Abby. "She must have hated him." I wondered if it wasn't yellow fever at all but the Spanish pox that killed Carl Franks. Blanche's letter ended with an afterthought, how were Isidore and dear, dear Max?—to which, Abby promised not to respond.

With the war over, our thoughts turned to the matter of sab- otage. Zak feared the old crew might wreck the Costanza Court now that it was near completion. I thought Mishka was the most likely vandal and owned to having tossed his last blackmail letter into the coal burner. Zak said he'd have done the same. Even so, we'd be wise to keep a night watchman. Marco agreed, but said not to worry about the old crew. The men were fools, not cow- ards. Mishka was the sneak who bided his time. A man like that was a stalking animal, a fox returning to familiar haunts. Unless you heard the geese honk in alarm, you didn't know he'd been lurking until the damage was done. I thought of Zipporah Gelb and her battered face behind the veil. I hadn't seen her for months. I'd ignored the flyers she sent for meetings against the war and the appeals for money. I didn't care to argue my position with fire-eating *pacificos*. I'd fallen away from the Cause. Fanny said I should stay that way, a fallen angel. Nevertheless, I went down to Allen Street to call on Zipporah, our sentinel goose in the ghetto.

The names Alice Ward and Daisy Osgood were no longer on the mailbox. Zipporah opened her door cautiously only after she'd recognized my voice. "It's you," she said, and slipped something into the slit pocket of her skirts, I thought perhaps her gun. I couldn't help looking directly at her face. "Stare as hard as you like, Max," she said. "Don't be shy. It's actor's greasepaint to cover the scars." I said I wouldn't have guessed, she was the same girl I'd always known. Zipporah waved away my lie and responded with one of her own: "You don't have to pretend." In fact, what I saw on her face weren't scars at all, but the chisel-cuts of fear. I asked after Daisy and Alice. They'd gone, she said, run off to hide from Mishka. Good luck to them. "He's here again?" I said. Zipporah nodded yes, then shook her head no. He was here and not here, there, everywhere, and nowhere. The girls had received word from Boston concerning their uncle, the drunk. "Osgood?" I blurted out. "He's dead!" Zipporah asked how I knew. That was precisely what Daisy and Alice had learned from their family. An anonymous letter told them the fool had been murdered. The family could have the details suppressed, for a price. Otherwise the circumstances of Osgood's death and his degradation would be dragged into the open. The girls thought only Mishka could have written such a threat, and fled. Zipporah's voice became shrill. "Max," she said, "if you know about this, tell me!"

I confided everything to her respecting the murder at Stump Lake. Zipporah heard me out, then rose, tight-lipped and with dignity, to be sick in the kitchen sink. "Max," she said wheezing, "please, take a walk around the block." I picked my way through the heart of the ghetto. Children born in America ran up to me and in the accent of Slobodka asked for money. I pretended not to understand. They circled me, pulling at my coat, and asked again in a gutter gibberish of which I caught only the word "penny." I gave them a few cents, and they rushed away like howling Yahoos. On Allen Street, the prostitutes shouted and stuck out their legs to trip me, a Yankee, they laughed, come looking for real Jewish delicatessen. When I returned to Zipporah's flat, I told her she should move uptown. She was composed, wearing a clean middy and fresh greasepaint. "To hide from him, you mean?" she said. "Never." I answered that she mistook my meaning. She should get away from the filth of the ghetto. These streets were a lower world between hell and heaven, not Europe, not quite America. Her work was wasted here. Her revolution, if it were ever to happen, would take place out there—I gestured—where recognizable English was spoken. "You're crazy, Max," Zipporah snapped in Yiddish. "Revolutions don't start uptown." Then she returned to English and added: "I belong here. I'm not like those sisters of yours, Miss La-de-di and Miss La-de-da, their feet in the muck and their noses in the air, or that other one, the Goldman girl, who doesn't speak *der Jargon*."

Zipporah had a plan. She'd asked among the comrades about Mishka's International Revolutionary Order and its Central Council. No one knew of it, but there was a reluctance to dismiss the group's existence. Inquiries would have to be made abroad. That would take time. Communication with European circles was necessarily secretive and slow. Only Zipporah's Russian friends ridiculed the idea of an International Revolutionary Order. The name was suspiciously like Nechayev's false fronts, the Secret Revolutionary Committee and the so-called Russian Section of Bakunin's World Revolutinary Alliance, of which he claimed to be member No. 2771. It was recalled that Nechayev was able to fool Bakunin himself and bilk even Herzen of thousands of francs. The comrades eventually came around to the Russians' view. "We are agreed about Mishka," said Zipporah. "We will have him removed." I wasn't to suppose the decision was reached easily. She wasn't normally this high-strung and edgy. So much could go wrong and, of course, money was needed. "Be an angel, Max," she said. She leaned back in her chair, like her old self, and smiled.

When Mishka was born, a boiled turnip, I'd found him repulsive. Some feelings never die. Now Zipporah would have me conspire in his murder. I'd have preferred to hear about it after the fact. I said if she and her friends succeeded in killing Mishka, whether or not they were found out, they would have sunk, all the same, to his brutal level. "Max," she said, "I'm already there," and touched her scars. She asked who was I to preach. Hadn't I kept silent about Osgood? Hadn't I admitted to bankrolling

Mishka? I said I had no choice. Zipporah answered, "Neither do I." She reminded me that the deed was a collective undertaking. It might be months before they tracked Mishka down. Nevertheless, revolutionary justice must prevail. I asked who, exactly, were Mishka's judge and jury. Was a vote taken by a quorum of the Pioneers of Liberty, or perhaps the Russian Progressive Union? Was the outcome a majority or a mere plurality in favor of the murder of the murderer? How long was the debate? No, I said, a cabal made up of a few friends met right here in the kitchen. I wondered how they dared try to make me an accomplice. "Max," said Zipporah, "you already are." Whom did I think Mishka was likely to implicate in Osgood's death? Not himself, surely.

Sophie's voice came to mind—not peremptory, as it was now, but concerned, the way it sounded that day outside the bathhouse after I'd killed Bobelis and she saw me covered with blood. How good it felt when she said, looking at the grave I'd dug, "Very well concealed, comrade." I came nearest then to embracing Sophie's Cause. When I hesitated, she didn't seriously dispute me, except for a sisterly kind of mocking. She kept Bobelis's death in confidence and never held it like a knife against my throat. What Zipporah took for my sisters' airs I understood was a certain restraint. Mutual aid implied a modicum of mutual respect. I closed my eyes the better to catch Sophie's words, but they were drowned by Zipporah's laughter. "Pull your head out of the sand, Max," she said. "I'm still here."

Zipporah went on with her scheme. Daisy's and Alice's family was the surest link to Mishka. One of her people was in Boston even now to convince them to pay what he asked. My role was to provide them the money. "Mishka takes the bait," said Zipporah. "He comes back for more. Sooner or later, we'll find him. And then ..." She reached into her pocket and withdrew her little gun. I didn't suppose Zipporah would actually carry out the deed herself. "We shall see," she said, and shifted comfortably in her chair. "Meantime, Max, you know what you have to do." The matter was settled. I should allow myself to be fleeced once more, this time at second hand, by Mishka.

IV

1900

WHERE WAS MISHKA? I saw his hand in every disaster: in the
fire that December which swept lower Broadway and those the
following spring which destroyed grand hotels and mansions, on
Fifth Avenue and at the seaside of Coney Island, and especially
the Vanderbilt house on Long Island, its name, "Idle Hour," an
invitation to arson. A section of the elevated railroad was blown
up in July, during a strike in Brooklyn. Mishka was not among
the arrested dynamiters. The Costanza Court went untouched.
Zipporah Gelb said not to worry, just keep the money coming,
she was on Mishka's track. We met regularly at Schwab's, as I
used to meet with my sisters, to dole out cash. I didn't care to be
alone with her again at Allen Street, where she could toy openly
with her gun. Once, cousin Emma happened by, between tours
again. She broke away from her friend Ed Brady when she saw
us, shaking off his arm, and plumped herself down at our table.
"Don't let me interrupt anything serious, dears," she said, and
then solicited for the Alexander Berkman Defense Fund. There
was a final appeal to be made to the Board of Pardons, and if
that failed: escape. I said I seemed to have heard that before.
Zipporah sat back lazily and watched me, I thought, amused.
Emma said she wasn't asking for what I couldn't give. If I

doubted her word, I should think of what our support meant to Sasha, after seven years in prison—seven years of the dungeon, the straitjacket, and solitary confinement, with the prospect of fourteen years more of the same. If it was to be escape, she said, this was the time. She was going abroad for some months. With her out of the country, the prison warders were sure to relax their scrutiny of Sasha's contacts with the outside, easing his getaway. I understood her reasoning. The police read Emma Goldman's signature in every labor riot, every act of political violence, just as I read Mishka's mark. It was a wintry day. I thought of Sasha as a boy in Kovno, the strategist of snowball wars on the Nemen, the free spirit who challenged *gimnaziya* with his essay "There Is No God," something I might have written myself. There were places, I thought, even in America where they'd be happier to put you in a straitjacket for penning such an idea than for actually killing a Henry Clay Frick. I imagined myself helpless, in the dark, while rats nibbled at my face and toes, and pledged ten dollars to the Berkman Fund. Emma kissed my cheek and said she knew I gave from my heart. Ed Brady stood at the bar and coughed. Emma got up and joined him, and they left Schwab's after a whispered exchange of words. "She's soft on you, Max," said Zipporah. She'd been sipping a beer and now moodily drained the glass.

The opening of the Costanza Court was delayed until Marco's family settled in. The building had an actual courtyard, not for privies and trash, but laid out with a trellised garden and blossoming shade trees planted by Marco himself. The day he brought his family home, an Italian string band played in the courtyard, and the tenor with the mandolin sang "Bella Costanza, Amore Mio." We invited the crew and tenants from the Abigail Arms and the Frances Arms. There were strange cheeses and melons, red Italian wine, greenish noodles, and other foods Basya eyed without tasting. Marco's daughter, Tina, showed Joey and Elizabeth how to suck up spaghetti. The children had a hilarious time running among the legs of the dancing grown-ups, Tina shouting funny English words and Joey and Elizabeth funny Italian ones. Marco had furnished a spacious apartment on the second floor. From her windows, Costanza waved to the band and the revelers below and took possession of her rooms, her courtyard, her building, as a queen bee her hive.

Costanza ruled the tenants. Zak and I were of no consequence. By her sufferance we collected the rents in her Costanza Court. Marco was the happiest drone alive. There was little talk from him now of the Cause, only Dante, Tina, and Costanza, whom he called his Beatrice. Abby was disappointed. She'd supposed Marco was more manly. Fanny said, "The woman thinks she's still in Italy." Costanza would learn soon enough what country she was in when that daughter of hers talked back to her only in English. Zak said no matter, so long as Marco was on the spot and the rents were on time. Nevertheless, we all felt sad for Marco. Abby determined to leave the shop and return to social work. She took a position with the same Hebrew Immigrant Aid Society that came to Basya's rescue at Ellis Island. Everything was splendid between Zak and her, she confided to me, flushing. She thanked me and said I was the best cousin a girl ever had. "To tell the truth, I was never really needed in the shop, was I? Besides"—she sighed—"it's become a little dull, with the new crew, no strikes, and the beautiful revolution come to nothing."

Whatever Mishka was up to, and Zipporah Gelb entangled with him, it wasn't revolution. These were prospering times. Ida kept Stump Lake filled the year round and raised the rates for the summer and holidays. Silver & Kraft owned three fully rented apartment houses. Zak played his chessboard game on the city map, along the projected subway line into Washington Heights. The crew was never idle. Fanny saw no difference between the heralds of revolution and the tub-thumping millenarians shouting "Repent ye, sinners, the twentieth century is at hand." She found both equally disgusting. Abby said, "How pitiful! You'd think humanity would have learned by now to separate its hopes from its expectations." Nina's letters sounded almost happy. She looked forward to several trips to Paris come the New Year, in preparation for an international anarchist congress. "Maxie," she wrote, "even I have my dreams. Who knows what I shall find there?" Zak supposed she meant by this to break away from Sophie for some private adventures. I understood it wasn't opportunities for love she'd be seeking, but Mishka. Zipporah agreed with Zak. "Believe me, Max, she's itching. I know about these things." Then she said: "If Nina does find Mishka in Paris, you'll know I'm dead."

About this time, Basya gave up looking for her husband. Zak

had gone with her several times to Rivington Street. At Selig Gittelman's former address, no one recalled the man. Abby said people passed through the ghetto as if it were an annex to Ellis Island. With the help of the Hebrew Aid Society, she searched immigration records and the registries of the needle-trades unions. She found no trace of Selig Gittelman, the garment maker, and concluded he'd changed his name. Basya spit three times and announced she needed a bigger kitchen. In my stepfather's villa, there was room for Ruth the cook and Basya herself working side by side, with Marya the housemaid scrubbing the pots. If such was the case in Kovno, how much the more so should it be in America. Zak said to consider it done. Basya knew that he and I had purchased a lot on East Seventy-ninth Street, where we intended to build a proper residence. With the children, the present house was cramped. It was dark, being mostly gaslit, while Costanza Pacifici looked down from her apartment, brilliant with incandescent light, onto a flowering courtyard. Abby wanted a garden like her mother's, with magnolia trees and climbing vines. Fanny missed the furniture we had to store when we moved to East One Hundred Fifth Street. The house should have not just an Oriental corner but a separate den for the ottomans, the hangings, and a new divan. She'd have a tailor make for me a smoking jacket and cap. I could put aside my smelly briar and pull on a water pipe. "Xanadu," I said, "our dream haven." "Yes," Fanny warned, "for private dreams, not revolution." Zak worried over the rough plans at the shop and talked about his village. "Bigger than the house of Mendel Chalfin, the moneylender, and of Yankel Gritz, the miller." "Also," I added, "of Pyotr Mikhailovich, the landlord." Zak asked by how much. I thought perhaps two rooms, counting the bathhouse outside. He bent silently over the sketches for a few minutes, then looked up, grinning. "Bigger by three rooms," he said, "counting Xanadu, which we almost forgot."

We celebrated the New Year at Delmonico's, six of us, including Marco and Costanza. Reservations were difficult to come by. Marco persuaded his wife that she could hardly refuse the invitation, which Abby had extended with reluctance, in a formal note Costanza couldn't read. Marco interpreted the menu for her. She stared speechless at the *potage au tomate,* as if it were a bowl of blood and the caviar heaps of offal. We drank half a case of champagne. Before long, Costanza was feasting and roaring with laughter. I toasted Marco and presented him with a bonus of stock in Silver & Kraft. Zak explained to Costanza in Italian the meaning of the shares. "*Sí, capsico!*" She waved her butter knife at Marco. "*Mutualità!*" Marco beamed and said, "*Proprio,*" telling us with his smiles how wise she was, the wife. Graciously, he accepted his shares. "*Una porzione giusta,*" he called them. I said it was an observation worthy of Kropotkin. At midnight came an explosion of cheers from other parts of Delmonico's and the popping of champagne corks. The strains of "Auld Lang Syne" rose up and drifted in from all around. Zak lifted his glass. "To the American century," he said. The phrase was Colonel Roosevelt's, whose Rough Riders had drubbed the papists at San Juan Hill. He added: "May the past be forgotten. America is our revolution." We drank to America and wept, remembering the years gone by. Fanny supposed it was the same in every room at Delmonico's, from the hush that followed the outburst at midnight, and said as much to our waiter. "Begging your pardon, ma'am," he answered. "With all respects, the guests have got back to the business at hand, their dinners."

V

Bookish Considerations

THERE WERE DIFFICULTIES with the library. Uncle Henry had
been proud that all his books were in English. It was a matter of
principle I wanted to maintain, but couldn't. I recalled Sophie's
amusement at seeing *The Communist Manifesto* in Yiddish. Since
then, the foreign books had increased to a measure of several
shelves. The problem was how to arrange them when we moved.
Zak bought for me the same edition of *Dieu et l'état* I lost over
the side of the *Massapeag*. Should we put it next to *God and the
State* or among the French books Abby was reading? She'd discovered Zola's *Germinal* serialized in Yiddish. It was nothing like
the silly fables and maxims she had to read as a schoolgirl, and
not because of a special grace, as I tried to joke, lent by the language of the ghetto. Abby insisted her French moderns be kept
together. Zak felt as strongly about his German poetry. We had
an Edison phonograph set up in a corner of the parlor. Often
after dinner Zak sat and listened to lieder, holding a volume of
poems in one hand, in the other a cigar, which he waved while
humming to the songs. On the floor beside him lay a pile of books
a foot high, which he carried back to its niche when the evening
was through.

Fanny claimed to have a sixth sense about Russian. She could find what she was looking for with one glance around the room. For herself, it didn't matter how the books were arranged, but she disagreed with my wanting the entire library in strict alphabetical order. She held up Chekhov in Yiddish. "Which alphabet, Max?" she asked. It was a selection of stories and short plays. I answered, "Which category?" Basya was watching us. "What is to argue?" she said. "It goes here." She pointed to a gap among the Yiddish books. Basya's English was improving, but reading it was an agony. She shook her finger up at me. If I took the Yiddish books and put them with the rest, how could she find what she wanted? Even in Kovno, Basya reminded me, in my stepfather's villa, there was a place, downstairs, for the Yiddish books she and Ruth the cook could read. I remembered in a dark passageway, between the kitchen and the larder, a small bookrack filled with translations of the Law and the Psalms and other Hebrew works, mildewed and bound in black cloth. Basya stopped scowling and stood proud when I suggested that in the new house, all the books in Jewish should be in her care. Abby could hardly object, but said how sly of me it was, contriving to keep Yiddish in a domestic ghetto. I thought, Precisely where it belongs.

There was one book in Italian, *La Divina Commedia*, a solemn household gift from Marco Tullio Pacifici. We deciphered the poem with progressing horror, and then set it on the low dark shelf we reserved for other unwelcome works that, also being gifts, we couldn't discard. The poetess Blanche Viereck Franks sent from Venice her *Sorrow Songs and Grecian Odes*. From Julius Schapira, M.D., the family physician, we received his privately printed *Free Inquiry into the Scientific Basis of the Religion of the Hebrews*. He supposed that, as modern thinkers, we would appreciate this rationale for superstition.

Marco branded the papist imperium the great debaser of mankind. It was a puzzle how he squared Dante's unrelieved medievalism with the revolution he still held in his heart. One day in the shop, he explained. "I was an aerialist," he reminded us. With his brother Quinto on his shoulders, he rode a unicycle along the netless high wire. Before him, like a guiding angel, danced his sister Emilia. Below was an abyss. It was a vision of heaven and hell. Up high on the wire was a world in exquisite balance. Down there were the rich patrons' upturned faces, their harsh breathing and gaping mouths. Eternity was shattered in Milan when Emilia fell from *paradiso* to her death. Her leg cramped. Marco saw her wince. The words *o dio* formed soundlessly on her lips, and she dropped into the shrieking *inferno*. "God did not save her," he said. "She was fifteen years of age." Some newspapers in Milan proclaimed "MURDER." In his confusion of grief, Marco thought the headlines referred to Emilia, not the Haymarket martyrs in Chicago, who had just been hanged. They, too, he realized afterward, were dropped into hell on account of the bosses. "*Ecco!*" Marco lifted his eyes to the ceiling of the shop. "*La luce di verità.*" Dante in his time shone the light of truth as he understood it. He set himself against the pope in Rome. We must not imagine that because he lacked our knowledge of science he did not know that only man can take the true measure of man. Why else would he have written his great work in the language not of the Church but of the people? By calling the poem a *commedia*, he announced its humanity. Someone else, not Dante, added the word *divina*. "Therefore, my friends," said Marco, "I will hold with Bakunin that the mission of science is to light the road of liberty, that nevermore, '*Nel mezzo del cammin di nostra vita,*' shall mankind find itself in a dark wood."

Zak applauded Marco's explanation. It was like one of the brilliant feats of Zusya, the village rabbi's son, who could stick a pin through the pages of a book and weave the skewered words into a seamless argument. Marco was unsure of the compliment. "It is nothing," he said. In the end, what mattered was *la poesia* Dante composed in *la bellissima lingua italiana*. A man who could sing like so must, *profondamente*, place man before God, didn't we think. I said I couldn't agree more. No doubt Dante would also hold with Bakunin that if God existed, we should kill him. That was, after all, the essence of Christianity.

Abby didn't think it was right to tease Marco. "The poor man has thorns enough in his side from that greedy, ignorant wife of his." Zak said not to worry, Marco was a bully sport, a freethinker like us, only at times a little sentimental. We were eating in the kitchen, even the children. The rest of the house was a shambles in preparation for our move. Basya stood by the stove, stirring pots and grumbling in Yiddish at our conversation. She mistrusted Marco because of his magnificent mustache, which to her made him a Gypsy or a Cossack. Fanny was in a black mood, because of the house's disarray. She hated upheaval and dreamed at night of the long wagon ride when her family fled from Shavl. She caught Basya's mutterings. "*La bellissima lingua italiana!*" She laughed grimly, then added, in Yiddish, in the children's hearing: "*Ghetto*, that's an Italian word."

I conceded the arrangement of the books, so long as Basya took the Yiddish. The library at East Seventy-ninth was to have a pair of bay windows that took in the north light and looked out over the broad two-way street. Another set of bays was to face the garden in the rear. The library was to open onto the parlor, the parlor to lead to the dining room, the dining room to overlook the garden. Zak had completed a correspondence course in architectural drawing. He planned the house in near symmetry. There were to be two stairwells, front and back, and on each floor two telephones, two full baths, two WCs, everything ample and up-to-date. And so it was. Our last day at One Hundred Fifth Street was a Sunday in November. Marco came by with his daughter, Tina, to take the children off our hands during the final packing. He was pensive. His thoughts kept turning to his sister, who had died on that very day thirteen years ago. It was also the anniversary of the hanging of the Haymarket martyrs, a saints' day in the calendar of the Cause, with speechmaking and other money-raising memorials. For the first year I could remember, I hadn't heard from Zipporah Gelb. Our telephone was disconnected and mail delivery stayed. No one was regularly at the shop. Zipporah had no way of reaching me easily for the annual Haymarket donation or even to tell me Mishka was dead. I smiled to think of myself as a misbehaving angel.

I'd seen Zipporah last in Schwab's three months before. She announced, "We've got him nailed," but precisely where or how, she wouldn't say. She thought I really didn't want to know, and, in point of fact, I didn't. Zipporah was hardly triumphant. When I gave her the usual, she stuffed the bills in her bodice and complained that these should be for the revolution, not running down a mad dog. She ought to be going to the anarchist congress in Paris instead. I said not with my money she oughtn't. Zipporah sank back in her chair and pretended to laugh. "What you mean is," she said, "I should do the dirty work for both of us and let you know when it's finished." She drank two whiskeys with her beer and left in a hurry, as if she, and not Mishka, were the one being hunted.

Zipporah's silence since then I laid above all to the failure of Sasha's escape. The newspapers were slow to report the discovery of a tunnel, under the prison courtyard, leading to a house on Sterling Street across the way. The plan was so much like Mishka's, I wondered if there hadn't been some truth in his scheme after all. Zak said absolutely not. As Basya would put it, how many ways were there to pluck a chicken? How much the more so to break out of the Western Penitentiary. Nevertheless, Zipporah knew how I'd been bamboozled. She could have given the idea of the tunnel to cousin Emma, Modska the Twin, and whoever else was behind Sasha's real attempt. The warden informed the press of a foiled anarchist plot. The police came to a different conclusion. Not Alexander Berkman, but the notorious forger William Boyd was the would-be escapist. The warden then wavered and fixed on Pat McGraw, the desperado who had once worked his way through the prison roof. Amid the conflicting stories, it seemed prudent for Sasha's accomplices to lie low. That last time at Schwab's, Zipporah must have known all about the botched undertaking in Allegheny City. She might have told me. Sophie's voice admonished, "What do you expect, trust? Angel you may be, Maxie. Even so, you cannot buy your way in." I answered back that I couldn't seem to buy my way out, either.

When our mail delivery resumed, there was a letter from Bromley. "My dearest brother," Nina wrote. "We have just now returned to England after several exhausting weeks in Paris. You can well imagine what it was for me to consort with comrades who even now call Vilna, St. Petersburg, and our own Kovno *home*. Sophie one evening assembled something like our youthful circle, though we missed Fanya, and you hovering about, and M——, whose name I forbid myself to utter. We laughed to remember you, Maxie, with your ear to the door. Rest assured, our latter-day company included a fair complement of *men*. Olga Stepanov was there with her brother, your boyhood friend Sergei. They make an amiable pair, unassuming and quietly devoted to the total destruction of tsarism and the end of the era of the knout. We often have them down to Bromley. Emma came with her newest love in tow, Hippolyte Havel, whom we know from London, a jumpy, bearded little fellow with wild hair. Like her, he must have the last word on everything, especially when he's in his cups. They shan't get on together long, but clearly she has parted from that Brady brute at last. (I think sometimes of my sweet Arshag in Volkova.) With Emma, too, were her Ruttenberg cousins, Fanya's brothers Lev and Fedya, as stolid as when they were boys. Upon these rocks, says Sophie, shall the social revolution be built. They called Emma 'little cousin Chava.' She called them Hinz und Kunz, we assumed not without affection. They asked after various comrades in New York, the Gelb woman especially, though I don't know why, thinking she would be in Paris. They have been underground for months, due to the unfortunate discovery by the secret police of their press in Riga, whence they removed themselves two years ago after the death of their parents. (I convey their apologies to Fanya for not sending word sooner.)

"The authorities in Paris (who call themselves socialist!) withdrew permission for the congress at the eleventh hour, so that all the meetings were held in secret. Gathering amidst the danger of imminent betrayal, ever concerned about informers, we might have been in Slobodka, at Kazimierz Wojcicki's flat, and not the land of the first great revolution. Suspicion naturally fell on those highly ardent spirits whom, upon inquiry, no one seemed to know. One Russian lad, not unattractive but with rather too much of *une manière insinuante*, approached Sophie and me, separately. His suggestive mien bespoke familiarity, though I certainly could not place him. I thought he meant to slip away with me to some intimate *estaminet*, but no: his expressed passion was for propaganda by deed, and his allegiance to a certain International Revolutionary Order. He said a rendezvous could be arranged between myself and the group's leader, who goes by the *nom de guerre* of Michel Bourg. I of course refused and told the young spy his *soi-disant* International Order was nothing to me, and, further, for an anarchist of any true stripe, a 'leader' does not signify. I needn't tell you with what words Sophie dismissed this scum, who slunk away, not to be seen again. It is to our shame and horror that Michel Bourg translates to Michael Borough. But I must not continue! Concerning M— and his brutalities, let me, at least for the moment, think *no more*.

"With some others of our sister comrades, we stayed on in

Paris a few days longer to attend a conference of the banned Neo-Malthusians on birth limitation. Yet another gathering forced underground for the people's protection! Emma quite rightly bridled at remarks, directed at the Americans, deriding 'their' benighted Anthony Comstock. She reminded one and all that we met in hiding by the courtesy of *la république française*. As a nurse and midwife, she took an especial interest in the practical application of devices that, I confess, I would blush to describe. Sophie rose to contend that poverty is above all a matter of the equitable distribution of the common wealth, the spectre of overpopulation being something of a mote in the Malthusian eye. The shock of her statement provoked cries of 'For shame!' Sophie stood her ground. Moral restraint, she averred, is an individual choice even in this age of science, provided the choice be made free of governmental and religious coercions, not to mention the body's spring tide of vital impulses. A rare free choice indeed! So long as 'moral restraint' remains a woman's one and only choice, she will be the slave to endless childbearing and ever vulnerable to insidious diseases, an ignorant, ineducable breeder, a replaceable cipher, in short, a mere chattel. 'Not overpopulation but undervaluation of half of all humankind—it is that aspect, precisely, of the social question we are here to address.'

"Sophie was moved by the 'Bravos' she received from the comrades, who, led by Emma, rose to their feet. There is some irony in her consideration of 'moral restraint.' How often has Sophie chided me for my *un*restraint! How often has she said, thinking of Kazimierz and her lost child, it was given her once to love with body, mind, and heart; that season of life was past; her body, mind, and heart she now devoted to the Cause.

"A striking woman, in a shirtwaist suit of rich green velvet trimmed with Belgian lace, came over then to speak with us. Amongst *toutes les femmes*, she was by far the most excellently appareled. She introduced herself as a delegate from Alsace but conversed in perfect Russian. She put out her hand and said in the frankest manner: "A brilliant speech, Sophia Petrovna—but from you I would expect no less. I am Ariane Lévy-Mendès. Perhaps you know my name." Maxie, I must say! Little wonder you followed her all the way to Paris! After the day's session, we three repaired to a *bistro* nearby, already *fast friends*. She spoke of you not unkindly, nor was she incurious to hear of your life in America and lovely children, and said she couldn't have hoped for more. She herself is childless, as a matter of principle, though married to a physician in Strasbourg, a distant cousin, also a Lévy-Mendès. It was her stay at Kovno that decided her against child-bearing. A prosperous family, a house full of children, and so much unhappiness! She of course intended no offense, and we took none. As Sophie observed, all bourgeois families are alike, happy or unhappy, in that they must add to the general unhap-piness of the working class. Ariane has studied nursing in London and, you will be pleased to know, speaks English well. She works alongside her husband, Alois, and administers a clinic for women, in which gynaecological capacity she was now in Paris. I am dis-tressed to say, she then broached the subject of M——. Two days previously, whilst taking her *petit déjeuner* in a café off the Boulevard St.-Germain, he appeared out of nowhere and sat him-self down at her table. She knew him the moment he said with derision, 'Madame Ariane.' He hinted that he'd been following her for days and was privy to her dossier. A woman like her, said he, would be useful to him and his group. Ariane answered coolly, 'And what dossier, *mon homoncule*, is that?' He grabbed at her wrist as she rose to go and said, 'You were good enough for Maxie.' She rapped his knuckles with a knife handle and strode off ... Terrible to hear! Sophie had the presence of mind to advise Ariane to depart from Paris without delay, whilst I——I could only avert my eyes. From the quiet urgency in Sophie's voice, Ariane understood the danger she was in and determined to leave for Strasbourg that very night. She promised to write upon her safe return home——which she has done!——and to call on us next spring at Bromley, following a planned lecture she is to give at the Nightingale School, St. Thomas's Hospital.

"Brother dear, I am weary from these past weeks, and you will forgive me, I know, for declining to speak of them further. I have given you, as Sophie would say, *the sum and substance*. With loving affection, &c., to you and yours, Nina."

I read the letter in the dull light of a December afternoon, standing by the bay windows in the library. Like a Greek chorus in the ancient plays I studied at *gimnaziya*, my mind weighed rumors from afar. The letter in my hand was a herald bearing reports from offstage, from the field I'd long ago meant to abandon and forget. As drama, *Maximus Rex* wasn't quite tragedy or comedy, but something in between. That day, a choral refrain echoed and reechoed these words of Zipporah Gelb's: "If Nina does find Mishka in Paris, you'll know I'm dead."

VI

The Gravedigger's Tears

ZIPPORAH GELB'S NAME was gone from the mailbox on Allen Street. There was no one I could find who would talk about her disappearance. She never let on which Russians, precisely, were party to the hunt for Mishka. In Schwab's Saloon, the comrades who knew her dropped their eyes and shrugged, as if I'd turned from angel to informer. Sach's Café was shut. I told Zak I'd been paying Zipporah to find Mishka. He was surprised she'd strung me along, it didn't seem her way. I explained that I'd gone along with it on account of him and Ida. Zak looked grim. He said we could only hope Mishka stayed in Paris and someone over there finished Zipporah's job. We made inquiries among the landlords to whom we'd sold our ghetto properties years before. We learned that Zipporah's rent was in arrears since August. In November, her flat was cleared out. Of the furniture and effects, what wasn't sold off to the junk peddlers was left in the street for scavengers. I wondered what happened to Zipporah's little gun.

Fanny pored over Nina's letter. She didn't care that Mishka might be a secret agent. My sisters and cousin Emma she dismissed as tiresome show-offs. What infuriated her was the mention of her brothers, and also of Ariane. "Max," she said, "say you've forgotten her." I hesitated, searching for the proper words.

She groaned and held her stomach as though she'd been kicked. I told her not to upset herself. Ariane was a distant memory from half a lifetime ago. If we didn't have that photograph with her in it, I'd hardly remember how she looked. Fanny tore the Kovno grouping off the wall and threw it out the window into the garden, where it fell face down in the snow. As for her brothers, it was unspeakable that they would send the news of her parents' death two years late and at third hand. For all Fanny knew, her mother and father were cut down in the street by Cossacks—not that it meant anything to her, not really, after they'd slighted her all these years. Dead was dead. Her brothers were oxes. Sophie was a fool to think they'd so much as blink if an actual revolution broke out in front of their eyes. Fanny wept and couldn't sleep for days. Dr. Schapira came and prescribed a treatment of chloral to relieve what he called an acute temporary anxiety hysteria common to women her age. "What she wants, Mr. Kraft," he said, "is another child."

The Kovno portrait wasn't damaged. I took it to a retoucher, who made enlarged copies of Pyotr Mikhailovich and my youthful self, framed in silhouette. These we hung in the dining room. The original photograph I saved in a leather case kept for miscellany—old letters, Uncle Henry's stereopticon postcards of America's great views, and the like. Basya was triumphant to see Vera Andreyevna and her darlings removed at last. Fanny, when she was herself again, made no comment but straightened the new pictures, as if they'd been there all along and been knocked awry while she wasn't looking. She didn't mention Ariane. Except for the occasion of that one outburst, we'd never discussed her before. Fanny must have pieced together the story from what she heard from my sisters, or perhaps Zak and Abby. I always referred to the young woman in the back row of the family portrait as, simply, the French governess. Certain things were better left unspoken and, so I thought, the easier forgot. As Fanny said, talking wouldn't stop the hand of history from seizing you by the throat. Everyone wanted a retreat from life. In Xanadu, our Oriental den, she decreed a paradise: no history, no children, no revolution. There I wore my smoking jacket and cap and read aloud from Coleridge, the *Rubáiyat*, and even, in English, the Song of Solomon, since it had no mention of God. Fanny made up her face with white rice powder and said she was the Queen of Eden. I'd hardly have thought to bring up Dr. Schapira's advice if Fanny hadn't done so first, one evening while she was smoking fragrant Egyptian cigarettes and nibbling on marzipan and nougat. She blew a series of smoke rings. "Look, Max," she said, "a circle in a circle. You know what some people would say." I thought she meant the game our children played, and answered: "What goes up the chimney ... Smoke ... May your wish ... Never be broke." Fanny's hand cut through the loosening rings. She laughed sharply and said that wasn't how Dr. Schapira put it. She should try to be aware of the symbolic expressions of her unconscious wish. I said he'd broached the matter with me as well. "Did he?" said Fanny. "So nice of him to tell me." The previous year, Dr. Schapira attended some lectures on psychology in Vienna. Since then, she said, he'd been insufferable, as if none of us knew what was really on our minds. He should stick to proper medicine. Instead of Vienna, he ought to have gone to that Malthusian meeting in Paris. Fanny insisted the only wish-fulfillment fantasy she had was to own a good supply of those little devices that supposedly made Nina blush. After that, we found symbolic expressions of our unconscious everywhere. Zak and Abby joined in the play, and it became a family joke.

I hardly thought of Zipporah Gelb without her there to dun me. I supposed myself coldhearted, as I'd sometimes been told. Zak said not at all, otherwise why would I question myself. In his village, there was a saying, "The gravedigger's tears are the most terrible of all." We could put a private detective on the case, but to what purpose and on whose behalf? If we learned for sure that Zipporah had been murdered, or even that she'd gone back to Russia, like Fanny's brothers, for the police that would only mean one red agitator fewer to spy on. It was better to let the details surface as they might, without our stirring up muddy waters. I recalled that the body of Ivanov, the comrade Nechayev shot, rose from the bottom of a pond in Petrovsky Park, despite the stones that weighed it down.

When Nina, in the dead of winter, wrote with terrible news, I saw the name Zipporah, somehow, where it clearly read Ariane. She enclosed a story from *Die Elsässer Nachrichten* that was sent to her anonymously. The newspaper clipping said the doctor's wife, a Polish-French Jewess and known feminist radical, fell from an upper-story window of her husband's clinic, an apparent suicide. Sophie and Nina sent their condolences to the bereaved Dr. Lévy-Mendès. He wrote back and called the inquest a reactionist sham, by a coroner who held to the insane race theories of Gobineau. The report did not mention that the window from which Ariane had purportedly jumped was an overhead transom through which she could only have been pushed while unconscious. Nor did it say that her broken neck showed signs of strangulation, and that her body was bruised as if kicked. Perhaps the followers of Herzl were right: we Jews might hope to survive only in a country of our own. Here, for us, there could be no justice.

"Maxie," wrote Nina, "we are *desolated*. Sophie cannot bring herself to discuss this nightmare with anyone, Comrade Kropotkin least of all. There are private matters that fall beyond the pale of general scrutiny. She has simply informed Pyotr Alexeyevich, without explanation, that we shall be sorry not to accompany him on his next tour of America, for which he is, as you surely have heard, shortly to depart. In his kindly way, he has expressed regret and asked no questions. The pall that hangs over us now conjures up those dark days when we were taken back to Kovno with Kazimierz Wojcicki's body bag at our feet, the guards eyeing us, whilst we grieved; likewise the start of our second exile, going on foot from Tomsk to Chita, kept apart from the rest of the marchers, the soldiers wives and the convicts in chains, who whispered, not quite out of hearing, '*Jewess*.'"

Only once did Nina allude to Mishka, and then with constraint. She said that while Kropotkin was away, she and Sophie would go abroad, albeit with foreboding, to attend to our troubled family affairs. I understood by this that they would return to Paris soon and make themselves available for an interview with the elusive Michel Bourg.

Grief seized me all at once. It picked me up and threw me down. I dosed myself with Fanny's chloral and dreamed I was on the Nemen again, which was the Styx frozen over, skating around the world. Two hands grip me at the waist. I turn my head and see the dead trailing behind, linked in a mournful, swaying chain. The hands that hold me are my mother's. Following her,

crouched, each at an arm's length from the other, are my father—Jurgis Bobelis—Aunt Libby—Uncle Henry—Pyotr Mikhailovich—Osgood—Carl Franks—Daisy—Alice—Zipporah—
Ariane. Their eye sockets are hollow. A thin twitter comes out of
the closed black slits of their mouths. Their bare feet scrape the
ice like steel blades. In the Sachs's Café that is the garden of my
stepfather's villa, I sit with the dead at a long table, directly across
from Daisy and Alice. No one speaks, but a voice, my own, says
to the girls: *Forgive me, I pray ye. I knew not.* A rise of whispery
twittering responds: *Never do they know.* Now it is Zipporah and
Ariane who sit opposite, their mouths broken open in soundless
laughter that turns shrill and shrieking: *His mother died when he
was but five years of age!* Bony feet rub against my legs. I reach
out for Fanny's hand and pull awake, shouting. I sat on the edge
of the bed while Fanny rocked me with her arms. "Max," she
said, "forgive me."

VII

Michel Bourg

THE RISE OF the Paris Commune, like Haymarket, was a yearly remembrance. The thirtieth anniversary came and went without Zipporah importuning. Fanny thought she'd gone back to Russia. "And may she be happy underground, with my brothers," she said. "But there at least she's safe from Mishka." I didn't worry the point, not wanting to rouse forebodings. Mishka could be anywhere and everywhere at once, or so he'd have me believe. Ariane's murder was an ugly shock. Abby asked how we could know for sure that Mishka was the one who did it. Even as she spoke, she knew it was so, and added: "Max, you don't think he'll go after your sisters?" I remembered Mishka clinging to Sophie and Nina that Sabbath eve we were driven from the village of Chassidim, near Vitebsk. For years he trailed them, all the way to Blagoveshchensk, and planned their escape down the Amur. I told Abby he wouldn't kill them; he wanted to prove he was their hero. Me, I thought, Mishka hated. He wouldn't kill me either, on account of my money, but I didn't say so.

Zak had second thoughts about letting matters lie. He went down to the ghetto, to the offices of the *Free Workers' Voice*, hat in hand like a greenhorn, and asked after Zipporah Gelb. He'd grown a bristly mustache like Colonel Roosevelt's and didn't think anyone would recognize him. No one did. Who was it, he was asked, that was looking for Comrade Gelb? Her cousin Isaac from Vilna, said Zak in the proper accent, only two days in America. Zipporah hadn't been seen for months. Perhaps she'd gone back to Vilna and passed him going in the other direction. Zak was told to try the Russian Progressive Union. Zipporah was homey with Russians. There Zak was able to convince a Comrade Rogovoy that he was no spy and, after a glass of schnapps at Schwab's, not Zipporah's cousin either, but the business partner of Max Kraft. "The next glass is on me then," said Rogovoy. "I'm paying with your partner's money."

The Russian was privy to Zipporah's counterplot. He'd gone to Daisy's and Alice's family in Boston and delivered the blackmail to lure Mishka. More than once Rogovoy thought he had him, but Mishka always sent someone in his place to pick up the money from its hiding hole. One time, Rogovoy followed a lean, small man with a big head all the way to Milford by train. The fellow turned on him with a knife at the station platform and shouted "Thief!" in Italian. Last August, suddenly, Zipporah vanished. "Back to Russia?" said Zak. Rogovoy shrugged. It could be. Or she might have wanted everyone to think she'd gone back, to draw Mishka into the open. Zipporah was becoming sly and didn't necessarily reveal her full intentions. "On the other hand," said Rogovoy. He drew a finger across his throat. Zak told him that was our thinking as well, that Mishka had done the deed and slipped off to Europe. Nina's letters were the brutal evidence for the Russian. He called Mishka a rabid wolf that should be shot at all costs. "Exactly," said Zak. Zipporah knew it. Wherever she was, we mustn't let her down. Rogovoy rubbed a thumb and forefinger together and wondered who would cover the expense of his going abroad. Zak reminded him who was paying for the schnapps. They drank to the angel Max.

After meeting with Rogovoy, Zak went to the shop. Marco and I were figuring payroll expenses and materiel for the coming season. Silver & Kraft had subcontracted demolition work along the new subway line up the West Side. Blowing up houses was brainless labor that paid well. I said too bad about the old crew; the men would have been in their element. Marco didn't smile. "Please, Mr. Kraft," he said. "For me, this is no joke. Remember

Gaetano." He meant Gaetano Bresci, a comrade from Paterson who returned to Italy the summer before and shot the king of Italy. Marco was worried the immigration authorities would still link him to the assassin. He'd met Bresci once at a May Day picnic—a very gentle man, he said, who had done a sad, brave, and useless deed. Zak arrived a little drunk and full of his plan. He wanted me to wire my sisters immediately at Bromley to find out their Paris address. I said it was pointless. Kropotkin left for America weeks ago. He was in Boston now and would be in New York in a few days. Cousin Emma was taking on Sophie's role, making all the arrangements and telling everyone what to do. It was all in the newspapers. Zak smacked his forehead. He'd forgot. I said there was another thing he didn't remember. My dollars didn't cross borders. I wouldn't pay Rogovoy or anyone else to leave America. I wouldn't now and never had.

Marco took out his Dante. He turned a page or two and said without looking up, "Life outside society, says Bakunin, is death to man. And I say, man against life is death to society. This principle goes beyond national borders, which—*non è vero?*—have not to do with ethical significance. It is not for ourselves that we must do this thing." Zak approved Marco's reasoning. He followed the trail of money from my pocket to Zipporah, from Zipporah to Rogovoy, from Rogovoy to the family of Daisy and Alice, thence to Mishka via his doubles. If Mishka was in fact traveling back and forth between here and Europe, with whose dollars did I suppose that half brother of mine prowled his murderer's path?

I allowed that there was some truth in their arguments. I owned that Mishka had put himself out of the reach of compassion. He had no pity for others and would accept none for himself. Nevertheless, I refused knowingly to give this Rogovoy, whom Zak had only just met, the wherewithal to quit the country. Zipporah was another matter. She never told me precisely what she was up to. "And you never asked?" said Zak. I explained that she and I had an understanding. At that moment, her voice came into my mind, with a clarity that promised it would come again. Zipporah repeated what she said that last time at Schwab's: "What you mean, Max, is I do the dirty work and let you know when it's over." Marco, still looking into his book, inquired as to the nature of this understanding between Zipporah and me. "Europe wasn't in her reckoning," I answered, to cut the matter short. "Zipporah said to me, if Mishka went to Paris, I'd know she was dead." I left the shop. This time, let Zak pay. There was still the question of Ida and what Mishka knew. Rogovoy could reconnoiter the Poste Générale until he found Michel Bourg. Afterward, let him sit with a friend over a bottle of wine and laugh about the American moneybags, the angel Zak.

Kropotkin was speaking at the Grand Central Palace on the last afternoon of March, a Sunday. Cousin Emma organized a dinner party for friends to follow. She invited Fanny and me, to fill the seats my sisters should have taken. Something told Fanny we ought to attend. "This is respectable," she said, laughing. "This is America. Here, a 'comrade' becomes a 'prince' and writes his memoirs in *The Atlantic Monthly*." She could talk this way now, even in Xanadu, our Oriental den. What happened to the poor French governess made her realize that the dark side of the revolution wasn't revolution at all, but a matter for Dr. Schapira's professor in Vienna. Capitalists and revolutionists called each other deranged criminals! It was really very funny when you thought about it—Fanny laughed again—as if the whole of anything were defined by the shabbiest part, any more than coffee and wine were by the dregs. Why shouldn't we instead judge the whole of everything by the sum of its happiest effects? Surely, that was at the heart of Kropotkin's thinking. "Of course we'll go, Max." Fanny lighted a cigarette and lay back on the divan. She blew a stream of smoke at the ceiling, laughed once more at the follies of mankind, and then was seized by a fit of coughing, followed by the onset of a migraine that split her vision in two. I sent Emma our regrets, along with money toward her spring lecture tour through the Midwest. "My dear comrade Max, bless you," she wrote back. It was pleasant for once to be thanked.

Julius Schapira, M.D., repeated his concern about Fanny's wanting another child. He'd finished making a call upstairs and sat with me in the library, looking through the parlor and dining room to the budding magnolias in the garden. I told him what she really wanted was rest. Dr. Schapira observed the house. He knew the children were enrolled in private school. On several occasions, Fanny had the livery send the surrey for him, to save her the trouble of visiting his offices. "Rest from what?" he asked. Sophie's voice admonished me, "History shall give no rest." Zipporah echoed, "No escape." I said, aloud, that it wasn't easy running so large a house. We also owned a hotel upstate, and Mrs. Kraft kept a careful eye on the business. As I saw him to the door, we passed Sadie Mirkin, the housemaid Basya had insisted on hiring, with a tray of noodle soup and egg bread for Fanny. "Business indeed," said Dr. Schapira.

Fanny lay propped up in bed to prevent the blood from rushing to her temples. The curtains were drawn against the daylight. She wore dark goggles but knew me by my footsteps. The tray of food was untouched. She whispered that we needed a new doctor. There must be more to modern psychology than this one had to offer, if—she sighed—psychology in fact had anything to do with these headaches of hers. "New doctor indeed," I said, in Julius Schapira's basso profundo. Fanny asked please not to make her laugh. I thought how soon we might dispose of the *Free Inquiry into the Scientific Basis of the Religion of the Hebrews*, Dr. Schapira's hypocritical tract. "Eat this," I said, and fed Fanny small spoonfuls of soup and bits of bread. I told her everything was set at Stump Lake. Just as soon as she was on her feet, we'd take the pleasure boat up the Hudson. Fanny asked, between swallows, what Ida had to say. In the monthly accounts, Ida had enclosed a note protesting that through the summer was already too short a time for Mrs. Kraft to stay. She should remain through the Jewish high holidays, for the roast beef after the fast Ida was introducing in place of the customary chicken and fish. "The guests should remember, shouldn't they, Mr. Kraft, that this is America." Fanny began to feel better. She said, "I'll be home before then. This year, Max, instead of Delmonico's, we'll throw our own Yom Kippur ball."

Zak and Marco were relieved to have me out of the shop for a while, though they didn't say so. They didn't talk about Rogovoy in my presence, and wouldn't until he'd done away with Mishka, or Mishka him. When Fanny and I arrived at Stump Lake, the dogwood was in flower. Ida had planted a path of trees from the manor house down to the lake. We celebrated my birthday at Kraft's Hotel. Ida announced to the dining room, "Thirty-five years of age, and almost half of them in America!" I blew out the candles on a colossal cake all in one breath. The guests applauded and tried to sing "For he's a jolly good fellow" without an accent. Ida's Barnard scampered about making faces, but no one paid him any mind. He ran against my arm as I was cutting the cake, and half the topmost layer slid to the floor. A groan rose from the guests. Barney disappeared under a table and didn't come out until he was assured, with many pleas, that it wasn't his fault Uncle Max's birthday cake was ruined. He looked at me with liquid eyes but kept his distance, as if he guessed I'd have dragged him through the dogwood by his Fauntleroy locks and whirled him into the lake. I told Fanny to watch out for that boy or she'd never get her proper rest. "Max," she said, "you exaggerate."

The plan was for me to stay at Stump Lake every other week and, once school was over, to park the children there for the summer. When I went up for the second time, Barney had worked his way into Fanny's good graces. "What a charmer he is," she said. "The way he tricks pennies from the guests—it's really very clever. He goes from one to the next, saying guess what Mr. or Mrs. So-and-so gave me. Let me see, they ask, licorice, jelly beans? A penny, says Barney. Only one? Here's two!" I quoted Poor Richard. A penny saved was a penny earned. Honesty was the best policy. The boy was a regular little Benjamin Franklin. I wondered how many pennies he got from her for his candor, but Fanny wouldn't say.

While the children were with Fanny, I heard from my sisters. Pyotr Alexeyevich was in poor health, wrote Nina. The strain of his American tour was taking its toll, for all the admiring newspaper accounts. Yes, there were successes, but failure lay hard upon his heart. Perhaps I'd learned of his attempt to see Comrade Berkman at the penitentiary. It was not enough that a man of Pyotr Alexeyevich Kropotkin's renown was refused the visit. The prisoner himself, already in solitary confinement, was sent to the dungeon for days afterward. "Thus bourgeois democracy silently comments upon itself," was written in the margin of the letter in Sophie's hand.

Nina continued. "We have not troubled our ailing comrade with a report of our own encounter with (shall I say it?) Mishka, nor even now do we know whether to call that, too, *success* or *failure*. You will recall, dear brother, my telling you of a young Russian fire-breather at the clandestine congress last autumn who proposed to lead us to 'Michel Bourg.' This same fellow again made an appearance, at our pension, in response to a letter for MB we left at the Poste Générale, and this time the meeting was arranged. We made our strange rendezvous at a shabby *bistro* in the Faubourg Saint-Germain. Mishka held to the guise of Michel Bourg, I suppose for the benefit of his *aide-de-camp*, speaking atrocious French. The Russian would not leave us, but sat silently the while, building tiny hutches out of matchsticks and then, with a smirk, collapsing them. He is called Comrade Gorovoy, a name that jarred me into recollection. Years ago, a certain Rogovoy, a pretty fellow, attended meetings of the Russian Progressive Union. The Gelb woman straightway collected him for herself. This Gorovoy is surely he, transposed into a twin anagrammatic self. Sophie concluded the same. She taxed the Russian point-blank, in English, with his and Zipporah Gelb's cliquism of years ago, adding politely, 'That is, if memory serves.' Gorovoy and MB both were made uncomfortable by the mention of Zipporah's name. I do believe that she has taken the entire spear side of the revolution to bed with her. (You know full well, Maxie, that I of all people do not disapprove of her exercise of free love, but merely the *saloperie* of her practice.) Gorovoy pretended not to understand, and with a wild gesture of incomprehension swept away a matchstick house. MB pursed his lips and, shrugging in the Gallic manner, said, '*Inconséquente.*'

"Just then, a motor car came jouncing along the street and let out a sudden clap, like a gunshot. A waiter dropped his tray at the sound. The customers started in their seats, all except MB and Gorovy, who crouched momentarily to the floor, the latter holding a small pistol. '*Ah,*' I exclaimed, '*c'est beau, le petit pétard! J'aime le travail exquis.*' The Russian could not but hand the object over. It was of American manufacture, a lady's gun with a wrought barrel and carved handle of ivory. I gave it back with an expression of admiration. Sophie placed her foot on mine, as if to say, '*Comrade Gorovoy's memento of New York.*' "

Better *memento mori*, I though. Now I knew who in fact killed Zipporah and what happened to her gun. The Roman funeral procession came to mind. Mishka and Rogovoy shuffled along, with donned masks of their own faces. Zipporah's voice rang in my head. "The Brothers Kraft; everyone does their dirty work for them. Get in line where you belong, Max. The long march to nowhere."

"Almost in the same breath," Nina wrote, "Sophie asked what derring-do Gorovoy intended with his toy pistol, and MB what this International Revolutionary Order of his might try to effect that were better accomplished openly. The Russian bit his lips and made no immediate reply. MB recited the articles of Nechayev's *Catechism of a Revolutionary*—with Gorovoy joining in by snatches—sitting straight in his chair, chin up, like a proud schoolboy. 'You have proposed a means,' said Sophie, 'outdated and discredited, toward an uncertain end divined a generation ago, when we were children. The scope of revolution is all-inclusive.' MB challenged us to name our revolutionary successes of the last thirty years, *barring Volkova*. Sophie would not rise to the bait. In quiet reproof, she demonstrated the provincialism of the *Nechayevsti*. 'Russia,' she said, 'is not the world.'

"MB responded in Russian. Even now, he said, the vanguard of the revolution was preparing for the inevitable. Student protests in the streets of St. Petersburg and Moscow, the assassination of Bogolepov, the minister of so-called education—did we think these were without design? Sophie and I have become soft from Western ways, corrupted by pandering to the liberal bourgeoisie. When the great upheaval comes, as it must within the next few years, the world will look to Russia and heed the call of the International Revolutionary Order. 'You mean to return then,' said Sophie. 'It is our dearest wish also, when the time is right.' To which he countered, 'I mean to return tomorrow. The time is now.' Sophie shook her head. Impulsively, I reached across the table and took both his hands in mine. He pulled away, with a mad, cold look in his eyes. Our interview was at an end—and not a word said of Ariane Lévy-Mendès. We do believe Mishka has indeed quit Paris and gone to Russia, Gorovoy with him. We have lost a brother. Henceforward, we will neither speak nor write of him *again*.

"Your loving sisters. Nina. Sophie."

Zak read the letter with unease. "I don't believe it," he said. He didn't like to lose money. I supposed my sisters had their means of learning where Mishka and Rogovoy went after skipping France. That Sophie signed her name, and even underlined it, twice, was another way of saying all of the above was true. Marco thought Sophie was likely to get word to her comrades in Russia of the rogue informers' coming. If so, Zak's money was well spent. I didn't argue, relieved no longer to be the prize dupe of the revolution. "Revolution?" The voice was Zipporah's. "The revolution didn't murder me, Max. Don't blacken our great dream.

VIII

Fanya and Chava

I BROUGHT FANNY and the children home before the high holidays. Joey and Elizabeth wept on leaving Stump Lake. They hid in the woods in one of Barney's secret places, a platform perched among the branches of a beech tree, not far from the now forgotten Gypsy's grave. It took me all morning to find them. I called up to them, and they climbed higher, losing themselves in the leaves, the way I scrambled from Bobelis that time in Kovno, but without giggling. Barney was with them; otherwise they'd have come down the moment I appeared. Fanny was weary from children's antics. She wanted to stay for a month in Xanadu and sleep. "Forget our Yom Kippur ball, Max," she said. "This year, not even Delmonico's." Put American children in the country and they became savages. Barney was a devil, a regular Apache. Just picture him with a little paint and his blond curls dark. It was Ida's fault, spoiling the boy and letting him run wild. Abby said at dinner, "Don't be too hard on her, dear. She's all alone in the world and has to do the best she can with him. Sometimes I think we don't really appreciate how fortunate we are." She smiled at Zak and squeezed his hand. I said not to worry about Ida. Kraft's Hotel was filled all year round and in the black, thanks to her. The small capital she had from selling her millinery she invested in the local telephone concession, which she now owned. She held the mortgage on the biggest furniture factory and repair shop, used by the sanatoriums and other guesthouses. Her son was going to be an attorney. He was going to study at Harvard. If the law school maybe didn't welcome our kind now, she said, when Barnard Sussman's time came, it would. I didn't add what Ida also told me: "Isidore will be proud of the boy, don't you think so, Mr. Kraft."

Because of the weeks I spent at Stump Lake, the shop accounts were in a muddle. I was going over receipts early on a Saturday morning. Zak was apologetic. He'd been out on the job too much, to keep his mind off Rogovoy. He found the demolition work exciting. I joked, quoting Bakunin: "The passion for destruction is also creative." Zak said, "Exactly. It brings in money." We agreed that if the books were in a mess, it was better due to gains than losses. Profits looked to be so good that Zak expected he and Abby would do some touring when the building season was over. I cautioned that winter was no time to see America. Zak grinned in the boyish way he had when he intended mischief. "We're going to Europe, Max," he said. "I've already booked passage for the first of December."

Zak sketched the itinerary. While he talked, I remembered falling in with his group on the road to Brody, Zak writhing on the ground with his twisted ankle, how we carried him across the Austrian border at night, the two of us on the train to Berlin, our quarantine in the German barracks, the farewell we said in the English I'd taught him: "Good-bye, we shall see each other again soon, in America." Abby wanted to visit all the cities where Uncle Henry had lived, Geneva, Königsberg, Kovno. She thought it was especially important for her, American-born, to experience the places her immigrant brethren were leaving in such great numbers. They'd be going to Brody and even Zak's village, from which he'd run away so long ago. I was speechless. It was eighteen years since we arrived in America. Zak said he'd never meant to see his village again, but Abby's heart was for it. He owed her so much, how could he let her down? I shrugged, thinking there were easier ways to distance himself from Ida. Zak put his hand on my shoulder. "They can't hurt us over there, Max," he said. "We're Americans."

Marco rushed into the shop, leaving the street door swinging wide. Zak shouted, "What! An accident?" Marco dropped a newspaper on the table. His face was ashen. The headlines announced that President McKinley had been shot in Buffalo by an anarchist named Czolgosz, a follower of Emma Goldman. A police search for her was on. "She's for it now," said Zak. Marco could barely speak. "*Sì*," he choked, "*e la tutta Causa.*" I said nothing. I ran my eyes over the page, looking for any mention of Borough or Bourg or Kraft, and was relieved to find none. I told Zak he couldn't leave the country now. What if he weren't allowed back? At home, Fanny groaned at the news, as if the hand of history were already gripping her neck and the police were at the door. She sat in the parlor with her arms tight across her midriff. "But I have to talk to Emma," she said. "No one else can help." Fanny confessed she was expecting a child. Abby hurried over and hugged her. "Don't worry, dear," she said. "We can find another midwife. It doesn't really have to be her, does it? Just imagine, a new baby in the house!" Fanny burst out, "I'm not your substitute! I'm not going to have it! It will kill me!" Abby ran from the room.

In the next weeks, Fanny purged herself with salts, took hot baths, and threw herself down the stairs. She refused to see Dr. Schapira. Known anarchists were beaten in the streets and jailed. The *Free Workers' Voice* denounced the assassination. Its offices were smashed to pieces nevertheless. Cousin Emma was arrested in Chicago and held without bail. Only she among the American comrades spoke with concern about the fate of the assassin, whom no one seemed to know. She was released on the day of his conviction, not three weeks after the shooting, and dropped from sight. Fanny said I had to do something to find her, but there was nothing I could do. The ever prominent Red Emma had gone underground. Abby obtained in the ghetto the names of some women said to perform illegal operations. She handed the list to me, to do with it what I liked. Fanny and Abby weren't talking. A month after Leon Czolgosz was electrocuted, Zak and Abby sailed for Europe as planned. I misplaced the paper Abby gave me. I wondered if losing it wasn't a symbolic expression of my unconscious, as in the family joke, but didn't say so to Fanny. I made quiet amends with a fruitless search for Emma, not even knowing if she was in the city. Schwab's Saloon was shut, the owner having died. Comrades made themselves scarce in those months after Czolgosz's trial and execution. In the end, cousin Emma came to us.

Fanny was sick but still wouldn't see Julius Schapira or any other doctor. She remembered the medical advice from the time she carried Elizabeth and drank copious amounts of water and ate no fruit or sweets. Her swollen face was made up with rice powder and paint, like Zipporah's after being pounded and kicked by Mishka. In her discomfort, Fanny was impatient with the children. Basya hired a governess to watch over them. We now had three servants living in: Sadie Mirkin the housemaid, Celia Wilner the governess, and Basya Gittelman as reigning housekeeper and cook. They all spoke the Yiddish of the Baltic provinces, but minded my rule to do so only in the kitchen. It was Sadie the housemaid who opened the door one night in January to a small, shivering woman who called herself Miss E. G. Smith.

Emma was distraught, her clothing untidy and her talk incoherent. She'd always been neat and articulate. I told Sadie to bring a glass of tea to warm our guest, Miss Smith. Emma said whiskey. After two shots of bourbon, she began to cry. Emma had always been tough. I caught the word "Worcester." She remembered harrying me out into the night, when my arguments had been so right about violence, about revolution having to be made in the language of the place. Now she was the pariah, deserted by her comrades for speaking with any compassion of that unfortunate boy who killed McKinley, who said before they threw the switch on the electric chair, "I did it alone. I did it for the American people." Emma took another shot of whiskey. She handed me a letter from Sasha, smuggled out of the Western Penitentiary. "I haven't slept. For days, Max," she stuttered. "Not since I got this." The letter was several pages long, filled to the margins in a minuscule hand, a meditation on propaganda by deed and Sasha's own sore experience resulting from his attempt on Frick. It seemed that his sentence had been shortened in a general commutation. With four years left in prison, he would not now try again to escape. He also disagreed with Emma about the worth of what Czolgosz had done. Since the importance of an *Attentat* lay in its public perception, McKinley's assassination was of no value, no matter the pure motives of the youth who felt driven to it. "I regard my own act as far more significant and educational than Leon's," wrote Sasha. "It was directed against a tangible, real oppressor, visualized as such by the people."

I wanted to say both acts were futile, links in an endless chain of human brutalities. I was ready to resume the argument at Worcester, but was checked by Emma's furious look. She took back the letter. Three whiskeys had restored her tongue. She rose to her feet and spoke to the library as if to a crowd. "These words," she said, flicking the papers with her fingertips, "these are the words of a Johann Most condemning an Alexander Berkman! These are the words of hypocrisy! These are the words of betrayal!" Then she collapsed onto her chair. "Sasha," she sobbed, "how could he, of all people?" I poured Emma a fourth bourbon, and her story flooded out. After returning to New York from Chicago, she could find no work and no place to live. All doors were closed to the murderess Emma Goldman. She changed her name to Smith and moved from one furnished tenement room to another. For money, she did piecework and took up her nursing in brothels and among the poor, where at least she was welcome. It seemed at any rate a useful way to live, until she lost Sasha. Everything was empty now. She was no good to anyone in this vain world.

"You can be of help to me, Chava." It was Fanny speaking. She stood just inside the library doors, behind cousin Emma, swathed in loose clothing, her puffy face ghostly with powder. "I sent Max for you. I knew you'd come when you could." Emma turned and took in Fanny's condition at a glance. She turned back to me with eyebrows raised, as if to say she'd been roaming the city in her despair and merely happened to be on East Seventy-ninth Street. Then she'd realized she might find a haven here— and a good thing for us she'd come, too. She went over to Fanny and hugged her. "We'll talk things over together, Fanya dear," said Emma. "You and me, the way we did as girls."

The two of them went off the next morning in a hired carriage. While they were gone, I took the children over to the Costanza Court, without their governess, to stay with Marco's family for a few days. Fanny and Emma returned late in the afternoon. "Max," whispered Fanny, "it would have been a girl. No matter." She was half-conscious and bleeding heavily. Emma called for Celia the governess and Sadie the housemaid to help carry Fanny to bed. Basya in the kitchen was boiling towels and sheets. The women bustled up and down the stairs. Antiseptic smells and Yiddish filled the house. I was surprised to hear Emma speak jargon. She told me not to fuss. "We're family," she said. "When I speak in public, I make the revolution in the language of the place—as someone I know once advised me."

Emma was in a fine humor, having taken charge of the house. She moved briskly about and sometimes bumped me playfully on the stairs. The library, she said, was a very masculine room. I contrived to keep her out of Xanadu, which was Fanny's place, saying it was just a storeroom for rubbish from the shop. "If it's junk," she said, "throw it out. If not, then give it to the poor. You don't need to lock it up." I shrugged as she rattled the knob. Zak saved everything, I explained, because of his poverty-stricken childhood in Russia. Emma left off trying the door and nodded gravely.

Fanny slept for twenty-four hours. I stood by the bed with Basya, and once more saw another Fanya, my mother, with a damp lock of hair against a pale face. For Basya, it was the same. "Maxie," she said, "I won't say who she looks like. God forbid it should happen again." She left the room, wiping away tears and, I supposed, rising memories she thought to have buried an ocean away. Cousin Emma came in. Fanny opened her eyes. "What have you two been up to?" she said. Then she added, "Don't tell my brothers. I don't want to see them just yet," and fell back to sleep. Later in the evening, she woke up ravenous and ate two platefuls of Jewish crêpes with sour cream and a large slice of honey cake, while Emma and I sat by the bed. Emma looked at the food doubtfully and asked, if Fanny didn't mind, for a little bite. Fanny said it tasted grand. "Hunger, dear," said Emma, "will make anything taste good."

The following day, Fanny was on her feet and Emma in the kitchen, instructing Basya how to prepare Jewish crêpes. By then, the other servants knew that the Miss E. G. Smith whom Mrs. Kraft called cousin Chava was the anarchist ringleader Emma Goldman. Sadie the housemaid and Celia the governess were impressed but frightened. Basya said they had nothing to fear. Emma was still the chubby friend who came to Pyotr Mikhailovich's villa to play. She was a good girl and came from fine people. Mr. Kraft, too, came from fine people. The bad ones in the lot were the half brothers, Mishka the sharper, and Vera Andreyevna's trash, the three converts. Basya spit three times. All of them were in Russia now, and there they should stay. Just as Emma was descending the stairs, Basya quoted a saying of Zak's from his village: "A woman in her kitchen is the queen of the universe."

Emma said of Basya's crêpes, "I have one criticism to make. Too many eggs in the batter and not enough water. Your results are too thick and doughy." The rest of the disputation was in Yiddish. Basya said, "One egg and two hands full of flour ground, Moist be your noodles and your pancakes browned," and looked to Sadie and Celia for support. They dropped their eyes. Fanny thumbed through a notebook of recipes and didn't look up. Emma said, "If you please," and thinned the mixture. Everyone agreed that Emma's crêpes were finer. Basya blamed Vera Andreyevna's chef for making her halve the amount of flour for every egg, for a richer, yellowy, French batter. She pointed at me with the mixing spoon. If her crêpes were now too heavy, it was Maxie's fault for not saying so.

That night was Emma's last in the house. On the strength of her crêpes, Basya allowed her, just this once, the run of the kitchen. We ate cold beet soup with steaming potatoes, stuffed fish, roast chicken with dumplings and carrot stew, and a dessert of custard with almond cookies. Fanny noted down Emma's recipes to send to Stump Lake. Afterward I brought out a bottle of plum brandy. Sitting at the kitchen table, the women sang, while I would only hum, ballads and lays in Jewish and Russian. Emma took up a German workers' song. Sadie and Celia joined in, after a tentative glance at me. Even Basya sang the fighting refrain, which she'd never have done in my stepfather's kitchen. "This is America," she said in Yiddish. "Here, I consider myself maybe a socialist." She read the *Jewish Daily Forward*. Emma said that kind of socialism meant giving ground to exploitation. Why the *Forward* when she could buy the Cause's own *Free Workers' Voice* just as well? Basya pondered the idea. She declared that from now on, out of respect for Emma's cooking, she'd read them both.

If one such newspaper was good, how much the more so were two.

Later we sat before the parlor fireplace, Fanny, Emma, and I. The coals cast low light and shadow on our faces. Fanny and Emma shared a sofa. In daylight, they'd always looked more like sisters than Sophie and Nina, each with the same clean jawline and wide blue eyes. Even I could scarcely tell them apart in the glow of the fire, except for Fanny's lingering accent. She thanked Emma for everything she'd done. "Chava, dear," she said, "you musn't think the less of me for it." Fanny seemed to be gazing directly into the fire, talking almost to herself. Emma said never! A woman's risk meant a woman's choice. She reminded Fanny what the doctor they'd gone to said: Bringing forth another child would surely have killed her. Emma insisted it was she who must thank us, for taking her mind off Sasha, if only for a while, and restoring her trust in the ties of seasoned friendship. She felt ready to pick up her life again and confront the comrades with their cowardice and suspicions. "It isn't true that Leon Czolgosz was completely unknown to us," she said, "but we denied him, to our shame." She held her head for a moment, and then went on. It was he, calling himself Nieman, who'd come up to her at a lecture that spring in Cleveland, to ask advice about his reading. He approached Emma again in Chicago, where they talked hurriedly on the elevated train. She commended him to the comrades, and they put it in print that Nieman was a spy. "He shot the president," she said, "to tell us it wasn't so. We have spies enough, but never that beautiful boy." I said yes, they had Mishka and Rogovoy.

Emma looked up and corrected me. "You mean Gorovoy, don't you? The one in Paris who kept trying to turn the discussion to bloody *Attentate*." She said he was a fool, not a spy, though a handsome one. Sophie sent him packing just as he was about to sneak off with Nina. Those sisters of mine, for all their talk of free love, kept each other on a short leash. Then she asked what the recluse had to do with it, meaning by this, Mishka. I told her about Michel Bourg and the International Revolutionary Order, about Rogovoy, late of the Russian Progressive Union and now become Gorovoy, possessor of Zipporah Gelb's little gun. Fanny said, "She's dead then, not in Russia with my brothers?" and put her hands over her ears. Emma brooded silently, stroking her underlip like a bearded elder. Come to think of it, she did remember Rogovoy from a meeting years ago of the Russian group, before Zipporah took him up for herself. How terrible for her that she'd fallen for Mishka, too, once again an emancipated woman losing her heart to sick and battered souls. Siberia was a forge of the revolution, but many were broken on the anvil. She could tell me now that the comrades kept a distance from Mishka not because they thought he was an informer, but that he was off his head. The International Revolutionary Order smelled fishy to anyone, but who'd have guessed Mishka was its Nechayev?

I was reminded of what Kropotkin said, likening Nechayev and Dostoyevsky to twins strugglng with each other in the womb of the revolution. Emma said I couldn't have heard that directly from him. I answered no, it was Sophie, who'd reported it to Nina. "As always," said Emma, "lifting their noses above the muck." If our old comrade had compared the two, he'd have been honest enough to add that he didn't think that highly of all the writer's work, finding much of it tedious and eccentric. Fanny was astonished. She said no one but Dostoyevsky had so plumbed the depths of the human heart and bared its vileness to the world. Emma didn't deny it. "There's only one hope, Fanya dear," she said in Russian. "Only one.

IX

Abby's Confession

AT THE END of January, there was a dynamite explosion along the unfinished subway line. Buildings in the area were damaged and several people killed. Zak wired from the Hôtel de France in St. Petersburg. "Not to worry," I wired back. "Accident only. Silver & Kraft not involved." I chose my words carefully, so that Zak and any other parties reading my telegram would understand it was a business communiqué, not evidence on a trail of sabotage. Colonel Roosevelt, the new president, had vowed to rid the country of anarchists and other foreign criminal types, just weeks before the one held most dangerous of them all, cousin Emma, found refuge at our house, carrying with her a smuggled letter from the would-be assassin of Henry Clay Frick. Marco said I, as an angel, should remain incognito, an unrevealed spirit. He feared some of the old crew might turn informer, and that would be the end for him in America and for the shop. He was disappointed by the president's remarks, *tanto barbari, anche imbecilli*, coming from the hero of San Juan Hill, the man who had humbled the Church of Spain. Marco was agitated and took out his Dante to fidget with while we talked. I said that in America even the president had the right to speak foolishly; his words didn't straightway become law. One bad idea canceled out another. The panic about McKinley would pass and common sense prevail. "In theory, *sì*, Mr. Kraft," said Marco, "but in practice—*finito*." He shut his book with a slap. Ariane's voice came into my mind. "Maxim," she said, "there is a certain low criminal type about whom you and I and your president wouldn't disagree. Mishka wasn't broken on any Siberian anvil. He was a vicious little brute from the start." She was right. If America was already rid of him, and of Rogovoy, too, in their case I'd have to be on the side of the tsar's hangman.

Zak wired a second time from St. Petersburg. Abby was ill. They were coming home. Fanny and I met them at the dock. Zak waved exuberantly from the gangway. "America!" he shouted. "I'll kiss the ground!" Abby was peakish. She tottered into Fanny's arms and said, "Forgive me, dear." Fanny wept and insisted herself on being forgiven. In this way, they put to rest the matter of the baby and talked about the ship's stormy crossing. They'd been forced to make port at Stockholm and Amsterdam, but all the passengers were relieved to be out of Russia. Even in the first-class dining rooms, the talk was of students rioting in the streets of Kiev, Moscow, and St. Petersburg and of the mounted troops let loose against them. Zak's new Kodak attracted attention from the moment they landed. The Germans in Königsberg were as wary of his little detective camera as, later on, the Russians were. He was careful to take pictures only of tourist sites when he thought they were being watched. Fortunately, he hadn't had the camera with him when they happened on the soldiers cutting the students down. Abby fainted, and Zak's hands were free to carry her back to the Hôtel de France through the screaming crowd. There she became feverish and lay in a stupor. The hotel doctor wanted to bleed Abby for her distemper. Zak refused to let him, she was so thin and wan. For three days, she could take only beef tea and Holland rusk. On the fourth day, she walked around the room. On the fifth, they sailed for home.

Abby remained semi-invalid and was unable to return to her work in the ghetto. Our new physician, Elias Pereira, was a distant cousin of Abby's on her mother's side, a bachelor, and belonged to the same Masonic temple as Zak and Marco. He found nothing the matter but respected the evidence of her fatigue. "There is much that science doesn't know," he said with assurance. "Our understanding of microbial disease is in its infancy." It was certain, however, that there could be no physical symptom without a physical cause. He surmised Abby had picked up an unclassified Asiatic germ abroad, though not a highly virulent one, since it hadn't spread. Zak thought it must have been at the flea-bitten inn between Vilna and Kovno.

Celia the governess divided her time between Abby and the children. Dr. Pereira called twice a week. Celia hurried to answer the door when he rang. With both hands, she carried his black doctor's bag upstairs, and later brought it to the front hallway and lingered there until he left. Zak and Marco and Elias Pereira began forming a free-thought circle among the Masons, to meet in our library at least once a month. I of course was invited to attend. Fanny said, "What, no women?" Celia flushed at the news and told Basya she didn't mind the extra duty of waiting on the men.

Zak's snapshots were a muddy nightmare, as close to Europe as ever again I intended to come. I'd made for him a rough map of Kovno, drawn from memory. The pictures he'd taken there Zak showed first. We gathered one afternoon in the library, where the winter light was best. Fanny called Basya and Sadie the housemaid from the kitchen. Celia the governess held the children between her knees. "Pyotr Mikhailovich's villa," announced Zak. It looked small, more like a summer cottage than the house and grounds I remembered. Where once had been a lawn, there was a veranda, with icy bushes up to the top of the railings. I said this wasn't the right place. Fanny turned away. "It's been so long," she said, "who can tell?" Basya corrected me. She pointed to what she said were the parlor windows and Vera Andreyevna's rooms. The veranda was built the summer after I'd gone to America. Zak said it was my stepfather's villa for sure. In the neighborhood, when he asked for directions, people still called it the Jew's house. Abby elaborated, speaking faintly. "The Jew's house, where the murder was," she said, meaning Bobelis. Next Zak brought out photographs of the Nemen frozen over, with clustered dots of children playing on the ice, then a tiny span that was the Jurbarko bridge, and finally a pair of high wooden doors I recognized as leading to my stepfather's place of business, off the cobbled streets of Slobodka. Fanny stood up and paced the room. She lighted an

Egyptian cigarette and blew out the smoke with a hiss. "Well,"
she said, "if we've finished with Kovno, let's get on with the rest."

From the boat was a view of the port of Danzig, on the
estuary of the Vistula—downstream from where Kazimierz
Wojcicki was shot while my sisters looked on. Here was Zak, in
Königsberg, next to a bronze statue of Immanuel Kant. There
was Abby beside the door to Kant's house on Prinzessenstrasse.
The university had been rebuilt since Uncle Henry's student days.
There was no imagining Papa on those streets, said Abby. Zak
passed around a picture of regimental guards on drill in the
Parade Platz. Abby said everywhere they went were men in
uniform: German soldiers, customs inspectors, Russian police.
"Cossacks," said Fanny, "all of them. Now you know, dear, why
we're here, in America." Abby pressed a pale hand to her eyes.
She said yes, now she knew.

Celia the governess pointed excitedly to details in snapshots
of Vilna. She made out what she said was the Hebrew school her
brothers attended, near the Green Bridge over the Wilja. "And
your brothers," said Abby, "they're here in America?" Celia answered no. One was in Palestine, another a conscript in the
Russian army, she thought somewhere in the Far East, and the
third—she shrugged and said, "Who knows, maybe Siberia,
maybe underground." Dead or alive, I wondered. I heard
Zipporah's voice: "Tell the one again, Max, about being on the
side of the tsar's hangman." I saw her in my mind's eye, slowly
leaning back in her chair at Schwab's, fixing me with a mocking
smile.

After leaving Vilna, Zak and Abby traveled northward to
Shavl and then to Riga, the cities where Fanny and I were born.
To reach Shavl by railway, they had to return to Kovno. There
was a delay overnight while the ice was cleared from the tracks.
Zak showed a picture of a line of railway cars against the flat
countryside and men in fur hats posing with pickaxes and shovels.
I remembered being stopped, stripped, and disinfected during the
journey from Brody to Berlin. Zak said just there the railway line
passed by a market crossroad. The scattering of houses was so
small it had no name, or so said the Jew who ran the inn where
Zak and Abby had to stay the night. When it became known that
Reb Silver and his wife were Americans, Jews from a village a

few miles away came to ask after relatives and friends. Zak and Abby were taken by cart to dine with the village rabbi, who for the occasion wore splended furs in his little stove-heated house. He declared that he would one day visit America. His brother was the butcher in Philadelphia. Abby, who was seated with the women at a separate table, asked why he wouldn't come to America to live. The rabbi said to Zak, "You wonder why I wish only to visit?" He removed a thick gold pinky-ring with a charm engraved on the inside in a Hebraic gibberish. The ring was a gift from the rabbi's father, who had received it from his father, and so on for ten generations. The rabbi recited the names of all the givers and receivers. Far be it from him to raise the wrath of the letters and bring their curse on the next ten generations, he said, and spat three times. He spoke with Zak as one reasoning man to another, while the women listened in silence. Children peeked in at a half-opened door. The air was choking. The narrow windows were fogged, and through them could be seen now and then a blurred hat brim or beard from among the crush of villagers surrounding the house. "It was as if," said Zak, "he and I were deliberating the coming of the Messiah, instead of the price of a train ticket from New York to Philadelphia."

Sadie the housemaid said she came from a place like that. Her father was a horse trader and also the village cantor. She still wasn't sure which it was that drove her out, his singing or his refusal to give up one of his nags for a dowry. If she couldn't marry, she'd have to stay there and listen to the old man's crowing forever. "So," she said, "I ran away to America." Abby wouldn't laugh. She confessed that she used to think all those stories Zak told about his village he made up for our amusement. She'd been curious to see for herself if it really could be that foolish and benighted. Her work in the ghetto had shown her a different sort of Jew—ignorant and poor and, yes, often superstitious, but eager, restless, and young! Now she understood there was no need to seek out Zak's village more than any other. She'd found it, or one just like it, a hamlet from the Middle Ages five miles from the railroad tracks beween Vilna and Kovno, *Anno Domini* 1902.

I recounted the adventure in the summer of '78, near Vitebsk, when one Sabbath eve my sisters and Mishka and I were shooed out of a Chassidic village. "They thought we were Russian children from the city, come to make fun of them," I said. "We thought the ones without beards looked like Red Indians." Everyone laughed, except Abby. If the villages were in the Middle Ages, she said the Chassidim were from before the Crusades. We had our history wrong. The Crusades were the beginning of the end for the Jews. "I know what I'd have done in those days," she said. Her voice was weak but insistent. "I'd have become a Christian, instead of being burned alive or slaughtered like a dog." It was pointless to cling to one set of hocus-pocus in preference to another equally dark and absurd. I said it was pointless to hold to any without compulsion, such as a cruel Inquistor or government or God. "Yes," said Abby, "you've always said so. I ought to have taken better heed. How ridiculous I must have seemed, running down to the ghetto while everyone else was trying so desperately hard to come uptown." Fanny said, "Not at all, dear. What could be more important than teaching English to the greenies?" We all nodded in encouragement, but Abby disagreed. All these years, she'd forced herself on the immigrants, ostensibly for their good, but in fact for her own contrary purposes. "I wanted to speak jargon, like a real Jew," she said, dropping her eyes. Then she added: "I was slumming." Zak said, "Don't talk nonsense." He spoke in Yiddish with Basya's accent, joking. No one found it funny, though everyone tried to smile, even Abby. She answered in English, "Present company excepted, of course," but didn't look up at Zak as she said so.

The children were fretful. Fanny said if they couldn't behave like grown-ups and hold their tongues, Celia would take them to the playroom. They cried and wanted to see more pictures. "Please, let them," said Celia. Fanny put her fingers to her temples, indicating she might have a migraine coming on. Celia said to the children, "Sit and be quiet." A heavy snowfall in Shavl made the figures in Zak's snapshots into mounds of white. Fanny said the snow made no difference, she couldn't tell one place from another anyway. She was four years old when her family fled from Shavl. The dreams she carried with her of that night were more vivid than any photograph could be. What use was a Kodak, if you couldn't take pictures, in color, of your dreams? Zak hurried on. Here was Riga: the port, the moat around the Old City, Abby muffled from head to toe, an ancient castle rising behind her. What I remembered of Riga I didn't care to say. I heard my mother screaming "Osip! Osip!" The taste of the rock candy our neighbor made rose in my throat. Zak held a final group of snapshots. "St. Petersburg," he said. From the windows of their suite in the Hôtel de France, they could look in one direction along the entire length of the Nevsky Prospect. When they turned their heads, there was the Winter Palace and beyond, on the farther side of the Neva, the spires of the Peter-Paul Fortress. Straight ahead was the spot near the Mikhailovsky Gardens where the tsar had been blown to bits. Sophie's voice said, "We were in the Litovsky prison. Papa came every day, always with hopeful news that was lost as he shouted across the visiting room. It made no matter what he said. My thoughts were on Kazimierz and his child growing within me. Nina wanted to know if they sent girls like us to the Peter-Paul Fortress. I told her, 'Don't be silly,' but of course I didn't know. Perhaps I'd be put in the cell next to Nechayev's. I wanted to live for Kazimierz's sake. But when I called to mind our heroes and martyrs in the dungeons of the Peter-Paul—Dostoyevsky, Bakunin, Chernishevsky, Kropotkin—to tell you the truth, Maxie, I envied them."

Fanny looked at the snapshots of St. Petersburg and saw the hand of history reaching out from every one. Zak asked how that could be so. The camera eye received the light-waves bouncing off the objects in its range. Zak subscribed to *Scientific American*. He said photographs were simply reflections of light fixed in black and white on a silver emulsion. They were images of the reality at a given time and place. Whatever else we saw in them was like a camel in the clouds or, he added, the color in our dreams. The Kodak was a great American invention. Celia herded the children out of the library. "No more pictures today," she said. "Come, dears, let's go to the playroom."

X

The God Debate

WHAT WAS TO be a Masonic free-thought circle at East Seventy-
ninth Street became Fanny's and Abby's salon. They said the secretive practice of the brotherhood was intolerable. If our library
held the necessary books for discussion, then our house held the
necessary people. They would not be excluded as women from
any meeting in their own home. Dr. Pereira didn't object. As a
professed freethinker, his principal cautions concerned not women
but God. "It's the scientist in me," he said. "Test and verify,
test and verify!" That year, I heard nothing from my sisters in
Bromley, nor of Mishka. Cousin Emma, after her brief stay, vanished once more. With a mind unvexed by the troubles of the
revolution, I redoubled my fight against God. My boyhood declaration to Pyotr Mikhailovich, "No compromise, never," I held
in my heart. I told Elias Pereira his scientific rationalism was
misdirected. It was like the investigations of archeologists to find
in the remains of extinct reptiles evidence of the Flood or the Age
of Titans. I showed him the little treatise by Julius Schapira, M.D.,
Free Inquiry into the Scientific Basis of the Religion of the Hebrews,
which I'd spared from the rubbish for such a demonstration. Science shouldn't be wasted on attempted proofs, or disproofs, of the
existence of God. Elias was agreeable as always. He said, "Ah,

but you see, Max, I subscribe to a hierarchy of matter and all that it implies. I haven't a spiritual bone in my body." God was simply a convenient term for the topmost entity of the natural order, whose existence every Freemason was bound to acknowledge. I suggested that this supreme being of his, on its perch at the farthest end of the universe, no doubt sported a big white beard, knew our thoughts, and brooded over our destinies. Elias laughed. "If you say so, Max! If you say so!"

We met in the first and third weeks of every month, except for the summer. The day was changeable, according to the weather and Abby's health, exigencies of the shop and Dr. Pereira's medical practice, or Fanny's frame of mind. Now and then, a guest joined the discussions. An ideal circle would have taken in a wider gathering of the living, and also the dead. I imagined them sitting with us in the parlor: among the living, my sisters and the Worcester ménage of Emma, Sasha, and Modska the Twin; Pyotr Mikhailovich, Ariane, Zipporah Gelb among the dead. Sophie's voice proposed Kazimierz Wojcicki as well. The absent living needed no spokesman. Out of respect for the absent dead, I sometimes brought their argumentation into play, in the evolving debate, not over the unprovable existence or nonexistence, but the utility, of God. I conjured up Pyotr Mikhailovich's position as bait for Elias Pereira. God was mankind's compromise with the universe, a negotiation with eternity. As my stepfather might have said while ruminating over jellies, "Between the One and the many, Maxie, lies the path of words." I countered with Mr. Wojcicki. "Empty words, futile compromise. Consider this: Socrates pledges a cock for sacrifice to Asclepius— he still must drink the hemlock. What does this tell you about the dialectics between heaven and earth?" Ariane would be charitable. She'd say the opium of the people served to bring a little heaven into a living hell. Not cynicism but kindness led Voltaire to say, "If God did not exist, it would be necessary to invent him." Zipporah, sinking back into the sofa, would say how ironical that Dostoyevsky's Grand Inquisitor must agree with Bakunin: "If God existed, it would be necessary to kill him."

Celia the governess could scarcely restrain herself when I dismissed Dr. Pereira's amiable doubts. I held there was no middle ground between mumbo jumbo and the measurable world. A man with his head in cloud-cuckoo-land left his feet dangling in the air. Celia cried, "Oh, not so!" and then flushed, mindful again of her position. I didn't care, so long as she protested in English. Elias was unperturbed. He offered the writings of Professor William James, an American, to show that religion had its uses. I suggested that the stand was the familiar one, simply in a psychological disguise, that took the symptom for the cause. "God is real since he produces real effects" was no more an advance in scientific thinking than "I am that I am." A Voltaire would give this the twist it deserved. "If God did not exist, it would be unnecessary to disbelieve in him." Elias smiled. "If you say so, Max. If you say so."

One afternoon, Ida showed up unexpectedly at the shop. She'd come down from Stump Lake on private business and had time before the next train back. Marco and I rose as she entered. Ida said please, since when should we get up for her. Then she added, in a voice not quite her own: "But where is Mr. Silver? I haven't seen him for I don't know how long." Zak promptly walked in through the door. He'd been out of the shop all day, without leaving word, and seemed astonished to find Ida there. In a voice not quite his own, either, he said, "Ida Sussman, what a surprise," and asked after her Barnard. Ida took a studio photograph from her handbag. Zak said to her, "A handsome little fellow," according to their script, and passed the picture to Marco and me to admire. The boy's hair had been cut. Without his Fauntleroy locks, he looked to me like an impish miniature of Zak, but I didn't say so. It was coming into summer, late in a day reserved for Fanny's and Abby's salon. Zak invited Ida to attend. "Thank you," she said, turning to me, "but I have to catch the train home, don't I, Mr. Kraft," knowing I could hardly agree. Zak avoided my eyes. Ida, half-joking, said to Marco that she didn't expect Mr. Kraft would fire her because she spent one night away from the hotel. She could maybe find a place with friends, in the Frances Arms or the Abigail Arms. Marco, the gentleman, said such a thing as this was unthinkable. Ida must stay with his family at the Costanza Court. He rang up his wife then and there. Zak was at least good enough not to offer Ida a bed under the same roof with Abby.

That evening, I meant to give my summary of Huxley and

Spencer, having previously disposed of Professor James. As I began my talk, Elias Pereira whispered to Ida that he hoped she wouldn't be bored. Celia watched them uneasily. Ida said, "God forbid. A learned mind is the most precious treasure there is, don't you think, Dr. Pereira." I'd never seen Ida flirt before. She smoothed her skirts on the sofa beside him. With an uncharacteristic giggle, she excused herself to hoist her hems and loosen the buttons of her shoes. Elias glanced at her ankles. Zak sat in his chair unconcerned, loading tobacco in his pipe, while Celia gasped and dissolved in a faint. This cue wasn't in the scenario. I supposed Zak brought Ida to the house to avert suspicions about the two of them. If she started a little false romance with Elias, who would be the wiser? Celia's disheveled skirts rode up higher than Ida's, almost above her knees. Elias was immediately on the floor. He pulled her skirts down over her stockings and undid the buttons at her neck. Celia opened her eyes and took hold of his hands. "Elias," she said softly. "Elias," she repeated, and put her arms around him. Dr. Pereira lifted Celia and carried her to the sofa. Ida scrambled out of the way. I shelved my discussion of Huxley and Spencer until fall.

Abby rang for Basya and Sadie the housemaid to help Celia down to her room. Elias, already lovesick, followed to wait upon his new patient. When he was out of earshot, Fanny declared the girl would have to be let go. Her disgusting behavior in front of a guest was unforgivable. This would be Celia's last night in the house. Ida protested that no one should suffer on her account. Zak still avoided my eyes. "Mrs. Kraft," said Marco, "with your permission: 'Love he moves the sun and all of the stars.' This is Dante speaking, not I." Abby recalled for us Aunt Libby's disapproval of Zak. With all due respect to Dante, love might not move Elias Pereira's widowed mother and two unmarried sisters, pillars *sans reproche* among Israelitish exiles from Portugal and Spain, for whom Uncle Henry was "that little German." "What!" said Fanny. "This chippy a fancy doctor's wife?" She put her fingers to her temples, as if to push an emergent migraine back. The voice of Zipporah said, "That's no headache, Max, just the idea of free love." And so it was, or something like it, that brought Fanny back to herself. She dropped her hands. "Oh, well," she said, "let the girl. What's the harm?"

Elias and Celia spent their honeymoon on a private yacht. They sailed up the Hudson and the Mohawk as far as Little Falls, stopping overnight at Stump Lake on the way back. The captain married them on deck in sight of the Statue of Liberty. In the wedding party was our entire salon. I was relieved Elias didn't compromise our freethinking principles on the question of the ceremony. Zak gave the bride away and continued to avoid my eyes. Abby stood in for Elias's mother and sisters, who refused to attend the wedding for fear of noxious summer gases rising from the river. Abby had tried to dissuade them. They lectured her on the God of their fathers and the Sephardic rite. "You shall explain to this young woman," they said, "her duties." Abby told Celia, "Welcome to the family!" Sadie the housemaid wept, while Costanza Pacifici arranged and rearranged Marco's tie and the bows in Tina's hair. The children all held flowers. As the yacht pulled away with the tide, Celia waved her handkerchief and threw blossoms plucked from the bridal bouquet. We cheered from the landing, and the captain rang the ship's bells. Basya grumbled that it wasn't a real wedding without a canopy and the groom stepping on a wineglass. It was a breezy afternoon in July following a bad heat wave, but in no way like the one ten years ago, said Fanny, when Sasha tried to kill Henry Clay Frick. She was glad we were finished with all that. I said nothing to remind her of cousin Emma's visit in the winter, not wanting to spoil the happy day.

Fanny and I were there to greet the honeymooning couple at Stump Lake. They were comfortable with one another, communing in small gestures and easy looks. Fanny supposed they belonged together after all. You could always tell that about people from their relaxed manner: take, for example, Zak and Abby. We were sitting in the Oriental corner in our hotel suite. Ida smiled coldly and couldn't agree more. "But sometimes I have to ask myself, Mrs. Kraft," she said, "can we know the yearnings even in our own hearts"—a thought that might have come from Fanny herself in one of her moods. Fanny laughed, thinking Ida was jealous of Celia. She said not to worry, one day soon, among all the hotel guests, Ida was sure to find an unattached doctor. "Thank you, Mrs. Kraft," said Ida, "but I wouldn't change my situation for the world." Then she asked after Mrs. Silver's health in the absence of Dr. Pereira. "Perfect," I lied. "She's fit as a fiddle and taking the sea air at the Jersey shore. Why do you ask?" Ida's face tightened and tears came to her eyes. "No reason, Mr. Kraft," she said, and left. Fanny wondered why I'd want to hurt the woman's feelings, when she'd asked a perfectly civil question. Her service was extremely valuable to us. "Exactly," I said. "Let her manage the hotel and keep out of our personal affairs." The only situation Ida would change was her own for Abby's, but I couldn't say so.

Ida hired a governess for the children of the hotel guests. We were able to leave Joey and Elizabeth at Stump Lake for the rest of the summer and not watch after them during our visits. Elizabeth didn't recognize Barney without his locks. She cried and said he looked like a rat. He revealed to her and Joey the secrets of the new boathouse down by the lake, and they were fast friends again regardless of his rodent looks. Tina Pacifici went up for three weeks. Her mother released her from the Costanza Court after much weeping and exacting from Marco in exchange something of which he dared not speak, or so Fanny guessed. When Dr. Pereira and bride arrived, a pack of children ran to the carriage, led by Joey, Elizabeth, and Tina. Celia was delighted and said soon her own children would be playing with them. Tina said, "Are you going to have a baby?" Celia flushed, and the children giggled. Elias smiled down at them all, already the contented father. "Max," he said, "if children didn't exist, it would be necessary to invent them." I withheld my thoughts concerning the necessity for Barney Sussman. Before Elias and Celia were settled in their rooms, the boy managed to wheedle from them a nickel each. By the time they left, the following afternoon, he'd milked them upward of half a dollar. I watched him do it. He returned my gaze with his cold little eyes and kept out of my reach. Ida, too, held her distance. She walked away if she saw me coming and contrived never to speak with me unless in Fanny's presence or that of some of the guests or the staff. Only at the end of the summer season did she seek me out, expecting that the circumstances of the last salon might now be recalled in jest. I said I wasn't laughing. Ida was solemn. "Then let me tell you, Mr. Kraft," she said, "it was my idea to be there, and you can dismiss me if you like," knowing I wouldn't. She looked away from me and as much as confessed that Zak was Barney's father.

"I have very little of Isidore, except for the boy, don't I, Mr. Kraft. Mrs. Silver has all the rest of him."

I gave my summary of Huxley and Spencer at last. Because of the delay, I was able to refine my arguments with reference to Kropotkin's new book, *Mutual Aid*. I'd have thanked Celia for her time-winning swoon, dedicating my talk to Mrs. Elias Pereira, if I thought she'd be amused. In Celia's absence, I stiffened my attack on Elias's insipid agnosticism, driving him to a flicker of resentment. "But, Max," he said, "we are agreed. The existence of God per se cannot be demonstrated either way. Isn't that enough? Why insist on absolute nonbelief? Why sit here always at each other's throats?" I said I had to laugh. Didn't he call himself a social Darwinist? Elias answered he did indeed. Then, I said, he must with Messers. Huxley and Spencer subscribe to the war of each against all. Elias chose his words hesitantly, trying to forestall a trap. "In nature, yes," he said, "and, by inference, in society at large, the war of each against all, as you put it, obtains, as the universal mechanism of selection. But surely, Max, surely not here, among friends." I had him. "Precisely," I said. He had only to consider Kropotkin's critique of the survival of the fittest to understand how corrupting of mankind was the least suggestion of divinity. The idea of God debased the cooperative instinct behind the struggle for existence. Kropotkin was as confident in his atheism as he was in his science. Mutual aid among flocks, herds, tribes of men, or nests of ants, even schools of fish, never depended on divine inspiration or duress. "You social Darwinists, on the other hand," I said, "are wishy-washy on the subject of God, and with what result? You see a bloodthirsty world animated by sheer malevolence."

Abby came to Elias's defense. Much as she agreed with me about God, it didn't follow that a godless universe was a kind one. She asked what benevolence impelled me always to ridicule Elias's position. Could there not be a double impulse, the urge to kill and the urge to save, as in war? Marco recalled Bakunin's words, that the passion for destruction was equally a creative drive. Fanny paced the room. "Max, I'm sorry," she said. "We know how people are. If God existed, why would it be necessary or right for him to believe in us?" Zipporah's voice said, "Tell me again how the war of each against all is over." She lifted the veil away from her ruined face.

XI

Kishinev

AT CHRISTMAS, THE Costanza Court was strung with lights. Marco on his hands and knees laid a crèche beneath a decorated trellis. We realized what payment he made for Tina's weeks at Stump Lake. This was not a topic for the salon. At dinner, Zak quoted a saying from his village, "The King of the universe is everywhere but in the marriage bed," again avoiding my eyes. Since coming to America, Costanza had taken up the religion she renounced after marrying Marco. Fanny said it only went to show how faith in God wasn't sure to make anyone a better person. Costanza Pacifici was changed into as gentle a saint as a Spanish inquisitor. I held my peace. Fanny's remark about the vaunted reforming powers of belief was the clincher I'd meant to spring on Elias Pereira. Instead, I was compelled to leave my argument half completed and extend my hand. Our reading and discussions took on a more general character. We honored the principle of free thought in its broadest sense, recognizing no authority in matters of opinion. Abby said that whatever Mr. Anthony Comstock condemned for us should be an open book. Elias was relieved. I supposed he still feared a renewal of my assaults. Not until the last gathering of the year did he confess that he and Celia had quietly been married a second time, by a rabbi, for his family's sake. He smiled hesitantly: "Even Max should understand." There was silence in the parlor. A wind from the garden rattled the windows in another room. I said, "If you say so, Elias."

Dr. Pereira bought a house on Riverside Drive, as far from his mother and sisters as he dared, a few blocks nearer to the water than they were. Celia came to Basya for advice. Basya said, "Feed them." People like those in-laws of hers always needed to eat. What else did they have to do? Whenever Vera Andreyevna saw a starving beggar, she thanked God for her own good fortune and put a bite of something in her mouth. Basya took Celia to the ghetto, to show her where to bargain for fresh foods. Never mind the fancy groceries uptown, she said. Here was better. It was among the pushcarts and stalls on Hester Street that Basya chanced on her husband, selling old clothes. "You!" she cried. We had the story from Elias, who heard it from Celia, corroborating what Sadie the housemaid reported to Fanny and Abby the afternoon Basya stormed into the kitchen. The women in the crowd held the man when Basya shouted in Yiddish, "My husband! Selig Gittelman, the deserter!" He was shorter than she remembered and no longer had a beard. "I'm Harry Shein," he insisted, in English, "and I've never seen you before in my life." Basya laughed. He'd changed his name, too. "Selig," she teased him, in Yiddish, "your mother in Bialystok—what about the money she left you when she died?" The man stopped struggling, wanting to hear how much. Now that Basya had found the cheat and knew he wasn't dead, she could divorce him. Zak and I sat with her in the library. He told her it was pointless and complicated. All the records of the marriage were in Bialystok. Here in America, no one cared. Basya disagreed. What if she wished to marry again? She said far be it from her to bear such iniquity in her heart, meaning by this, adultery. Zak said nothing, thinking no doubt of Ida. It had to be a Jewish divorce, said Basya, the one that counted. Everything could be arranged through the Bialystok immigrant society, if Mr. Silver would write on her behalf. "I read," she said, "but even Jewish I don't write so good." She knew I would have nothing to do with the matter. Dr. Pereira offered himself as a witness at the ceremony. When the time came, he described it in detail at the salon, until Abby stopped him. She asked, who here was about to get a divorce, let alone a religious one, and turned to Zak.

It was clear Elias Pereira was going too far. If he and Celia

must have their firstborn circumcised according to the desert custom, that was their affair. For him to invite the salon to the rite
was obtuse. Fanny and I found we had to rush up to Stump Lake.
Abby felt her weakness coming on. Marco had to oversee the
rebuilding of a wall that had collapsed on the job. Zak grimly
stood in for us all. He supposed this religiosity would end now
that there was an heir to the Pereira name. I said Elias was beyond
hope. He was no better than my stepfather, Pyotr Mikhailovich,
whom I would honor above all men except for his accommodation
with God. The seed of belief if it grew became a poisonous weed
that intoxicated the best of minds and stupefied the least. I picked
a volume of Bakunin's works from the library shelves and translated, " 'All religion is nothing but the deification of the absurd.' "
Then I added: "No compromise, never!" Zak applauded and said
I'd have made a bully preacher, but owned that I was right. The
Mason he once knew, Elias Pereira, who only meant to credit a
rational order in nature, was ready to make blood sacrifices on
the Temple mount, if that were asked of him. Again I opened
Bakunin. The Masons of today were not like the heroes of yesteryear. At the time of the French Revolution, Freemasonry was
a conspiracy worldwide among radical bourgeois against the tyr-
annies of monarchy, feudalism, and the established Church. " 'It
was,' " I read, " 'the International of the bourgeoisie.' " And now?
I closed the book. Zak joked, "Well, that explains the kind of
revolutionist I am." His village was still in the Middle Ages. He'd
left it and traveled forward in time as far as 1789. How much
farther in one lifetime must a man go? I said not to worry, no
one could call Zak Silver a throwback. But Elias Pereira was born
an American. He had no excuse for relapsing into a revolutionary
condition earlier than 1848.

Marco one afternoon in the shop suggested an answer to the
question of Dr. Pereira. He was turning the pages of his Dante
and explained why it was that he read the *Commedia* in English.
He said, "I know the Italian in my heart, Mr. Kraft, as a perfection. With the English, I bring it to earth and understand better
the language of America." I remembered how I learned English
with my circle of friends in Kovno. We used *The Young Lady's
Accidence*, Flügel's *Wörterbuch*, and the King James Bible to read
against the Hebrew, German, and other versions of the so-called

Holy Writ. Not once in our studies did the topic of religion or the subject of God arise. We were boys and could be that judicious. For Marco with his Dante, it was the same. I determined our salon should be as wise and no longer provide Elias with a pulpit, whatever the matter under discussion. It should be possible to divert him from his sermonizing with some genial banter. We were reading the utopian imaginings of Bellamy, Morris, and Butler, and also Theodor Herzl's Mitteleuropean fantasy, *The Jewish State*. Abby invited to one of our evenings a young man she'd known from her work at the Hebrew Immigrant Aid Society. The fellow, Marcus Fisch, was now a fierce Zionist and a money-raiser for the Jewish National Fund. He brought with him photographs gotten out of Russia of the Easter pogrom at Kishinev the month before. This was butchery, he said, on the scale of the Cossack massacres of Bogdan Chmielnicki. Nothing had changed in two hundred fifty years. It was time for Jews everywhere to defend themselves and resolve to return to their homeland, there to live as a free people once more. I heard myself echo Sophie's question to me as a boy concerning the emancipation of the serfs. "Free to do what?" I said. Fisch asked, "You are Jewish, are you not, Mr. Kraft." He knew the answer. I wouldn't deny or affirm it to his face, sensing the kind of trap I'd been setting for Elias. I said, "Have I not eyes and hands and organs, senses and affections?" "Then, if pricked," said Fisch, "you must bleed, and if wronged, you must take revenge." He caught me.

Fisch revealed the plight of the Jews in Europe as if it were news to us Americans. In the parlor at East Seventy-ninth Street, he heard no foreign accent but Marco's and his own. Even Fanny now spoke with scarcely a burr, except when headachy and feeling bleak. The pictures of the dead at Kishinev were terrible to see, the shrouded bodies lying in the spring grass in row after row. Those of the injured were worse, most of all, said Abby, the blank faces of the ravaged girls. "Forty-five dead," said Fisch, "six hundred maimed and wounded, ten thousand left without homes. It is enough for us. We know what is to be done." He saved for last a photograph of the self-defense group formed after the slaughter. The men, with knives tucked into their belts and holding muzzle-loading rifles, were staring the camera down. The women were defiant, their backs straight and chins high, like Sophie entering an argument and cousin Emma bracing for the attack. Fanny said, "Don't they look glorious?" and wept. Elias began to preach. He said the pogromists had desecrated the Passover. It behooved us henceforth every year at this season to memorialize our brethren of Kishinev. Elias knew he sat in a house where no religious ceremonies were held. He broached the feast at Passover nevertheless. I could hardly joke it away, according to plan, while we had in our hands pictures of the Russian carnage. Fisch was curt. "Dr. Pereira," he said, "the memorial that matters we already have: 'Next year in Jerusalem.'"

Zak surprised Fisch by speaking Yiddish. It was near Kishinev that he'd been discovered as a Jew traveling with a Ukrainian circus. "Should I say what was done to me?" he asked. "I still have the scars." He was resettled by the police not a hundred miles away, in Mogilev-Podolsk, and from there made his escape, to America. Zak continued in English. "To America, Mr. Fisch, not to Palestine." To America, where he could live as a free man among free people, not as a Jew among free Jews. In this Jewish state of Fisch's, what was to become of the secularists and freethinkers, the men of the twentieth century who looked to science and not Zion for the betterment of all? Zak wrote Fisch a check for one hundred dollars. "For self-defense," he explained, "repeating rifles to replace those muskets. Not for Palestine." Fisch replied, "Palestine is self-defense, and self-defense is Palestine, Mr. Silver." He returned the check and left, with a few sharp words, barely under his breath, to Abby. He'd see us again when the American pogroms began. Zak was furious. When he gave money to a cause, it wasn't to have it shoved back in his face. The Cossack didn't worry where his gun came from—why should the Jew? Once you were dead, you couldn't emigrate to Palestine or anywhere else: *do svidanye*, Marcus Fisch.

Ida enclosed a note with the monthly accounts from Stump Lake. Fanny read it aloud after Fisch's exit. At the news of the massacre at Kishinev, wrote Ida, the White Russians, Ukrainians, and Poles boarded up their stores in town and hid in their churches from the Jews. We couldn't help laughing. Fisch should have stayed to hear. The Jewish boys lined up on Main Street and marched. "Hep, two, three, four, left, right"—where they learned this, Ida didn't know—"halt, about face, spit." And so they did, in front of the Ukrainian Catholic church and the Eastern Orthodox church, where the peasants were. In Woodville, in Liberty, in all the towns in the area, it was the same. Barnard Sussman, though he was the youngest and smallest, was at the head of the marchers. He told Ida he did this for the sake of his grandfather, after whom he'd been named, Baruch Fogelman the carter, who'd been hanged by the roadside in the old country. The boys vowed to march every year at Easter. Fanny smiled. "Marcus Fisch should know: in America, the pogromists run and hide from Jewish children." Then she added: "Elias, never mind the prayers. This is your memorial."

XII

The Great Storm

SADIE THE HOUSEMAID became the children's governess. This was after her sister Lena arrived in New York unannounced, with nothing but a sack of clothes and the East Seventy-ninth Street address written on a worn envelope. I went with Sadie to Ellis Island. There once again I stood as a guarantor for a new American. I showed my citizenship papers to the immigration officials and swore that Lena Mirkin was to be a housemaid in my family's employ. Sadie hugged her sister when she saw her. Later, on the ferry, she slapped her. Why didn't she write to say she was coming? The girl whined in Yiddish that there hadn't been time. I waited to hear another wretched tale of the new wave of pogroms that began at Kishinev. "It was Papa," she said. Drunk and singing, he had horsewhipped her for no good reason. That same night, when her father fell asleep, Lena dug up his strongbox under the stable, took the money she needed to come to America, and escaped. Sadie said, "You'll pay it back, every kopeck." Lena's face fell. The sky was black with autumn thunderclouds. "How?" she wailed. I supposed she thought Sadie would order the boat to turn around and have her sent back to Russia. I said, in English, I would take care of the matter, then listened to make sure Sadie, in Yiddish, didn't qualify my words with threats. It started to rain heavily, sheets of water washing across the ferry. We were soaked through even before reaching the landing. There was no free carriage in sight. We walked a half hour in the downpour until I found one. Splashes of mud beat against the windows. Lena sat shivering, her soggy bundle in her lap. The sewers backed up and flooded the streets, slowing our progress home. Sadie took the opportunity to lecture her sister on how to behave in the Golden Land.

We arrived home after dark. As Sadie hurried her sister into the service entrance, the girl looked at me, her Ellis Island protector, in despair. "Tcha," said Sadie, and cuffed her. It was the first week in October but not an evening planned for the salon. Nevertheless, there were guests in the house. I stood dripping in the foyer and heard Russian voices drifting from upstairs, and then the measured tones I knew as Nina's. In an instant, I was in the parlor and holding her in my arms, wet as I was, welcoming her and Sophie back to America. Nina disengaged herself and took both my hands in hers. "Maxie, I must tell you," she said, "I am not here with my sister." I glanced around the room. Where I thought to find Sophie, there instead sat a small, bearded man who regarded me large-eyed through thick spectacles. Basya wrung her apron while muttering charms in the language prohibited upstairs. She had never expected to see either of my sisters again, not since the day twenty-two years before when the tsar was killed and they fled. Nina said there was tragic news to tell. She and Sophie had broken with Kropotkin's circle. "And I," she added, "have broken with Sophie. Maxie, she and I no longer speak, terrible but true to say." Fanny announced I'd catch my death of a cold if I didn't change my clothes. She could barely hold in her laughter until we reached our rooms. "If your sisters' not speaking is a tragedy, tell me: what is a comedy?" Zipporah's voice answered in my head: "Mishka's International Revolutionary Order. It's a regular Punch-and-Judy show."

Back in the parlor, Nina's companion held forth. She stopped him now and then to interpret for Abby, addressing the man as Georgi Matveyich. It turned out he was the former engineering student she'd known in Tomsk, the brother of her schoolfriend Sonya Rashin. I'd imagined a sturdier sort. He'd recently made his way to London, to attend a congress of the new Russian

Social-Democratic Labor Party. There he and Nina had found each other again. "You may wonder at our presence at this meeting, my sister and I," said Nina. The question hadn't come to my mind. The doings in London of an assembly of émigrés we'd never heard of were of no concern to us. We were finished with the revolution, so Fanny said, though Zipporah's voice teased, "Max, don't be so sure the revolution is finished with you."

Lena in an oversized housemaid's uniform brought up a tray of finger foods and stood stricken at the top of the stairs. Sadie propelled her into the parlor. I said to Sadie why press the girl her first day in America, perhaps she needed rest. "The sooner she learns," she said, "the better," and abandoned her sister to a room of strangers while she and Basya prepared dinner. Georgi Matveyich talked on. Tears rolled from Lena's eyes. "Where am I?" she whispered in Yiddish. She'd come all the way to America alone, in steerage, to find herself in the service of Russians arguing revolution. She could have run away more easily to Kovno instead. "Here, dear, come sit by me," said Abby. She took the tray of food from the girl and passed it around the room herself. Georgi Matveyich was too intent on his words to eat. He went on about maneuvers and countermaneuvers, the majority faction, the minority faction, and who was allied to which. Zak made a show of attention while writing notes in the margins of *Scientific American* on the future of reinforced concrete in the world of tomorrow. Rain drummed against the windows. Fanny kneaded her temples. In this way, we first heard of the Mensheviki and the Bolsheviki and made acquaintance with the names Lenin and Trotsky. The children were allowed at dinner on account of their aunt Nina. She gave them a bag of jellies. "These are real Russian candies, my darlings," she said. They pretended to believe her. Georgi Matveyich in garbled English instructed them how to share equally, just as the children of Russian peasants and workers would, but stopped in mid-lecture when someone kicked him. I supposed it was Fanny. His eyes bulged at the injury, and he went silent. Elizabeth thought he was glaring at her and started to cry. I told Sadie the children could leave if they wished. They slipped off their chairs and raced downstairs to the kitchen. Lena looked as though she'd follow if she could. "You are not to leave," said Sadie, and walked stately after her charges, now liberated from the revolution.

Nina frowned. "When we were children, Maxie," she said, "even then the revolution was our all in all." She recalled our uprising in the schoolroom, how Sophie hurled a dictionary at Madame's head and we barricaded ourselves against the household and drove Vera Andreyevna to a fury singing the "Internationale." Not once in her retelling did she mention Mishka. Without a word, Georgi Matveyich quit the table to sulk in the parlor, limping as he went. From the smile on Zak's face, I understood who it was that kicked him. Nina called out in Russian, "*Dushechka!*" my soul, "*galubchik!*" my dove, and then shrugged. Without his monologue, she could return to the breach between herself and Sophie. It began with their falling-out with Pyotr Alexeyevich. They were helping him correct the galley proofs of *Mutual Aid*. Sophie commented that the book was hardly a blueprint for revolution. She suggested a final paragraph to anticipate the inevitable Marxist critique, especially by Lenin and his circle, concerning the political efficacy of anarchism. "At the mention of Lenin," said Nina, "our usually generous comrade commenced to tremble convulsively. The galley proofs slipped from his lap. We thought it was his heart, but it was his fierce temper showing, of which he rarely loses control. He managed to say 'Sophia Petrovna, I have already refused to see in private this man you speak of. Should I now recognize him and his cabal publicly, in print? Enough of the *Nechayevsti!*" Sophie objected to the suggestion of conspiracy. Lenin's ideal of revolutionary organization, *What Is to Be Done?*, was a tribute to Chernishevky's work and the *narodniki* of yesteryear, as well as an answer, though not the final one, for our time. "We are in the twentieth century," she said. "Perhaps these Social Democrats you shun mean to build a roomier party than you suppose, comrade." Kropotkin took it that Sophie and Nina were deserting the Cause. He looked at them darkly. "Beware the blandishments of state power," he said, and turned away. My sisters were all at once unwelcome at the Kropotkin cottage.

Lightning flashed all around the house on East Seventy-ninth Street. Thunder rolled overhead. The windows rattled. Lena wept. "Just so," said Nina. "My sister and I felt cast out into the storm, into another exile." They grieved remembering that day long ago when they fled with Kazimierz Wojcicki. Before the thrilling and fearful news came of the tsar's assassination, they had been about to print, on the underground press, Comrade Kropotkin's "The Spirit of Revolt." As they made their way home in Bromley, Sophie said, "We have lost the dream of our youth." Nina feared her sister would begin to despair, as she had after her baby died. The irony was, they had as much to do with Lenin as Pyotr Alexeyevich himself—that is to say, nothing. Not they, but my boyhood friend Sergei Stepanov, and his sister Olga, had gone over to the Marxists' camp. "I now welcomed their importuning for Sophie's sake," said Nina. "Before long, we found ourselves accepted among the London émigrés and gave up our place at Bromley."

A fresh downpour swept the house. What I thought were Lena's sobs, now turned into hiccups, was Zipporah's chuckling. "Max," she said, "here comes the whitewash. 'We didn't abandon the Cause. It was the Cause that abandoned us. Surely the end envisioned by the followers of Marx is not so different from our own that we cannot find the common means to achieve it. Of course there will be violence, a passing necessity. How else will the workers and peasants seize their moment? You cannot make an omelet without breaking eggs.' And so on. Just listen." In Nina's vocabulary, the revolution became an *omelette soufflée*, the party organization the collective chef. Abby protested that people weren't eggs. Nina said, "Did you say something, dear?" and then took up the account of her estrangement from Sophie. The quarrel arose over what *noms de guerre* to assume as new party members. They rejected Borova, which was on the passports they used when escaping Siberia. The name, said Nina cautiously, had difficulties, meaning by this, its ties to Mishka. For Sophie, the choice was a rebirth. She fixed upon Kazimierska. Nina refused the pedigree; Kazimierz Wojcicki was never her teacher, her lover, or the father of her child. She took instead for her namesake Timofey Timofeyich Yakovlev, their warden in Tomsk. Sophie was disgusted. The man was a nondescript bourgeois. Yakovleva was of no significance. "That was my point, precisely," said Nina. She was inspired by Trotsky, that fiery young eagle, born Bronstein, who offhandedly borrowed the name of a jailer in Odessa. Then she added, without a smile: "I have to laugh. The revolution will have its little jokes. But, of course, Sophie never did have a sense of humor."

Few party members knew Sophie Kazimierska and Nina Yakovleva as sisters. When the London congress split into factions, their severance was complete. Sophie went to the Bolshevik side, Nina to the Menshevik. Here I was, I thought, an American, born in Riga the son of Osip Abramovich Diamant, raised in Kovno as Maxim Petrovich Kraft, and now the only one of my stepfather's seven children to keep his name. If my sisters had done the same, would the rift between them have been possible?

Fanny stood up suddenly and shouted. With her eyes on Nina, she circled around and around the dining table. Lena shrank against a wall, and still the rain came, hammering the garden windows. "Don't talk to me of your revolution!" said Fanny. "Kropotkin was right. You betrayed it, both of you, you and Sophie, betrayed the beautiful ideal." Georgi Matveyich rushed in from the parlor, no longer limping, an arm uplifted as if to strike. Zak and I seized the little man and sat him down. Fanny was unrelenting. "What are you," she said, "a Cossack princess, to speak of crushing people?" Then she uttered the forbidden name. "You're no better than Mishka, that murderer. Next to the bunch of you, my brothers are saints." Georgi Matveyich bellowed and squirmed. Nina cried, "Fanya!" and made protestations in Russian. Fanny waved them aside. She said that when they were girls together in Kovno, the talk was of sacrifice, not butchery, for the Cause, of defense on the barricades of freedom, not attack. Even a foolish *Attentat* had a lofty aim and a single target; not so this omelet revolution of blood, like Kishinev, but all over Russia, a field day for the peasants and workers, drunkards all of them, and how would this party of theirs protect them from that, the biggest pogrom in history? No, the dictatorship of the proletariat wouldn't include Sophie and Nina Kraft, even if they tried to pretend they weren't Jews. Was Nina here to raise money for the slaughter? "You won't find it in my house, in America, Miss Whatever-your-name-is," said Fanny. "For me, your revolution stops on the other side of the ocean." She held her head and dropped into a chair.

Several times in her tirade, I thought Fanny would break into Russian, German, or Yiddish, or even somehow all three at once, but she didn't. In the language rooms of my boyhood, English was lavish with the furniture of words, the others of gestures that

Fanny was using. Georgi Matveyich declared he and Nina wouldn't stay another minute in the house of these self-serving bourgeois sentimentalists, these two-faced parlor liberals. I laughed and said this wasn't the first time I'd been so accused, remembering Johann Most's scorn for me in Schwab's. We released Georgi Matveyich. He ran downstairs to poke his head into the storm, and returned sodden to tell Nina they must sleep on the foyer floor and leave in the morning. "Maxie," said Nina, "it needn't have turned out this way." I answered of course not, they could sleep in the guest room and still depart at dawn.

It rained the next day, too, but not heavily enough to prevent their going. Nina and Georgi Matveyich spent the night not in the guest room or the foyer, but in front of the parlor fire. I heard their bickering and the groans and twitters of the dead Jews all over Russia, as I skated on thin ice along the edges of sleep near the banks of the Nemen, which was the Styx frozen over. In the morning, the front door was opened and then shut. I looked for a note from Nina but found none. Georgi Matveyich had emptied the candy jar we kept on the tea table and drank off Zak's best brandy. "The Slavs are all barbarians," said Zak at breakfast. He rang for the food. There was yelling downstairs, the clatter of mounting footsteps. Basya and Sadie rushed into the dining room to report that Lena had disappeared. "They kidnapped her," wept Sadie, meaning Nina and Georgi Matveyich. "Tcha," snapped Basya. Sadie said all right, when she found her sister, she'd kill her.

Fanny and Abby joined the search. We looked everywhere, from the pantry to the attic and even the garden shed. Abby said the poor girl didn't speak a word of English. We should telephone the police. "Never," said Fanny. "No Cossacks in this house." The telephone lines were dead anyway, because of the storm. Marco came to let us know he'd already closed the shop and sent the crew home from the job, which was flooded. The old brickwork under the surrounding sidewalks was filled with muddy water spilling into the foundations. The newspapers said this was the greatest rainfall recorded in the city. There would be the greatest mopping up, *subito*, when it was over. I told Marco of our visitors the night before, and also about the new housemaid missing. He shrugged. My sisters were never anarchists truly in their hearts.

They believed in the revolution, yes, but for Russia first and so long as someone was boss. "Of this kind of revolution, Mr. Kraft," he said, "there is no need." Then Marco, too, began looking for Lena. He put his hand on the door to Xanadu. Fanny and I were used to keeping it locked, ever since cousin Emma tried to force her way in. "What is this?" he asked. I said it was a private room. Lena couldn't possibly be there. Marco turned the knob, and the door eased open. "Max," said Fanny, "I remember. Yesterday, I lost my key." Lena was curled into a ball, asleep at the foot of the divan. I carried her to the guest room, where Sadie couldn't kill her. After the storm ended, Fanny took her to Stump Lake. Ida made a position for the girl at the hotel, far away from her father's whip and far enough from her sister. Lena was safe in America at last.

XIII

Which Side Are You On?

ZAK WAS BECOMING paunchy. He took pride in his girth. The fruit of hard work and prosperity, he said, was no disgrace. There was a saying in his village: "The poor man puts away a pot of chicken fat for the winter season; the rich man puts on flesh for the wintry years." He was light on his feet nevertheless and still ran along the beams, joking with the crew in all the languages the men spoke. They were mostly Germans, Italians, and Irishmen. For a short time, there was a Russian, Yarchuk, a hod carrier, whom Zak was uneasy about hiring because of the pogroms. "Mister Zak," said Marco, "forgive me, but this boy, he was twelve years of age, came to America with his mother and sister in '97. What has he to do with the butchery?" Then Marco discovered that Yarchuk was pinching copper tubing and scrap from the job, and fired him. Afterward the crew let on that the Russian had tried to stir up trouble. Zak asked what kind of trouble. The men shrugged and wouldn't say. I suggested that Yarchuk was a union man, but Marco said no, an organizer wasn't a sneak thief. Zak grinned and mimicked Elias Pereira: "If you say so, Marco, if you say so."

There was a new bridge over the East River, connecting Williamsburg in Brooklyn with the ghetto. The subway line up the West Side was almost finished. Tenements, row houses, and larger apartment dwellings were going up all around. So much work and cheap immigrant labor were goads to the unions of the building trades. Silver & Kraft was good to its crew. The men on our payroll got whatever the unions were demanding and, so we thought, remained loyal. Not we, but the big realtors and builders were out to break the unions. These were the companies from whom Silver & Kraft subcontracted business, and the talk among them was of a summer lockout. The day was set for August 8. We often stayed late in the shop, reasoning our way through the coming disaster, like a trio of aerialists, said Marco, trying to outpace an unraveling tightrope.

Zak said he came to America to make money. He was against whatever interfered—right now, the big contractors as much as the unions—and was for whatever helped. We had to close during the lockout, but we should give private assurance to the crew that when the charade was over, the men could come back to work. They'd understand we weren't the only shop forced to play a double-edged game. Marco said he came to America never again to walk the tightrope, and here he was, so to speak, on the high wire again. In this country, he meant to fight the bosses, and here he was, a boss. We must support the men, yes, but also not forget Yarchuk and even the old crew. "*In tempesta*," he warned, "*vendetta*." I came to America to be left alone, but didn't say so. I suggested that after the lockout, Silver & Kraft pull out of construction and keep to real estate. Zak answered that no matter how this stupid business was settled, we were in the midst of the greatest building boom in history and should seize the day. Faint heart never bagged a cool million. Sophie's voice said, not for the first time in my life, "Maxie, which side are you on?"

We shut the house on East Seventy-ninth Street for the summer. Zak and I stayed in a flat in the Frances Arms, and ate ham sandwiches and drank sarsaparilla, as we used to in the days when Silver & Kraft was starting out. Abby took Basya with her to the Jersey shore. Fanny and the children, with Sadie the governess, went up to Stump Lake. Tina Pacifici was with them, at what new price exacted by Costanza I didn't know. Then one afternoon on the job, Marco removed his collar, opened his shirt, and a gold saint's medal swung out. "The wife," he explained. "She says this

will ward off *tutti gli agitatori*." He added: "We shall see," and
tried to laugh. We had a contract for a pair of row houses several
blocks north of the subway terminus, away from the main sites
of the lockout downtown. So far as we knew, there was no union
organizer among the crew, or a rat for the builders come to spy.
I suggested both sides would forget us. Zak thought not. In times
of trouble, it was the cities that got the attention and the outlying
villages that got destroyed. He bought a revolver for each of us
and hired watchmen for the job and the shop. Marco returned
the gun. "I will not shoot a workingman over the question of
property," he said. The aerialist must keep his balance or fall to
his death, so, too, the man of principle. Zak answered it wasn't
going to be the crew out there against us. Property had nothing
to do with the case. We were simply contractors protecting the
livelihoods of our families. If Marco needed a principle to take a
life, he should recall the principle of mutual defense. "*Sì*," said
Marco gloomily, "*capisco: mutualità*." Zak handed back the revolver. I didn't hear him mention self-defense, or the revolution
either. Of the three of us, only I had ever killed a man. I remembered Bobelis's ponderous climb, my stabbing him in the hand,
his crashing fall, and Sophie's saying over the grave, "Very well
concealed, comrade."

The week before the lockout, Sadie the governess showed up
at the shop. Ida insisted she leave Stump Lake for disrupting the
staff. Fanny concurred. I received a letter from her saying to expect the girl and to put her on the ferry and train to the Jersey
shore, where Abby was. Ida wrote in a separate note that Sadie
put on airs with the hotel's own live-in governess and other employees, ordering them about as if she were a guest and raising
her hand against her sister, Lena, everyone's favorite. "I don't
have to tell you, of all people, do I, Mr. Kraft, that in an American
hotel, among themselves the staff are equals. That's democracy."
Even worse than riding her high horse, Sadie had taken a hair-
brush to innocent little Barnard. Bully for her, I thought, but
Sadie denied beating him. She just threatened the little weasel,
for peeping at her in the bath and, she flushed, going through
her linens.

Because of the approaching lockout, there was no time to send
Sadie off to the safety of the shore. Zak and I were on the tele-

phone with the big realtors and builders, in the hope they'd call off their plan or, if not, assure us of help in the event of trouble. They did neither. The lockout was going forward, they said, and Silver & Kraft was on its own. The only help we'd get were wooden barriers and rope to cordon the job. Marco told the crew over and over not to worry, this thing will pass, and so long as there was work, the men would have jobs again. They hardly believed him once the rope and fencing arrived. Zak said if the the crew was locked out, we were locked in, but no one would stop a woman from coming through with our daily bread. Sadie Mirkin was recruited. She was horrified and objected that she was a governess, not an errand girl, and didn't know anything about strikes and unions besides. I told her I put complete trust in any-one willing to give Barney Sussman a thrashing. We were de-pending on her. If she liked, she could have Fanny's surrey all to herself in which to go about town. Zak was puzzled and asked me what I had against the boy, but Sadie consented to be our lady bountiful.

The lockout was set for a Monday. I handed out in silence what might be the crew's final pay envelopes. The men pocketed the money and lowered their eyes. Sadie stayed at the Costanza Court, helping to lay up provisions. On Sunday, we cordoned the job. There was no sign of the crew, but Zak spotted Yarchuk watching us from the cover of a weedy lot, and with him was Rogovoy, Mishka's foul-playmate. I looked and saw nothing. "Are you sure it was Rogovoy?" I asked. Zak answered, "If not, then Gorovoy." Whatever he called himself now, with him here, it was likely Mishka, too, was skulking nearby and not in Russia any-more. We cocked our guns. Nothing happened. Zak and Marco camped down for the night in the half-finished row houses. Sadie in the surrey let me off at the shop. While the watchman slept, to distract myself from thoughts of tomorrow, I sat reading *The Last of the Mohicans*, my favorite book of yesterday. I dropped off toward dawn and dreamed of Cossak-Hurons who were Russian nihilist pickets for the American building trades. Then I awoke to the sound of shattering glass. Someone had thrown a brick through the storefront and run. The street was empty. A shower of splinters roused the sleeping watchman from his bench. He refused to help me glue newspaper over the broken window glass.

"It's not my duty," he said, and I fired him. I waited alone in the shop. No picket line formed outside. The time for Sadie to appear came and went. I discovered the telephone was dead and assumed the wire was cut. As I was about to leave, no matter the circumstances, a police van arrived with Sadie, looking wild-eyed, up front. She pointed at me. "That's him," she said. "That's Mr. Kraft." I was told politely to come along. There'd been an accident. The driver cracked his whip, the van tore through the streets, heading toward the job with its bell clanging, and before we got there, I understood that Marco Tullio Pacifici was dead.

The bewildered crew stood across the street, their signs protesting the lockout dragging in the dust. When the men saw me, they called out that Marco was their friend, they had nothing to do with it. The body was covered by a tarp where it had fallen from an upper story, said the police, into the rubble of the backyard. Marco had tripped on a slack mason's line and pitched over a low course of bricks along an uncompleted outer wall. Impossible, I told myself. Marco was an acrobat. He didn't stumble; he was pushed. From the look on Zak's face, I knew he thought the same. I raised the tarp and saw Marco's open eyes and heard my mother's voice screaming "Osip! Osip!" but it was Costanza keening on the ground nearby, clawing at herself and gasping in grief. Whatever happened, Zak was in the other house at the time. I asked him where the watchman was, thinking of the touchy slumberer in the shop. "On his rounds," said Zak. "He didn't hear a thing."

Slowly the crew quit the picket line. The men drifted away one by one, with a shrug, and left their discarded placards behind. The police appropriated the cordon and offered to post a guard at the shop. We said thank you but no. Zak and I were interviewed at the station. The detectives were civil and unsuspecting. They dismissed the shattered storefront as minor union mischief at worst, but since no bricks followed, more likely the work of some drunk, what with the niggers moving uptown and the greasy foreigners just off the boat. We were happy to agree. They took us for Americans. Known anarchists were now liable to deportation if they weren't citizens, or surveillance and jail if they were. Cousin Emma had been in the newspapers recently, still as Mrs. Smith, for trying, unsuccessfully, to prevent the expulsion of

John Turner, an English libertarian on a lecture tour. The fight went to the Supreme Court before Turner lost his appeal. Because she wrote to ask, I sent Emma money, with a note from "An Anonymous Angel." If a man came to America to speak his mind in English, I thought he should be allowed to stay. Mishka was another matter. Zak and I gave the detectives nothing to suppose we weren't native-born citizens, or had any connection with alien agitators and dynamitists. They asked about the "dead dago." Zak nodded sadly. In his best cracker-barrel accent, he said there weren't no loyaler American than old Marco. In my head, a voice—this time my own—asked: "Max, which side are you on?"

We left off work on the row houses and closed the shop until after the funeral. By then, the lockout was over. Both sides claimed victory, and neither, in fact, had won or lost. For Silver & Kraft, the outcome hardly mattered. Without Marco, we would have difficulty finishing the job, and there was no one we trusted among the crew to replace him. We'd have to give up construction, after all. Costanza arranged for a requiem Mass and determined to return to Italy for good with Marco's remains. He would have wanted a Masonic burial on American soil. Costanza wouldn't hear of it. Did she not know what was in her husband's heart? She raised her eyes to him in heaven, and turned away from me to fan herself, as if I weren't there in the darkened parlor at the Costanza Court. The funeral was at All Saint's Church in Harlem, another medieval make-believe of the kind that troubled my first days in America. As a small boy in Kovno, Marya the housemaid used to take me by the cloisters in the Old City to hear the nuns' chanting. She liked to sing the way they did, through the nose. But never in my life had I set foot in a church until Costanza made it a widow's imperative. The place was a sepulcher, a boneyard for saints. Images of the the dying God hung on the walls, demonstrating once more that, exist or not, it was necessary to kill him. Fanny was outraged. She whispered, "Max, this is eternal life?" She'd come down from Stump Lake with Tina. The girl told Fanny on the train she was going to return to America by herself when she was grown and marry our Joey. She kissed him before she left the hotel. All the other children ran away, shrieking with embarrassment, except Barney, who waited for a kiss, too, but didn't get one. Once upon a time,

I was going to run off to Paris with Ariane. Now Tina sat beside her mother on the pew closest to the open coffin and stared ahead unblinking, but, I hoped, not seeing her father's rouged cheeks and his lush, unruly mustache clipped and waxed.

Fanny returned to Stump Lake. Abby, who had come for the funeral, went back to the Jersey shore, taking Sadie the governess with her. Zak and I opened the shop and found it wrecked. The stove and desks were overturned and flattened into junk. Papers coated with coal ash were strewn all about. The telephone wire was ripped from the wall. Every page of Marco's Dante and my *Last of the Mohicans* was torn out, it appeared one by one, and stuffed down the used water closet. I remembered the summer of 1878, coming home to my stepfather's despoiled villa, the gold candelabrum fixed in excrement. "Mishka," I said. Who else would care so about the *Leatherstocking Tales*? "The old crew," said Zak. Who else would take so much trouble with the Dante? Then Zipporah's voice said: "Why not both? Yarchuk and Rogovoy, too? The International Revolutionmary Order can't make a revolution, Max, but what it did to me it can do to you. Look," she moaned, "look how the ideal is made filth, our great hope a poison." I offered this as an afterthought, without crediting the dead Zipporah. Zak said if I were right, we'd be hearing soon from the International Revolutionary Order. He spun the cylinder of his revolver. We had three guns between us. The detectives had returned Marco's with a wink and pocketed a pouch of gold eagles. It was understood by this that the police approved the weapons for the defense of property, remote as they thought their use might be. We shook hands all around, like real Americans, and said, "So long, pals." Zak and I cleaned up the wreckage in the shop and kept the matter to ourselves. We whitewashed the walls and bought new desks and a gas heater. The storefront and windows were wired to an electric alarm. Zak altered a pair of mechanical clocks and rigged them to the lights, to confound intruders. All night long, as one lamp shut off, another came on. Inside the refurbished shop, there was no trace left of Marco's presence. Outside in the dark, the silent, steady round of lights conjured up a ghostly Marco Tullio Pacifici searching for his lost Dante, though I told myself that couldn't be so. Marco's shade was already in my dreams, not in the shop, the last in the train of the dead trailing behind me on the icy Nemen.

Costanza refused on any terms to give up Marco's stock in Silver & Kraft. We thought she'd understood that holding the shares was contingent on his employment, though as gentlemen we foolishly hadn't put it so in writing. "I know nothing of this thing," she said. "What was his is mine." She took the certificates with her to Italy. Zak said she'd ship the Costanza Court, too, brick by brick, if she could. As it was, she uprooted from the courtyard every transplantable growth, and took cuttings of the rest. She sailed with her booty and Tina and Marco in his coffin at the beginning of October. It was not an unhappy send-off, the tenants at the Costanza Court celebrating their emancipation. Zak said good riddance and stayed at the shop. Abby and Fanny felt unwell. I went to bid a bon voyage and took the children with me, for Tina's sake, so that she'd remember her promise and return one day to America. "The land," I bent to whisper to the girl, "where your Papa wanted you to live."

XIV

Minding the Shop

I RAISED A mustache as a memorial to Marco. It was not so splendid as his was—I didn't want to be taken for a foreigner— but full enough that I could give the ends a little twist. This was my first mustache since Mishka burned the old shop and later murdered Osgood, because the drunk in his delirium talked about the fire. Dr. Pereira said Marco lent a dignity to the salon evenings that could be felt only now in his absence. Fanny asked if Elias would be more precise. Surely, she said, the horrendous news from Russia was nothing to be taken lightly: thousands of peaceful petitioners slaughtered in front of the Winter Palace, women and children cut down by Cossacks, the revolution begun. "If I've said anything amiss..." Elias submitted. Fanny answered it was not for her to say, and lifted her eyes toward where Abby lay asleep upstairs. Coincidental with the massacre in St. Petersburg was the recurrence of the illness Abby had contracted after witnessing another bloody riot there three years before. Dr. Pereira was careful not to draw unsure conclusions. "Science tells us," he said, "that correlation is not causation. Disease must be treated according to physical symptoms, not unverifiable criteria—no matter," he added in his friendly way, "how appealing those criteria may be." He offered this confidence in place of a remedy, and advised bed rest. Basya had her secret nostrums. She bought the ingredients in the ghetto and, late at night, prepared the soups and potions she spooned to Abby behind a closed door. Zak wanted to know what was in these concoctions, but Basya warned him in Yiddish to stay away. Abby told Zak not to worry, she wasn't going to swallow anything foul, and confessed with a weak laugh that her health seemed to improve and worsen with the revolution's changing prospects. Zak tried to show it wasn't so, comparing the rise and fall of her fever with newspaper reports from Russia. He hardly believed his words himself. Abby rallied nevertheless. Only the revolution failed. Basya was triumphant at Elias's expense. "Doctors," she told me, "what do they know? They know nothing. A doctor killed your poor mama. I could have given her a little something, and things would have turned out different." She wiped away a tear. A vista opened on a happy life at my stepfather's villa: no exile for Sophie and Nina, Mishka growing up a jolly boy, no English for me, no America. Ariane's voice added: "No Vera Andreyevna and her brats, no Madame, no Ariane Rahel Lévy-Mendès." Zipporah chuckled. "No tsar assassinated, no pogroms, this year no revolution. The hand of history was never on the throat. Max, how different can things really be?"

Through most of the year of the revolution that failed, someone was trying to break into the shop without tripping an alarm catch. After each attempt, Zak modified the mechanism. He changed the position of the lamps and reset their clocks. Eventually, he replaced the clocks with electric regulators and connected these with the alarm, so that the entire system was electrified. When the lead outside was damaged, Zak contrived an automatic changeover to a storage battery of his invention that would keep the works in operation for twenty-four hours, safe from short-circuiting and sabotage. He determined to apply for a patent in the name of Silver & Kraft. We toasted the company's grand new future at our Yom Kippur celebration at Delmonico's for the year 1905. There wasn't a storefront business that wouldn't buy our security device. The U.S. Patent Office required a detailed blueprint and a working model. For these, we found a firm in Detroit that specialized in patent applications, Emil Braun & Sons. German artisans were so meticulous, they'd be at least a year in

perfecting our order. We were pleased to confirm that their services were much in demand. Meanwhile, there were sure to be
consultations. "Detroit!" said Zak. We'd see America at last.

That summer, Sasha was released from the Western Penitentiary and sent to the county workhouse for the remaining months
of his prison term. Cousin Emma was raising funds for the flag-
ging revolution in Russia. She wrote to Fanny and me, not for
money but about the approaching end of her dear boy's purgatory.
The note was penned on an announcement to "Dear Friends,"
informing them of her new address, now above ground, at East
Thirteenth Street. She also wrote: "Max—be Anonymous if you
like, but to Angel I object; it is crude." I was surprised at her
fastidiousness. An unbeliever who invoked purgatory should
hardly reproach me for an angel. Fanny asked how much I'd been
giving Emma and put her hands over her ears when I explained
it was a year since I donated five dollars in behalf of the
Englishman John Turner, then awaiting deportation. "We'll be
the ones to be deported!" she cried. I said Emma respected my
anonymity. Fanny asked, "And what of the police, what do they
respect." In her dark moods, she referred to all police everywhere
as if they were Cossacks, or from the tsar's Third Section, even
our American pals, the detectives at the station. In this, at least,
she and Emma were agreed, though I didn't say so. Fanny insisted, "No money for her, Max." I said of course, and sent none.
To be an angel when no one asked was to play the fool.

Zak took the first trip to Detroit, while I managed the shop.
He wired me: "System flawless says Braun. Return delayed. Not
to worry." Our alarm was proof against intruders in the night,
but not daylight visitors. Ida arrived unannounced the morning
after Zak left. She approved of the refurbishing and laughed to
see the security device. "Isidore is so clever, Mr. Kraft," she said
happily, "a regular Thomas Edison." She got down to business
and took out a letter, in Yiddish. "Read," she said. It was from
a relative of hers in Russia, writing to say that Jake Sussman was
dead, murdered and mutilated on the road from Pinsk to Turov,
in case Ida cared to know. "Killed, like my father, Baruch
Fogelman, of blessed memory," said Ida. "I'd never wish such a
death even on Jake. But look how it says here," she pointed, "that
he meant to divorce me, for abandonment. What, I should go

back to Russia and with a Jake Sussman? I didn't know he'd gone, did I, Mr. Kraft. This for him." She spit and declared herself a free woman. "Free to do what," I asked. Ida smiled. She was on her way to Detroit with the good news. I understood the reason for Zak's delayed return. Her luggage was checked at the Grand Central Terminal. Boarding time wasn't for two hours, so she decided she and I should have a heart-to-heart talk about Isidore. Ida sat down at Zak's desk and in a wifely way went through his drawers. She fished out his pipe, sniffed it, and knocked out the caked ash. Outside, through an open window, I heard the cries of flying geese and remembered another heart-to-heart years before, with Abby at the Meer. I said, "After Detroit, what?" Ida closed the desk with resolution and then turned away to shield her tears. "Mr. Kraft," she said, "I trust you to understand. The boy should have his father's name." I thought, The little rat doesn't deserve it. To Ida I said, "You know it's not possible. Zak won't acknowledge him, will he? He's no Jake Sussman, either. He doesn't hold with desertion." Then I asked: "What does the boy think?" Ida said, "He doesn't think anything. I have my pride, don't I." Ida got up and slowly paced the shop. She faced me dry-eyed to say it was just a matter of time: Sick or not, sooner or later that woman would have to know. I suggested that there were certain things best not said. Ida listened stonily and blinked only when I added: "If you tell her yourself, it will kill her. What kind of man would marry the woman who murdered his wife, even with words?" Ida looked at her wristwatch. She answered that Isidore wouldn't want her to miss the train, would he, Mr. Kraft.

Another day, Yarchuk and Rogovoy sauntered through the front door instead of tempting the alarm. They glanced around the repaired shop, as if surprised to be there after months of looking in from the outside, and, I thought, to find no trace of their damage. I knew Rogovoy, though I'd never seen him before, from Zipporah's description of his pretty face, and also by her derringer, which he pointed at me while asking in Russian if I'd be good enough to open the safe. Guarding the storefront, their backs to the shop, were two short men, Italians, to judge by the wide, flat brims of their hats. From the old crew, I thought. The entire International Revolutionary Order, except for Mishka, was at the shop. As I leaned down to the safe, I heard Yarchuk rummaging through the desks and laughing as he came upon one, two, then three revolvers. "Leave them," said Rogovoy. "It is a useless arsenal." They were here to collect a debt owed to the International Revolutionary Order. Let them proceed with the expropriation. Yarchuk did as he was told, after emptying the cylinders and pocketing the cartridges, making the guns useless in truth. He cut the telephone wire and the connections to the flawless alarm, patent pending. It was shortly after the first of the month, when the cash on hand from rents was greatest. Rogovoy tallied up the take and said it would have to do, for now. I should remind my business partner, Mr. Silver, that the iron hand of the people reached everywhere, from the smallest peasant village to Moscow to St. Petersburg, to New York, even to Stump Lake. I wondered what Ida would say to being a pawn in Mishka's shadow revolution. Underground groups in Russia were expropriating money from enterprises owned or backed by the government and bombing their offices. I'd seen these direct actions alluded to in the Yiddish *Free Workers' Voice*, which Basya continued to receive, but read unhappily, because of her agreement with cousin Emma—and a promise, she said, was made to be kept. Rogovoy was hinting at a kinship with these Maximalist ex's so-called. As he talked his disguised blackmail, I recalled the language rooms of my boyhood, and also the touted international language of revolt, whose phrases I now heard mouthed. Mishka and Rogovoy had broken into a room called revolution. They'd gutted and refitted it. The meaning of the high-flown words that they spewed out was petty and criminal. Rogovoy left me loosely trussed with my own suspenders, I supposed as a matter of form, but ungagged as a matter of trust. "You'll keep your mouth shut," said Yarchuk in English. "We'll be back," and stuffed an envelope into my shirt. It took me a minute to worm myself free. I opened the envelope, expecting a letter at last from Mishka, however cryptic, but a letter nevertheless. Written instead, under the letterhead of the International Revolutionary Order/Central Council, was a receipt for the money taken from the safe and the rubber-stamp signature, "M. Bourg."

Cousin Emma also came to the shop. "Am I intruding?" she declared as she strode in. I was reading Whitman's *Leaves of Grass*.

She glanced at it with approval. Emma was no intrusion at all, I said. Her timing was fortunate. To myself I thought, Better now than when Rogovoy and Yarchuk were here. I imagined the gleeful headlines: "Red Emma Foils Russky Revolutionist Stickup." She had in tow her niece Stella Cominsky, a serious-minded girl from Rochester who spoke without an accent. The two of them were selling tickets on behalf of a Russian theatrical troupe stranded in America. Any profits would go to benefit victims of the Black Hundreds, the antirevolutionary pogromists. Because Emma asked, I paid for two tickets, but wouldn't take them. Plays, I said, were trivial, except, I added, for those of the Greeks and Shakespeare and Chekhov, and even they were better when read than performed. Emma snapped, "Spoken by a man who knows. Lift your eyes from your books, Max." She favored me with a lecture on the modern drama. The stage was the mirror of life, whereon were displayed human failures and aspirations great and small. The playwright was not a social theorist but a man among men. By tapping the wellspring of his emotions, his deeply felt dissatisfactions with the wrongs of the world, he expressed for us all the longing for justice that lay in our hearts. She mentioned names, some of them I hardly recognized, stabbing the air repeatedly to drive their significance home to the audience that wasn't there. Hauptmann, Wedekind, Sudermann, Shaw, Galsworthy, Ibsen, Strindberg, Zola, Brieux, Becque, Gorky, and, yes, Chekhov—these were the prophets of our time, and who dared turn a deaf ear to their cries and lamentations? I asked, "Are there no Americans worthy of your list?" "The American stage is in its infancy," she answered, "but has hope." Before long, the American people would awake to the radical ideas that paved the way to freedom, to life's open road. Then she said, "Well, dearie, you mustn't think I came here only to sell tickets," and pushed a chair near me, our legs touching when she sat, her face too close to mine. Zipporah's voice reminded me, "She's still soft on you, Max." I was relieved that niece Stella was there as chaperon.

Emma's feeler touched upon personal affairs. "You know how warm I can be," she said, "when it comes to things near to me." She put her hand on mine. Stella stood up and went to look out the storefront, her back turned to us. Under her breath, Emma confessed she really came to talk to me of matters of profound concern to herself and regarding the fortunes of the Cause, here, in America. I suggested her visit had to do with money after all. Emma withdrew her hand. "Only in part," she said. I wasn't so much of a parlor liberal that she couldn't trust me in a strait to admit which side I was on. She came to confer with me about Sasha, and about the magazine she hoped soon to start. I listened as she explained the need for a journal, in English—she'd hear no objection—that would disseminate to the American people the revolutionary thought, in literature, the arts, the social sciences, that was already changing the world. I remembered the night in Worcester when Emma's ménage of three expelled me from their midst for insisting that revolution was made in the language of the place. It seemed she'd forgotten now who it was who told her so.

Stella came back to report that two men, Italians by the look of them, seemed to be watching the place from the street. She thought they might be police, members of the red squad following Emma again. I said not at all, they were just a couple of neighborhood toughs who often hung around near the shop. Zak and I didn't mind; they scared off prowlers. Stella was relieved and sat down. "Now, Max," said Emma, "we can put you down as a supporter?" I reminded her I preferred to remain anonymous. The magazine itself didn't yet have a name. "I was coming to that," she said. My opinion was valuable to her. Any name that appealed to me was a potential catchphrase for other, like-minded bourgeois. I asked what of the workers. "The American workingman," she said, "is uneducated and poor, everything you are not." She meant to enlighten him, it seemed, with middle-class money. Stella had a list of possible names. Some, such as *The Rebel* and *The Alarm*, I dismissed because they recalled journals of former years. Others I rejected, *The Dissenter* and *The Nonconformist*, for example, because they had a religious ring. What Emma wanted, I said, was something as bounteous and big as the American continent itself, as generous as the dream that brought us here. Emma laughed, "You're a poet, Maximus." The three of us regarded *Leaves of Grass*, its pages spread at the "Song of the Open Road." Emma picked up the book and read, " 'Afoot and light-hearted I take to the open road, Healthy, free, the world before me, The long brown path before me leading wherever I choose.'" Then she added: "The open road, Max, the paved way to freedom. I think we have something here, camerado."

Concerning Sasha, Emma was apprehensive. He was to be released from the workhouse in May, unless the dispensers of so-called justice in Allegheny County found a way to prolong his agony. How would he take to the changed world he'd be walking into? The dear boy had never seen or heard a motor car! He was out of touch with the Cause, after fourteen years of hearsay and smuggled mail. Look how he'd belittled Leon Czolgosz! Leon, who was as much the martyr Sasha meant to be himself, on that long-ago day when he shot and stabbed Henry Clay Frick. One thing was certain. Emma shouldn't meet him at the workhouse door, or anywhere near it, for that matter. "Think of the reporters following me," she said, "the cameras flashing and exploding, while poor, bewildered Sasha blinks in the sunlight!" No, it was better if he left prison quietly, alone, and met her elsewhere, far from Pennsylvania, for their momentous reunion. Emma's spring speaking tour would find her in Michigan about then. They could meet in Detroit. I said her thinking was wise. Rip Van Winkle in real life wouldn't have more of a shock upon his awakening. "His resurrection," Emma corrected me. "Sasha—my Lazarus, come forth from the grave." She added, perhaps as an afterthought: "But someone must watch after him, unobtrusively. You could do it, Max." Once again, Emma put her hand on mine, then gripped it as she told me that, in fact, I must do it. Sasha wouldn't recognize me, not after so many years, not with that overgrown mustache I now sported, and the police wouldn't know me either. I might have given my no then and there, but thought the better of it with Emma and Stella crowding me with their gaze. "You'll think about," said Emma, and I answered of course.

The last visitor at the shop, before Zak came back, was Mishka. It was eight years since his apparition at the dock, when my sisters and Kropotkin sailed for England. He'd grown a beard. His big head now brought to mind a hairy coconut, the kind children try to bowl over at carnivals. He sat down at Zak's desk without a word of greeting and cleaned his fingernails with a penknife. I determined not to play his waiting game. "I thought you were in Russia," I said. Mishka shrugged and responded that he was here. "Before that," I said, "in Russia, in Paris, in Strasbourg." "Could be," he said. "I go where I got to. I been around." I said he hadn't spent much time in America, otherwise his English might have improved. "I been out west some," he answered. Beyond that, Mishka wouldn't say. I brought up Michel Bourg and the International Revolutionary Order, Rogovoy and Yarchuk and the Italians from the old crew, and elicited nothing from him. I hinted that I knew something of the fate of Zipporah Gelb and Ariane Lévy-Mendès, and of others I could mention. Mishka laughed and told me to shut up. I didn't know nothing. This wasn't one of them books of mine with Red Indians and dam-o-zels. This was the revolution. "Listen," he said, "I got a new plan about Sasha," and unfolded a sketch of the streets around the workhouse in Allegheny City. Then it was my turn to laugh. I reminded him we'd been through this years before, with the tunnel that didn't exist. Besides, there was no point in Sasha's escaping, now that he was about to be released. Mishka persisted nevertheless, speaking in Russian. It was a relief to me not to hear his English anymore. He supposed I understood the conditions in Russia. The craven bourgeosie had lost the revolutionary opportunity to sham reformism, as of course it was bound to do. The fight was left for others to carry on, until the tsar and his countless lackeys, the exploiters of the people, were swept off the face of the earth. I asked if by others he meant the International Revolutionary Order. Mishka conceded there were several underground groups that must rally under a temporary war leader. To my surprise, he discounted himself, saying he hadn't the gift to unite the factions of unruly anarchists. He was even candid. Not a Nechayev was needed, he owned, but a Bakunin; not a Mikhail Petrovich Kraft, but an Alexander Osipovich Berkman. Mishka was prepared to turn over the International Revolutionary Order to Sasha—Sasha, the chief strategist in the school gang fights on the frozen Nemen. "You, Maxie," he said, "will bring him to me."

XV

The Hand of History at Detroit

ZAK RETURNED FROM Detroit a little portlier and well pleased. He said America was grand. All the energy for the national enterprise—the factories, the farms, the railroads, the great cities rising—was due to our abundance of beef. The best porterhouse in the world was served in the dining cars of the New York Central. He already could see the look on my face when I had my first bite of steak and then washed it down—he sighed—with real Milwaukee beer. Braun & Sons promised the preliminary work on the patent would be finished in May, and Zak suggested we go out to Detroit together then. He recalled our first long train ride, from Brody to Berlin, when I taught him to count in English. That was more than half a lifetime and half a world away. "This time," he said, "we travel in style." We were in the shop. Zak opened his desk and found his pipe cleaned of its ashes. "Ida," I said. He understood from this that I knew she'd been with him in Detroit. He took out his revolver and saw it was emptied of its cartridges. I said, "Yarchuk." Then he opened the safe and discovered it was empty. "Rogovoy," I said. Zak asked who else was here while he was gone. "Just Emma and her niece," I said, "and Mishka." While Zak held his head, I explained how, on our way to Detroit, we'd be making a short detour to Allegheny City, and why.

Mishka's scheme was insane, and Emma's unnecessary. Both required the same thing of me, up to a point: that I trail Sasha from the moment he left the workhouse, a free man, until his train arrived at Detroit. Emma would have me keep him out of harm's way. Mishka would have me do harm. Emma wanted me to see that Sasha reached her waiting arms, gratis, for the good of the Cause. Mishka warned he'd be there at the station in a motor car, waiting for me to guide Sasha to him, in return for the cancellation of Zak's debt to the International Revolutionary Order. He indicated that every step I took would be watched. I had only to reveal myself to Sasha shortly before the train arrived and lead him to understand there was a change of plan: I'd be taking him to cousin Emma instead of her being at the station platform. If I failed, Abby would receive a letter that detailed the adulterous entanglement of one Isidore Silver with a certain Ida Sussman. Zak tried to laugh. He said Mishka contrived to have a blackmail letter like that delivered once before. Abby refused to believe it. She slapped Alice's face, if I remembered, until the girl screamed and bled. Why would she credit another one now? I answered, "Because Ida will tell her it's true," and explained that Mishka also threatened to send a letter to Stump Lake. Then I added: "Mrs. Sussman doesn't need any strong-arming, does she, Mr. Silver."

Zak was perplexed. There was a saying in his village: "For every question, an answer. For every answer, a doubt. For every doubt, a question. Trust only the One, blessed be His name, for the beginning and the end." I suggested we see where this village logic would take us, barring the theological conclusion. Zak spun the empty chambers of his revolver, as if to say he was already going around and around. "Question," he said: "I question if all by yourself you can stop Mishka and his thugs from kidnapping Berkman." "Answer," I said: "Then I'll need your help." "Doubt," said Zak: "It would take more than the two of us to do it." I responded with a question: "You mean the police?" He answered: "Better, the immigration authorities." I was dubious, thinking just then of Mishka's crimes, his murders and extortion, rather than his illegal entry into the country under an assumed name. Even a legal immigrant could be deported within three years if he were discovered to be an anarchist. "Question," said

Zak: "All we have to do is whisper 'alien reds,' and don't you think every immigration agent between here and Detroit will be on the train with us or at the station?"

We talked in circles until we devised a counterplot to Mishka's trap. Nevertheless, I was uneasy about playing the informer and worried that, because of us, Sasha and Emma, America's most infamous alien reds, would be hounded at their first private moment together in fourteen years. Zak said that was nothing to the hounding we'd prevent. Emma wanted me to look out for Sasha, and I surely would. However, our first concern should be that Mishka and his gang get picked up by immigration agents. Emma Goldman's spring lecture tour was no secret, nor was Alexander Berkman's release. There was no need for us to bring them into our story. "Question," said Zak: "Don't you think they'll both have police tagging after them whatever we do?" "Answer," I said: "Our coach won't have an innocent passenger aboard, except for Sasha."

Twice that winter and into spring, the shop alarm system was set off, we supposed as little reminders that the International Revolutionary Order was still there, watching. Zak spared me from exposing Mishka to the immigration authorities. He said I'd been troubled enough. He'd go about the thing his own way. I agreed. Ariane's voice came into my head. "Not your brother's keeper, Maxim?" she laughed. "*Bien, un point d'honneur*, no doubt." The big realtors with whom Silver & Kraft did business had government connections they'd used during the August lockout of 1904. They passed on a few names and introductions to Zak. The Department of Commerce and Labor had charge of immigration, as a protection for American business and, so it was said, the workingman. Zak went down to Washington coincidental with Ida's absence from Stump Lake on a personal matter. "Woman trouble," thought Abby, "yet she never complains, Ida Sussman is the salt of the earth." When Zak came back, he announced he had some real estate tips from the boys at Commerce. He'd put money down on some old houses in the Foggy Bottom due for demolition to make room for government buildings. "Max," he said, "we're part owners of the capital of the United States of America." He didn't mention at the time that our mortgage on these patriotic properties was held by Ida. I asked what of Mishka: Did the immigration authorities question why we were meeting him in Detroit? "Not at all," said Zak. "We were praised for our patriotism." The government was duty-bound to follow every trustworthy lead. An Alexis Rogovoy and a Mike Borough, alias M. Kraft, were already on a wanted list of potential deportees. Foreign agitators were everywhere, in the mines and lumber camps and factories, the spreading tentacles of the anarchist Industrial Workers of the World. The International Revolutionary Order obviously fit into the bigger scheme afoot in the heart of the country.

Niece Stella came to the shop alone. She was selling seats to a benefit theatrical performance by the Russian troupe to raise money for Emma's magazine. Again I bought two tickets but didn't take them. Zak did the same. He preferred music and the opera to the theater. "I'm a romantic," he said to Stella. She looked at me and moved her lips with a silent question, Could she trust him? Like a brother, I mouthed in return. Zak caught the mute exchange and laughed, perhaps thinking of Mishka. "If you'll excuse me, comrades," he said, "back to work," and went for a walk. He understood that Stella was there on Emma's behalf. What she had to tell me was likely to affect our roundabout expedition to Detroit. If the plan was off, only I could argue it on again. It would not be easy now to dissuade the immigration authorities from their duty. I said, "About that matter, concerning Sasha. I've been thinking it over. You can tell Emma I'll keep an eye on him as she asked." Stella leaned toward my desk. "Good," she whispered. Then she asked, in confidence, if I would attend a meeting at Emma's apartment to discuss the magazine. She frowned when I declined and said family could be such a complication. I gathered from this that Emma had cautioned her how skittish cousin Fanny Kraft could be about the Cause. Closeted with Emma and her circle, I'd feel in the present circumstances no better than a spy, but I didn't say so. Instead, I reaffirmed my anonymous support for *The Open Road* and took a subscription in Basya's name. The voice of Ariane commented in French on Maxim's delicate conscience.

The magazine that arrived in March was not the one I expected. Basya said, in Yiddish, what was this? If this was a joke, it was too American for her. I told her I didn't know what it was either. We were at breakfast. The pamphlet she dropped on my plate had a strange cover, a fairy-tale drawing of an Adam and Eve, naked under a tree, with cast-off chains nearby, and looking toward a rising sun. Across the top, in inch-high type, was the title *MOTHER EARTH*. Perhaps it was a nuditarian tract. Then I noticed in small letters at the very bottom: "Emma Goldman, Publisher. 10c. a copy." *The Open Road* was a path not traveled. It was abandoned, a note to readers explained, owing to the existence of another magazine by that name. Fanny took *Mother Earth* from my hands and leafed through it. She said about the title that Emma was thinking of herself as usual. The childless woman must insist she was the mother of us all, telling everyone what was right and what was wrong and what was to be done. Abby said stiffly, "Perhaps you're being a little simplistic, Fanny dear. Barren isn't of necessity brazen." Fanny made no reply. I don't believe she heard. She was absorbed in the magazine and sat reading it through breakfast. Afterward, she took it with her into Xanadu.

In April, the Italians began lurking near the shop again, after a winter's absence. "'Springtime,'" quoted Zak, "'then lean comes the bear, And the ravening wolf from the lair,' as they say in my village." One night, a reminder in Russian, penned in revolutionary red, was slipped under the door: "18 May. Be there." I received something similar, though more friendly, from Emma, with the departure and arrival times of Sasha's train. She was already on tour. Newspapers reported her speeches *in memoriam* of Johann Most, who had recently died—Most, whom she'd flogged in public for the sake of Sasha's honor; Most, who'd insulted me in public; Most, of the twisted face, who doubled in my dreams as Bobelis, climbing. Fanny noted how generous Emma's praises were now that he was dead and she, Mother Earth herself, was the Cause's undisputed voice. "I don't mean this to be funny," said Fanny. "Think if it were the other way around and Most, not cousin Emma, were alive. He'd have said nothing at all, as if she never existed."

Zak and I left for Allegheny City with the feeling that the rushing waters of history were rising to the throat. Currents converged behind us were sweeping us toward fated narrows. Zipporah's question repeated itself: How different could things really be? Zak confessed he was a socialist. When I laughed, he did too, and added: "A socialist in principle. I've always thought the day was sure to come, so let it—tomorrow. And look where we are today."

We sent our heavy luggage ahead to Detroit and traveled by coach to Pittsburgh. Lunch was ham sandwiches, apples, and sarsaparilla bought from the porter, the same as I had my first day in America, on the train from New London to New York, when I was robbed. Porterhouse steaks and Milwaukee beer were for later, on the hoped-for return home. A trunk line took us to the Allegheny City station. From there, it was a short walk to the squat cube we were told was the best hotel in town. Our room had a view of the leaden Ohio River and, on its banks, the dark palace of the Western Penitentiary. Morning found us outside the county workhouse. "Look," said Zak. Half a block away, in the mouth of an alley, were the Italians. They saw us watching and backed into the shadows. Bored newspapermen smoked and told jokes. Silent detectives in plainclothes avoided one another's eyes by checking their wristwatches. A dozen people waited in straggly groups for Alexander Berkman, the Russian anarchist fanatic who once shot Henry Clay Frick. If Emma were among them, there'd have been a crowd.

He appeared. Zak whispered, "My God." We remembered the sturdy boy who drove off the Orthodox hooligans outside the first Yom Kippur ball. Against the high doors of the workhouse, Sasha stood small in an ill-fitting suit. He was half-bald. The rest of his head was shaved. His goggling eyeglasses reflected the flashing cameras. Reporters shouted questions. How did it feel to be a free man? Was he repentant? What were his plans? Sasha didn't answer. A detective showed his badge and gestured with his thumb in the direction of the railway station. Sasha walked uncertainly through the open spaces of the streets. The reporters and detectives followed, with Zak and me and the Italians trailing behind. As the loose procession approached the station, the reporters fell away. Sasha lurched into a trot and turned left when he should have turned right, right when he should have gone left, and then bolted from nowhere into a railway car, he must have hoped, alone. His pursuers piled in after him. He looked up at my face as I passed him in the aisle and showed no recognition, just as Emma predicted.

In Pittsburgh, Sasha jumped from the car before the train came to a halt. Not all the detectives followed him. Those who did seemed unaware of Zak and me, or the Italians dogging us. Sasha looked repeatedly over his shoulder. I expected him to stop, turn, and shout, "Go away!" but he didn't. The streets were noisy and crowded. Sasha bumped into the people around him. A motor car spun by. He stopped dead on the sidewalk to watch it, and a man hurrying behind walked straight into him. He ran for a trolley and rode one stop, likewise the detectives, Zak and I, and the Italians. He ducked into a hat shop. Zak reconnoitered and spotted a side entrance. He motioned me to follow him around the corner and across the street. The detectives waited at the storefront. Sasha came out of the side entrance wearing an oversize bowler that sat on his ears and wobbled on his head. He saw no detectives, and fled. We lost him. It wasn't for us to make a show of close pursuit. We were to protect, not frighten him. The Italians glared at us and threw up their hands. No matter; we'd wait for Sasha at the railway station. Whatever his business in Pittsburgh, it would be brief. He was on his way to Detroit and had to catch the early-afternoon train. "Forward the revolution," said Zak, and glared back at the Italians.

A new set of plainclothesmen was at the station, along with immigration and other federal agents. We didn't detect them, nor did Sasha when he arrived, nor did the Italians, but Zak insisted they were there. In the matter of alien reds, the government's word was good. This was not a matter of conscience but of self-defense. The aim of government was to perpetuate itself. I suggested Zak lower his voice; he sounded like an anarchist. The immigration men were to pick up Mishka and his cohort, not us. Zak said not to worry, the agents had sketches of everyone. He'd made them himself. He stopped talking nevertheless. His mouth was as dry from the day's tension as my own. When the call came to come aboard, we gave each other a light punch of encouragement, as if to say, No worse than Brody to Berlin. Zak had me take the window seat, since he'd been through the countryside before. My thoughts drifted into memory as the landscape glided past. What I saw were not the fields and towns and woodlands of America unfolding in the late afternoon sun, but crab-apple trees under a crescent moon, Russian forests, myself half-carrying Zak across the border into Austria.

Two seats in front of us was Sasha. The Italians were directly behind us. Ranged around the car were other passengers; the agents, we supposed, were watching, ready to move. The conductor announced the approaching arrival at Detroit. The Italians cleared their throats and kicked the back of the seat to remind me to engage Sasha in conversation, to lie to him that I'd be leading him to Emma when I meant to deliver him to Mishka's motor car. Zak nodded. I rose and went to the lavatory, according to our plan. The Italians would think I made my way up the aisle so Sasha could see me and not be too startled when I spoke to him on my return. Instead, I waited behind the locked door until the train was pulling into the station and I knew that Zak had turned quietly to the Italians with his revolver in hand.

As I came out of the lavatory, Sasha brushed by me to exit the railway car. He was oblivious to the scene at his back. The Italians sat, already handcuffed and gagged, growling curses at Zak, and then me, in their muffled Apulian dialect. The fellow passengers who stood over them identified themselves to me as immigration police. I looked through the window. Beyond the station, a hundred yards distant, was a motor car surrounded by a press of men. Climbing down from it with their hands up, one by one, I recognized Mishka, Yarchuk, and Rogovoy. The agents told Zak and me it was safe to leave the train. There on the platform another pantomime was played. To our left stood cousin Emma as if turned to stone, one hand against a pillar, in the other a bunch of flowers. She stared past us at Sasha in his immense bowler and eyeglasses. He walked awkwardly toward her. He raised his arms, lowered them when she didn't move, then raised them again. Suddenly she threw herself against him, and wept without a sound. Sasha buried his face in the flowers.

Part Five

I

Ida's Accounting

WHEN I WAS a boy at my stepfather's villa in Kovno, Sophie used to ridicule my gallery of heroes. They were men. They were Americans, except for Moses, who never existed, and the tsar, who was no kind of hero at all. My son, Joey, had no heroes until he and his sister Elizabeth went away to school. Then, at home on holidays and vacation, he papered his room with pictures clipped from newspapers of college football players and professional baseballers. They were men. They were Americans. Elizabeth derided them. Her own room was decorated with coloring-book cutouts of girls' heroines: Judith, Molly Pitcher, Betsy Ross, Clara Barton, Sacajawea. They were women, said Abby, and Americans, except for Judith, who never existed, but a little mythology would do the girl no harm, provided God was kept out of it. Abby had taken charge of the children while Zak and I were in Detroit. She discovered Sadie the governess beating them with a razor strop for using dirty words. She told her, "Nobody raises a hand to my niece and nephew. We don't flog children in this house." East Seventy-ninth Street wasn't a filthy hovel in a Jewish village. This was America. Here, free speech began at home. I agreed, so long as the dirty words were in English and not spoken at the dinner table. Sadie was fired. Fanny at this time was dosed with chloral. Reading *Mother Earth* perturbed her and disrupted her sleep. She dreamed of her brothers and hidden dynamite, of cousin Emma cutting Johann Most with a horsewhip, of Sophie's circle in Kovno, and of her family's nightmare flight from Shavl. The children's voices irritated her, and she spent her days in Xanadu. She continued to read *Mother Earth* nevertheless and fretted whenever a Post Office seizure prevented an issue from arriving in the mail. "Max," she said, "I don't know what I think anymore. I agree. I disagree. Tell me," she pulled at her hair, "what is my opinion?" She reminded me that I always said she and Emma could be twins. What if she, too, had traveled the open road? It was possible. Look where she was living when we met again in America—in an anarchist commune.

Joey was a small, good-natured boy. Early that summer at Stump Lake, he fell from a tree and broke a leg. He spent the next few weeks immobile with a plaster cast, reading adventure novels on the hotel porch. When he rose to his feet, he was another Maximus. Elizabeth was sly. She made Barney Sussman her champion and, in return for a kiss, took a share of the money and candy he got from the guests. Ida said they made a lovely little couple. Who knew what happiness someday might be theirs? I told Ida she was a sentimentalist. "Am I?" she said. "I only wish for my son and your daughter what Isidore and I can have at best in snatches. You think I don't understand? We don't get what we want in life, do we, Mr. Kraft. We get what we get."

Abby went to Stump Lake when summer was over to take the children directly to their boarding schools. Ida was called away on sudden business, with no time for apologies, but Abby was understanding of Ida's hard life. The North River Academy for Boys and its sister Academy for Girls were near Dobbs Ferry, on the slopes of the lower Hudson. Abby learned of them through friends at the Ethical Culture Society. Like the boys' and the girls' *gimnaziya* in Kovno, the schools shared some classes. The dormitories and dining rooms for each sex were a half-mile apart, at opposite ends of the grounds, which were bisected by a high stone wall with playing fields on either side. The academies proclaimed intellectual perfection through clean habits, *Mens optima per integros mores*, and a transcendental philosophy after Emerson. Cousin Emma reckoned Emerson an original anarchist of the

New World type. I considered what she'd have to say about the schools' answer to the sex question. Boys and girls were allowed to mix outside the classroom once a week at voluntary Sunday chapel, which was devoted to contemplation and discussion of the Oversoul. "Not quite God," said Zak, "cold baths every Saturday, and they take Jews. Not to worry, Max. That's how it's done in America."

Fanny was herself again by late winter. Our salon evenings started up. The stock market dropped. Abby recalled Ida's genius at cards and said that if we came out ahead after the panic of '93, we could surely do the same now. Though she didn't hold with gambling, why waive the advantage of that admirable woman's iron will. Zak said nothing. I was thinking of the mortgages Ida held on Silver & Kraft's properties in Washington, which would sit idle if the banks failed. She'd already foreclosed her loan to the furniture factory and repair shop near Stump Lake and taken it over for herself. Elias Pereira said gambling was among the highest of survival instincts, born of mankind's boundless font of hope. He thought I would approve this generous proposition. "Hope," I said, "is a mirage." Elias's face fell. I added: "Yet a mirage is real to the thirsty man and impels him to crawl from point A to point B." Elias thanked me for saying so. That was his argument, exactly. Fanny disagreed. "You'd have us believe," she said, "the man crawls across the desert, endlessly from point to point, for a greater purpose than his own need—but there is none, not even if a point here or there proves to be not a mirage but an oasis. Take the revolution, which may or may not happen. Beyond that oasis, when it dries up, Dr. Pereira, lies another mirage." Sophie's voice came into my mind: "Your Fanya has forgotten, Maxie. You shall remind her: the true revolution is the historical necessity that will make the deserts bloom."

The patent for Zak's electric alarm system was rejected. There was nothing in the parts and wiring that warranted protection, he was told. Only the storage battery was original. It was also original with someone else, as often happened with an idea whose time had come. Zak blamed Emil Braun & Sons for taking too long to prepare the blueprints and model. "A year's wait for those Heinies," he said, "more than a year's for the Patent Office, and someone else gets there first. We wasted our time and money going to Detroit." We were in the shop. The newspapers reported the country's financial collapse. Between the lost patent and the bank failures, Zak thought it was the end for Silver & Kraft. I said the situation wouldn't appear quite so bad if we looked at it rationally. Zak knocked the ashes from his pipe and shattered the stem. He threw the fragments on the floor. "Rational," he said. "Max, you've never been poor." He listened quietly to my reasoning nevertheless. First, I disposed of the matter of Detroit. I said Zak should forget for the moment the pleasures we took in the train ride home: the wide American landscape, the grand porterhouse steaks, the Milwaukee beer. Since he favored socialism not today but in the by and by, he should forget, too, the revolutionist love tableau at the railway station. But he must not forget Mishka and his gang, picked up and deported for having false immigration papers, even Yarchuk, who Marco once thought came to America as a boy. The French were holding Mishka and Rogovoy on charges of extortion. The Germans wanted to extradite them for the murder of Ariane Rahel Lévy-Mendès. The Russians claimed they had committed acts of treason against the tsar. We must conclude, then, that going to Detroit was hardly a waste. Zak conceded the point. Zipporah's voice said, "You informed on your own brother, Max, even if he deserves to be shot, with me pulling the trigger." I recalled Vera Andreyevna's brats sneaking up on Ariane and me through the bramble bushes at Mishka's direction. I answered that if I'd informed on that half brother of mine sooner, she wouldn't now be in the long line of dead skating on the frozen Nemen. "Justice," she twittered. "Justice in the hands of the state will not be done."

Continuing my rational analysis, I turned to Silver & Kraft's balance sheet for the previous year. It no longer balanced. Our liabilities outweighed our assets by far. Zak was right about our finances. We had loans outstanding on all our properties. The two in Washington, one in Washington Heights, and three in the Bronx were undeveloped and worth less than their original appraisals. We intended to sell them at a profit, but there would be no buyers for a while. Our buildings in Harlem—the Abigail Arms and the Frances Arms, the Costanza Court—had to carry our debts. If the tenants' rents fell off, we'd be bankrupt. Zak said things were worse for us now than in the last panic. We were older. There were children in the family. We had more to lose. It was back to the gambling dens for us. "Just you and I, Max," he said. "We don't need Ida." Thinking of her interest in our houses in Washington, I agreed.

Wherever the places for gambling were, without Osgood we had difficulty finding them, and when we could, our way inside was barred. The house on Thirteenth Street was still there, where Carl Franks gamed and whored after children. The Bowery boys at the portal conceived in their small brains that we were spies for Comstock's vice raiders and threatened us with clubs. November's rents dribbled in. We spent our days knocking on our tenants' doors and our nights hunting for a betting room. We found one at last with the help of our pals at the local station house. They said we should have come to them sooner, and gave us a couple of addresses under their protection. At a basement joint off St. Nicholas Avenue, we sat down to a game of open poker. Zak never played better, nor did I forget the odds myself. We guessed at every card not shown and how every hand must be played. It took only an hour, nevertheless, for us to lose our entire stake. The game was rigged. Zak said we would have known if we weren't out of practice. Instead of going home to East Seventy-ninth Street with our bitter news, we bought a bucket of beer to drink at the shop. Zak tried to joke. "Let's have one final look around, Max," he said, "before this becomes Sussman, Silver & Kraft."

Fanny and I went to confer with Ida. Zak said best the two of us, since Ida was in our employ, even if she could buy the hotel twice over. Fanny asked what made him think we were selling. "My advice," said Abby, "was to bring in Ida Sussman from the first. Only Zak wouldn't hear of it." Kraft's Hotel wasn't hurt by the bank panic. Visitors of patients in the Catskill sanatoriums needed lodging. Failed guesthouses nearby increased the trade at Stump Lake. Ida had no use for bankers and bargained the monthly expenses with cash. She quoted her father, Baruch Fogelman, that a kopeck in debt was another man's hand in your pocket and the eviction notice on your door. With the profits from her management, we paid off what remained of the mortgage on Stump Lake and improved the buildings and grounds. She always welcomed us with something special from the kitchen. On this occasion, it was Mrs. E. G. Smith's Original Kosher Crêpes filled with spiced apples and raisins, a favorite dish of the guests. Afterward we drank tea from glasses in the Oriental corner of our suite and went over the hotel accounts and those of the shop. Fanny wondered why both concerns shouldn't prosper. "It's the system," said Ida. "The banks and the trusts, they've got all the money locked away, Mrs. Kraft, and make their profits on the credit of the workingmen and the middle classes." I told Ida she was a socialist. Far be it from her, she answered. This wasn't Ida Sussman talking, it was the president of the United States, Colonel Roosevelt, who said so. But here at the hotel, there was no credit given, no credit asked, and a dollar was a dollar. She added: "What's owed me, I take, and people respect me for it, don't they, Mr. Kraft."

The holidays were past. There were no children at Stump Lake except for Barney, and he spent his days at school. It was natural to think of business during a quiet walk in the woods and around the lake. The Gypsy's grave was overgrown with shrubbery. Ida called it pennyroyal. The plants in the damp ground by the boathouse were moneywort. When the late-afternoon sun was on the water, and a wind came up, rippling the surface, didn't the reflections, asked Ida, shine like pieces of gold. She broached the reverses of the shop one evening at dusk when a full moon hung low in the sky, like a silver dollar. As with business, so it was with the moon. Each waxed and waned. In the end, a business disappeared under its weight of debt, and the moon would fall into the sea. I told Ida she was a philosopher. "Do you think so, Mr. Kraft," she asked. "This is my father talking, Baruch Fogelman the carter. He also used to say the only philosophy you need in life you learned by keeping your eyes and bowels open and your mouth shut. Forgive me if I offend." Fanny laughed and said no offense meant, no offense taken. She couldn't agree more. "Thank you, Mrs. Kraft," said Ida, and repeated further sayings of her father, to the effect that the moon's inevitable plunge was an act of nature, whereas bankruptcy was an act of man that might be prevented. If a cart was overloaded, its wheels groaning and about to crack, the wise driver made two trips or lightened the burden with a second cart. "Mr. Kraft," said Ida, "I am this Fogelman's daughter, and I offer myself as the other cart for the shop." She proposed to refinance the mortgages on all the undeveloped properties at a lowered rate of interest, in return for a quarter of the shares in Silver & Kraft. She was prepared to meet us any time to settle the details. The offer was generous. I said I'd take it up with Zak. "Please do," said Ida. I should remind him that a debt wasn't only measured in money. Everything she had in America she owed to Mr. Silver and me. What we were owed, we should take: "In my accounting, a kindness for a kindness, Mr. Kraft."

It was visitors' weekend at the North River Academies. Fanny and I took the steamer from Newburgh to Dobbs Ferry. Zak and Abby were at the pier with the new Reo motor touring car they'd bought to celebrate our success with Ida. We were obliged to sit through voluntary chapel. The headmaster, Dr. Cornelius Beinhorn, commented at great length on Emerson's short essay "Prudence." There were no diverting images of the dying Oversoul. Zak whispered that if Beinhorn didn't exist, it would be necessary to kill whoever wanted to invent him. The sermon concluded with an invitation to an outdoor performance on the garden lawn by the older girls. They danced and sang a Victory Ode of Pindar, to a medley of processionals by Sir Arthur Sullivan, arranged and played on a pump organ by Mrs. Cornelius Beinhorn. This was followed by a football exhibition. Our Joey carried the ball half the length of the field before he slipped and disappeared under a pile of howling boys. Fanny closed her eyes. "Animals," she said. "Dogs. Why does he have to be a hero?" I joked to Fanny that I was her hero once in school, when I sharpened her pencil stub with my pocketknife. The boys closed around me afterward like wolves. "That was Russia, Max," she said. "They can't get enough of heroes. That's why we're here, not there." Tea and cakes and lemonade were served in the assembly hall of Emerson House. A chorus of younger children, our Elizabeth among them, sang Beethoven's "Ode to Joy." Abby supposed we should have a piano in the parlor, now that we knew the girl could carry a tune. She regretted her own lack of a proper musical education. "Mama insisted I play," she said. "Naturally, I refused." Fanny said did we really need more noise when the children were home? Must we always be hostage? First, it was the pogroms. Then, it was the revolution. Now, it was to be music. If Elizabeth showed a gift, let the school nurture it. As we were leaving for home, Abby said to the girl, "You all sang like angels." Elizabeth answered that she hated chorus, and the academy, too. Why couldn't she live at Stump Lake and go to public school, like Barney? "We're only doing what's best for you," said Fanny. "You should be grateful for the finest school, not a place for ignorant peasants." Every day, Barnard Sussman and his friends got into fights with the White Russian and Ukrainian boys. Elizabeth said nothing, but looked at her brother. Joey stood next to the motor car and ran his hands over the fenders in admiration. His cheeks were bruised, and one eye was thickening. Abby said, "He was injured in a game, dear. The boys weren't really fighting. They were building character. Isn't that so, Joey?" But Joey wouldn't say. The children cried when we drove off. Fanny said we mustn't feel bad for them or they'd be spoiled. What did they have to be sorry about? She wasn't much older than Joey when she came to America, all alone by steerage, and her father covered himself in ashes and recited for her the prayer for the dead.

Fanny and Abby insisted on driving the Reo. A motor car didn't know whether a man or a woman was at the wheel. How different was it from Fanny's surrey? It went forward and backward and around in circles. It turned left and right. It stopped. Zak explained the workings of the pedals and the hand levers. Then he and I sat in back, out of the wind, while up front Fanny and Abby took turns driving and sang songs of the open road. We halted for farm animals that wandered from meadows and barnyards onto the highway. Fanny shouted over her shoulder, "Is this the Siberian or the Boston Post Road?" When Zak and I weren't shooing cows and pigs away, we talked about the shop and Ida. He asked if she'd mentioned his name at all out of Fanny's hearing. I said once, in passing. "I'm disappointed," he said, but looked relieved. "We have a new understanding: no past regrets, no future prospects, everything strictly business." He asked what it was that Ida said, then changed his mind and asked that I not tell him. I answered nevertheless. She only observed how much her boy was growing to resemble Zak. Truth was in the eye of the beholder, I joked. Fanny thought Barney took after Jake Sussman, a cheat. Zak said, whether or not I liked him, Ida certainly wasn't risking so much of her capital simply for the boy's sake. He knew her finances and how she drove a bargain. He'd expected no more than a short-term loan. She owned the furniture factory and the local telephone concession. What could she get from Silver & Kraft that she didn't already have. I said, "You don't really know?" Zak was quiet for a moment. The headlamps threw light on the frame houses along the roadside. "We're in the Bronx," he said, as if I wouldn't recognize the streets where we'd looked at property together countless times. Then he protested: "It can't be. There's an understanding. Strictly business from now on." Long after dark, we crossed over the Harlem River into Manhattan.

II

The Waters of Lethe

FANNY DETERMINED TO give up the surrey for a motor car of her own. For her forty-first birthday, I bought her a Waltham-Orient in which to bounce around the park. She enjoyed the astonished look on men's faces when she blared her horn and their horses shied. "This is real emancipation," she laughed. "Never mind the vote." Fanny and Abby disagreed about woman suffrage. At the salon evenings, Fanny took cousin Emma's position. The political arena was a circus, and the candidates were the clowns. Universal suffrage, where it existed, was a sham. It merely allowed women to make the same foolish mistakes as men, so long as the choices were dictated by the upholders of God and the state. "We should all have the right to make mistakes, dear," said Abby. "We make them anyway. I cannot believe that you'd deny the vote to those who've struggled for it, or not cast the ballot if it were yours." Fanny answered that the vote was an empty gesture. She felt sorry for men having to choose seriously between a Tweedledum and a Tweedledee, a William Howard Taft and a William Jennings Bryan. Whichever of them won the election, it was a William in the White House. Elias Pereira said Fanny made some telling points. He, for one, found himself voting year after year for the lesser of two evils. "To what extent that makes me an accomplice of evil," he said manfully, "isn't that the crucial question?" Surely we oughtn't to force our women to take on a wretched responsibility for which, perhaps, by evolution they were as yet unprepared. The moral force of humanity's better half was most effective, indeed ruling, in the home, where the still, small voice of goodness prevailed. Elias's eyes became teary as he spoke. Fanny snapped, "Unprepared? Dr. Pereira, we all take on the responsibility of history, whether we vote or not. Who voted on the bank panic? A Cossack with a knife at a girl's throat and his knees under her skirts doesn't ask if she's prepared." Zak tried to joke. He quoted a saying from his village: "Go to the rabbis for talk, to the women for work." If practicality was the argument, then the vote should have been women's natural prerogative, and it was men who should have had to prove their worth. "If you say so, Zak," said Elias, but not laughing. "The world turned upside down." Basya wheeled in the tea service. Ever since Sadie the governess was let go, she'd been doing all the housework. No American girls would put up with her, and the greenhorns these days, she said, all had big ideas. When she found the salon discussions of interest, she delivered her opinion. When not, she rattled the dishes and groaned with her rheumatism. "Who should vote?" she said. "Why is this a question? In a democracy, the people should vote. Who are the people? The working people. Who is the candidate for the working people? Mr. Debs, the socialist. Who, then, should the workingmen vote for? Mr. Debs, and how much the more so because, when the president would be a socialist and not a clown, the workingwomen also would get the vote, and it wouldn't be a waste." Basya fixed us each with a look, and left.

Our salon evenings weren't meant to be devoted exclusively to political questions. Elias Pereira played second violin in a string quartet of Freemasons that welcomed the opportunity to perform at East Seventy-ninth Street. Abby remained friendly with her former colleagues at the Educational Alliance and was a patroness of its art classes. She invited young Jewish painters whose work she admired to talk about art and the promise of America. We read aloud the plays that cousin Emma recommended, each of us taking several parts, sometimes using translations we made ourselves. The theatrical evenings were especially lively. Fanny and

Abby were both great hams and lost themselves in their roles, even when they were feeling unwell. I wondered aloud if Fanny's migraines would go away, and Abby's lingering malaise also, if for a few days each stopped being Fanny or Abby and pretended to be someone else. Abby was offended. Fanny said if she tried it, how would she know to come back to herself again. "I might be almost, but not quite, me. I might be Emma. Is that what you'd like, Max?"

Zak and I arranged a series of evenings called "Is America the Golden Land?" though none of us doubted it was so. We read the novels of Stephen Crane and Jack London, the memoirs of Ulysses S. Grant and William Tecumseh Sherman, and were proud to be Yankees speaking English. Abby suggested the stories of Abraham Cahan, Jacob Riis's *How the Other Half Lives*, and Hutchins Hapgood's *The Spirit of the Ghetto*. Fanny laughed. The ghetto was hardly news. We moved uptown to get away from it. What could these books tell us that we didn't already know? Elias Pereira was shaken in reading them. He confessed that not once in his forty-three years had he been anywhere near the ghetto. His medical practice didn't take him there, and slumming was never to his taste. Delancey Street might be as near to him as Breite Gasse in Vilna, where his wife, Celia, was born. "And yet," he said, "far flung and, in some cases, impoverished though our ancestry may have been, we meet here, month after month, year after year, for intelligent conversation. A golden land, indeed." Fanny dedicated an evening to the Leaden Land, meaning by this, Russia. To prepare for it, she made a translation of *The Seven That Were Hanged*, Leonid Andreyev's story from the revolution that failed. Afterward Abby was sick for a month. Not even the prospect of acting a comedy by Oscar Wilde could draw her out. At the next salon, we had to read *The Ideal Husband* without her. Zak mimicked various ladies to add to the humor. This voice was Emma's, that one Abby's, another Ida's.

Basya found a housemaid at last. Lena Mirkin, the sister of Sadie the former governess, left Stump Lake on account of Barney Sussman, but precisely why no one would say. Ida came down to the city for the monthly business meeting of Silver & Kraft. She brought the girl and left her at the door of the house before going to the shop. "My Barnard," she said, "is a healthy, growing boy.

What can you expect? This Lena Mirkin is no little innocent."
We soon learned about Lena. Basya held she never had a better
helper, only why did the girl stand there when her work was
done, smiling and saying nothing? What was she, waiting to be
hit? "Far be it from me to do so, Maxie," said Basya, "not with
these fingers," and flexed an arthritic hand. It turned out that
Lena and Sadie maintained correspondence, in Yiddish, and had
been from the day we'd sent the younger sister away to Stump
Lake for her protection. Basya claimed the right to open Lena's
mail. Lena didn't say no. In this way, we learned that Sadie was
now in San Francisco, looking to marry a rich man, the way Celia
Wilner had done, only better: Sadie was going to marry a real
American—a Gentile. She intended to change her name and also
get rid of her accent, which was why she went out West. "If you
stay in New York," she admonished her sister, "in the employ of
Yids from the old country, you'll always talk like a greenie. When
I'm Mrs. Big Noise, I'll send for you, my Lena girl, and you can
live by me on Nob Hill." Fanny and I called Lena into the library
and told her how wrongheaded Sadie was. Lena said nothing,
and smiled. Except for Basya in the kitchen, I explained, no one
here spoke jargon. Even Mrs. Kraft had lost her accent, and in
her case, it had been more Russian than Jewish. If Lena wanted
to learn proper English, East Seventy-ninth Street was the place
to do it. Lena smiled, and said nothing. Fanny rose, I thought
perhaps to strike the girl, just to make her blink. Instead she said,
"When you write your sister, dearie, you should remind Mrs.
Sadie Big Noise, the anti-Semite, that there's a name for a woman
who marries for money." Fanny quoted some of cousin Emma's
remarks on the hypocrisy of respectable prostitution. Lena hung
her head, said nothing, then looked up and smiled.

Fanny was becoming an expert motor-car driver. She even
cranked the starter and changed the tires without help. Her
Orient was the one-cylinder buckboard model. After a year, she
was ready to give it up for a more elegant and powerful machine
and set her heart on a four-cylinder Knox. Her accustomed routes
were around the park and up Riverside Drive as far as the
Harlem River and back again. These were much the same as her
rides in the surrey, but the speed, she said, made her feel electric.
If Fanny sensed a dark mood coming on, she had the motor car

brought around and galvanized herself at the wheel. Otherwise she was content to spend her days in Xanadu, reading and smoking, attending to matters of the house, the hotel, and the salons. She reflected, perhaps a little sadly, that the Cause wasn't what it used to be, and recalled the meetings of the Autonomie and Freiheit groups, where the arguments raged in any language but English. The Cause was American now. Sasha had become the principal editor of *Mother Earth*, while Emma spent much of the time raising money for her magazine. She lectured to large audiences all over the country and published reports from on the road. "If Emma would only stay put," said Fanny, "what an evening we could have: 'Anarchism in the Golden Land.'"

That was shortly before the presidential election. At our first gathering after Taft had won, Zak and I owned to feeling foolish, having voted for a man that embodied the figure of a fat cartoon plutocrat in Emma's pages. On the other hand, we couldn't support Bryan, who brought God into every issue and had him as his adviser. Abby conceded that Fanny might be right about the vote after all. Elias Pereira pondered whether woman suffrage would result in an improved selection of candidates from which to choose, and decided yes, that was a possibility indeed, provided, of course, the candidates themselves were men. "Broaden the vote," he said, "without violating the sanctity of the home." The parlor went silent. I waited for Fanny to make her attack. She began kneading her temples instead, then gasped with pain. Dr. Pereira helped me carry her up to Xanadu and prepared a dose of chloral. She and I spent the night on the divan. In her drugged sleep, Fanny talked to her brothers, I supposed about expropriations at gunpoint and *Attentaten*, muttering about oxes and slaughter. The next morning she was subdued, not from the chloral, she insisted, but the aftereffect of the migraine and the sinking gloom that went with it. It was a bright autumn day. Fanny said what she needed was a spin in the motor car, and then she'd be herself. I was surprised she took the election so hard. "It's not the election, Max," she said wearily, "only the headache. I'll be all right. You can go to the shop." Then she added: "Not to worry; it's not a baby again," though if she were keeping a secret from me, I wouldn't suppose it was that.

Abby telephoned the shop later that morning to say there'd

been an accident. Fanny was in St. Luke's Hospital, unconscious, but with no broken bones or serious internal injuries, so far as the doctors could tell. She'd hit her head on the steering wheel of the Orient, after running it against a tree on Riverside Drive. The police telephoned the house, and Abby rushed to the hospital without thinking to let me know first. "Forgive me, Max," she said, "and get over here fast." Zak's Reo was parked outside. We were across town, so it seemed, the instant after I locked the shop door, and walking the corridors of St. Luke's, past silent nurses dressed like nuns, looking for Fanny's room. We found her asleep, her head swathed in towels. Abby was sitting at the bedside, holding Fanny's hand. The pale face of my dying mother came into view. Dr. Pereira arrived and the hospital physician with him. Fanny opened her eyes. She gazed unseeing at her visitors, then closed her eyes again. Elias patted my shoulder and said, "It's just a concussion, Max. She'll be home in a day or two, up and about and her old self in no time at all." The attendant physician echoed, "No time at all, indeed." I remembered the brawl years before outside the Yom Kippur ball and my weeks of recovery. I was a young man then. I wondered what of Fanny now, and heard her say in my mind, "How will I know to come back to myself? I might be almost, but not quite, me." A nurse came to inquire who was the husband. She handed me Fanny's handbag, hat, and jewelry and suggested I take them home. I found that night, folded into the change purse, a short letter to Fanny and me from Sophie, postmarked Geneva and dated three weeks earlier. Fanny must have carried it with her for days. Sophie had never written to us before, except for little comments appended to Nina's correspondence. Whatever she said, the news couldn't be kind if Fanny kept it to herself. I read the letter and returned it to the purse.

Sophie wrote in Russian, her handwriting small and clear, her words formal but blunt even when devious. I missed Nina's flourishes and polish. The signature at the bottom read S. P. Kazimierska. It was a moment before I recognized it as Sophie's *nom de guerre*. She addressed me as Maxim Petrovich and Fanny, her esteemed sister-in-law, as Fanya Abramovna. Her letter was a chilly catalogue of miseries. She understood that Nina, whom she referred to as the woman Yakovleva, had visited us during the time of the abortive revolution, so that there was no need to dwell on the change in their allegiances. It would suffice to say that Yakovleva had now abandoned the revolution and was living with her manikin lover among decadent artists on an island off Italy. It was not that woman, however, who was the subject of this letter, but recent intelligence from Russia which had reached Sophie's circle of exiles in Geneva. Fanya's brothers were dead. They'd been seized by the police two years before in a roundup of Maximalists in Bialystok and executed while still awaiting trial. "There is little to add in the way of details," she wrote. "Grief is not a matter for individuals. We grieve only for the revolution."

Then Sophie brought up Mishka without once mentioning a name, not Borough, not Bourg, not Kraft. There appeared among the jailed Maximalists a certain police informer with a hero's reputation, who was said to have lost his youth in Siberia. He hinted at having had the honor of first being deported from America to France, then extradited from France to Russia. This same man was put in the cell with Fanya Abramovna's brothers. Not long afterward, the two were taken into the forest and hanged. Other prisoners with whom he spoke received severe sentences. The hero himself was not brought to trial and, so it was said, vanished before court proceedings began and the information he gave concerning his fellow comrades was used against them. Sophie concluded: "Hearsay requires corroboration, and corroboration, action. We shall wait, and we shall see what is to be done. S. P. Kazimierska." In a postscript, Sophie wrote that she was soon to leave Geneva for Paris. We would hear from her shortly, when she was settled again.

I realized what Fanny said in her sleep the night before the motor-car accident: "The oxes gone to slaughter." The two that were hanged came into my dreams. They join the wavy line of the dead on the Nemen, which is the Styx frozen over. The river widens, the shoreline on either side become a darkening at the horizon. I am skating around the world into the Sachs's Café that is the garden of my stepfather's villa. Fanny sits beside her brothers. She looks almost, but not quite, like cousin Emma looking almost, but not quite, like Fanny herself. Lev and Fedya are chewing their cud. Nooses dangle from their broken necks, and beneath the ropes they bear the yoke of the revolution. Nina crawls from table to table, nuzzling at everyone's knees, while Georgi Matveyich follows on all fours, sniffing her from behind. The marble statue that is Sophie watches them through blank, lidless eyes. Out of her unmoving stone mouth comes judgment: *Thus shall the hand of history delighteth to do unto the dogs that have forsaken her.* A voice, my own, says: *There hath been a misunderstanding. My mother died when I was but five years of age, and lo! the dead will be with me now always.* Fanny's brothers try to roll their heads. They join in the Greek chorus of protesting twitters. The dead will not be faulted. It was I who dragged them along the frozen Styx into Sachs's Café, when they would return to the river of oblivion. Fanny pleads with her eyes: *Better for thee and me that they, yea, even we, drink of the waters of Lethe.* I reach for her hand, clutch at air, and wake, alone on the divan in Xanadu, only an empty phial of chloral beside me.

Fanny remembered nothing of the accident and little of what preceded it. She had no idea at all what could have made her lose control of the motor car. I alluded to the letter only after she returned home, not wanting to roil her mind abruptly with the recollection that her brothers were dead. "I don't understand," she said. "What letter are you sorry about?" I said the one in her purse. Fanny rummaged through the whole of her handbag and declared no letter was there. What was so important about it anyway, this letter that didn't exist. I suggested we forget the matter if the thing couldn't be found. "Max," she said, "I've forgotten already." I wondered what it really was that I saw her burning in the parlor fireplace the day she came home, her hospital thoughts, as she mysteriously called them, going up in flames. In time, when no further word came from Sophie, I began to question my memory and supposed her letter was just part of a vivid dream brought on by the chloral. Without corroboration, as Sophie might say, there was no call for action. So far as I knew, my sisters still lived in London and no longer spoke to each other, Mishka and Rogovoy were rotting in a French dungeon, and Fanny's brothers were harnessed to the cause in Russia. I thought: Let them remain silent, wherever they are, and not disturb our peace in America.

III

Doings at the Brevoort

ABBY SENT IDA a standing invitation to stay at East Seventy-
ninth Street when she came down from Stump Lake. Ida declined. She preferred to put up at a hotel and be a guest for a
change instead of the manageress. Abby respected Ida's independence and called her the salt of the earth. Ida favored the Hotel
Brevoort on lower Fifth Avenue. After a posh dinner in the restaurant, she enjoyed sitting in the basement café and watching
the Greenwich Village radicals argue. For her, she said, it was an
education. If she had to live her life over again, who knew, I
might see her on top of a soapbox in Union Square, Red Ida
making speeches to the masses. I said she liked money too much
for that. "Do I," she asked. "But not for itself, only for what it
can buy. If there were no need for money, this would be a happier
world." I said she was a true communist. Ida laughed. "I said in
another life, didn't I, Mr. Kraft."

When Silver & Kraft required legal counsel, our monthly
meetings were held at the Brevoort. We retained as our attorney
Elias's elder brother, Julian Pereira, Esq., who found the libertarian atmosphere of the café even more educational than did Ida.
He cautioned us regularly to lower our voices, so that we might
take in the conversation at a table nearby. "Quiet, my friends,"

he said, "I do believe they are discoursing upon free love." On one such occasion, we met to discuss the threat of a lawsuit. A letter from Italy had come to the shop. I thought it might be word from Nina, and that Sophie's curt missive months before was no dream after all. But the postmark was from Naples, not a Mediterranean lotus isle, and the squat handwriting belonged to no sister of mine.

The letter was from Salvatore Ricatto, advocate for the family of the late Costanza Pacifici. He demanded forthwith an accounting of the sums of monies due the heirs from dividends, goods and chattels, sales of property, appreciation, "*eccetera*," and all other accumulated earnings derived from the American estate of the deceased. I said to Zak, "Greedy even beyond the grave." He wasn't so sure. One of the richest men in his village made his shabby fortune with this confidence trick, claiming to speak for his brother's heirs and then slowly defrauding his orphaned nieces. Who was this Ricatto? How and when did Costanza Pacifici die? What of Tina, why was there no mention of her? We took up the matter with Julian Pereira at the Brevoort. He studied the letter through his pince-nez, and chuckled. "An Artless Dodger," he said, "all phumph and fanfaronade." Provincial lawyers were the same everywhere. One simply called their bluff, and their return silence settled the case. Julian remarked that the heirs themselves were not named. Who, precisely, was this man representing? I said the only heir we knew of was Tina Pacifici, Marco's daughter. The girl was an American, her father having become a citizen at the time of the Spanish war. Julian took notes. "Very good. And there is no property, I suppose?" Zak said nowhere but in the woman's imagination. She must have trumpeted the Costanza Court as her own. "A charming lady," said Julian. "I quite understand the depths of your grief. In fact, then, shares in Silver & Kraft are the only goods and chattels, *eccetera*, in question. The income from these has been held in escrow for two and a half years, Signora Pacifici's whereabouts until now being unknown." He proposed to write a monitory *ad rem* counter to Ricatto's, demanding a copy of the death certificate and the names of Costanza Pacifici's heirs. We agreed to convert the account in escrow into a trust for Tina and inform Ricatto of its existence should he make a satisfactory response. I said, trust or no trust, the girl would return to America, the land where her Papa wanted her to live. "Grant that it be so," said Ida, in Jewish. Julian Pereira cleared his throat. Our business was done. "Quiet, my friends," he said, and gestured to a noisy table in a far corner. "I believe they are arguing the sex question."

Seated at that table were cousin Emma and three men, who sported loose collars and Windsor ties. Sasha was among them. The others I didn't recognize. Emma became aware of us listening to their conversation and waved us over. Ida and Julian were hesitant. They preferred to be unnoticed observers in the Brevoort café. I said none of these people carried bombs under their clothes. Emma put on a show of greeting me in front of her men. She introduced me as her old comrade and supporter they'd heard so much about, Mr. Anonymous, sometimes known as Max Kraft. The men smiled. They took their measure of me, and then of my companions. What they saw was money. Only Sasha laughed warmly. "It's been too long, Max," he said. With fourteen years in an American prison behind him, he still spoke with an accent. I realized, when he rose to shake my hand, that he had no memory of the tall, mustachioed man who was near him in the railway car from Pittsburgh to Detroit on the day of his release. The two seated men stood up, reluctantly, I thought. "Havel," said one, swaying. He held a glass of whiskey in his hand. The other drawled, "Reitman." We'd chanced upon a meeting that concerned *Mother Earth*. Here were the publisher and the editor, Emma and Sasha. With their private nods and scowls, they were more like brother and sister than the Tristan and Isolde I saw on the railway-station platform. Emma's love interest, from her expression, was now Ben Reitman. He was a slick-looking fellow who managed her tours and, she said, the finances of the magazine. Zak prodded my ribs, as if to say, Alas, poor *Mother Earth*. Reitman extended his hand. "Put her there," he said. I noticed a black line of grease under his fingernails. Hippolyte Havel I knew from his literary articles in the magazine, and also from a letter of Nina's years before: a jumpy, bearded fellow, she called him, and also Emma's lover. Zipporah came into my head to remind me, not for the first time, "She's soft on you, too, Max." I answered, Alas poor Emma, I wasn't joining that harem of hers. Zipporah leaned back in her chair. "Not even for the Cause, Max?" she said. "Still the Individualist."

We joined their table. The discussion was not about free love at all, but deportation. Emma's citizenship was in question. She had with her the manuscript of a piece she wrote for the magazine, "A Woman Without a Country," referring to herself. She explained that more than twenty years ago, in Rochester, she'd married a man named Kershner. Her divorce from him was never finalized. Kershner's whereabouts were unknown, but federal investigators had discovered he'd given a false birth date on his citizenship application and the wrong year of entry into the country. For all anyone knew, the man was dead. Nevertheless, for his grand lies, they'd revoked his citizenship, and Emma's with it. "The government swine," said Havel, "they care nothing about this goddamn Kershner." If Emma Goldman left America now, they would never let her return. So she must stay, because they wanted her out. "It's a joke," said Emma, not laughing. I hardly sympathized with her leaving, but didn't say so. For my companions, it was the same. Sasha pointed up the irony in the words "naturalized" and "denaturalized." Citizenship was no state of nature. To lose one's citizenship was to regain the freedom of natural man. It was then that I mentioned our gatherings at East Seventy-ninth Street and Fanny's hope for an evening on "Anarchism in the Golden Land." Zak gave me a surprised look. The salons had lapsed since Fanny's accident. Havel said, "Ha! The goddamn irony of that!" meaning, I supposed, that the suggestion came from the mouth of a goddamn bourgeois. Emma silenced him: "Max and Fanny go back to my early days." She brought up my sisters, and also Fanny's heroic brothers, Lev and Fedya Ruttenberg. Heroic in what way, I wondered, but had no chance to ask. Havel looked at me with little less contempt. He'd met them all years ago, he said, at the underground anarchist congress in Paris. He snorted. My sisters had gone over to the other side. Sophie would have replied, "The only true revolution is the one that shall succeed." Of Lev and Fedya, he said nothing.

Reitman was seated next to Ida. While Havel talked, he whispered in her ear. Her face flushed to the frills of her collar. She bolted from her chair and strode out of the café without a word. Zak was on his feet immediately. He stood with balled fists, glaring at Reitman, ready to brain him, hesitated, and followed Ida. "If you will excuse me," said Julian Pereira. He, too, took his leave, but not before Havel, perhaps with mockery, tried to touch him, and then me, for a loan of five dollars. Reitman pouted at Emma like a naughty boy. "Mommy," he whined, and left his plea hanging, doubtless that he meant to *épater les bourgeois*, or words to that effect. Sasha, and even Havel, had to turn away. The look on Emma's face was daggers blunted by resignation.

I caught up with my companions in the hotel lobby. Ida was leaning against a pillar, fanning herself. Julian was saying such buffoonery belonged on the vaudeville stage. If these people wanted support for their Cause, they should begin by learning manners. Zak put his arm around Ida, then removed it, remembering where he was. Julian dropped his eyes. "Mr. Kraft," said Ida, "I take it back. Never in another life would you find me on a soapbox. This revolution of theirs, if ridicule and disrespect are what it's about, we don't need it, do we." Emma came hurrying up the stairs. She declared, "I will not apologize for my comrades. That they must do for themselves, as they shall." My companions said nothing. Emma took my hand and drew me aside. "Let's not be strangers, Max," she said. "I'll remember: 'Anarchism in the Golden Land.'" Then she sent her condolences to cousin Fanny, for her martyred brothers, and returned to the café downstairs. "That little woman," said Julian, "the formidable Red Emma. *Mirabile dictu*, she could be Mrs. Kraft's sister. Though to be sure"—he laughed—"the less pretty of the two." I thanked him for saying so, while in my mind's eye, I reinstated Lev and Fedya among the line of skaters on the Nemen, with Costanza Pacifici behind them. I wondered what I should say to Fanny now.

Zak and I determined to walk all the way uptown to the shop. He was angry, he said, and couldn't sit still. It was a fine spring day, the trees in flower. Without deliberating, we turned west when we left the Hotel Brevoort and marched in silence until we stopped in front of what was once Uncle Henry's house along the row of Rhinelander Gardens. Zak gripped the wrought-iron fence. His knuckles became white. "I'll kill him," he said, "and the other one, that drunken hunky, too." I said Emma guaranteed their apologies. Zak predicted how heartfelt these would be. He recalled hopeful days at Uncle Henry's house, when we were young. Even revolution held a promise in the by and by. Now, we had everything, he said, except hope. What happened? Zak answered himself. In those early years, we weren't there anymore, meaning Russia, and not entirely here, either. Never-never land was where we lived, the land of dreams, but thought it was America. I disagreed. If there was ever a man with plans and two feet on the ground to carry them out, it was Zak Silver, who started to learn English on the train from Brody to Berlin, so he could become rich in the Golden Land. A dog came growling out of Uncle Henry's former house and barked at us from behind the fence. "The Golden Land," said Zak. "I was talking about hope, Max, not dollars." How could I have suggested a salon evening with those mangy curs present, Reitman and Havel? He kicked at the dog, which cringed and set to howling as we walked away. "Like that," he said, "in the seat of the pants, if they show up at the door."

I told Zak I'd mentioned the salon for Fanny's sake. Arranging an evening on "Anarchism in the Golden Land," with Sasha and cousin Emma, might bring her back to her old self. Zak understood how she was since the accident. She'd written to Ida to warn of the Gypsies, who hadn't been seen at Stump Lake for seventeen years. Her vision was often blurry. Instead of a Knox, I bought her a Ford motor touring car, a simpler machine, but she was afraid even to sit in it. She had a new sort of headache, persistent, for which she took aspirin pills every day. "Lena," she would call out from Xanadu, "fetch me a Bayer!" What Zak didn't know was that Fanny's memory was stray, as if part of her mind were bathed in the waters of oblivion. Zak was troubled to learn of Sophie's letter. All these months, he said, and not a word from Fanny about her brothers. Why hadn't I told him? I said I wasn't sure of my senses. Did I dream the letter, did Fanny burn it and forget, or was it lost? I hoped to hear again from Sophie, or from Nina, but it was cousin Emma's remarks that confirmed the truth. Lev and Fedya Ruttenberg had been hanged, and Mishka had betrayed them. Zak and I found ourselves in Central Park, threading our way through the shaded maze of the Ramble. I thought of Marco, and said, quoting Dante, " 'In the middle of the journey of our life, I came to myself in a dark wood, where the right road was lost.' " Zak said he could see Marco in the shop, turning the pages of his book, and hear his considered advice, " 'The right road, like the tightrope, is walked step by step, Mr. Kraft, *passo a passo la dirrita via.*' " I took Zak's point. Fanny would recover herself by degrees. He said not to worry, if the revived salon was her road, he could put up for an evening with a Reitman, a Havel, or anything else Emma dragged in.

At dinner, Fanny said, "'Anarchism in the Golden Land'? How did you two think of that?" She hardly believed it at first when I told her the idea was her own, before the accident. Except for Emma, who was family, she said, why should she want those people in her parlor? Reading *Mother Earth* was one thing; inviting dynamitists was quite another. "Max thinks I've forgotten everything," she said, "but I remember when my brothers tried to make our house into their bomb factory." That was all she said about her brothers. Zak joked that dynamite was Old Style, like the Russian calendar, and had proved of no use to the Cause in America. Fanny wondered when Zak became a revolutionist, to talk that way. Abby said it wasn't revolution as such, or socialism as such, at the heart of anarchism New Style, but liberty: free speech, free thought, free love. We raised our glasses to the three freedoms, and Fanny confessed she was beginning after all to entertain the notion of the salon.

Another letter arrived from Italy, not at the shop this time, and not from Salvatore Ricatto, but from Nina. "Dearest brother," she wrote. "I greet you from *Circe's isle*. Scordevola it is called, a jewel in the Tyrrhenian Sea. There is a legend here that deep amongst the volcanic caves runs a branch of the sweet river Lethe, trickles of which, percolating into the springs and wells, cause a touch of forgetfulness in all who drink thereof. How else explain the careless lethargy in native and visitor alike? Georgi Matveyich awoke one morning with a start. 'We are forgetting the revolution,' said he, and fell asleep once more. He has not thought of the revolution since. Nor have I, except as it were some restless beast pacing a distant shore. The wine-dark sea surrounds us. The dot on the horizon is Ulysses' cutter, not the battleship *Potemkin*. How came I here, or why, does not signify. Whither I shall go, or when, is no question. I have spent the better part of my life amongst people with answers, and the world has heeded them not, nor I think will it ever. I dream now not of red banners but of the rosebushes in the garden of Papa's villa, and open my eyes to a cascade of blossoms outside my window. Here one dwells with *eternal things*. There is a poetess on the island, an American widow of the Sapphic persuasion, who writes in images. Words, says she, are icons of the mind. With her encouragement, I have begun to paint. She says there is a visual metrics to my brush-strokes and calls them verse. I believe you know of her, Maxie: Blanche Viereck Franks. At all events, she intimates your paths may have crossed long ago in her other life in America, but does not expatiate upon *the past*. As it is said, *A Scordevola, solamente il presente*. Your loving sister, Nina." The postscript was crossed out with a thin line of pale ink and so remained legible, I supposed intentionally. It was a request for money. The wherewithal for the timeless moment was needed even on Circe's magical isle.

Fanny expressed no surprise at Nina's words. She read them stone-faced, dropped the paper on the tea table in the parlor, and left the room. All she said was, "How coy—not a dime for the flirt," and nothing to show that Sophie's letter had been no dream. Abby announced herself unnerved. Never, in all the years of their friendship, did Blanche Viereck betray an unusual predisposition. She remembered, in point of fact, that Blanche found even the common schoolgirl crush infuriating. "It must have been something to do with Carl Franks, I wouldn't wonder." Yes, I thought, he paid for children. Zak was reminded of a pious young man in his village, an ascetic who denounced any deviation from the Law as blasphemy. He would burst into a house, like one of Comstock's raiders, and point an accusing finger at some starving wife for cooking an egg with blood in its yoke. He searched schoolboys for modern books. He died of malnutrition, barely out of his youth. Hidden among his few possessions were discovered several volumes of Spinoza, a chemistry manual, a German grammar, and a sheaf of erotic poems in Hebrew by medieval Spanish pederasts. Abby said Zak was making the story up, just to tease. He grinned and admitted yes, but only to the part about the egg. "So, Max," he said, "now we know what happened between you and the poetess." I said I never denied it, the poetry was rotten, and changed the subject to Fanny. We lowered our voices as Basya came to collect the tea service. She stopped to listen to our conversation nevertheless. Abby suggested that if science, as Dr. Pereira avowed, had little to say about the material workings of the mind, then it shouldn't trouble us to feel that Fanny's amnesia was, somehow, selective. Zak said if only Emma confirmed the salon, there was sure to be a turn for the better, even as Fanny began the arrangements. Memory thrived on exercise. How else did children learn or an otherwise senile man in synagogue know to recite by heart, year after year, the whole of the Law and the readings and the ancient prayers? When Hippolyte Havel ridiculed my sisters, or Emma alluded to Fanny's brothers, one thought would give rise to another, and the welcome light of recollection would flash. "Not so," declared Basya. Already she couldn't remember the given name of what's-it?—Gittelman, the husband who abandoned her. She spit three times. How was this a curse and not a blessing? "A person forgets what she wants to," she said, "so it wouldn't hurt so bad anymore."

IV

Anarchism in the Golden Land

IT WAS NOT until the fall of the following year that cousin Emma and her comrades came to East Seventy-ninth Street. During that time, when she wrote, she humored my anonymity by sending her letters to no one in particular, simply the "Resident," whom she addressed as "Dear Friend." The first arrived a few weeks after the incident at the Brevoort, a typewritten appeal for money. The local police were frustrating her lecture plans. "I face the alternative," she said, "of either again calling on you for financial aid or suspending *Mother Earth*." At the bottom, in her rapid scrawl, she added: "The challenge of our Cause in the Golden Land!" A circular in June announced the advance subscription for a book of Emma's lectures. Though sent to more than one "Dear Friend," the one we received had a personal note. Alongside the statement that she might substitute one or two lectures for those mentioned, Emma wrote: "Perhaps a new piece, Max: 'A. in the Golden Land.'"

With each letter, Fanny's spirits quickened, but not her memory. She followed Emma's itinerary as it was reported in the newspapers and in *Mother Earth*. Just reading about the endless demonstrations, lectures, and arrests, she said, made her feel like a spinning leaf at the edge of a whirlwind. She lost count. There must have been more than a hundred lectures, many of them, I was sorry to learn, in Yiddish, in at least half as many cities, and everywhere, so it seemed, a standoff with the police. Fanny was surprised that Emma found a moment at all to think of the salon. Zak said not to wonder, it was a question of money. Emma knew enough to call her angels home to their dovecote, so they wouldn't go astray. Abby supposed it was also a question of stage vanity. The woman was an actress and couldn't pass up the opportunity to perform. "Just remember," she said, "how she stole Johann Most's show with her horsewhip."

Another of Emma's angels had bought her a retreat near the city, a farm, she called it, in Ossining. From there, she wrote to say she was finishing her book, and also to set our evening for the middle of November, in a quiet time before her next lecture tour. Quiet, for Emma, meant fighting the Canadian customs office for seizing her magazine, and speaking in defense of anarchists and union organizers suspected in the recent bombing at the Los Angeles *Times* that killed twenty people. Quiet meant mocking Anthony Comstock at public meetings for his vice crusades, his confiscation of nudes at the Art Students League, and, of course, his attempts to suppress *Mother Earth*. I wrote Emma to say Zak and I would interrupt her solitude the day of the salon to drive her from the farm to East Seventy-ninth Street. On the way, we'd be stopping to pick up the children. The North River Academies were ten miles from Ossining, and Fanny thought Joey and Elizabeth should be allowed to attend the gathering. "When we were their age," she said, "we'd already put Russia behind us. Never let it be said that I spoiled my children and tried to hide them from the hand of history in the Golden Land."

We had no difficulty finding Emma's house, which was set not far from the road, amid orchards and hills. A tent was pitched on the highest knoll. She explained it was Sasha's retreat. He was trying to write about his prison years and often had to come to the farm to be alone. Emma offered us food, but we couldn't linger. The children were waiting. "The children!" she said. Her little cousins, whom she scarcely knew. It was commendable of the school authorities to give them leave to meet Emma Goldman, rather than expel them. Zak looked at me and winked. So far as the North River Academies knew, and the children, too, their coming home involved a family matter, unspecified. Emma admired the Reo. She sat up front with Zak and me on the open road to Dobbs Ferry, singing "Hallelujah, on the bum" and other I.W.W. songs, while urging us to join the chorus, as Sophie used to do the servants in the kitchen of my stepfather's villa, when she took up the "Internationale." The children were astonished to see Zak and me, the top rolled back, with a woman between us they didn't recognize. "Say hello to your cousin Emma," I said. She gave them each a kiss, Elizabeth a motherly one, Joey's accompanied by a squeeze that made him flush. "My, what a pretty boy he is," she said, looking up at him. "He takes after his father." They sat in the rear of the motor car. "Now, dears," said Emma, "what do they have you study in school," and then, all the way to East Seventy-ninth Street, explained to them what they ought, and ought not, to be learning.

Some guests were there before us. Abby hired a harpist for the evening. Standing in the foyer, I made out a celestial rendition of the "Marseillaise." The parlor floor was open from end to end, from the library through the dining room. A buffet table was laid alongside the bay windows overlooking the garden. Hippolyte Havel was at the caviar as we came up the stairs. Ben Reitman in the parlor was distracting the lady harpist by mimicking her hand motions and rolling his eyes to heaven. Havel shouted out, "Hello, my friends! My little parlor liberals! Little monkey-faces!" He was drunk already. Reitman stopped torturing the harpist and swaggered over. "Long time no see," said he, and held out a sticky hand. Zak caught my eye, as if to say, At last, those heartfelt apologies for the insults at the Brevoort. Sasha was in the library, a lively young woman with him, the two of them studying the bookshelves and talking *tête-à-tête*. He introduced her as Becky Edelsohn, his companion. She wasn't much older than Elizabeth, and flashed, when she moved, stockings of revolutionary red.

The brothers Pereira arrived, Elias with Celia on his arm, her first visit to the house since leaving our employ. Reitman looked her over and introduced himself to the husband. "Dr. Ben L. Reitman," he declared. "Pereira, doctor of internal medicine," said Elias, and inquired of Reitman's specialty, or was he, perhaps, in general practice. "Generally, the syph and abortion," Reitman replied. Elias guided Celia to the other side of the parlor. Next came Bolton Hall, the man who gave Emma the farm. Julian Pereira recognized in him a fellow attorney, no doubt by his formal dress, and drew him aside to discuss the merits of the case against the McNamara brothers, accused of bombing the Los Angeles *Times*. I heard them agree that those boys were blameless as babes. Before long, the remaining guests made their appearance, Emma's niece Stella Cominsky, Hutchins Hapgood, whose book on the ghetto Abby so admired, and the first violin, viola, and cello of the Freemasonic string quartet with their wives. Fanny greeted the guests in the foyer or at the top of the parlor stairs. She led one knot of them over to another, and urged them all to sample the buffet before the serious talk began. Not a single invitee failed to show. Fanny was radiant. Her salon would be remembered for years to come. Beside her, Emma in plain dress and pince-nez seemed more of a maiden aunt than a near twin. Fanny wore a turban. She smoked Egyptian cigarettes. Her face was delicate with white rice powder, like porcelain, said Abby, with a blush of rose. Emma said to me she didn't flatter herself; Fanny had made the evening in honor of her brothers. I said perhaps, but there was no intended memorial. "Of course," said Emma. "The pain she feels for them cannot be expressed in words. When I mentioned their names, Max, it was as if she didn't hear me. She turned away."

Fanny determined that I should make the opening remarks. Sofas and chairs in the parlor were set in a loose circle that called to mind Sophie's student gatherings in Kovno, where she demanded of each and every one there that they be equals. Among the faces waiting for me to speak were some that had seen the inside of prison. It hardly seemed right to claim equal revolutionist credentials, to say that I was once a courier for the People's Will. Nevertheless, no one laughed when I did, except Zipporah in my head, who observed: "A reluctant courier." I pointed out to the guests that so far that evening I hadn't heard a word of German or Russian or Yiddish. These were the languages some of us spoke thirty years ago, the day the tsar was assassinated and my sisters fled with Kazimierz Wojcicki on what would be the start of their long exile. On that day, too, I said, the Russian door closed behind us, and the door to America swung open, with these words above it, in English: "Abandon all false hope, ye who enter here." What this meant, I said, was the dream of a European revolution in America. If "Anarchism in the Golden Land" signified anything, it was the cause of freedom not bound by Old World considerations and the languages that preserved them.

Sasha said he'd heard this argument from me before, on a certain night in Worcester in 1892. My ideas hadn't changed much. I thought, Nor have yours. He quoted me as insisting the revolution was made in the language of the place, as if the social question everywhere were not the same. Economic injustice and international capitalism went hand in hand. The elimination of one spelled death for the other. International revolution, therefore, was the only means to that end.

Zak rose up in defense of my stand. It was Kropotkin who held that at the close of the century, the right of the lord over the peasant no longer existed in Europe. But was a workingman's birth and ancestry so obliterated that he no longer wore the invisible mark of serf, or the Jew his yellow star? So long as there were kings and queens, lords and ladies, the abolition of feudalism was not, in fact, absolute. The social question in America didn't bear such medieval freight. Here a workingman was a workingman and the social question was answered in an American accent: Every man for himself, every man for his brother.

Havel applauded wildy. "In this Paradise," he said, "every man drinks wine under his own willow tree, until the day of Judgment. Then, my little bourgeois friends, you know who will hang from the lamppost, while the dogs of war lap the blood of the individualist swine!"

The Freemasonic cello addressed a question to Emma on the matter of violence. In the light of Mr. Havel's considered remarks, he asked if she would clarify the difference, if indeed there was one, between the chaos of anarchy and anarchism as such. Becky Edelsohn jumped to her feet and said, "I can answer that!" She understood the man's apparent puzzlement as a provocation, but would not be goaded. What the newspapers reported as desperate acts of anarchist violence were reasoned responses to the brutal power of the state. She shook her fist. Government was organized violence. It was government that sent a boy to war and threatened to shoot or imprison him if he refused to take up a gun and kill. In whose pay were the militia and police that cut down workers—even women with children in their arms—meeting openly in view of a millionaire's mansion to protest hunger and degradation? Such was the cowardly machinery of the state. Its destruction meant not chaos but the cooperative society that always existed when the people were left free to live as they choose. "This," she said, "is what we call anarchy. Anarchism is the philosophy of this social order, liberty unconstrained by unnatural laws. Have I answered your question, sir?" The Freemasonic cellist said yes, and then asked another. "What of regulation? Without government, who would make the trains run on time?" "The trainmen," Becky Edelsohn snapped, "who else?"

The children watched Becky. Here was a girl who might have been at school with them, playing sports, obeying rules, attending Transcendentalist chapel. Elizabeth whispered to Joey, pointing to Becky's red stockings. Joey nodded. The look on his face was much like mine, I supposed, the day that Ariane Lévy-Mendès strode into the parlor of my stepfather's villa and told me to help her with her bags. A smile from Becky Edelsohn, and Maximus the younger would fall in love. She ignored him and turned to Sasha as she sat down. I heard Elizabeth say to her brother, "What an ugly old man!" Cousin Emma took it all in, while seeming to make notes, and gazed gently upon Joey. Zak laughed under his breath. "If she can't have the father," he said, "she'll have the son."

Reitman shifted his chair close to Elizabeth and began to play with the ribbons on her dress. She let him. Emma thanked Comrade Edelsohn for her useful, though somewhat simplistic, remarks. She, too, recalled that night in Worcester when I came to visit, and said that of course I was right, revolution could only happen in the language of the place, but disagreed that the false hope of America was an Old World dream. The American people were half asleep, lulled by the illusion of democracy propagated by the state, with the help of its twin handmaidens, religion and capital. She herself once held the promise of the Golden Land in her heart. Her first shock was the hell of Castle Garden. Over its doors truly belonged the words "Leave all hope behind who enter here." Next came the sweatshop, slavery at two and half dollars a week. Even in Russia, workers were treated better. "And then there was Haymarket," she said. "When those innocent martyrs were hanged, what a cruel farce was this 'land of the free and home of the brave'!" The Freemasonic viola asked, if such was the case, why hadn't Miss Goldman returned to Russia. Emma said she might have, but for Homestead and her growing realization that the Cause had native roots in the soil of the New World. Sooner or later, the American people were going to wake up to their true history. "This is the challenge of our Cause in the Golden Land. Not a dream, but the trumpet call of reality."

The Freemasonic first violin asked, "Once the American people are fully awake to their past, what then? Does Miss Goldman think they would all sell whatsoever they had, give to the poor, and follow the Cause for righteousness' sake?" The good news had been proclaimed before, and the hearts of men were yet to be overcome. Elizabeth, glassy-eyed, removed Reitman's hand from her lap. He turned his attention to Lena the housemaid, who was passing a tray of cordials among the guests. Emma was momentarily distracted. Hutchins Hapgood said, "If I may be allowed," and responded to the first violin. He reminded him that the wealth of this land was so distributed that, upon the day of awakening, unless there were giving by the few, there would likely be taking by the many. Clearly, without economic fairness there could be no social justice. Violence was not the preferred means to achieve that aim. Education was surely more practical, he said, and praised Freemasonry as a bright light of tolerance and change.

Lena gathered the empty cordial glasses. She carried her tray to the dining room, to send it down the dumbwaiter to the kitchen. Reitman worked his chair to the periphery of the circle and made after her. Emma followed. Bolton Hall, in her absence, introduced himself as a single-taxer. The question, he said, was how to encourage the spirit of self-reliance and ensure the equitable distribution of wealth, while realizing the Jeffersonian principle that the government which governed best governed least. "Or perhaps," he added, "governs not at all, if that were possible." The answer lay in a levy on the rental value of land. Emma returned with Reitman in tow and sat him down beside her. Joey raised his hand, as if in the schoolroom. He asked Hall how a government that governed less, or not at all, could still impose and collect taxes. "An excellent point," said Hall. I was proud of the boy, remembering that night in Schwab's Saloon when I held my own against Johann Most. Emma beamed at Joey. "Your question, dear," she said, "goes straight to the difference between reformism, no matter how well intentioned, and anarchism," and took back the floor from Bolton Hall.

As a boy in Kovno, I spent hours in my stepfather's study arguing with him about God. Pyotr Mikhailovich ended the discussions with a piece of candy and the observation that between the One and the many lay the path of words. He meant by this that through talk, not silent meditation, a Jew found his way to the Holy One, which was why we even recited our prayers and read the Law aloud. I declared myself an exception. "Yes, Maxie," he said, "if a mule balking on the straight way amid the passing traffic is an exception, then you are one." Now Emma said much the same about the reformist, the social gospeler, the puritan, and the like. Such well-doers appeared so often to think as you did, to talk as you did, but of a sudden they stopped in their tracks on the open road of freedom: thus far they would go, and no farther. But the wide road once taken, there was no turning back to the narrow path. Emma quoted Whitman. "Allons! the road is before us! Camerado, I give you my hand! Will you give me yourself? will you come travel with me?" The Freemasonic string quartet and their wives nodded yes, pleased not to be counted among the foot-draggers and obstructionists.

It was then that she brought up Fanny's brothers. I should have expected it. With Emma, there'd be no gentle stirrings of remembrance. Two camerados, she called them, workhorses for the Cause, whose fate could not go unmentioned in this house, though their names would not be found in newpapers, only in the files of the tsar's Third Section. Lev and Fedya Ruttenberg, brothers to Fanny Kraft, didn't seek martyrdom, any more than those countless others who heeded the call of the revolution and followed its road. Emma was eloquent in describing the steely courage with which they must have faced the hangman's noose on a cold morning in the forest outside Bialystok. She didn't say it was Mishka who betrayed them. It was possible she didn't know. Even Sophie, in her letter, wasn't certain on that point. Emma looked in Fanny's direction. All eyes followed hers. The children cried out, "Mama!" The chair in which Fanny sat was empty.

Abby asked everyone please to keep his seat. The harpist began to play. I found Fanny in Xanadu, lying on the divan, listening to the faint music. "What an evening, Max!" she said. There was a phial of chloral in her hand. She'd had to slip away without disturbing anyone. It was only for a few minutes, until the dizziness and double vision passed. I wondered if she heard Emma eulogize her brothers and asked her who was speaking when she left. She smiled groggily and giggled. "Imagine Lena and that bum," she said, meaning Reitman, and fell asleep. I covered her with a blanket and returned to the parlor. Sasha was holding forth on prisons as schools for crime, and schools as prisons for children's minds. He fell silent. I motioned to him that he should go on.

V

Free Love

LENA THE HOUSEMAID was in love. She told Basya that Ben Reitman would come back and take her away, and what would her sister Sadie say to that, her marrying a doctor. Basya spit. "Another Gittelman," she said. Abby explained to the girl that Reitman was already spoken for, by Miss Goldman. Lena shook her head. That couldn't be so. If they were betrothed, why did Dr. Reitman say nice things to her at the dumbwaiter? "He didn't mean what you think, dearie," said Abby. "He just believes in free love." Lena smiled and said nothing. Abby had to laugh at herself, and dropped the matter. She was supposed to believe in free love, too. She told the story on New Year's Eve. We celebrated with Elias Pereira and his wife at their house on Riverside Drive, in way of return for Celia's first attendance at a salon evening. Julian was there as well. He said, without mentioning Ida, that because he no longer consulted with Silver & Kraft at the Brevoort, he had no opportunity to observe the routine antics of free-lovers. The denizens of the Ritz-Carlton and the Waldorf-Astoria were, no doubt, equally libidinous, but contrived to cover their Yahoo instincts with the mask of civility. "That," he said, "is called hypocrisy, and I raise my glass to it. Free love behind closed doors, sans kiss-and-tell." Fanny added some words in praise of the sleep that follows. It was her joke, ever since the last salon, to say ruefully that she could sleep through anything, even the revolution. The morning after, at breakfast, I told her the guests left late, with a long round of cheers for Fanny Kraft, which failed to awaken her. She wondered if that doctor in Vienna wasn't right after all, that the greater part of our mental life was consigned to oblivion and only occasionally dribbled out disguised as dreams. I asked if she heard the applause in her sleep. Fanny answered, "You mean like a distant flock of birds." Then I asked if perhaps she dreamed of her brothers. "What a question," she said, and rang for the eggs.

After Julian gave his toast, Celia suggested that the trouble with so-called free love was that people confused it with wanton sex, on the one hand, and true love, on the other. Didn't the sex-and-love question, in point of fact, break down into matters of choice. How terrible for us if we'd been forced into arranged marriages, the way our grandparents and even some of our parents had. Was that not a kind of prostitution? I thought of Ariane. Her grandmother's first marriage was arranged. The old woman told her that the wedding night was like making love with a beautiful stranger. Celia reached out to hold Elias's hand. "And if I find and choose my true love," she said, "isn't that free love?" Zak was quiet, as always when conversation turned to fidelity. Julian smiled at his sister-in-law, as if to say, would that everyone were so fortunate. I took a letter from my pocket that concerned, I said, another case of true love freely chosen. It was from Tina Pacifici and arrived that morning at the shop.

"Dear Papa Max," she wrote, "(I think of you as my papa now), this letter comes to you by the goodness of my friend Sister Maddalena Angelica, the teacher of geometry, music, and English at the convent school of Santa Maria Annunziata in Naples. In English, I am one of her pupils, even though I speak the language better than she, because of my years in America. She says that when I leave this place, she will hate to see me go, because she will have no one with whom to practice her English. I have been in the convent school four years, sent by my mama and her friend Signore Salvatore Ricatto. Now Mama has died of a burst appendix, and Signore Ricatto wants to keep what was hers for himself, when all the world knows he should not do this. He has promised the convent a big donation, says Sister Maddalena, for keeping me here beyond this summer, the time for finishing my education, so that I do not stand in his way. While Mama was alive, I did not care so much that I was here, because every time I saw her and Signore Ricatto together, I thought of my Papa Marco and, if there were a heaven and he looked down, how sad and angry he would feel. But now that she has died, I will stay no longer. I am my father's daughter and have determined to leave! Maddalena Angelica and many other of the sisters side with me, especially those whose families forced them to take the vows, and say they will help me when my studies are finished. I have told them I have a young man in America who is going to take me as his wife. I long to know if Joseph still waits for me, but dare not receive letters from America at this time and arouse the suspicions of Signore Ricatto and his supporters in the convent. Papa Max, please tell my Joseph for me that I will soon be with him, and he and I shall grow old together in happiness, the way we said we would. I kiss you and Mama Fanny, Aunt Abby and Uncle Zak, Auntie Ida, and Barney, too. I love and miss you all. Your Tina."

Abby said this was out of those dreadful romances she read as a girl, and began to cry. What could we do to save her? Julian dabbed his eyes. There was nothing we could do, he said, that we hadn't already done. Since Marco Tullio Pacifici was a naturalized citizen, so, too, was his daughter. Copies of the appropriate records were filed at his firm's offices. The monies coming to her from the inherited shares in Silver & Kraft were being held in trust, out of the reach of that blackguard Ricatto, a leech of the basest order. "He durst not reply to my letter," said Julian, "lest he reveal his coward's game." Elias suggested hiring an investigator to inquire about the convent school of Santa Maria Annunziata. Julian asked to what end. Tina Pacifici was clearly a young woman of resolve. She was in no physical danger. A year from now, she'd be sitting among us, or, if not, she'd let us know the reason why. The real unknown was Joey. The boy's head might be turned, he said, by an upraised hem and a redstockinged ankle. Just how far was Miss Goldman's farm from the North River Academies, that he mightn't be spirited away one afternoon to the bower of free love? I imagined Maximus the younger ravished by cousin Emma in Sasha's tent: "Come in here, dear, I've got something interesting to show you." I told Julian not to worry, Joey was good-natured, yes, but cautious. He wasn't the kind to act without thinking or let spill whatever came into his head. Elizabeth was the impetuous one. Besides, Emma was about to start on another long lecture tour. By the time she returned next summer, school would be over and Joey would have been graduated and be far from Dobbs Ferry. "Bravo," said Julian. "We don't want the young woman to return to these shores, after her travail, to find damaged goods awaiting her." At midnight, Elias popped the champagne. We drank to prosperity in America, and to the true lovers' reunion, in the New Year of 1911.

The children were home for the winter school vacation. I sat with Joey in the library. We were discussing his future. He was soon to turn eighteen years of age. I thought, Some things are missing: a beard on my face, a bag of sourball candies, the smell of flowers and the sound of voices drifting in from the garden of my stepfather's villa. I remembered Ariane, how we were discovered together, and heard her say, not unkindly now: "All the way from Kovno to America, twenty-seven years gone by, and you still haven't left your stepfather's study, have you, Maxim?" Joey said he took an interest in engineering and was thinking of attending Columbia University's School of Mines. "And afterward?" I said. He shrugged, a little shyly, and said he'd like to come into the shop. Maybe Silver & Kraft would return to the construction business. "We shall see, Joey. We shall see." I was pleased to learn he had some determination. I told him that when I was his age, I was resolved to come to America and had taught myself English. Joey smiled patiently. He'd heard the story before. It was then that I brought up Ariane. I'd followed her to Paris, and meant to take her with me to America. "But," I said, "the young lady wouldn't go. I thought she was waiting for me, but she wasn't." Joey was unsettled. All his life, he believed his parents had loved each other since they were children, from the moment in that little schoolhouse in Kovno when Papa sharpened Mama's pencil stub with his pocketknife, the same one he carried unto this very day. He recalled the figure of the young woman in the family photograph that once hung in the dining room, before Fanny threw it into the snowy garden, and said he always thought

Madame was beautiful, the way she looked right at the camera, not like a person in service at all. I said it was a terrible thing to hope for something that wasn't there and never would be, such as God or an expected revolution. "Most of all," I added, "a waiting love," and gave him Tina's letter to read. Joey flushed. He excused himself and went into the parlor to stare at the coals in the fireplace. He came back into the library, the letter in his hand. "What does Tina look like now?" he asked. "What if she's—" I finished the thought for him. "Ugly and fat, not like Madame. It doesn't matter, Joey, so long as you're waiting when she arrives. That's all I ask." After that, they'd be free to choose. This wasn't the Old Country. We didn't arrange marriages here, in America.

Elizabeth sulked in her room for the rest of the winter vacation. She said everybody in this house talked about free love and free choice, but we were all pretending. If Joey could marry Tina Pacifici, why couldn't she marry Barney Sussman? Why couldn't she stay at Stump Lake? It wasn't as if she'd be running away from home. We owned the place, didn't we? She locked her door from the inside and shouted, "Becky Edelsohn is my age and lives with Mr. Berkman, and they aren't even married!" Abby commented that we had ourselves to blame. Thus was come down upon us "Anarchism in the Golden Land." Elizabeth was unprepared for the salon and shouldn't have been allowed to attend. Fanny disagreed. She tried not to spoil her children, but young people in America were willful and ungrateful. I suggested that so were we in our day, and gave as evidence Sophie's circle, the People's Will, and emigrating alone in disregard of our elders. "Yes," said Fanny, "but that was Russia. That was the revolution. That was the pogroms." Nevertheless, she had to coax Elizabeth from her room with a promise that we'd consider her living at Stump Lake. I imagined the girl debauched by Barney the rat in the tree house near the Gypsy's grave: "Hey, come up, big surprise for you!" It was my bounden duty to consult, however tardily, with Ida. I determined to delay until school occupied Elizabeth's attention again and the matter was less urgent, even forgotten. She complained in her weekly letters home that she was as much a prisoner as Tina Pacifici in the convent. If we didn't talk to Ida soon, she threatened to throw herself into the river, and then we'd understand how serious she was, when it was too late. Dr.

Cornelius Beinhorn, the headmaster of the North River Academies, wrote to inform us of his concerns about young Elizabeth.
Her studies were suffering. She lacked discipline and was disrup-
tive. For several Sundays running, she refused to attend voluntary
chapel, alas, for contemplation of the Oversoul might indeed
prove a proper physic for her bilious temperament. Unless her
conduct changed for the better, she would be asked not to return
after the termination of the school year and to pursue her education elsewhere.

Ida declared that Elizabeth should think of Kraft's Hotel as
home. Who was this Beinhorn to talk this way? What kind of a
doctor was he? "You know the happiness I wish for the girl," she
said. "The same as I'd wish for a daughter of my own, and—
who knows?—one day she may be. We don't have to be red
anarchists, do we, Mr. Kraft, not to stand in the way of true free
love." I imagined Ida boosting Elizabeth up into the tree house.
This was at the monthly meeting of Silver & Kraft, a Saturday
toward the end of March. Ida now stayed at a different hotel each
time she came down to the city. She preferred the smaller estab-
lishments on lower Fifth Avenue to the uptown palaces. She
didn't have to act the grand lady; knowing she had the money to
do so was enough for her. We sat in her suite talking over the
business of the shop. I mentioned Joey and his hope that we might
return to building. Zak said that, walking the side streets today
to Ida's hotel, he'd seen at least a dozen clapboard boardinghouses
near collapse. Why not buy two or three, let the boy collect the
rents, then tear them down in a few years and see what he could
do. Julian said if it were done wisely, 'twere well it was quickly,
while property values were low. Our radical friends were making
Greenwich Village a desirable place for overeducated, underam-
bitious youth. Ida said no. The cost of real estate hereabouts was
already inflated. Everyone was too confident these days. It was
better to play a safe hand, as in cards, until the next panic started
and the old houses could be had for half what we'd pay for them
now. "It's not the reds who raise and lower the ante, is it, Mr.
Pereira. It's the bankers. If we wait, we'll beat them at their own
game." Julian bowed and deferred to her pecuniary wisdom.

Our business was done. Zak made it known with a slight nod
that he and Ida wanted to be alone. Julian glanced at me, as if to

say, Behind closed doors, sans kiss-and-tell. He proposed we walk south to Washington Square, and from there east to Broadway and then down to his firm's offices near City Hall. There was time for me to sign before witnesses an affidavit concerning Tina Pacifici's citizenship, attesting to the fact that she was her father's daughter—this, in case the papers she had with her when she arrived were insufficient proof of her identity. As we neared the square, fire engines clanged by, some horse-drawn, others motor-driven. Black smoke rose up and dimmed the late afternoon sky. People around us began to run, and we ran with them, past the private homes on the north side of the park, past the arch, through the park itself, until we reached the blazing factory building at the edge of the square where the girls, one after another, were dropping from the uppermost floors to their deaths on the pavement below. The police held back the nearest onlookers. Julian and I were able to see over the heads of the people in front of us. The fire ladders extended only to the sixth story, and the eighth, ninth, and tenth were in flames. The life nets broke under the weight of the falling workers, some with their skirts ablaze. Word went through the crowd that one of the biggest garment-makers in the city, the Triangle Shirtwaist Company, was on fire. Bodies by the dozens lay sprawled on the sidewalk, and every one of them was Zipporah Gelb. On the ninth floor, a man was handing young women through a window. One turned to kiss him, and he followed after her in a lover's leap. Their clothes billowed as they turned in the air. They hit the cement together. The conflagration was put out within fifteen minutes. By then, so the newpapers reported later, there were one hundred forty-six dead.

"I am shattered, shattered," said Julian, and grieved in the taxicab all the way to his firm's offices. He was too anguished to remember I was to sign an affidavit on Tina's behalf, and I was too perturbed to remind him. We sat behind closed doors, amid law books and leather furniture, and drank neat whiskey to calm ourselves. In my head, I heard the screams of one hundred forty-six women and men burning, suffocating, falling. Julian said the ghastly irony that such a disaster should happen within sight of the homes of America's finest families was almost enough to turn a just man into a revolutionist. "Max," he said, "they may be outrageous, those friends of yours, but they are innocents, I tell you. Their anger at least is righteous, and their Cause pure." He added: "Never will you hear me mock them again," and he quoted Oscar Wilde, that "where there is sorrow, there is holy ground." We poured out more whiskey and pondered the queerness of life: our comic devotion to its everyday trivia, our blessed ignorance of its impinging tragedies, even at the moment they struck—oblivious at birth, unconscious at the moment of death, blind in between. "The Greeks well understood," said Julian. "The action is offstage. Unhappy the man who blunders beyond the wings." That night on the icy Nemen, which was the river Styx frozen over, the heavens opened up. Roundabout the line of the dead falls a silent hail of fiery bodies, pairs of free-lovers hurled down by the hand of history from the upper stories of the burning sky.

VI

Our House Divided

SADIE MIRKIN, THE former governess, sent for her sister Lena to come live in Walla Walla, in the state of Washington. She was Sally Kellum now, married to a rich American rancher named Bill, a genuine Unitarian. He'd never been east, didn't know a Yiddish accent when he heard it, and believed his bride was an orphaned farm girl from a family of Pennsylvania Dutch. The letter was written in English and contained railway timetables and a postal money order of fifty dollars that was supposed to cover traveling expenses but, in fact, would not. "When you would be here, darling Lena girl, on my kettle ranch the Billy K, you would make good by me for the money with the work." Lena asked me to explain the letter to her, since she couldn't yet read and write English so good. I sat her down in the library and told her to be careful. She didn't have to go all the way to Walla Walla just because Sadie summoned her. She could return the postal order. She didn't want to be her sister's slave, did she? Lena smiled, and said nothing. I said, "You're not still waiting for Ben Reitman?" She nodded her head, then shook it, wiped away a tear, said nothing, and smiled.

After Lena left, Basya complained more than ever about her rheumatism. No housemaid she hired stayed longer than a few weeks. The children's rooms were empty, and the house was vast. Joey entered Columbia College, preparatory to the course in engineering, and lived in a dormitory there. Elizabeth attended the local high school in Woodville, near Stump Lake, one grade below Barney Sussman. She was first in her class among the girls in Latin, algebra, history, and cooking, and was allowed to enroll in the honors class in elementary Greek, all without meditating on the Oversoul. There were no more salons. Fanny said what was the point of them if she was asleep and couldn't remember the discussions. Let Dr. Pereira and his wife continue the evenings if they liked. Abby said the salons weren't necessary for us anymore. She was on friendly terms with Hutchins Hapgood, ever since our last gathering. He introduced her to a wider circle of writers and artists—thinkers, she said—than our limited associations made possible. She only regretted her health wasn't better, so she could get out more often. Not a month went by without her relapsing for a few days into lethargy. It was a recurrence, she said, of her St. Petersburg illness, nothing mental. She explained to Fanny, "Hutch and his bunch respect the work of that man in Vienna, Dr. Freud, and recognize the difference between real and imaginary disease. No offense intended, dear." Fanny remarked how sensitive this St. Petersburg germ must be, flaring up at the slighest exposure to talk of the revolution that failed and of Cossacks and pogroms. Perhaps the germ understood English. I recalled the unbridgeable silences in my stepfather's villa, between Vera Andreyevna and her brats and us children of Pyotr Mikhailovich's from his earlier marriages, among the servants when they spoke Yiddish and Lithuanian, between my sisters and me when they spoke the language of girls, between me and Mishka. There were similar silences now in the house at East Seventy-ninth Street. In my mind, the voice of Ariane reechoed among them, sadly I thought: "No, Maxim, you haven't come very far."

Zak said the difficulty would work itself out as always. This wasn't the first time the women weren't talking to each other. Ida, when she heard, said how sad, and took an apartment at the Chelsea Hotel. She was there at the end of the month for Silver & Kraft and on occasional days betweentimes. The staff at Stump Lake affirmed that Mrs. Sussman was away on private business and was expected to return tomorrow. Zak told Abby he had to work late at the shop and couldn't attend that evening's reception, lecture, concert, play, exhibition, debate, or soirée. I looked forward to having a comfortable dinner at home with Fanny and the run of the place to ourselves. We listened to the phonograph in the parlor, took a turn in the garden, journeyed upstairs to Xanadu, without crossing zones of cold silence. I smoked my water pipe while Fanny read aloud poems by Coleridge and mysteries by Conan Doyle. She said it was like the old days, when it was just us together under one roof, at the beginning of the world. She wondered why we continued to keep house with other people at all. She also noticed that Zak's late nights at the shop coincided with Ida's private business. "I'm not saying I think anything, Max." She smiled thinly. "But if I did, who could blame him?"

Ida requested that Fanny come to the next meeting of Silver & Kraft. This was toward the end of the year. She telephoned me at the shop to say it was a personal matter that she preferred to discuss in comfortable surroundings. Zak looked at me and shrugged, as if to say he didn't know what it was about, though perhaps he did but didn't care to say so. Fanny, when I told her of the invitation, said, "You'll see I was right. They're going to declare themselves, she and Zak. What else?" Then she laughed. These things really did happen in life. How could I work with Zak every day at the shop and never suspect? I suggested Fanny's anger was giving her imagination free rein. Ida was all dollars and cents. Whatever she had to say to us both must have to do with mortgages and property and concern Stump Lake. Fanny said, "Max, how can you be so naïve?"

After the Triangle Fire, Julian Pereira's hair turned gray. He grew a beard, took notes on his cuffs like a sorry notary, and rarely said anything witty. Nevertheless, I was relieved to see him at Ida's apartment. I thought his presence meant that even the personal business of the meeting would remain in the unmelodramatic and measurable world of money. Fanny gathered the same. Her expectant expression changed to matter-of-fact. We went through the usual agenda, accounts, rents paid, rents in arrears, the price of real estate, building repairs. Then Ida said we should congratulate ourselves. We were all soon to be grandparents. Elizabeth was going to have a baby. Julian looked up from his cuffs with interest. Zak was startled. Without saying as much, the way Ida put the news included him as well. Fanny said, "Must she?" The look on her face was near disgust. No one asked who the father was. Everyone knew. Ida ignored Fanny's question. She confessed there was a difficulty about the wedding. "Difficulty indeed," said Julian, something like his old self. "There hasn't been one." Ida ignored Julian's remark. She said, "We hope for our children the things we never had, don't we, Mr. Pereira. More than anything, they want a big home wedding, a canopy, a rabbi, dancing, a celebration. I married Sussman on the boat." The problem was where to have the wedding, here in the city or at Stump Lake. Fanny was blunt: "At the hotel, Ida. We don't allow rites of religion in our house." Ida said far be it from her to dispute the wishes of the mother of the bride. She only wanted to point out that, speaking as the mother of the groom, it was proper that Isidore should be there. "And what my feeling is," she added, her voice starting to choke, "my feeling is that he should come without that woman." Zak spoke to her in dialect. Julian didn't understand Yiddish. I gave him the gist of the plea. Ida should be reasonable. What she was asking was impossible. Abby respected and admired Ida and considered herself a second mother to the girl. To all of this, Ida said nothing. It was a brisk day. A gust of wind from the street blew in soot and the smell of chimney smoke. With the back of one hand and then of the other, Ida wiped her eyes, which were smarting, she said, from the city air.

Fanny was shaken. How much longer must she live in the same house with the adulterer and his cold wife? How could she look at Abby anymore without thinking of Ida? How was it that all these years I knew and never told her? "Max," she said, "what else haven't you told me?" and when I began to speak, covered her ears and walked away. Yet somehow that week at East Seventy-ninth Street we managed to sit down at dinner together, Zak and Abby, Fanny and I, and talk. Abby was upset for Elizabeth. "Her schooling," she said, "doesn't anyone care about that?" Here was a girl almost seventeen years of age. She was too young to vote even if there were woman suffrage. She was ignorant of the idea of birth limitation. Now she would be without a complete education. What was left for Elizabeth in life? What did she have? Zak suggested money. Abby said this was no time for his jokes. "My daughter has made her choice," said Fanny, "and she must live with it. I was younger than she is when I left *gimnaziya* to come alone to America. I learned on my own. Are you telling me, dear, that I am uneducated? Or Zak? Never let it be said that I stood against my children's intentions the way my family did mine." Abby flushed. That wasn't the point. So far as I was concerned, the real affliction was Barney, my son-in-law to be, the seducer, the father of my grandchild, the wolf who was making himself my heir. With Zak there, I didn't say so, but broached instead the matter of religion. That a daughter of mine, raised in a household without superstition, who had never set foot in a synagogue, should want a rabbi to officiate at her wedding was beyond my understanding. Abby asked if I were proposing that not all of us attend. Zak brightened. Then she said, "I'm certainly not going to add insult to the girl's ruin, out of a misplaced stand on principle." If Fanny and I let Ida Sussman turn Kraft's Hotel into a Jewish establishment, for the sake of profit, well, dears, one must reap what one has sown. Basya was grumbling by the dumbwaiter. She stood unbent to deliver her opinion. "Tcha," she said. "So we give them what they think they want, a big wedding, something nice to remember before things go bad and they get old." In this way, she invited herself to Stump Lake. We agreed to hold the ceremony in January, when the guests at the hotel would be few and Elizabeth's appearance, said Fanny, still slender.

It was then, after Ida set the wedding for the week following New Year's, that I received a telegram from Tina Pacifici, in Hamburg. "Papa Max. Sailing today on Kaiser Wilhelm 2nd class. Arrive Monday. T." Julian gathered the necessary documents, the record of Marco's citizenship and my affidavit, but said he expected we wouldn't need to show them. Second-class passengers had the privilege of going through customs and immigration aboard ship. A young woman adroit enough to decamp undetected from a convent and circumvent Ellis Island had her effects in good order. Nevertheless, he determined to meet the *Kaiser Wilhelm* in case of trouble. "The sins of the father," he said, meaning, by this, Marco's having once been a red anarchist. I didn't suppose the authorities could exclude her for that. Julian said, "I shall be there if they try." The greeting party was small, consisting of Julian and me and a bashful Joey, in anticipation of a long wait and arguments on board. But when we arrived at the dock, the passengers were already moving slowly down the gangplanks. I craned my neck to find bobbing among them the dark-eyed girl I remembered as Marco Pacifici's daughter. A tall nun in a black habit walked in front of me and stood in the way of my full view. I suggested she remove herself and her valise. I wished to see the passengers as they disembarked. To my surprise, she laughed. Then she cried, "I fooled you with my disguise!" and hugged me. It was Tina. Julian said, "May I have the pleasure," and kissed her hand. She curtsied. Joey stood shy of her, I thought perhaps because of her clothes. Tina smiled at him, taking in his height. "Joseph," she said, "you've changed." He answered so had she. He'd been holding a bouquet of flowers and gave them to her now. "Roses," she said, "*tante grazie*," and kissed him on the cheek. Joey reddened and stepped back. People nearby gazed curiously at the deportment of this affectionate nun. The moment we settled in a taxicab, Tina pulled off her wimple and, sighing, shook out her hair. She lifted off the crucifix that hung around her neck. "The game is over," she said. "Papa Max, can't I just toss this thing in the trash somewhere?" It was worthless, a one-lira street item made of papier-mâché coated with silver paint and shellac. Joey said it would light a terrific blaze in the fireplace, with shooting flames. Tina pressed his arm. "Let's do it!" They should rip up the rags she was wearing and throw them in, too, and make of her lost years in the convent of Santa Maria Annunziata an *auto-da-fé*.

That day at East Seventy-ninth Street, the rifts of silence were breached for a time by the merriment of Tina's homecoming. Her crucifix and rent nun's habit made royal fireworks in the parlor hearth. Longtime tenants at the Costanza Court came by to welcome her back to America and sing "Bella Tina, Amore Mio." Elias Pereira and Celia were there with all their children, four girls and the first-born, Nathaniel. Basya prepared piles of cousin Emma's stuffed fish, platters of her roast chicken with dumplings and carrot stew, loaves of holiday bread, and two large honey cakes. The little Pereiras ran through the house and made themselves sick with sweets. A number of Marco's Masonic brothers and their wives, the string quartet among them, called to pay respects and stayed long after dark. A welcoming telegram was received from Stump Lake and the messenger sent off reeling on his remaining rounds from a glass of schnapps. The open house lasted far into the evening. When it was over, I had pieced together from Tina's conversation the story of her escape and flight.

Wearing the nun's habit was the idea of Sister Maddalena Angelica. It would allow Tina to travel without arousing suspicion and the curiosity, or worse, that a young woman alone and in plain dress would. Her studies were finished. She reached school-leaving age, but was compelled by the mother superior to start preparing for the novitiate. Salvatore Ricatto had promised the convent a handsome gift if Tina were kept cloistered. The gift, said Tina, would be from her papa's money. It was her money now, if she could put her hands on it somehow. She was her father's daughter. The only thing Marco Tullio Pacifici would have donated to the Church was a mouthful of spit. More important to her than money were her family's passports, her papa's American citizenship papers, and the stocks in Silver & Kraft. Ricatto kept stacks of cash on hand. He stuffed his pockets with rolls of lire the size of his fists and peeled off the bills to give to his friends. Sister Maddalena's family also had friends, who happened, as well, to be friends of Ricatto's enemies. Among honorable men, favors were given and favors returned. Sister Maddalena's cousin Gianni had a favor due. Perhaps Tina knew where Ricatto stored his *perfida valuta*. A man of honor didn't claim what was not his own. Tina recalled the location of the safe in a corner of Ricatto's wine cellar. A few weeks later, a box of music paper was delivered to Sister Maddalena for her classes. At the bottom were American passports in the name of Pacifici, Marco's citizenship papers, the stock certificates, and a bundle of lire. That very night, Tina walked out unimpeded from the convent of Santa Maria Annunziata, dressed as a nun. The guard hardly noticed. He was told to keep strangers out and schoolgirls in. Sister Maddalena and her coconspirators were to say nothing at first, and then admit that Tina Pacifici had hinted at wanting to slip off to the port of Naples and stow away on the first boat leaving for America if she couldn't beg the money for steerage. Ricatto's friends would search the docks, while Tina boarded the train north to Switzerland, then into Germany, and made her way to Hamburg in three days' time. Customs officials at the borders addressed her as sister and waived inspection. Fellow passengers moved to give her a window seat. She shared a cabin on the *Kaiser Wilhelm* with three other women, Bavarian immigrants crossing to join their husbands, who dropped their eyes and whispered in her presence. "A path opened for me from Naples to New York," said Tina. "The most beautiful sound I've heard in years was today, when the immigration man said in his American accent, 'Everything's O.K., sister, you're on your way home.' And the most beautiful sight"—she laughed—"Papa Max at the pier, on the lookout for a little Italian girl."

The day before Elizabeth's and Barney's wedding, there was a skating party on Stump Lake. Ida said it was good to take our minds off all the preparations for tomorrow and make of the whole occasion a time of happiness. I asked if she were worried. "Not I," she said, "but take a look at yourself in the mirror, why don't you, Mr. Kraft. Mrs. Silver is also a little peaked, may she fall through the ice." I said now that we were family, Ida should call me Max. As for Abby, she was simply concerned for Elizabeth's future. "What concerns can she have?" said Ida. "The girl is in good hands, or doesn't that woman think, not really, that mine are as capable as hers. This for her." Ida spit. "This for her admiration and respect." Hot cocoa and sandwiches were served in the boathouse. Barney and his friends showed off, skating backward and making figures of eight. They formed a chain of the wedding party, which snaked over the ice. One by one, everyone joined, even Abby, although she felt weak, even Tina, who was shaky on skates, even Basya, bent as she was. "Come on, Max," they shouted, "don't be the spoilsport!" I hooked on to Julian, who was the last to attach himself, protesting, before me. Our skate blades scraped the thick ice as we circled the lake. The women's laughter echoed in the cold dry air like the twittering of the dead on the Styx frozen over. It was curious bringing up the rear of the line. In my dream, I was always at the head, with no one and nothing in front of me. Zipporah's voice said, "Once more around the Nemen, Max."

Their wedding was hilarious to Elizabeth and Barney. They giggled over everything, the Hebrew prayers, the crunch of the wineglass under Barney's foot, the scowling looks the rabbi gave them. After the ceremony, the band struck up and a hired Yiddish funnyman sang and gibbered and urged everyone to dance and eat. There were champagne and caviar, sweet liqueurs and plum

brandy, a huge cake, and trays of the hotel's specialties, Mrs.
E. G. Smith's Original Kosher Crêpes and her Genuine Butter
Almond Cookies. The newly wedded pair was hoisted up and
carried on chairs. Basya capered around them waving a handkerchief. She said to me, breathless, there hadn't been such a wedding
since my mother and Pyotr Mikhailovich were married, and then
cried. Ida took the opportunity to dance flirtatiously with Zak
right before Abby's eyes. Amid the to-do, Joey and Tina slipped
off somewhere hand in hand. I danced with Fanny. She was
bright with excitement and wine, the blush of her face shining
through the white rice powder. "Max," she said, "I know this is
terrible, and I disapprove of the whole thing, but I'm having a
wonderful time!" During a break in the music, Elias Pereira and
Celia took the groom and bride aside, respectively, for an intimate
heart-to-heart, as if either of them needed any instruction. The
funnyman announced I was to dance with the bride. Everyone
laughed and shouted, "Be careful, Barney. Don't let her run off
with him!" Elizabeth hugged me and said thanks for the swell
party. Barney punched my arm and presumed to call me Pop.
Afterward I walked outside alone and went down to the boathouse. It was a night of moon and stars, hoarfrost, and glitter on
the clear ice. Someone tapped me on the shoulder. It was Abby.
She said, sadly I thought, that something very wrong was going
on. I supposed she meant between Zak and Ida, but I didn't say
so. The house, she continued, would never again be what it once
was. We couldn't be what we'd been. She cleared her throat and
confessed that she and Zak had considered giving up their share
at East Seventy-ninth Street and moving to a place of their own.
I told her that for Fanny and me it was the same. "You and Zak
will still have the shop," she said. "Fanny and I have nothing
together anymore, not even the salons. You and Fanny have this
lovely hotel. You've got the children. I have Zak." Abby paused.
She picked up two small stones lying at her feet, threw one, and
then the other. They skittered along the frozen lake. "Yes, I have
Zak. Tell me that's enough." The funnyman's voice called out
through the megaphone, "The groom's mother dances with the
father of the bride." I left Abby contemplating the stones, which
had come to a standstill far apart.

VII

The Question of Violence

TINA SETTLED INTO Elizabeth's old room at East Seventy-ninth
Street. She removed from the walls the coloring-book cutouts of
girls' heroines and put in their place pictures from fashion magazines. Abby was surprised that the daughter of Marco Tullio
Pacifici would take an interest in such trivialities. Tina reminded
her that she'd been six years in a foreign country, in a Catholic
convent school where all the students had to don the same drab
uniform every day. She wanted to look like an American again
and, for that, must study what clothing to choose. To me she said,
"Aunt Abby thinks because all the women in the bunch she goes
with wear a shirtwaist and skirt, everyone else should, too. My
papa always dressed like a gentleman." I suggested that Abby was
looking for a friend in the house. Tina answered that a bossy
mother superior didn't have friends, only allies and enemies. Who
was Aunt Abby to run her life and tell her what to do? If Uncle
Zak worked late at the shop, why must she, Tina, go to those
gatherings instead, with all the talk that got nowhere, and the
men, the goats, laughing at her when she explained to them she
wasn't against free love but was, in fact, engaged. Fanny was
sympathetic. "Ideas, even good ones, won't change the human
heart. You'd think that woman would know it by now. Just be

patient, dear. Stay out of her way, like I do. We'll all be moving soon."

Zak was unhappy about giving up the house for which he'd drawn up the plans. Ida said nonsense, if we were going to sell, the time was now. We'd make a killing before the market fell. She found a prospective buyer and invited him to a meeting of Silver & Kraft. Julian was there and Tina as well, because she owned shares in the shop. The man called himself Shady, which he was, and spoke with a thick accent I couldn't place. Zak thought afterward it might be Syrian. Shady admitted he was a purchasing agent for a party he couldn't yet name, who had no interest in the house, only its location. His offer was all cash and nearly half again what the property was worth. This was Ida's kind of deal. She fixed her eyes on Zak until he laughed. "Why be sentimental?" he said, and he and I shook hands with Shady and left the details for Julian to sort out with the man's lawyer. Ida was triumphant. She said to Zak, after all the business was finished, "Stay a while, Isidore," and patted the place beside her on the sofa. Tina looked at her, then at Zak, and said under her breath, "Of course," but seemed shaken. Julian and I took her to a tearoom across the street. As we talked, her eyes kept drifting to the hotel and upward to the curtained windows of Ida's apartment. She asked if this was what it meant when Uncle Zak worked late. I nodded. Tina pointed to her stomach. She said, "I think Aunt Abby feels it down there," then pointing to her head, added, "but doesn't know it up here." Julian said it was a wise observation. "I am my father's daughter," she said, "and I know how to watch." Tina also thought that Ida believed that by selling the house, there would be less to hold Zak and Abby together, and that was why she was so eager for him to accept the offer from Shady. "But Auntie Ida is wrong. He will never leave her. I know this is true"—she pointed to her head and then her stomach—"because I understand it both here and there. It is all so very sad, isn't it, Papa Max?"

Once the house was sold, Fanny and Abby started to speak to each other again. There was work to be done and another wedding to be arranged, for Joey and Tina, before the packing and moving began. Abby said, "Just a small affair," and drew up an invitation list of over fifty. Tina took it from her and reduced it by half, but allowed a couple of people to remain from Abby's circle of friends. Cousin Emma wasn't among them. She was still out West with Reitman on her speaking tour, and didn't approve of marriage anyway. "The gentlemanly ones," said Tina, "Mr. Hutchins and Mr. Hall." Mr. Berkman was a gentleman, too, but ticked like a bomb, and his companion, Becky, was like one of those fierce young nuns she'd known, zealous and quick to judgment. It was a question of violence. If a man had a gun, sooner or later he'd use it, just as the man who made threats would carry them out. These people armed themselves with words. I asked what if the words they spoke were true. We were sitting in the library, Tina and Joey, Fanny and I, going over the invitations. Tina answered my one question with three of her own. "Forgive me, but true for whom? The killing starts with words. What does truth mean to a dead man? My father turned his back on the talking, because of the blackness of the human heart that Mama Fanny says will never change, and they murdered him, didn't they?" I gathered she meant the old crew, but couldn't bring myself to ask her with Fanny there. "Didn't they, Papa Max?" she repeated. Fanny froze, ready to cover her ears. I thought of Mishka, as I always did when it came to butchery and betrayal, but this wasn't the time to bring up his deportation and that of his International Revolutionary Order. Joey and Tina passed a look between them. Tina said, "Never mind, we know they did," and we returned to the matter of invitations. Ida was already crossed off the list. She'd told Tina she couldn't come on account of Abby, but also in order to be near Elizabeth, who was nearing her term and too big to travel. Joey understood. I was relieved not to have to explain. Barney would be the lone family representative from Stump Lake. Better that American-born rat, I said to myself, than any from the foreign branch, Sophie, Nina, Mishka, souls lost in the European abyss.

A few days before the wedding, a letter from Paris was delivered to the shop. The mailman apologized. He said it had sat in the post office for days because the address was incomplete and difficult to decipher. In fact, the envelope seemed to have been opened and resealed. The letter inside was from Sophie, in Russian. She was writing to me at my workplace, which she called up from memory, having lost her book of American addresses, and much of her baggage along the way, in her many moves from country to country. What news she had now to give was said more briefly than in her letter four years earlier, but was no less jarring. Mishka—she used his name—was dead. "Our people in Russia report," she wrote, "that he was beaten to death, as an informer, by fellow political exiles at a colony in Novosibirsk. That is all I know. It is enough. The will of the revolution be done. S. P. Kazimierska." There was not a word about Nina. Zak laughed harshly. "Gracious as ever," he said. "That's the end of his blackmail. The International Revolutionary Order, Central Council, clubbed to death in the Siberian mud." Then he added: "Can we believe it?" I thought there was no reason not to. Sophie might delude herself, but she didn't lie. Whatever she said was meant as a certainty, not an opinion, not a rumor. She loaded her cannon with facts. As Tina would say, Sophie armed herself with words. In my head, I heard again the girl's firm voice at the concealed grave of Bobelis commending my work. I saw Mishka, a purple blob in my mother's arms, and imagined his attackers with their cudgels, all of them women: Daisy Osgood and Alice Ward, Ariane Lévy-Mendès, Zipporah Gelb. "Forty-one years," I said. "I looked at him just after he was born, and his life came down to this." I held up Sophie's letter. Zak shrugged. "What I want to know," he said, "is who opened it before we did."

Joey and Tina were married by a judge, in the garden at East Seventy-ninth Street, on a warm Saturday afternoon in June. The last of the magnolia blossoms lay underfoot. The roses, azaleas, and rhododendrons were in full bloom. After the vows were made, Abby grew tearful. "Max," she said, "it's not the house I'll miss, not anymore, only my garden." As tenants from the Costanza Court struck up a Neapolitan wedding song, the sky clouded over and rain came down amid rumbles of thunder. Everyone retreated into the house and watched the storm from the bay windows. Zak raised his glass and recalled a saying from his village: "Rainfall on the wedding day, water for the fruits of a long and happy life." The guests cheered and toasted the bride and groom, who toasted them back and danced a brief two-step to imaginary music in the middle of the parlor. "A handsome couple," said Julian. "Indeed," said Bolton Hall. There were fresh strawberries and peaches, tea cakes, cousin Emma's cookies, and other finger foods, champagne, sherry, and Tokay. Barney attached himself to me. He asked where was the band and the funnyman and when would the party begin. He appraised the house with his weasel eyes and said it was a swell shack we were getting rid of. I realized my former good fortune. In the twelve years we'd lived at the place, never until now had he been there. He stuck his head in the library and asked what were all those books for. When I said for reading, he laughed, "You're kidding me, Pop," and jabbed me painfully in the ribs, in what might pass for a show of family affection.

The house was filled with the conversation of comfortable guests. A group gathered around Julian Pereira and Bolton Hall. The two lawyers were continuing the discussion of the McNamara case they'd had at the last salon. The brothers on trial for the bombing of the Los Angeles *Times* were no longer the blameless babes, having confessed to the deed that killed twenty people. "Another futile exercise," said Julian, "and then the betrayal of those among us who believed in them." Bolton Hall said not quite so. Those boys were still innocents in their way, misguided, yes, uneducated union men who didn't understand the consequences of their act. Their motivation was pure, even if their means were not. Because we once believed them to be without guilt, how in fact did that make of their confession a betrayal of us? If we turned our backs on them now, convicted prisoners, one of them for life, who were the real betrayers? To which Julian replied, "Is there no one, then, to atone for the dead?" Celia Pereira clapped her hands. "Good heavens, people," she said, "is this a wedding or a funeral?" Barney poked me again and joked that he was beginning to wonder the same thing. But Tina said no, please, let the talking go on. It wasn't so late in the day that we couldn't make merry again later. Joey and she never meant this to be a conventional reception. She had some thoughts herself on the question of violence, how it was, at bottom, a matter of words.

The chairs and sofa in the parlor were turned to form a circle. Joey and Tina's wedding became a near reprise of "Anarchism in the Golden Land." Fanny was on the alert, I supposed for the things she didn't want to hear. "I hate to say it, Max," she whispered, "but Elizabeth's party was a better time." It was Hutchins Hapgood who said that for the clearest connection between terror and words, one should look not to infrequent aberrations among unionists, libertarians, and their kind, but, rather, to the opposite, the accepted acts of their opponents. He cited Ben Reitman's recent ordeal in San Diego. The Freemasonic string quartet and their wives joked quietly among themselves. The only ordeal they associated with Reitman was that of being in the same room with him. Elias Pereira, speaking for them, asked if Mr. Hapgood would be good enough to explain. "With pleasure," he said. Perhaps there was in the house a copy of this month's number of *Mother Earth*? Fanny announced, "One moment." She went up to Xanadu and, on this occasion, returned, bringing with her the magazine. Hapgood held it up for everyone to see. "SAN DIEGO EDITION" was blazoned across the top and, at the bottom, "PATRIOTISM IN ACTION." In between, a masked top-hatted capitalist was holding a pole with an American flag and ramming its nether end into the mouth of a half-naked man staked to the ground. "If you will allow me," said Hapgood, and read with warmth to the wedding reception "The Respectable Mob," a firsthand report by Ben L. Reitman, M.D.

I knew the story already. The month before, cousin Emma and Reitman had taken her free-speech campaign to San Diego, to demonstrate support for the I.W.W., whose members were being murdered by local vigilantes. The hotel management lured Emma away from their room. Reitman was kidnapped by six men and driven at night twenty miles into the desert. His abductors took turns kicking and beating him in the motor car. They gouged his eyes and yanked his hair. Out in the desert, they were joined by another group of citizens. In the glare of the headlights, they stripped Reitman naked. They made him kiss the American flag and sing "The Star-Spangled Banner" and "My Country, 'Tis of Thee." They smeared him with tar and sagebrush, twisted his private parts, dug at his rectum with a cane, and with a burning cigar branded his buttocks with abbreviated words of terror, "I.W.W." He then ran the gauntlet of the fourteen men, that "respectable mob" of bankers, realtors, a newspaper reporter, small businessmen, and elected officials. Before they left, they returned his money, his watch, and, of his clothes, only his underwear and vest. It was not until the following evening that he reached Los Angeles, where Emma was. She'd been run out of San Diego and given him up for dead.

Hapgood paused at the end of his reading for dramatic effect. He looked up to find half his listeners gone. Something in the piece tickled them. It must have been the funny-paper image of Emma's two-faced lover howling amid the cactus and the purple sage. They tried to be polite and hold in their laughter, like schoolchildren in the classroom suppressing giggles, and then one by one fled, mute, into the library: the Freemasons and their wives, Barney, Zak, Fanny, even Julian. Hapgood, outraged, threw open the doors. He was greeted by astonished silence followed by helpless shrieking. He quit the house, Bolton Hall with him. Tina and Joey apologized all the way to the front door and returned to the parlor with tears streaming from their eyes, convulsed. By then, everyone was gasping weakly, except for Abby, who retreated to her bedroom in anger. Tina managed to groan, "Time for merrymaking," which started a new outburst, and Fanny whispered, "What a wedding! The best time I ever had."

VIII

The News from No Where

SHADY CAME THROUGH with the cash. It was delivered in a strongbox to Julian by an armed guard in plain clothes. The real buyer remained unrevealed. Julian hired a private investigator. The man found nothing illegal, but learned that Shady's operation acquired properties that in time the city always found to be attractive sites for schools, playgrounds, and the like. Among the investors in the realty concern were nieces of aldermen and wives of trustees of philanthropical institutions. Zak and I sat behind closed doors in Julian's offices and admired the trim bundle of thousand-dollar bills guaranteed by the gold of the Golden Land. "Benevolent graft," said Julian. "Your house will soon be a home for wayward girls." In fact, it went to rot and took on a haunted appearance, Bobelis's hutch in the woods grown to nightmare size. Zak couldn't bear to see it. He said that outside his village there was a ruined villa where beggars and bandits lived. "No Place," they called it, and told the police so when asked where they resided. Was that what our elegant house would become, a hobos' jungle, a shanty for bums? Fanny dreamed of the night she fled with her family from Shavl, just as she did when we first settled at East Seventy-ninth Street. This time, her father's house was in flames. She hadn't remembered the fire. I wondered if it were true. She said it was now. Only her brothers would know, and where were they for anyone to ask? Amid the packing crates and sawdust, it was hardly the moment to tell her, point-blank, "Under the ground in the forest near Bialystok." Instead, I said we weren't running from Shavl, simply hiring movers to take us from the east to the west side of town. Ariane's voice came into my head. "Not running, puppy?" she said. "Running in circles, you mean. You've been going from No Place to No Where from the day you left Kovno." I disagreed, and said I was an American. "It makes no difference what you say you are, Maxim. You are the boy on the river Nemen."

Ida, without asking, cleared away an acre of trees and shrubbery on the other side of Stump Lake. Over the forgotten Gypsy's grave, she built a cottage for Barney and Elizabeth and their baby, my grandson Rutherford Sussman. Ida said the cost of the house was hers. "It's an improvement of the hotel grounds—don't you think so, Max—and not a penny out of your pocket." This was in the owners' suite at the hotel, in the Oriental corner. Ida was minding the baby for the afternoon. Fanny and I had already moved from East Seventy-Ninth Street to an apartment on West One Hundredth Street and Riverside Drive. It was summertime, too hot to unpack, and we took the boat up the river for a holiday, the way we used to do. I asked Ida what other improvements she intended. She said, "I'm not a crystal ball, am I. But if what the other hotels offer, we can offer first, that's what we'll have to do, won't we." Fanny said that she and I still thought of Kraft's Hotel as our country home, our special place in America. It shouldn't be built up too much and spoiled. Far be it from her, said Ida, to leave such a legacy for Rutherford. She passed him to me and asked didn't I think he looked like Isidore. "To tell you the truth," said Fanny, "he's the spitting image of my father, Abram Isserovich Ruttenberg. May the poor thing grow out of it." To me, he looked the same as Mishka did after he was born, melon colored and all head, but I didn't say so. Instead, I told Ida she was a romantic. "Yes, I am," she said. "Do you think it's wrong of me to see what I love in the face of my grandchild?" She tickled him under the chin and cooed, "Rusty, how is my little Rusty?" a name that was beginning to take hold, because of the baby's hair and complexion. Where "Rutherford" came from was a mystery. Elizabeth, who'd studied Greek, thought the name was "swell." Barney balled his fists. He said, "When Rutherford Sussman bangs on the door, Pop, they'll know it isn't a little Ikey Sonofavichski coming into the room."

A letter from Nina was forwarded from East Seventy-ninth Street. It was delivered to the new apartment when Fanny and I returned from Stump Lake. The envelope was postmarked Tel Aviv, a town I'd never heard of, and looked to me to have been tampered with and resealed. "Dearest brother," she wrote. "A wind of history plays upon my life as on the stormy petrel, but how strange that it should turn out to be a wind blowing not out of the north but the *ancestral desert*. Do you recall, Maxie, our alarm whenever Papa, that most enlightened of men, showed signs of relapsing into the character of Jew? How incomprehensible it was, and *how repellent* ... I almost laugh to think of our youthful selves, you and Sophie in especial, sitting in judgment of that wise and weary man. I wish he were here with me now, in the settlement of proud latter-day Judeans, so that I might say to him: 'Yes, Papa, I am a daughter of Israel. I who sought the revolution amongst Russians have found it amidst the new Hebrews of Palestine. No, Papa, there is no God of the Jews, but there is a history which, if we follow its path, will redeem us from exile.' I refer, of course, to the literal return to Zion."

She went on to describe her shock of self-revelation. For some people, it was the massacre at Kishinev. For others, it was the Parisian mob howling for the death of Captain Dreyfus. For Nina, it was the morning on the isle of Scordevola when Georgi Matveyich awoke and remembered not to forget the revolution. He was sick with peasant brandy from the night before. His eyes were bloodshot, his hands trembled, and from his mouth spewed medieval curses. He accused Nina of casting the revolution out of his thoughts with her Jewish witchery. In her mind, she was again the captured fugitive being returned to Russia with Sophie, the bagged body of Kazimierz Wojcicki at their feet, the guards calling the sisters assassins, Jewesses, as if they were some kind of predatory female beasts.

Georgi Matveyich quit the island to rejoin Lenin's circle in Paris, not the Jew Trotsky in Vienna. There was nothing to hold Nina on Scordevola, an enchanted lotusland no more. The most interesting foreigners were gone already, fleeced and made pennyless by the islanders. Those that remained bickered among themselves and formed drunken, saber-rattling national cliques. The poetess Blanche Viereck Franks was in London, forced to flee the wrath of the family of a native girl whom she was supposed to have ruined.

"I made my way to Palestine," wrote Nina, "through North Africa and Egypt. Do not ask how. Suffice it to say, I allowed myself to be taken for a good Frenchwoman, a German *Frau*, an American adventuress, an English eccentric, a Russian countess, but never for a *Yiddish whore*. (I mention the last because of the grievous traffic in Jewish girls desperate to escape, for good reason, our degenerate ghettos and backward villages. Thus do they fall, further uprooted and debased, a diaspora within the Diaspora.) I arrived in Palestine in February of this year, on a mail packet from Alexandria to Jaffa. During the voyage, in a brief squall, I was overcome by seasickness and was tended by a fellow passenger, a physician. I took him for a Turk, until he addressed me by turns in perfect French and German. When I was recovered and able to speak again, we introduced ourselves. Though we had never met before, our names brought instant mutual recognition and the initial bonds of our *intimate companionship*. There before me was Alois Lévy-Mendès, the widowered husband of Ariane. Maxie, you will call it mere chance, but it was surely the wind of history that brought us together. He it was who first planted the seed of Zion in my heart, when in his grief and anger he wrote to Sophie and me that perhaps we Jews should hope to survive only in a land of our own, since in Europe there could be for us no justice. At the time, I dared not examine the thought, so much was I under my sister's uncompromising sway. It struck root nevertheless, and unbeknownst to myself, slowly germinated."

It was twelve years since Ariane was murdered. Alois had sold his clinic in Strasbourg. He emigrated to Palestine, where he became known as the French doctor—*Ha-Frantzi*, in Hebrew, said Nina—who traveled from colony to colony, town to town, administering to the women of the Jewish settlement. He made his home in the new suburb of Jaffa called Tel Aviv. Two or three times a year, he went down to Alexandria to purchase materia medica otherwise difficult to obtain. The national settlement was growing steadily, and he was now in need of an assistant. Nina offered her services, having gained some experience as a nurse, she told him, during her years in Siberia, at Volkova. "At Alois's side," Nina continued, "I have been the length and breadth of the land. Never in my life have I felt so immediately at home; never has a landscape, barren as it may be, become so familiar; never have I understood a people as so much *my own*. In Russia, the People's Will could hardly see beyond a necessary passion *for destruction*. In the Land of Israel, the will of the people is the necessity *to build*. There, we argued in vain that in the peasant commune were the beginnings of a brave new world. Here, on our agrarian collectives, I have rediscovered the beautiful truth of mutual aid, with no threats from Madame Hetman Sophie and her knout. You used to maintain, dear brother, that the modern solution of the Jewish problem, since in the age of Darwin God no longer signified, was for Jews simply to stop being Jews, a solution which at the time was scarcely possible anywhere but in America. I shall put a twist on your thought, Maxie. I agree: Our people must throw over their Jewishness, their wretched jargon—and become Hebrews once more, in Eretz Yisrael. America can be at best a way station in mid-journey.

"This said, I confess to a longing for Europe, not for Paris or London, but for Kovno and the sight of Papa's villa. I wonder, does the house still stand? Is it as grand as I remember? Thirty-one years lie betwixt me and the place I even now call home; thirty-one years betwixt the aging *voyageuse* I am and the girl of fourteen who left to follow her sister in exile to Siberia. Alois has determined I must make the visit. He says that only thus shall I extirpate false memories and sentiments that cannot share a heart with Zion. There is work to be done abroad for the National Fund in any case, so that my sojourn can have a *larger purpose*. I who have eschewed marriage shall be traveling on a German passport as the wife of Dr. Alois Lévy-Mendès. Parting from him will be cruel, though the separation be temporary: there has been too much of parting in our lives, Maxie. I plan to embark before the end of next year. Alois intends to join me within a twelvemonth, just as soon as his circumstances allow. My love &c. to you and Fanya and to the children (they must be quite grown now and doubtless barely recall their auntie). Your sister Nina."

The windows of the library on West One Hundredth Street looked out across the river to the Palisades along the farther bank. The sun had dipped below the cliffs. Nina's letter was in my lap. I sat with Fanny watching the sky turn from fiery to mauve, until with a blink the evening star came out. I told her I was thinking of how the wind of history had scattered the children of Pytor Mikhailovich. In my mind's eye, I said, a giant dust devil happened to touch down in the garden of my stepfather's villa, scooped us up because we happened to be there, me, my sisters, Mishka, even Nikki, Nakki, and Nokki, and sent us whirling out over the world. Fanny laughed. "What was that book of Elizabeth's?" she said. "*The Wizard of Oz*, where the tornado takes the girl to a promised land. It isn't history she's giving you, that sister of yours, just a lot of wind. She's riding it, the princess of No Where, on a magic carpet." Then she added: "The hand of history will pull her down." Fanny said nothing about Ariane. Nor did I, but I heard Ariane's voice, as if I were a boy in Kovno again, beside her on the bed in Madame's room. She'd told me once that Pyotr Mikhailovich wasn't so unattractive a man that a woman shouldn't find a way to love him for his money. I was jealous and confused. Now she said, "Nina took up with my Alois, when the one she really wants is you. She will ask him about me, then imagine us lying here together, and put herself in my place. Do I shock you, Maxim?" I said the thought was depraved. "But no less true for that, no? She's not your sister by blood, after all, and you do rouse a certain interest. Shall I peel back layers of depravity? Whose actual brother was it that strangled and bludgeoned me and pushed me through a window? You don't suppose Alois knows anything of that from the *nouvelle* Madame Lévy-Mendès." I didn't care for the turn of the conversation, and said so. Ariane twittered in chorus with the dead: "Then you'd better turn on the lights, Maxim. We are permitted to bring you news only in the dark."

IX

How We Lived Then

HOW TO DISASSEMBLE the library at East Seventy-ninth Street had seemed formidable but in the end was easily done. Abby claimed the books that belonged to her mother and father, and also everything in French, with the exception of Bakunin's *Dieu et l'état*, which Zak had found for me. Whatever was in Russian was for Fanny, if in German then for Zak. All the Yiddish, of course, was with Basya downstairs. What any of us bought for ourselves or received as a present, we kept if we wished. One of the happier moments in the sorting saw some dozens of unasked-for books hauled off to the public library, among them the *Sorrow Songs and Grecian Odes* of Blanche Viereck Franks and Julius Schapira, M.D.'s *Free Inquiry into the Scientific Basis of the Religion of the Hebrews*. Tina and Joey came to choose a hundred or so volumes as the start of their own library. *La Divina Commedia* that Marco tendered as a gift we gave to Tina in remembrance of her father. It would be the only thing of his she had. The vacant library was cavernous. I looked at it one last time and thought, If only we'd lived in this house as graciously as we moved from it. Zipporah's voice echoed in my head as if she were in the empty room, "Another lesson in mutual aid, Max? Why do you need me to say how petty the soul, how fragile its stretching?"

Zak bought a summer cottage where Abby could make her garden grow. She called the place Erewhon. It was less than a mile from cousin Emma's farm, so Abby didn't lack for company and busywork when Zak was in the city, which most of the time he was. Her lethargy recurred only at their new apartment while Zak was there to attend her. They lived at the Belnord on West Eighty-sixth Street, in a suite of twelve rooms all on one floor, so there were no stairs to climb. Their mail was delivered directly to them through a pneumatic tube and packages by the concierge's staff. They had a live-in English housekeeper and a cook, with a girl to help. Ida was enraged. When Abby was in the country, she came down from Stump Lake for days at a time. She berated Zak in the shop for a spendthrift. At the monthly meetings of Silver & Kraft, she appealed to Julian and me and Tina to talk sense into him, referring to Zak as if he weren't there. "I tell him, Isidore, remember the saying, 'The well that overflows today runs dry tomorrow.' He answers, 'No one dies like a prince who lives like a dog.' Far be it from me to lecture, but about dollars and cents I do know something, don't I." No one denied it. Zak said nothing. He never talked to Ida about Abby except in private. Once, in the shop, he complained that both women were wearing him down. "Sometimes," he said, "I feel it here." He thumped his chest over his heart, looking old and heavy as he did so. "If I were a younger man, I might cash in my chips and disappear. I did it before." He was thinking of how he ran away from his village and his father's house at the age of fifteen and never went back, of how he left Russia as Isaac Zilberzweig and arrived in New York as Isidore Silver. Then he tore a sheet from the back of my ledger and showed me how Ida was wrong. The difference between owning and renting a summer cottage, between living in a twelve-room apartment and one with eight rooms, between having three house servants and one came to a few thousand dollars. It wasn't he but Ida who wouldn't see reason. He threw up his hands, as if to say why. I had to remind him that in Ida's accounting, every entry for Abby was a liability. "Zak," I said, "what she wants is for you to liquidate the debt."

Basya was pleased with West One Hundredth Street. For the first time in her life, she lived in a building with an elevator and a dwelling without stairs, and supposed we moved there on her account. She declared that never again would she complain about her rheumatism. What were seven rooms to her compared with a house? If America was far from Russia, how much the more so was an apartment on Riverside Drive from Pyotr Mikhailovich's villa in Kovno. She remembered the oil lamps, the chamber pots, and the hot coals in the bathhouse, the woodstove and the constant fires in the kitchen to keep the pumped water boiling, the curing meats and the vegetable patch, every afternoon the sound of Kazys the gardener's ax in the woodpile, and Vera Andreyevna at the bellpulls at all hours, summoning one of the servants up and down, down and up the stairs. She had only one suggestion to make. Her room was too small for the Yiddish books and other publications over which she was guardian. They would have to go in the library now. I said better to throw them out. Basya drew herself up. In the purist German-Jewish she could manage, she said, "Maxie, would you deny me my *Forward* and the *Free Workers' Voice?* Would you deny me the literature that otherwise I am unable to read, because I am an old woman who has trouble with English, no matter how hard I study? Would you deny these to me, Basya, who held you crying on her knees when you were an orphan in your stepfather's house?" She helped me unpack the books and told me where to shelve them, not so high that she couldn't reach them, not so low that she couldn't find them with her rheumatism and failing eyes, but right alongside my American novels and my prized complete works of James Fenimore Cooper.

Tina and Joey took a small apartment in a brownstone on East One Hundred Seventh Street. Shortly afterward, the Ferrer Center opened down the street. This was a libertarian children's school by day, and at other times a gathering place for radicals, with lectures, concerts, and classes in art and literature, psychology and physiology, English and foreign languages. It was founded by Sasha and the Hutchins Hapgood–Bolton Hall bunch in memory of Francisco Ferrer. The Spanish educational reformer was executed a few years before, for allegedly masterminding a workers' uprising in Barcelona. The real reason was the success of his modern secular school movement in Spain. He was shot to death in the fortress of Montjuich, Mount Jew, where the Inquisition once held its *autos-da-fé*. Julian remarked at the time that the family Pereira was expelled from Spain in 1492. The land of his forebears apparently hadn't changed much in the past four hundred years. Tina was astonished at the sight of the children rushing in and out of the school at odd hours, swarming around their teacher, and whooping in the streets, she said, like Red Indians. Whatever they might be studying, they were at least learning to have a good time, which was more than she could say about her six years in the convent school of Santa Maria Annunziata. She thought of attending lectures at the Ferrer Center, but worried she'd see Hutchins Hapgood or Bolton Hall there, or, worse yet, Auntie Abby, who hadn't spoken to her or Joey for over a year, not since the riotous finale of their wedding. Zak said not to worry. Since Tina was working part-time at the shop, he'd bring Abby around to break the silence.

The opportunity Zak chose was a viewing of paintings donated to the Ferrer Center by art-class teachers—I remember the names George Bellows and Robert Henri—followed by a concert by the Modern School Trio. It was early fall. Fanny was up at Stump Lake, steeling herself to act the grandmother. Abby had her own motor car, a Peerless Roadster. She drove from Ossining with cousin Emma, who was back from another months-long lecture tour on the West Coast and looking to move herself and *Mother Earth* uptown, near the shop. What was it about me, I wondered, that made the Cause tag along after my life? Zak said it was my money, of course, and also my good looks. I had the wallet and the face of an angel, he joked, even with my mustache. "You'll notice it's the women who always come to sniff." Tina laughed. I asked why they kept coming if they didn't get what they wanted. Zak said that because I gave them half—the money—they expected sooner or later the rest would follow. In the world of anarchist free-lovers, he suspected I had the reputation of a gentleman flirt. "Not possible," I said. It was then that Emma and Abby walked into the shop. Tina tried not to smile as Emma, unable to pull me to my feet, bent down to give me an unexpectedly long and noisy kiss. I wiped my mouth and asked after Ben Reitman. She seemed offended. He was in Chicago with his mother, about to bring her to New York, the three of them to live together in Emma's new apartment. What a ménage, I thought. Emma took my arm. "I've got you to myself now, dearie," she said. "Maximus, don't be shy."

Emma was at me all evening. She was hardly a furtive se-
ductress. Everyone always knew her intentions. They were declared matters of principle and individual choice. As Julian once
observed, if a woman closed in on a fellow, boxed him in, and
urged herself upon him without surcease, he would most certainly
come to understand that the surest answer to the immediate sex
question was direct action, or, if one liked, a rigorous exercise in
mutual aid. The Ferrer Center wasn't Emma's domain the way
Mother Earth was, but she was prominent there. I'd have thought,
after her tour, that she'd have more concerns there than snar-
ing me.

Zak was amused by the game of cat and mouse, but I thought
he'd intervene. He didn't. I avoided empty corridors and shadowy
culs-de-sac. Emma trapped me nevertheless, in the cloakroom.
Just outside I heard Tina apologize to Abby, with dignity and
grace, for the behavior of the wedding guests the year before.
Abby said, "Thank you, dear, and now let's just put it behind
us." They hugged each other. Then they turned to hang up their
coats and remove their hats, and surprised Emma poised for the
pounce. I sent them an appealing look. Emma backed off, as if
to give them an entrée into the cloakroom, but waited restlessly
outside. When Joey appeared, she took no notice of him. Stump-
ing the country on the lecture platform, rallying strikers, standing
up to the police, or in the pursuit of free love, Emma was fa-
mously unflinching. My two guardian spirits tried to interpose
themselves between us. To draw her off, Tina asked to be introduced to Sasha. Emma took us both firmly by the hand and led
us over to him. He and Becky Edelsohn were in close conversation
with the schoolteacher Tina saw so often on the street, a former
seminarian named Will Durant. "Don't let me interrupt," said
Emma. "I want you to meet Tina Kraft. She spent six years in
an Italian convent." Young Durant was himself recently liberated
from the Church and overflowed with questions about Santa
Maria Annunziata. Emma left Tina there to talk about the nuns
and the corruption, and, still gripping my hand, edged toward a
darkened room off the gallery. "What could be in there, Max?"
she said. "Let's have a look, why don't we."

Abby descended from heaven, *dea ex machina*, directly in
Emma's path. With her was a thin exotic gentleman she presented

to me as Sadakichi Hartmann. I'd heard of him from Zak. The man was known for putting on light shows and perfume concerts and writing Oriental poetry in English; his mother was Japanese. He was charming, addressing me as the celebrated philanthropist and book collector, neither of which was quite true, but enough to engage me while Emma pulled at my arm. Then it was announced that the concert was about to begin. As we were taking our seats, Hartmann suggested that a man as generous as I was might tide him over with a few dollars. Fortunately, the music started. The program was all Beethoven, a favorite among libertarians, profound and soporific. Only the pressure of Emma's leg against mine and the buttons of her shoe digging into my ankle kept me awake.

I was never much for music. The longer a piece went on, the farther my mind drifted. At *gimnaziya*, when the students were assembled for a chamber concert, I closed my eyes to conjugate English verbs, lead a wagon train along the Oregon Trail, save a maiden from marauding savages. Now, in my reveries, I contended grammatically with the women's voices in my head. The subject was conjunctions and how to classify Emma's advances in a dim-lit hideaway below the Ferrer Center. Were they disjunctive, a syntax muddled by *however*s and *but*s? Were they a hesitant string of periphrastic *either ... or*s? Were they an unambiguous progression of copulative *and*s? Ariane and Nina agreed that parsing by the book was an unwelcome intrusion when it came to questions of intimate style. Sophie said the desired end alone must justify the means of desire. Zipporah sat back in her chair and laughed. "Oddly enough, it's a matter of gender. Max, be a man," she said, but the music was over before she could explain. I took it to mean I should speak up and remind Emma of her cousin Fanny. Her foot slowly unhooked itself from mine when I said it was time I was getting home: I was expecting a telephone call from Stump Lake. She seemed deflated. She searched my face, I supposed to find there a thread of interest she could seize. "Max, you're a puritan," she said sadly, "thus far and no farther," then stood up quickly and walked away. Now it was Abby who felt she had to apologize, for thinking to bring Emma to the shop. She'd never seen her so ferocious. "I wouldn't wonder," she said, "if it all had to do with that beast Reitman." I recalled for her the evening a ferocious Emma brought Johann Most to his knees with a horsewhip, in her lovers' quarrel on Sasha's account. Caught in the squeeze, for whatever reason, between Emma and her current love wasn't the place I ever wished to be.

Tina and Joey came to dinner two or three times a month. It was nice to have them, they were so lively, breaking into the newest dance steps in the parlor, the turkey trot and the Castle Walk. They stayed late and talked excitedly, the way young people did, about anything that came into their heads. Only the subject of Emma was forbidden, once Fanny heard how she went after me that evening at the Ferrer Center. Tina told the story, laughing, embellishing the scene with slapstick. "Look at Papa Max," she said, "he's blushing!" and then went silent as Fanny clapped her hands over her ears and closed her eyes. "She would do that to me!" Fanny shouted. She cursed her cousin Chava in Yiddish and said the name of Emma Goldman was never again to be spoken in her house. Joey surprised me by explaining to Tina what was said. Fanny's Yiddish was vulgar and incoherent, nothing that a son of mine, raised in English, should have understood. Tina was upset by what she'd done. I told her not to let it trouble her, we'd talk it over at the shop. The next day, she looked haggard, as if she hadn't slept, but said nothing about the outburst. She knew by now how Fanny was.

Emma must have realized that she'd gone too far. She still needed my money. The announcement of the removal of *Mother Earth* to East One Hundred Nineteenth Street was sent to the shop, as were Emma's circular letters to friends and the magazine itself, even though the subscription continued for a few more months in Basya's name, until I took it over myself. The sight of *Mother Earth* the one time I brought it home had a terrible effect on Fanny. Basya spit three times. She said far be it from her to insist on looking at the magazine just because it was addressed to her, not for the pain it brought, and her English wasn't up to it besides. Tina asked why I kept up the subscription and let M. Kraft remain on Emma's list of angels. We were in the shop with Zak. He said my connection with the Cause had never been so tenuous. I wasn't really an anarchist, was I, anymore than he was. I just didn't have Fanny dragging me to celebrations, speeches, and soirées the way that he had Abby. Wearily he enu-

merated the annual *Mother Earth* balls, Kropotkin's seventieth
birthday tribute at Carnegie Hall, the honored man absent, doings
at the Ferrer Center, Emma's Sunday-evening lectures, salon evenings at the apartment of Mabel Dodge, one of the Hutchins
Hapgood crowd. Now was the time for me to seize the chance
to make a clean break. "Max," he said, " 'Lucky the man who
knows to follow the path of his own luck,' " quoting a saying
from his village. I said I'd known these people all my life. "I am
my father's daughter," said Tina, my twenty-year-old daughter-
in-law, "and so have I." I was thinking of the uprising in the
schoolroom against Madame in '76, of Kazimierz Wojcicki's underground press and the People's Will, of Bobelis in his grave pit
and Sophie affirming, "Very well concealed, comrade," but said
nothing. I wouldn't have Tina joke that where the Cause was
concerned, Papa Max was a bourgeois sentimentalist. Ariane, in
my head, said, "Maxim is a bookkeeper, no? What other savor
does he have in his life but a soupçon of the libertarian spice?"
Nina disagreed. I was, as Zak suggested, a gentleman flirt.
Zipporah said there was a little truth in both remarks, but there
was also this: "In his heart, though he won't admit it, Max knows
what is right and which side he is on."

That winter, the real-estate market collapsed, as Ida said it
would. Business in general was in a slump. Jobs were scarce. People were turned out of their homes. There were soup kitchens
and breadlines, mass meetings in Union Square, and squatters in
the old house at East Seventy-ninth Street. Zak looked pasty. He
and Abby argued about the squatters. He wanted them out. She
said he should be pleased to see our former residence put to good
use by the people themselves. Her friends in the *Mother Earth*
bunch were rallying the unemployed. They led them into wealthy
churches to demand food and shelter and were arrested for in-
vading God's temples of charity. The organizers, Sasha among
them, were the heroes of Mabel Dodge's salon. Zak complained
he had to sit there, his mouth shut, and listen to them talk about
squatters' rights. Inside he felt sick, thinking of the house he so
lovingly designed and built occupied by vandals. Ida said the place
was Shady's concern. Zak had no call to make himself miserable
over what was no longer his. He was sitting next to Ida in her
hotel suite when she said, "Isidore knows what I want him to

do," and patted his stomach, meaning by this, a tightening of the belt. Property values were down. Now was the time to buy, not to eat up ready cash like a fat banker, as if it were profit, with no thought for tomorrow. For Silver & Kraft, it was a question of survival. I told Ida she was a social Darwinist. "Am I, Max," she said. "Well, it's business that should expand, isn't it, not the waistband. That's survival of the fittest." Then she added, referring to Abby: "I have to laugh. If that woman is so interested in the squatters, why doesn't she take in a few, the apartment is big enough, Isidore." She said this, knowing that Abby refused to move to a smaller flat in the Belnord, even after the market dropped. Zak of course said nothing, but sat there pale and drained.

Ida had a plan. She found two run-down tenements for Joey to manage, not downtown but in Harlem. Money was tight. She didn't believe in operating on credit for long. What she proposed was her buying into Kraft's Hotel and Guesthouses. The price she offered was high and would be a welcome infusion of capital into the shop. Fanny was hesitant and came to the next monthly meeting of Silver & Kraft. Ida was reassuring. This was money of her own that she meant someday for Barnard, when he started his law practice, but from where else now could it come? Not from Isidore, who didn't have a dollar to spare after his monthly bills and tips for the staff at the Belnord. Why should Fanny and I have to make up for that? Ida smiled sweetly. "It's all one family, isn't it," she said, "yours and mine," and glanced at Zak as if to say, "and his." "As my father, Baruch Fogelman the carter, used to say, 'You can shift the load so the wagon rides smoother, but it's the same load and the same wagon.' Fifty years from now, whose hotel will it be, whose realty company? They'll belong to our grandchildren and great-grandchildren, won't they." None of us, Tina, Julian, Fanny, or myself, made an immediate reply. Each of us, I supposed, contemplated an American enterprise unto the fourth generation bearing the name of Sussman. Then Fanny said Stump Lake might be in the family, but for her and me, it must always be our special place, so long as we were both alive. She added: "Fifty years is a long time. What we do now, we should do for ourselves." Ida's eyes brightened. She couldn't agree more.

Joey, at dinner that night, said that if business was so bad that we had to sell a share of the hotel to Ida, then he shouldn't be wasting his time in school. He shouldn't come onto the payroll at the shop either. He should get a job someplace else. He wasn't a boy anymore. He was a married man with responsibilities. I recalled using the same argument with Uncle Henry, when I wanted to leave City College, and told Joey so. "Well," he said, "you were right." He reminded me that Barney wasn't in school, but clerking in Liberty at an attorney's, where he was reading law, like Abraham Lincoln. I said that had to do with Barney's school marks, not his resemblance in character to the Great Emancipator. It took all evening to convince Joey to stay in college, to finish his four years. If he wanted to continue in engineering afterward, that was another matter. "I won't continue," he said. "What I need to know, I'll learn from you, Papa, and Uncle Zak." Tina cranked up the phonograph. "If it's all settled," she said, "let's dance. I'm glad nobody's asking me to go back to school," and crossed herself in mockery, from head to toe and shoulder to shoulder, spitting three times in the Jewish fashion, to express her opinion about her education at the convent. She and Joey did the one-step to a ragtime tune, then changed partners with Fanny and me and showed us how. Basya came out of the kitchen to frisk. Over the river hung a bright, happy, American moon. "Max," said Fanny, "why should we expect the worst anymore? It's 1914"—she laughed—"and the worst has never happened yet." For an instant, the Hudson looked to me like the Nemen. I thought of the snaking line of the dead with blazing bodies of working girls streaking down all around like shooting stars. I wondered what Fanny meant. "I'm talking about the revolution, of course," she said. "The hell with it!" and she spit the way Tina did about Santa Maria Annunziata, while we bounced to the "Maple Leaf Rag."

X

War!

FANNY AND ABBY were friends again. It was Tina who brought them together. She explained to Fanny how wary Abby was now of cousin Emma's answer to the sex question, which wasn't free love so much as free-range ravening. To Abby, Tina said we knew the way Fanny was, so why trouble her by mentioning Emma or the revolution. "What will we talk about then?" said Abby. Tina suggested food, Dostoyevsky, the weather, religion, Palestine, Stump Lake, the shop, anything at all, so long as the touchy matters weren't brought into it by name. Abby said this would be hard. Perhaps Fanny might show a hint of mutual regard and not make provocative pronouncements of her own, for instance, on the nature of Abby's invalid episodes or what a woman's childlessness implied. And so it was agreed. Zak and Abby began to come to dinner, on the excuse of missing Basya's cooking. Fanny and I returned the visits. Tina played the good-humored censor. At a signal I never saw, she and Joey diverted the conversation from disaster. There was the time the squatters were ejected from East Seventy-ninth Street and the house was torn down to make way for a public library. Not a word was said among us about police violence against the unemployed or that the new building would be paid for, by Andrew Carnegie's library fund, in

Homestead dollars. Zak simply commented that Shady's little circle must have made a pretty profit. Tina and Joey got up to dance the Texas Tommy.

In the shop, Zak complained of his boredom at Mabel Dodge's salons, something he couldn't do in front of Abby, or Fanny either. He said everyone was swelled up about being there, the nancy poets, the aesthete photographers, the mock artists, the drunken playwrights, the Hutch bunch, the Wobbly crowd, Emma's reds. He'd rather be home with his German lieder and *Scientific American*, or at the opera, where there was real artistry, than listening to these people preach their theories as if they were facts. Tina said the evenings at Mabel Dodge's were so talked-of, she'd like to see for herself what they were like. Zak shrugged. Then he grinned, on his sagging face a flash of his old mischief. "You can go in my place," he said. One time she and Joey did. The occasion was a debate between anarchists and socialists over the issue of direct action versus political action. "The same old stuff," Joey reported the next day. Uncle Zak was right: It was boring, a dull repeat of the gatherings at our old house. "Anarchism in the Golden Land" had had some excitement. When Tina and he married, it was even funny. He didn't understand where these people got their dangerous reputation. I said it had to do with Sasha shooting Henry Clay Frick. "All right," said Joey, "but the man deserved it. Who has Mr. Berkman tried to kill since?" Cousin Emma sounded like a schoolmistress. The fellow from the I.W.W., Big Bill Haywood, had marbles in his mouth. Everyone was waiting for Mr. Lippmann, on the socialist side, to stir things up, but he didn't. It was all very polite, except for Hippolyte Havel, who was drunk. No one there was interesting at all. Tina almost agreed. Among the speakers, that was the case, but not the invited guests. What about the other people? She laughed: "For example, Blanche Viereck Franks."

Mabel Dodge rented an apartment in a mansion across the street from the Brevoort. Abby treated Tina and Joey to a light dinner in the hotel café, and it was there, before the salon, that they noticed the imposing hulk of the poetess at a table with her girl acolytes. Blanche was so huge that Abby didn't recognize her until one of the girls came over to ask if Mrs. Silver and her friends would join Mrs. Franks's party. There were hugs and introductions. Blanche remained seated, too heavy to rise. She called her companions Drymo, Xantho, and Ligea, though two of them had English accents and the other was French. She studied Joey intensely and announced he was the image of his father, but hoped without the cold heart of Narcissus. To Tina she said, "You must tell me everything about yourself, Atalanta." She desired of Abby a full and frank recounting of all the years. Then, the preliminaries over with, she talked about herself until it was time to leave for Mabel Dodge's evening.

Blanche was just off the boat from London, where her life as a poetess had received a galvanic blast from meeting with Ezra Pound, H.D., and like-minded Americans there, *les Imagistes*. Before that, she lived in Florence and became acquainted with Mabel Dodge and her avant-garde circle at the Villa Curonia. Florence followed Blanche's expulsion from Scordevola, the accursed isle. "Doubtless you know the story, my dears," she said, "from Nina Kraft. Max's sister was something of my confidante there. A very warm person, very unlike her brother." Now Blanche was on her way to China and Japan, the lands of the quintessential verbal image, to perfect her verse. She wrote on the spot a Grecian sorrow song after the Japanese as a gift to Abby: "Lonely traveler, Callirhoë, look not back. Dusk obscures thy steps." Drymo, Xantho, and Ligea helped her up the café stairs and guided her, like towboats a laden barge, across the street to Mabel Dodge's. The last thing she said to Abby was: "I'm at the Brevoort for another three days. It would be kind of Max to call, though he won't of course. But you, my dear, must come for our heart-to-heart." All this was playacted by Tina at the shop. "Papa Max," she laughed, "you must have been quite the Lothario. Emma, Madame Ariane—even Blanche Viereck Franks can't forget you. Who else?" Joey flushed at the teasing. I said things weren't as they seemed. I didn't care to talk about what did or didn't happen long ago. Zak winked at me, as if to say he, too, remembered the platonic misery of my brief history with Blanche.

Fanny enjoyed the story. Tina repeated it at dinner that night with Zak and Abby, leaving out details of the salon, and also speculations as to Papa Max's love life in days of yore. Of the gathering at Mabel Dodge's, she simply said it was dull and you could guess who was there. To everyone's surprise, Fanny supplied most of the names and then sketched out the arguments. "Now tell me," she said, smiling, "how is this different from five years ago, ten years ago, and ten before that?" Abby said, "Fanny, dear, are you really asking? Because I can tell you." Fanny rose from the table. She walked over to the window and lighted a cigarette. Joey was already cranking the phonograph. Fanny turned back to us. "Very well," she said, and blew out a hiss of smoke. "You think I never want to hear what I don't want to know. But I read the newpapers, and I get the talk: not revolution, but war. Is there anything to add?" Abby answered just this: "It's Homestead all over again, and Alexander Berkman who's saying so." They were referring to the strike at the Rockefeller coal mines in Colorado. There had been a standoff for months. The strikers and their families, evicted from company shacks, were living in the union's tents at Ludlow, and the men were armed. John D. Rockefeller, Jr., declared that the question wasn't about money but free choice. The American workingman had the God-given right to work for whomever he wanted and not be subject to the dictates of orga-nized labor. The goverer of the state agreed and called out the National Guard to protect the miners from such unionist bondage as an eight-hour day, safety equipment, and wages paid in U.S. dollars instead of company-town coupons. Tina said, "Do you think he'd do it?" meaning, by this, Sasha making an *Attentat* on Rockefeller's life the way he had on Frick's twenty-two years ago. Abby couldn't say. He was thought to have renounced violence, but war was war. "Then I was right," said Fanny. "If Ludlow is Homestead to Alexander Berkman, nothing has changed after all." There was no more to be said. She kneaded her temples and pressed her closed eyes. Joey put a cakewalk on the phonograph, but Tina shook her head. She wasn't up to high-stepping.

The massacre at Ludlow on the morning of April 20 left twenty-two people dead. National Guardsmen broke up a Sunday ball game among the strikers. Words were exchanged. Before dawn the next day, the militia fired machine guns into the sleep-ers' tents and killed five men and a boy. Three miners were run down, beaten, and shot. The body of one of them, the strike organizer, was riddled with more than fifty bullets. Two women and eleven children died in the burning tents, which were splashed with coal oil and torched. By the end of the month, when federal troops came in, fifty-two more people had been killed, some of them Guardsmen, in the war at Ludlow over Mr. Rockefeller's great principle, the open shop. Abby and Tina stood with mourners in black in a silent vigil before the Standard Oil Building on lower Broadway where the Rockefeller offices were. On May Day, Zak and Joey went with them to a mass meeting at Union Square. I minded the shop. It was rent day, and someone had to receive the money. The mounted police charged the demonstrators with clubs swinging. Joey went down from a blow that cracked his collarbone. Tina threw herself on him as the horses bucked and reared around them, but wasn't injured. She managed to pull Joey clear of the panicking crowd and get him, half-conscious, into a taxicab and safely uptown. She telephone from St. Luke's Hospital to tell me what had happened. I asked what of Zak and Abby. Tina didn't know. Then Zak rang up. He was at home. Abby was asleep, feverish but unhurt. When the police attacked, it was, for her, like the soldiers of the tsar cutting down the students at the Winter Palace. She screamed, "Zak, where are we! Is this Petersburg?" and fainted. He got her from Union Square to the Belnord, he couldn't remember how. His heart was still racing. I closed the shop, concerned for Fanny, afraid of what she might do when she heard about Joey. As I entered our apartment, I heard the strains of a hesitation waltz. Fanny's face was thick with white rice powder. She was dancing with a bewildered Basya around and around the parlor. On the dining-room table stood a bottle of schnapps. The late-afternoon newspaper lay next to it, open to a picture of the May Day assault. "Max!" Fanny sang out. "Dance with me! I refuse to worry! It's 1914! The worst is over, and the best is yet to come!"

Abby's relapse prevented her from trying to picket Pocantico Hills, the Rockefeller country estate north of the city, near Tarrytown, and demonstrating in the village square. Sasha was the chief organizer of the protest group. He telephoned Abby two or three times at home. Her motor car would be useful, but only she knew how to drive it. Abby had to say no. There were days she could barely rise from bed. Sasha stopped calling. Tina said he was possessed. She and Joey occasionally stopped by the Ferrer Center in the evening. Joey had been something of a minor hero because of his broken collarbone, but now got scant attention for it. The atmosphere was electric around Sasha and his circle of young zealots, who determined to bring the war at Ludlow to the Rockefellers' door. In Tarrytown, time after time, they were heckled, stoned, beaten, and arrested. Abby complained that she should be there with them. What would her friends think of her? "Friends?" said Zak. He told her not to torture herself. What they wanted from her were the roadster and her money. They wouldn't give her much thought otherwise. He stayed home some days with her and missed two monthly meetings of Silver & Kraft. Ida was outraged. She came to the shop to give him her opinion of Abby's sham illness and, I supposed, just to see if he were all right, but found him gone. "What do I care about that woman's health," she said to me. "May she pine away permanently. It's Isidore I worry about. He has a responsibility to us, doesn't he, Max. And to me." I said he and Abby also had a legal responsibility for each other. Ida dismissed the idea with an angry laugh. "She could have gotten them both killed in Union Square. Responsibility!"

Joey's tenements were a difficulty, though I didn't say so. The buildings were in disrepair, the tenants poor, some now unemployed, and generally behind in their rents. Joey was new to the business and didn't yet understand its pace. He'd had school to see to, then his collarbone, and Zak had Abby. I stayed late at the shop and went in weekends to keep up with the work. On Abby's better days, Zak joined me for a few hours, happy to be there, he said, and out of the house. Dr. Pereira assured him that Abby would be her old self again by August. Zak hoped the wars at Ludlow and Tarrytown would be over and he could have some peace.

On the Fourth of July, we were both at the shop early in the morning, thinking to catch up on the accounts undisturbed. Around nine o'clock, we went out to buy some pipe tobacco. Our regular tobacconist was closed for the holiday. We found another a few blocks down on Lexington Avenue, paid for our pound of burley, and stepped outside just as the world exploded. Bricks, roofing, scraps of furniture, bits of metal, and broken glass fell like hailstones. A single human arm, with fist clenched as in a revolutionary salute, fell into the middle of the street. Zak slumped against me. I thought he'd been struck. His face was as white as Fanny's rice powder. He caught his breath and tried to joke, saying it was nothing, only the momentary shock from the noise of the glorious fireworks, or whatever it was, to his heart.

Then came the screaming, the clang of fire engines, police vans, and ambulances. People rushed into the empty holiday streets, shouting to know what happened. Was it a gas main that exploded or an anarchist bomb? Zak and I ran to the Ferrer Center. The police were already there, but it was closed for an Independence Day picnic. We knocked at Tina and Joey's door. They'd been thrown out of bed. Their bookcase lay shelf-side down on the floor, like a closed coffin. They thought it was a bomb for sure, a Fourth of July gift for the Rockefellers' gone off prematurely. I remembered how Zak and I disposed of the dynamite makings that Fanny's brothers left stored in two old valises, how with Marco we dismantled Mishka's chemical apparatus, how as a boy courier for the People's Will, I never questioned what was in the various packets Sophie gave me to deliver to darkened cellars and attics in Slobodka. I came to America to be left alone. After thirty years, it seemed I was still within the pale of someone else's passion for destruction.

It turned out that Tina and Joey were right. Not only the newspapers said so, but *Mother Earth* proclaimed the martyrdom of the three men and a woman friend who died in the blast, all but admitting that the bomb that destroyed the tenement on Lexington Avenue was meant for Pocantico Hills. The cover of the July issue was a drawing of the bronze memorial urn for the men's ashes, "CARON HANSON BERG KILLED JULY 4 1914," a pyramid topped with a clenched fist, like the one attached to the severed arm in the street. The police tried to link Sasha directly to the explosion, but couldn't. He frustrated them further by leading a mass demonstration for the dead martyrs, once again in Union Square, that drew twenty thousand people. Thousands more came to view the urn, which Sasha placed in the garden behind the offices of *Mother Earth*. Zak and I, along with Tina and Joey, were among them. We went not out of grief, nor to stand in the ranks of the workingmen in the widening war between capital and labor. We were pulled toward it, and the demolished tenement also, by the fascination with disaster, the way one gazed at the relics of a great fire or battlefield, or the site of an assassination. The hand of history that came so close to our throats, said Zak, was no longer alive and threatening, just a hollow metallic fist. Sasha saw us as we passed through the offices. He nodded to me, then turned to one of the staff, a woman I didn't know, to tell her who I was. I caught the words "good enough fellow," "anonymous," and "not really one of us." Zipporah's voice came into my head, laughing because my feelings were hurt. "You can't have it both ways, Max," she said, and hummed the Wobbly song, "Which Side Are You On?"

In all this time, cousin Emma was on the road with Reitman again, on a speaking tour out West. Publicly she stood by Sasha. Privately she was dismayed at his group's taking control of the magazine in her absence and its calls for violence, and wrote to tell me so. I received a letter from her at the shop, scribbled on hotel stationery and mailed from Portland. It was the first I'd heard from her since I responded in the negative to her sex question. "Dearest Max," she said. "No doubt you've read the recent harangues in *Mother Earth*, the paeans to force and dynamite. You well know, my friend, that these are not my views. I nearly threw the July issue into the fire! I've always kept the magazine free of prattle, but Sasha at heart is still the fierce boy you remember from that night in Worcester, the fanatical revolutionist of old. This shall not happen again, and I trust I can count on your support. Faithfully, Emma." I showed the letter to Zak. He said it was the usual stuff from her to me. If it wasn't about love, it was about money. He laughed to think that Red Emma and Abby were both repelled by the violent talk. As Tina said, in the beginning were the words. He said that Abby felt so torn by matters touching the Cause that she'd asked him to sell the summer cottage. It was too near Emma's farm, a retreat for the *Mother Earth* crowd. She wanted nothing to do with apologists for the Lexington Avenue explosion, any more than with advocates for law and order at Ludlow. She was sick of hypocrisy, of people and their rantings about war. She said that if Fanny or anyone else ever again commented on her being childless, she'd answer she was glad.

Zak sent Abby to the Jersey shore for the month of August and joined her on weekends. Fanny and I took three weeks together at Stump Lake. Zak thought it was time I had some rest.

When we arrived, Ida said, "I will not discuss Isidore." She was angry at him for missing yet another meeting of Silver & Kraft, while she had to come down to the hot city at the height of the hotel's summer season. It made no difference to her that he was selling the cottage near Ossining. "He'll have to do more than that," she said. "Until then, it's strictly business between us, and that's my final word on him." We didn't try to persuade her otherwise. Fanny and I determined to put the world out of mind. For the first time, we drove upstate, crossing the Hudson to Newburgh by ferry. Fanny hadn't dared sit behind the wheel of a motor car since her accident, but she found the country roads easy compared to city streets and the workings of the Model-T child's play after the Reo. She said driving made everything so simple. You were either on the road or off, going somewhere or coming back, and nothing else mattered. We could ride all the way to California like this, and forget the rest of life. I said I thought we were keeping it at a distance well enough already. Ida arranged for the city papers to be delivered to the hotel lounge. Even so, the news was late and felt remote. The morning editions arrived at night, the evening editions the following morning. Neither Fanny nor I bothered much with them. Some of the guests were troubled by the posturings of war in Europe, but only those who still had relatives over there. They assured one another that what the editorials had been saying for the past few weeks was true. The crowned heads were cousins. Families had their squabbles and minor vendettas, but in this modern age nothing to cause nations to clash with the might of arms. "Such pettiness is not in Clausewitz," said a book printer who had sisters in Prague. He explained the political theory of war. The guests tried to listen, yawned, and one by one drifted into breakfast, away from the lounge and the German invasion of Belgium.

At Stump Lake, only Barney was excited by the unfolding of the Great War. He said the fighting was for suckers, but if it lasted long enough, a guy could make a few dollars. "Big money, Pop," he announced. I asked how. He answered, "Maybe like the Rothschilds a hundred years ago," and bragged that he was actually reading a book. He held it up, a history of Jewish heroes, from Biblical times to Napoleon. This was in the cottage across the lake. Elizabeth was feeding baby Rutherford, the future heir of the banking house of Sussman. She said, "You'll see, Papa. It'll be swell. My Barney's a real sharper." I wondered where she learned to talk that way, my daughter who was once an honors student in Greek. For Fanny, it was much the same. "Why wait for the war to go on, Barney," she said, "be an undertaker if you want to make a fortune on death," and marched out to the lake. Afterward, in our suite, she said they were ruining our holiday, these American children of ours. Didn't they understand what war was? Where did this greediness of theirs come from? I said they must have picked it up from Ida. She was the only person we knew who had something favorable to say about the European war: not for or against it, just that it would be good for business.

It wasn't Barney and Elizabeth that marred our time at Stump Lake, but that war overseas to which we hadn't been paying attention. The other wars, at Ludlow and Tarrytown, and the Lexington Avenue explosion felt closer. I thought of my sisters: Sophie with Lenin's circle, wherever it might be in hiding now, evading martial law; Nina perhaps in Kovno, cut off from Dr. Lévy-Mendès, unable to return to Palestine. They came into my dreams. The Sachs's Café that is the garden of my stepfather's villa is also the hearing room at Ellis Island. A wooden barrier separates the living from the dead, both pleading wordlessly in the dream silence for the doors of America to open—all except Sophie and Nina, who keep aloof from the refugees and from each other. Sophie declares through frozen lips: *Our brethren, the workmen, have gone to war. They shall turn their bows and slings against their taskmasters, and capital standeth doomed.* Nina is a girl again. She sits in sorrow amid the garden flowers of her father's house. I hear her moan, though she makes no sound, the words of the Hebrew psalm: *If I forget thee, O Jerusalem.* A voice, my own, protests: *War hath not truly befallen us. There hath been but a misunderstanding among the families of kings, and neither can it prevail.* Machine guns rattle and bombs go off just outside the hearing room across the ocean, and there are flames. Fanny shakes me awake to tell me I've been shouting in my sleep again for the third night running, and tries to calm me by stroking my hand.

Ida opened the meeting of Silver & Kraft in September. Her manner was businesslike and cold. She addressed Zak as Mr. Silver and remarked on his absences since April. Zak shrugged.

"You know where I've been, Ida," he said. Then he added, "But last week, Julian and I were down in Washington, about our properties. I think we've got a deal." After eight years of dickering among rival groups within the Department of Commerce and Labor, the government was ready to lease the lots and pull down the old buildings. Commerce and Labor were now separate, and each needed space for its proliferating offices. "A lease, Isidore," said Ida, suddenly smiling. She held the mortgages. She laughed to hear the government's proposed term was for ninety-nine years. As Zak gave the details of the offer, Ida jotted down numbers, calculating, no doubt, the income for the next few generations of Sussmans if the mortgages were renewed until the year 2013. What Zak didn't mention was that his inside connections at the new Department of Labor were the immigration officials who had quietly contrived to deport Mishka and the International Revolutionary Order. Tina said that once it was known the properties were coming under development, their value on the market would go sky high. She suggested we sell them for the immediate profit. Ida said absolutely not. Tina asked how far could we trust the government to keep its word—surely not for ninety-nine years. "I am still my father's daughter," she said, "and I hear his voice: 'If we do this thing, this is the state playing with our life, this is walking the high wire for the bosses in Washington.'" She turned to me, "Don't you think so, Papa Max," and I agreed. I said I was still my sisters' brother, and surprised myself by saying so. "A revolutionist knows when he should fight," I explained, "and when he should lie low." In times of trouble, in this war, for example, it would be best not to call attention to ourselves, just take the money, as Tina said, and be gone. Zak and Julian reminded me that we weren't Jews in Russia. We were citizens of the Republic of the United States of America. The war was an overseas affair, our government was determined to stay out of it, and, in any case, it wouldn't last for long. My dreams told me otherwise, yet how could I, Max the rationalist, insist they augured truth? Tina and I were outvoted.

XI

Joey

THE WAR ENDED before New Year's at Ludlow when the miners called off their strike. The other war went on, and the news of German atrocities in Belgium was a nightmare. We celebrated 1915 nevertheless, at Elias Pereira's house, Zak and Abby, Fanny and I. Joey and Tina took Julian dancing, to show him how it was done nowadays. They promised to join us later for champagne. "The Hun must be stopped," said Elias. He wept to think of the rape of Europe by the barbarian. Fanny said it wasn't for the first time, was it. That was why we were here, not there. The newspapers weren't reporting the Russian atrocities in Poland. Why? Since when was a Cossack holier than a Hun? Who gained by such lies? Zak answered, "The people who make and sell the weapons. 'America Ltd.,'" he joked, 'Arms Purveyor to the World,'" but no one laughed. Celia said, "It's the women and children who suffer most." America wasn't even in the fighting, and already there was talk of preparedness and conscription. Those were our sons who'd be forced into the trenches.

It was near midnight when Tina and Joey burst in and did the tango. Julian shouted, "Olé!" Celia and Abby broke into tears. In a military draft, they said, a boy like Joey would be among the first to be called. He stood there bewildered, trying to catch his breath from dancing. Then he assured them, in his serious way, that he'd never have to go to war. What they were saying was impossible. The president, Mr. Wilson, was against our entering the fighting. So, too, were the Democrats and the Republicans, the Socialists and the anarchists, the unionists and the Wobblies. "If no one gives Johnny his gun"—he smiled—"then he can't go marching." Tina said the thumping about preparedness was empty bravado. When she was at the convent school of Santa Maria Annunziata, from the windows she sometimes watched the local militiamen strut in the street wearing plumed helmets and cuirasses, blowing bugles off-key, and brandishing their swords. "That," she said, "is preparedness." I popped the champagne. We raised our glasses to peace. "And may the Hun keep far from these shores," declared Elias, "if he knows what's good for him." It was Joey who said, "You can bet he does."

For her forty-eighth birthday, I bought Fanny a Ford Couplet de luxe and a pearl tiara in a Persian motif. Business at the shop and at Kraft's Hotel and Guesthouses had never before been so good, despite my bad dreams. The government lease in Washington brought in steady cash. America without fighting was helping the Allies defeat the Hun. The lines of the unemployed and the soup kitchens disappeared. The tenants in the buildings Joey managed found jobs in the war effort and paid their rent. Ida, through Zak's connections, obtained a manufacturing contract for her furniture factory and repair shop, to produce field-tent fittings and portable privies. Barney was making his dollars, having somehow passed his examinations for the bar. He put out his shingle in Woodville, "Barnard Sussman, Esq., Attorney-at-Law," and took on Ida as his first client. "Anytime the shop is ready for me, Pop," he told me, "I'm ready for the shop." I ignored him. It would be a black day for Silver & Kraft, following my death, if ever Barney the rat replaced the likes of Julian Pereira.

Joey finished school and came full-time into the shop. We bought him two more houses, tenanted by Negroes. He didn't mind and wasn't afraid of them, he said. He'd caught on to the work. It was only the war that troubled him. The sinking of the *Lusitania*, a passenger liner, by an *Unterseeboot* was cowardly and brutal. Drowning nearly twelve hundred civilians, he said, wasn't a strategic act of war; it was murder. The Hun had crossed the

Rubicon. Zak reasoned with Joey for weeks afterward, trying to convince him that the Germans were the same as any other nation, both good and bad. He invited Joey and Tina to dinner. Fanny and I went, too. We listened to lieder and Beethoven's "Ode to Joy" and the prisoners' chorus from *Fidelio* played on Zak's Victrola. We discussed the works of Goethe and Schiller, of Hegel and Nietzshe, and, above all, the philological investigations of Herder, Schlegel, Humboldt, and Grimm that linked language to language and people to people, to show all humanity as one, united in the beautiful gift of speech. Joey was deeply moved. I remembered the train from Brody to Berlin, the customs inspectors harrying the bewildered immigrants, stripping and searching them, shouting in German. I said nothing, not wanting to sway the boy back again toward belligerence. The women held their tongues as well. The English housekeeper poked a furious face out of the kitchen and yelled, "Tell 'em so at Ypres!" pronounced "wipers." She packed her bag and left that night, on account of Mr. and Mrs. Silver and their kind supporting the Boche.

On another occasion, at West One Hundredth Street, Joey and I were alone together in the library. Tina and Abby were at a demonstration for peace organized by woman suffragists. They'd persuaded Fanny into going with them, since the protesters would have nothing to do with Emma and the Cause. Joey had taken to smoking a pipe. The two of us filled our briars and talked about the war, Maximus major and minor having a heart-to-heart. He told me his confusions. I could hardly pretend I had none of my own, but I tried. What I said was that life required of us difficult, even terrible choices, but a man who walked the open road of reason would always be free. Sophie's voice asked, "Free to do what? These are the empty phrases of Pyotr Mikhailovich, with an infantile turn of Emma Goldman's." Zipporah said, "The boy doesn't mean what you mean, free to be left alone. He's asking you what he should do. Well, Max, tell him, why don't you."

Joey confessed that he and Tina wanted to have a baby, but were afraid. What if there were conscription and he died in battle? Barney said he shouldn't be a chump. Joey should have a kid so he wouldn't be called up. It wouldn't hurt him as much as blowing off a big toe or puncturing an eardrum. "Mama tells me," said Joey, "no son of hers is going to fight to save the tsar.

Aunt Abby tells Tina that no woman in her right mind ought to be bringing children into this world. Uncle Zak says the culture of the good Germans has been a light unto modern civilization. Dr. Pereira says they're all the same savages as of old, the men of the northern forests, only they've traded their animal skins for uniforms." He read *Mother Earth* at the shop. Even the Cause was split. The "International Anarchist Manifesto on the War" denounced both sides and the hypocrisy of the neutral states that profited from the fighting. Kropotkin didn't sign it. The most respected anarchist on earth said Prussian militarism must be crushed for the revolution to happen and the monarchies of Europe to fall. "Papa," said Joey, "we're Americans. We're against the war. But if the country gets into it, I have a responsibility, don't I, to come to the nation's defense. I mean, not to the defense of the state, but my fellow citizens. And if I do have a responsibility, I can still understand in my heart, can't I, that the war is wrong and that everyone's gone berserk." I respected him for saying so. But perhaps I should have told him that Barney was right: he and Tina should have their baby. Instead, I brought up my years at *gimnaziya* after the assassination of Alexander II. So many of us in school sang "God Save the Tsar" while making secret plans to leave Russia. We were young, willing to give up everything, but knew enough to keep our silence. "Your mama," I said, "simply disappeared one day. We guessed where she went. She was a courageous girl to come to America in those days alone." Joey nodded at the word "courageous." He drew on his pipe. "Courageous," he repeated. In my head, Zipporah said, "Max, you've given the boy your blessing if he should choose to die."

Ida thought we were worrying ourselves to no purpose. She quoted from the sayings of the carter Baruch Fogelman, her father. "The feud in Volovo," she said, "puts meat on the tables in Orlovo," meaning, by this, that in a time of trouble, not everyone must suffer. At the meetings of Silver & Kraft, she reminded the room of my opinions, talking about them as if I weren't present. "He's always said, hasn't he, 'Europe is the black hole,' 'We didn't come to the New World to fight the battles of the Old,' 'Revolution can only happen in the language of the place,' and who would disagree with him? Has anything changed? It's their war, and if it comes, it will be their revolution. If these things are so, then we don't have to be ashamed, do we, of making a dollar from their mistakes. The president says he'll keep us out of it, and you're wringing your hands over 'what if.'" Julian at last said that much as he esteemed Ida for her gifts at business, in the matter of war and peace she was simplistic, looking at the world from the perspective of Stump Lake, New York. "Am I," she said. "I won't deny it. I came here a Jewish girl from Turov. I don't demonstrate. I don't march with flags. And I don't throw bombs. It's foolish of me, isn't it, Mr. Pereira." Ida was referring to the Preparedness Day Parade in San Francisco the week before, when dynamite exploded among the onlookers. Ten people were killed and forty injured. The police tried to implicate Sasha. After Emma took back control of her magazine, he'd moved to San Francisco to start his own, calling it, without subtlety, *The Blast*. The natural suspicions of the police proved misplaced. Sasha mounted the defense for the unionists who were arrested, Tom Mooney and Warren Billings. For him, it was another Haymarket, innocent men being railroaded. For the police, it was the bombing of the Los Angeles *Times* all over again. Now Tina said to Ida, "A stick of dynamite goes off, and intelligence is blown to bits." Once the patriots started to march in Woodville, it would make no difference who threw the bomb. From hereon, there'd be no minding one's own business, or rational pacifism either. "Auntie Ida," she said sadly, "it isn't 'what if' anymore."

The war absorbed Fanny's attention more than *Mother Earth* ever did. Next to the library was our Oriental den; Little Xanadu, we called it. There she pored over newspaper reports of battles and diplomacy won and lost, and the arguments pro and con for America's entry into the hostilities. The New York *Times* published a rotogravure *Mid-Week Pictorial War Extra* and a periodic *Current History of the European War*. She read them both and scarcely ate or slept. She drank glass after glass of tea, smoked cigarettes continually, and lost weight. She looked haggard and ghostly white, her face made up with rice powder. I told her she was slender, the way I remembered her as a girl. She waved the compliment away as irrelevant and an attempt to divert her, which it was. Basya, with my consent, brewed a sleeping draft of herbs and added it to Fanny's tea. It had no effect. Details possessed her. Patterns overwhelmed her. She said they were like two hands of history. Once she fit the right and left together, she'd understand everything that happened from the night her family fled from Shavl until now, and perhaps know what would happen afterward. "I'm not crazy, Max," she explained. "I want us to be safe. The future is the sum of the present."

As it was, Fanny anticipated events far better than anyone else, better even than the choral voices in my head that warned without foretelling. There were hopes, she said, and there were expectations. She tried not to confuse them. Mr. Wilson ran for a second term as president with the slogan "Peace with Honor and Continued Prosperity." Fanny hoped he'd win and expected he would, because the married men would vote the way their wives told them, and the unmarried ones would vote to save their skins. I voted for Mr. Wilson. So, too, did Joey, Zak, Barney, Julian, and also Elias on account of Celia's pleas. After he was reelected, Fanny said she hoped he'd keep us out of the war as promised, but expected he couldn't with honor. She opened the *Mid-Week Pictorial* to a photograph of no-man's-land strewn with barbed wire and corpses. "That," she said, "is honor." In January, the Germans declared unrestricted submarine warfare. There could be no neutrality now. On April 6, Mr. Wilson announced we were at war. Fanny watched the Russian losses on the Eastern Front. She hoped they would continue and expected they would. No country in the world would drain its military resources for the sake of Nicholas Romanov. "Remember the anthem, Max?" she said. "Now it's truly 'God Save the Tsar.'" She laughed when he was deposed in March to think it took a war to bring on the revolution, not a spontaneous seizure of the means of production by the workers and peasants, which we supposed as children. Fanny could talk about the revolution again, and cousin Emma as well, as being among the pieces juggled by history's two hands. Sasha had returned to New York. He and Emma founded a No Conscription League and arranged mass protests against military registration. Fanny commented, "All hope, Max. No expectation." The one detail of the war she never mentioned was Joey.

Tina said the aura at the Ferrer Center was ugly. The children's day school, which used to leave sunny traces for the grown-ups at night, had moved to New Jersey. There was no good humor now. The police watched from the street and sent plain-clothes agents inside. There were scuffles and arrests made for seditious opinions opposed to the approaching draft. Even the regulars at the center argued among themselves, divided by Kropotkin's support for the Allies and Mr. Wilson's claim that America was making the world safe for democracy, which Emma said was enough to cause the devil to laugh. The police recognized Joey and Tina and harassed them as they came home from the shop. They decided to move and found an apartment around the corner from Fanny and me. I was glad to have them close by, so that one of us could always be near Fanny until she was herself again.

That was at the beginning of June. A few days later, on the eve of military registration, the No Conscription League held a demonstration at Hunts Point Palace in the Bronx. Tina and Joey went. So did Zak and Abby. Just that once, I thought to leave Fanny at home with Basya, but Tina insisted not. "Papa Max," she said, "I don't want Joseph to feel we've all come to protect him." "Protect him from what?" I asked. Tina wouldn't say. The meeting drew ten thousand people. Many were barred from entering by the police, for no apparent reason. Inside were groups of soldiers and sailors in uniform. They jeered at the speakers, threw lightbulbs, and threatened to storm the platform. Emma very coolly addressed the hall. She asked the audience not to be provoked, to file out singing, with dignity, and not to lose their heads, so as to give no excuse for a police riot and to set a splendid example, she said, for peace. The house did what she asked, to the strains of the "Internationale," which were echoed by the crowd outside. Tina and Joey came by on their way home, to tell us they were all right and how impressive the mass exit of singers was. I nodded surreptitiously toward Joey, and Tina winked, as if to say not to worry. The next day, he came late to the shop, and apologized. The registration lines were long, he explained, and besides, he'd enlisted.

Tina listened to Joey without saying a word. She looked at him, unblinking and resigned, the way she had at her father's coffin, while he assured us he wasn't the only volunteer. He and some of the other boys talked while waiting. Like them, he intended to do no more than register, as the law required, until his

turn came. The man behind the desk said Kraft, what kind of
name was that for an American, implying that it was German.
Joey declared it was as good as anyone else's who was there. The
name belonged to him, Joseph Peter Kraft, a citizen and the son
of citizens of these United States of America, born right here in
New York City twenty-four years ago. Then he surprised himself
by saying he was there not to register, but to volunteer for service
in the Expeditionary Force. "Papa," he said, "you and Mama
won't be angry. It's my responsibility," but his eyes were on Tina.
I waited for her to ask what of his responsibility to her, but she
didn't. Instead, she got up from her typewriter table and kissed
him. "Joseph," she said quietly, "how long before you have to
go?" They'd given him until August. After that, he'd have a few
months of military training. Zak said if they sent him to officers'
school, too, the war would be over before he could go overseas. I
thought of Fanny's distinction between hope and expectation, and
wished I'd urged Joey and Tina to have their baby. There'd be
no time for that now. Tina was concerned for Mama Fanny. How
would we tell her? It was then that Joey seemed about to break.
I said they shouldn't trouble themselves. I'd talk to her myself.

Fanny was in Little Xanadu. She'd replaced a wall-hanging
of the Garden of Eden with a map of the Western Front and was
sticking pins along the river Lys at the Messines Ridge. "If the
British take it, Max," she said, "they'll control all of Flanders from
there to the sea. I expect they will." I told her, gently I thought,
that Joey was going into the army in less than two months. She
lighted a cigarette, and said nothing. I repeated everything Joey
had said at the shop, and also Zak's remark that the war might
be over before the boy got into the fighting. Fanny turned away
and began shifting pins. She said we should expect Jerusalem to
fall to the British before the year was out, not that it would make
much difference to the outcome of the war. The sun was setting
behind the Palisades across the river. She watched it disappear.
She took a long swallow of tea, and still said nothing. The voices
in my head twittered, "Max, she hath drunk again of the waters
of Lethe."

After a third meeting of the No Conscription League in June,
cousin Emma and Sasha were arrested. They were found guilty
of conspiring to defy the draft law, and of urging others to do so

as well. What before was free speech was now defined as espio-
nage. They were each sentenced to two years in a federal prison,
to be followed by deportation. When they were released on bail,
the newspapers reported that it was the Kaiser's agents who put
up the money. That summer, *Mother Earth* died, killed in English,
the language I once supposed was for understanding, by the Post
Office authorities for its stance against the war and the draft. Joey
left for his military training in New Jersey feeling bitter. He said
he was ashamed of himself for volunteering, and of America for
what it was doing. He'd been seized twice on the street by squads
of vigilantes carrying flags and searching young men to see if
they'd registered. Those who hadn't were turned in to the police.
Joey and Tina had intended to spend three weeks at Stump Lake,
but couldn't endure Barney's mocking and Elizabeth's foolishness
for more than a few days. Barney told Joey he was a sucker and
suggested that if getting Tina pregnant was his difficulty, he,
Barney, would have been happy to stand in for him. It was the
kind of thing that was being done all the time to get around the
draft. "I could tell you stories, bo." The two of them were alone
by the lake. Joey confessed to me that he'd shoved Barney into
the water. I said I was pleased to hear it, but Joey wouldn't laugh.
He said Elizabeth dressed up little Rusty in soldier and sailor suits
and paraded him among the guests. She stood him up in the
dining room and coaxed him to sing "My Country, 'Tis of Thee."
Barney referred to the boy as his proxy draftee. Joey and Tina
took a steamer up the Hudson as far as Glens Falls, and from
there they went by train to Lake George. The Stars and Stripes
were everywhere, like stands of trees on the lawns, clustered in
flag bouquets on windowsills, displayed at the smallest docks
along the river. In one town, a pharmacy called Kraus & Pfeffer
hung a sign that read: "German Not Spoken Here." At a Sunday
concert on the commons, the audience shouted the music to a stop
when the brass ensemble played Brahms. The banner fringing the
bandstand proclaimed: "America Making the World Safe for
Democracy."

Whenever Joey came home on leave, he changed immediately
out of his uniform. He hated the look and the rough feel of it,
and he didn't want to startle his mother. Fanny still hadn't acknowledged his joining the army, anymore than she had her

brothers' having been hanged. At New Year's, Dr. Pereira assured me that she'd come to herself about these matters, just as she had about other things, in her own good time. He suggested I be patient. "Speaking as a medical man," he said, "science must respect the divinity, as it were, within." We happened to be alone together in the den, the smoking room at his house, for an after-dinner pipe. He had an arm across my shoulders, in his friendly way. I knocked it off. Elias put his hands up to protect his face. He thought I was going to hit him, and I was. Zak and Julian walked in and pulled us apart. I railed at Elias. I said I knew very well how Fanny was, and neither science nor divinity, as it were, would be any help to Joey when they shipped him off to Europe, to kill or be killed in the war Elias wanted him to fight, without a word or a kiss or even a tear from his mother. "Be patient?" I said. "When haven't I been? It's not patience I'm running out of, but time." Elias said he was sorry, perhaps he didn't understand. I realized then how unsteady I was. The war, Fanny, the world were wearing me down more than I supposed, and yet so far I'd lost nothing. "Nothing?" The voice was Zipporah's. "Nothing, Max? Tell me again the one about your right, in America, to be left alone." When Elias offered his hand for me to shake, I took it.

Tina and Joey telephoned at midnight to wish us a Happy New Year. He was on a holiday furlough, before being sent to artillery school. They'd been dancing all evening at home. He was due back at camp the next day and had to be up early. Besides, they didn't care to be out carousing among young men in uniform trying to enjoy what might be their final spree. One by one, we shouted our greetings into the telephone. Then Tina asked to speak to me once more. "Papa Max," she said, "I wanted to tell you: I'm going to have a baby after all. Please, tell everyone we're not unhappy about it. Far from it." She was crying. Elias opened a new bottle of champagne and made a toast to the Allies' victory in 1918 and to all children everywhere, the great hope of the world. We raised our glasses slowly, quietly, and drank, except for Fanny, who'd gone to the den for a cigarette while I was giving the news of Tina and Joey's baby.

Cousin Emma's form letters to "Dear Friend" still came to me at the shop, sometimes in envelopes that might have been tampered with. There were no more personal notes, but I responded to her appeals for money nevertheless. I asked Zak why shouldn't I. Reitman had left her, perhaps when she needed even the likes of him the most, gone off to marry a young woman who once worked in the offices of *Mother Earth*. Emma was putting up a battle against the foolish war we opposed, against her and Sasha's going to prison, against their deportation. I'd always said that if someone wanted to speak his mind in English in America, he should be allowed to stay and do so. In Emma's present case, I'd even forgive a little Yiddish now and then, as long as I didn't have to hear it. She was continuing to lecture on everything from birth control to literature to the revolution in Russia, while reviving her magazine as a truncated *Mother Earth Bulletin*. It didn't matter to me that she had only good words for the Boleshviki and believed they'd accommodate to the principle of mutual aid. Kropotkin himself had returned to Russia, and the government of the Soviets was rumored to be seeking peace. I imagined my sisters meeting by chance in the streets of revolutionary Petrograd or Moscow, or as two strangers in Kovno looking for the villa that used to belong to their father, wandering past an unrecognizable, tumbledown house, finding each other instead. In my reverie, old Kropotkin welcomes Sophie and Nina into his home, in a reconciliation wrought by the hand of a benevolent revolution. I didn't need the voice of Zipporah or Ariane to tell me my daydreaming could only turn hopes into expectations in a faraway landscape of such happy endings that once upon a time, as a boy, I would have called the place America.

In February, Emma and Sasha finally went to federal prison, she at Jefferson City, Missouri, he at Atlanta. Both of them had been in and out of jail over the years, but this would be the longest term for her, and also for Sasha since his entombment for his failed *Attentat* on Henry Clay Frick. In his published prison memoirs, Sasha detailed month after month in solitary and days at a stretch in a straitjacket, lying in his own filth, barely able to hold on to his sanity. I didn't suppose he'd be treated any better now, as a convicted enemy alien in wartime. In April, *Mother Earth* died a second death when the Post Office killed the *Bulletin*; the Ferrer Center closed; and Joey was posted overseas.

Basya cooked a farewell dinner of his favorite dishes, starting

with Emma's stuffed fish and ending with her butter almond
cookies. Zak and Abby brought him several pairs of thick socks
and an Italian salami, the kind he used to eat every day at the
shop. For once, Joey wore his uniform. Basya when she saw him
wrung her hands and wailed. Tina told him that if Mama Fanny
was ever going to say anything about his being in the war, it
would have to be now, and only if he appeared at the door with
his puttees and campaign hat. She was right. Nevertheless, conversation was trying. Fanny was silent until it was time for him
and Tina to leave. Then all she said was, "Joey, don't be a hero
if you want me to be proud." Joey hugged her. He answered that
he'd make Fanny the proudest mama of any man in the entire
American Expeditionary Force. For the first time that evening,
everyone laughed.

After that, Fanny was more herself again. She put on some
weight and spent the days, but not the evenings, in Little Xanadu.
Joey's letters gave no clue as to where precisely in France he was,
no doubt because of the military censorship. But Fanny had in
her map a large yellow pin that she said was Joey. She inched it
eastward from Cantigny, in May, to Château-Thierry on the
Marne to the Argonne Forest, and, finally, Montmédy on the
Meuse when the war ended in November. By then, Tina and
Joey's baby was six months old. Joey hadn't seen him yet, except
in the snapshots that Tina sent. He wrote that the boy looked just
like Marco, minus the magnificent mustache. On the day of the
armistice, Tina held little Marcus up to the map. "There's your
papa," she said, while he grabbed at the now meaningless pins.
We had a little party, ourselves and Basya, with honey cake and
plum brandy, to celebrate our Joey coming home. We replaced
the Western Front with the Garden of Eden and burned in the
fireplace the *Mid-Week Pictorial* and other reminders of the war.
Basya spit into the flames and muttered curses in Yiddish. Fanny
remembered that the day, November 11, was the anniversary of
the hanging of the Haymarket martyrs. How important we once
thought that was. "It's strange to think, isn't it, Max," she said.
It seemed so insignificant, especially now.

Two days later, as I was coming home from the shop, I found
Tina waitng for me in the lobby at West One Hundredth
Street. She had the baby in her arms and could scarcely speak.

"In my pocket," she stammered, "the telegram." It was an official communiqué from the War Department. Joey was dead. He'd been killed—the wire didn't say how—the month before, on October 5, in the battle for the Argonne Forest. His body was irrecoverable. Regrets were expressed. His personal belongings had been gathered and were being shipped home. We had to tell Fanny. She was watching the sunset from Little Xanadu. "Don't turn on the light," she said. Talking softly in the gentle twilight, we let her know the terrible news. I hoped she wouldn't hear. I wanted her mind to sink again into oblivion. There was only a heartbeat of silence before Fanny howled. She pushed her way into the parlor. She clawed at her face, her fingers raking through white rice powder. Her tears ran in blood-red streaks, as if she'd gouged out her eyes in grief.

XII

1919

THERE WAS A reading room in the manor house at Stump Lake where books and magazines were kept for the guests. Ida proposed to make it a memorial for Joey. I hung the plaque beside the door in January for the Joseph Peter Kraft Library. On the wall beside the fireplace, Tina put up some photographs: Joey and herself as children, standing by the boathouse; Joey and Barney in a canoe, holding paddles, Elizabeth seated in the middle, a picture I took in 1910; Joey in cap and gown at his college commencement ceremony, flanked by Fanny and Tina; Joey in uniform. Fanny looked dully at the display. She was stuporous from the sedative pills Dr. Pereira prescribed. He gave me the bottle, unlabeled, the night she collapsed and said, he'd keep us supplied as long as they were needed. He added, "Don't ask what's in them, Max," and I didn't. To tell the truth, provided they worked, if they were purportedly compounded of holy bread and the blood of saints and blessed by God, I wouldn't have cared. Elias didn't linger. He was exhausted. There was an influenza contagion spreading from Europe, and he'd been making house calls for days. I'd been fortunate to reach him at home. Among his fellow physicians, there was talk that it was the epidemic which in fact had brought the war to an end. "A microbial victory," he said.

"It is humbling. Joey was such a fine young man." I understood from this that Elias, in his own way, was recanting his former rant about the Hun.

It was at the next meeting of Silver & Kraft that Ida, as the first item on the agenda, brought up the memorial for Joey. The occasion was cheerless. She came down to the city with Barney. In the weeks since the armistice, the influenza had practically closed the hotel, as one by one the members of the staff were infected, then Elizabeth, Barney, and Rusty, but not Ida. "We count our blessings, don't we," she said. "Business has been slow, but no one there died." Here it was another matter. We'd lost Julian. He was caught one night in a rainstorm on the way to a friend's house, came down with a fever at dinner, and expired two days later in the guest room. For the moment, Silver & Kraft had no counsel. Ida, as the second item on the agenda, suggested Barney. In the circumstances, there was no objection possible. Barney puffed up, as if the position was due him for his merits, not the result of Ida's machinations and history's skulking hand stealing Julian away. He thumped me on the back, punched Zak in the shoulder, and kissed the air near Tina's cheek because she pulled her face back in time. "We'll be in the money now, bo," he said, boasting either to the room or to himself.

The ice on Stump Lake was brilliant with sunshine the day I nailed up the plaque. Tina and I walked down to the boathouse. It was seven years that week since Barney and Elizabeth were married. I recalled for Tina the skating party circling the lake and told her, the first I'd ever told anyone, of the lengthening line of the dead on the frozen Nemen. Then Elias and Celia joined us. They were thinking of the skating party, too, and smiled to remember Julian getting up stiffly from a bench to hook on to the end of the snaking chain. Elias chuckled. "The truth is," he said, "my brother had poured brandy into his cocoa. He always kept a dram in the head of his cane." Tina said it was a beautiful afternoon for memories, perhaps meaning, by this, that my dream wasn't of the Styx as I'd supposed, but of the river of life, which were the waters of unforgetting. Rusty dressed himself for dinner that evening in his soldier suit. He stood up by himself on his chair to sing "Over There." Ida put a finger to her lips. What guests there were turned away. Elizabeth snapped at the bewildered boy. Didn't he understand the war was over? Rusty should think of his Uncle Joey. He looked around the dining room. "Where is he?" he said.

Tina moved in with us at West One Hundredth Street. The nights alone, she said, were bleak. She took our guest room for herself and the baby. There were a few weeks of clutter, until we found where to put Tina's things. Joey's clothes she donated to a neighborhood settlement house. She kept only the two surviving pairs of thick socks that Zak and Abby gave him before he went overseas. These were returned to Tina by the War Department, together with her letters to Joey and the snapshots of Marcus she'd sent, one of them with an enormous mustache drawn in by her and the caption: "Marco Tullio Kraftifici." The jumble in the apartment was an unexpected tonic for Fanny. She found it something of a joke that we were having to rough it after all our years of wealthy living. "It's better than hope, Max," she said. "When you trip over the baby's rattle, that's no illusion." She also enjoyed how Basya defied me by singing lullabies to Marcus in Yiddish. Before long, Fanny was only taking Dr. Pereira's pills once a day, toward sunset, the hour, she said, when Joey always came to mind.

There were soup kitchens and breadlines again. Men huddled in the streets, dressed in shabby fatigues. Tina insisted on coming back into the shop in the afternoons, while Basya minded the baby. She walked across town if the weather was good and always kept spare change for the demobbed soldiers. "My husband was killed in the war," she told them. Once, a fellow knocked at the shop. It was a warm day in June, but he had an army coat wrapped around him, no doubt to cover his threadbare clothes. He was looking for work. "Silver & Kraft," he said. "I knew a Joe Kraft in the artillery. Blown to bits in the Argonne." Tina fainted. I hustled the man outside while Zak looked after Tina. He told me how his pal died in a direct hit on a gun emplacement. "Him and two other buddies. Hardly nothing left of them. Like that red bomber in Washington." Then he added: "Maybe they was better off not coming back to this." He looked down at his torn coat, and, after I gave him five dollars, walked away. The bomber he referred to was the one who recently tried to dynamite the town house of the attorney general and his family in Georgetown while they were at home in bed, but blew himself up on the doorsteps instead. There were seven more bombs set off that same day, in other cities as well. Zak had read aloud in the shop the newspaper accounts of a presumed Bolshevik plot. He sat at his desk and kneaded his chest, thinking of Lexington Avenue, the hail of debris, the severed arm that landed near us. Naturally, cousin Emma and Sasha were said to be involved, even though they weren't Bolsheviks and were still in prison. Tina said, "The truth doesn't matter. This is the attorney general someone was after. When the state feels threatened, then vengeance is mine, saith the state." As Joey's army friend disappeared down the block, I went back into the shop. Tina was hugging herself, shivering, and taking sips of brandy from a coffee cup, while Zak lied to her that this customer was just a bum with a line, angling for a handout.

What kept us going that year was the income from Silver & Kraft's leased properties in Washington. The Hotel and Guesthouses were rarely more than half filled, except on holidays and for the summer season. Ida confessed her own business was in trouble. The government had left her with a packed warehouse of tent fittings and privies and no buyer. If such was the case with her enterprise, we should consider all the others left suddenly in the lurch, their contracts useless, without enough money to meet payroll expenses and the costs of changing over from the making of swords to the making of plowshares. We didn't need to ask, did we, who was really responsible for the strikes and riots and bombs since the armistice. I told Ida she sounded like a Bolshevik. "Do I," she said. "Well, it wasn't the reds who got us into the war, was it, and those who did shouldn't turn their backs on the country now." That was what she'd written to the people in Immigration who leased our Washington lots, and just let them try to deport Red Ida Sussman, she laughed, for giving her opinion. This was at West One Hundredth Street, one evening when Ida and Barney came to dinner after a meeting of Silver & Kraft. It was early in October. Emma and Sasha had been released from prison and were appealing the orders that would send them back to Russia. Fanny stiffened at the mention of deportation. She had to stop herself from covering her ears. "This isn't a matter for joking," she said. "I wouldn't go putting ideas into the minds of the secret immigration police. We don't want them to think, do we, that you've even so much as discussed cousin Emma." Ida, very sobered, admitted that no, we didn't. Barney, our legal counsel, said, "Nah." These government guys were always waiting to be fixed, and they went dirt cheap. I wondered how he knew, but didn't ask. Tina drew herself up. She suggested that for people with principles, like Emma Goldman and Alexander Berkman, bribery was never a consideration. Barney said, "Yeah?" Well that was their lookout, wasn't it, and good luck to them.

It was a month later that a nationwide roundup of alien radicals was made. In New York, federal agents raided the Union of Russian Workers on East Fifteenth Street. The newspapers reported more than two hundred people arrested and held for questioning. That was November 7, a Friday. The following day, Zak and I were at the shop. Rents were in arrears, and Saturday was a good day to find our tenants at home, especially in the afternoon. Zak said that now we knew for sure the kind of people the attorney general was gunning for, and no bona fide Americans among them. The government had showed its hand. Fanny should have no more worries about a midnight knock on the door and a no-return ferry to Ellis Island, simply because she was a distant cousin several times removed of Emma Goldman. Neverthless, he became edgy when I repeated the newspaper description of the men and women who were being detained, as atheists, communists, and anarchists. "Mostly eyewash," he said. "Especially the first, and not grounds for deporting citizens anyway. Since when has it been a criminal offense in America not to believe in God?" He put on his hat. He was going out to collect back rents at the Frances Arms and the Abigail Arms. I said I'd wait until he returned before doing the same at Joey's tenements. With his hand on the door, he said, half-smiling, "If the police come to get you while I'm gone, Max, just tell them: 'I'm an American citizen. I've done nothing illegal.'" And that, in fact, is what I did.

There were three of them. I knew who they were when they walked into the shop. Their pushing swagger gave them away, and also the sameness of their dress, a common plainclothes uniform of bowler, tightly buttoned black jacket and vest, and no encumbering cane. "Silver & Kraft," said one. "Which are you?" I inquired who was asking. He answered, "The law," and flashed a piece of paper while his partners yanked my chair from under me and fastened handcuffs on my wrists. I tried to stand up. They knocked me down. I said, "I'm an American citizen. I've done nothing illegal," and was kicked in the ribs. They found my wallet. "It's Kraft," said one. "That's him," said another. The third said nothing and started to ransack the shop. Then all three pulled out the drawers of every desk and file and threw blueprints and papers on the floor. They had me crawl to the safe and open it with my manacled hands. They cleared out the cash, October's rents, putting it in a satchel, I supposed as evidence, but of what? Fortunately, Zak and I had sold our revolvers. Mortgage agreements and stock certificates, being of no subversive interest, were left in a heap. When the International Revolutionary Order made its expropriation, Yarchuk and Rogovoy showed more civility. On the floor in the W.C., a pile of reading was discovered: several issues of the dead *Mother Earth* and *Bulletin*. This was the greatest find, no matter that these were registered, licensed publications. I reminded the men that I was an American citizen and had done nothing illegal. They blindfolded me, stuffed a rag in my mouth, and led me stumbling to their motor car. I knelt on the floor in the back. The thought of Ben Reitman kidnapped and taken into the desert by vigilantes wasn't funny now.

I was alone in a windowless room with a concrete floor, a dim lightbulb hanging from the ceiling, and no furniture at all, not even a chair, just a rusty chamber pot in one corner. "How considerate," I said aloud, and tried to laugh at my little joke, but couldn't. My wrists were still shackled. I rested on the floor, my back against the stone wall, and waited. My pocket watch was missing. I had no sense of time. At last, two plainclothesmen entered the room. I recognized them from the squad that raided the shop. For a moment, they felt like old friends. They carried in a straight chair. They motioned me to get up off the floor and sit. I sat. They questioned me: when was the last time I entered the country? "November 1, 1884," I said. "I'm an American citizen. I've done nothing illegal." They told me to stand up and sit down again, and assisted by slamming me onto the chair, over and over, until it broke under me and I fell. They brought in another chair. "Sit," they said. I sat. They repeated their question. I repeated my answer. They repeated their chair battery until I blacked out.

I was skating on the Nemen, across the oceans of the world,

into the Sachs's Café that was the garden of my stepfather's villa, or was it jail? I lay on the floor, voices murmuring around me, and thought I was dreaming and could shout myself awake. I shouted. I was awake on the floor of a cell, amid murmuring voices. I asked where I was, and was told: "In the tombs." I was dreaming after all. I was dead, in a crypt that was Sach's Café. Then I remembered the name given to the men's house of detention, The Tombs. Someone handed me a piece of bread and a metal cup with weak coffee. I ate. I drank. Against a wall was a crusted toilet for sharing. I shared. My sisters in the Litovsky prison had a single slop bucket in their crowded cell, but this wasn't Russia; it was America, where there was a toilet that didn't flush. I was in a cell with a half-dozen men who, like me, had been picked up at work, or even at home. They were American citizens, they said, had done nothing illegal, and wanted to send word to their families. I thought of Nechayev in the Peter-Paul Fortress, said to have smuggled out notes scratched in his own blood. The Count of Monte Cristo learned to tap coded messages on the dungeon walls, and so had Sasha.

I was taken out again for interrogation by my friends the plainclothesmen. They told me to sit. I refused. They made me stand until my legs gave out, then returned me to my cell. The next time, I sat. I expected the chair battery again, but was beaten instead with a blackjack when I answered their question the only way I could, with the truth. Another time, they used just their fists. They broadened their grilling with questions about other matters and people that almost, but not quite, applied to me. I felt like another man named Kraft, off-center from myself. When they mentioned the International Revolutionary Order, I understood: They thought I was Mishka, the M. Kraft deported in 1906, as if he could possibly be the M. Kraft who was a "Dear Friend" correspondent of Emma Goldman's. I could scarcely speak, and was in no position in any case to tell them that in their stupidity they'd mistaken their man. Evidently they, too, realized something was amiss. I was taken back to my cell, this time still conscious. My handcuffs were removed. Perhaps a half hour later, I was released from The Tombs. There were no explanations or apologies given. Two uniformed policemen led me to a waiting motor car. I recognized Zak's Reo. "I'm an American citizen,"

I whispered on the sidewalk, "I've done nothing illegal," and collapsed.

Dr. Pereira found nothing broken. He and Fanny and Abby were in the back of the Reo, Zak and Tina in the front. Fanny was crying. She rocked to and fro, talking in a jumble of Russian, German, and Yiddish, but no English. I reached for her hand and spoke to her in kind. What was the language of America to me now? Abby stared at me in amazement and sorrow. I had no broken bones, but when the chair had shattered under me and I hit the concrete floor, something wooshed out with my breath and was lost forever in The Tombs: it was the small boy in Kovno who dreamed of being transported to the New World on an eagle's wings.

I slept for a day without waking and spent the rest of the year recovering from my three days of jail and interrogation. I had, in fact, endured very little: not Sasha's fourteen years, nothing like his and Emma's recent terms, not the life sentences Mooney and Billings received for the bomb that exploded at the Preparedness Parade. Tina said it wasn't right of me to make comparisons. These weren't figures in ledger book to be added up. "Papa Max," she said, "not all wounds are physical," and I had to turn away. Zak came to visit every day. He brought accounts from the shop for me to go over when I was up to the task, and explained how he'd got me out of jail. He'd seen me being put into a motor car by the police. His Reo was across the street, and he followed me all the way downtown. At The Tombs, he could get no information, but guessed I'd been seized in a second wave of roundups. On Monday, he telephoned his contacts in Washington at Immigration. He told them, "Do you want the newspapers to think your offices stand on property leased from an alien red?" They called him back the next day. Some overzealous fool of a clerk had taken it upon himself to read the subscription list of *Mother Earth* against a roster of deportees. He'd found two names that, without making a further check, he assumed were one. They wired my release immediately—no doubt, I told Zak, in the middle of my final third-degree, the one limited to fists.

Sasha and cousin Emma's appeals ran out. They were deported at the end of December. Almost on the eve of their leaving,

Henry Clay Frick died. Fanny said it was the clasping of history's two hands. The boat that took them to Russia, an outworn military transport, the S.S. *Buford*, was called in the newspapers a "Red Ark." It carried away two hunded forty-nine unwilling passengers, perhaps one or two from my jail cell and, too, a memory of a sometimes grudging angel for the Cause. I recalled Sasha in the offices of *Mother Earth* explaining about me to a woman there: "He's a good enough fellow, but not really one of us." But now, so help me, in my mind's eye I saw myself with them on the *Buford*, passing Ellis Island and the great statue in the harbor, whose raised torch had become a flickering sword.